About the Authors

A charity-working, dog-walking, child-wrangling, dust-ignoring bookworm, **Jessica Gilmore** lives in the beautiful and historic city of York with one patient husband, one daughter, one very fluffy dog, two dog-loathing cats and a goldfish called Bob. As day dreaming is her very favourite hobby and she loves a good happy-ever-after Jessica can't believe she's lucky enough to write romance for a living. Say hi on Twitter at @yrosered or visit sprigmuslin.blogspot.com

Brenda Harlen is a multi-award winning author for Mills & Boon who has written over twenty-five books for the company.

Being an author has always been **Therese Beharrie**'s dream. It was only when the corporate world loomed during her final year at university that she realised how soon she wanted that dream to become a reality. She got serious about her writing, and now writes books she wants to see in the world featuring people who look like her. When she's not writing, she's spending time with her husband and dogs in Cape Town, South Africa. She admits this is a perfect life, and is grateful for it.

Unexpected Surprises

Unexpected Surprises:
New Beginnings

JESSICA GILMORE

BRENDA HARLEN

THERESE BEHARRIE

MILLS & BOON

First Published in Great Britain 2021
By Mills & Boon, an imprint of HarperCollins*Publishers,* Ltd
1 London Bridge Street, London, SE1 9GF

www.harpercollins.co.uk

HarperCollins*Publishers*
1st Floor, Watermarque Building,
Ringsend Road, Dublin 4, Ireland

UNEXPECTED SURPRISES: NEW BEGINNINGS
© 2021 Harlequin Books S.A.

Her New Year Baby Secret © 2017 Harlequin Books S.A.
The Sheriff's Nine-Month Surprise © 2018 Brenda Harlen
Surprise Baby, Second Chance © 2018 Therese Beharrie

Special thanks and acknowledgement are given to Jessica Gilmore
for her contribution to the *Maids Under the Mistletoe* series.

ISBN: 978-0-263-30296-7

MIX
Paper from
responsible sources
FSC™ C007454

This book is produced from independently certified FSC™ paper
to ensure responsible forest management.

For more information visit: www.harpercollins.co.uk/green

Printed and Bound in Spain using 100% Renewable electricity at
CPI Black Print, Barcelona

HER NEW YEAR
BABY SECRET

JESSICA GILMORE

For all the amazing Mills & Boon Romance
writers—past and present.

Thank you for being so welcoming to new writers
and so generous with your time, experience
and wisdom, and thank you for writing
such amazing books.

It's an honour to work with you all. X

CHAPTER ONE

Early December, Chelsea, London

'WAIT! STOP! OH, NO...' Sophie Bradshaw skidded to a halt and watched the bus sail past her, the driver utterly oblivious to her outstretched hand. 'Just great,' she muttered, pulling her cardigan more closely around her and turning, careful not to slip on the icy pavement, to scan the arrivals board in the bus stop, hoping against hope the next bus wasn't too far behind.

She huffed out a sigh of disappointment. Tonight London buses were definitely not running in pairs—she would have to wait twenty minutes until the next one. And, to add insult to injury, the light snowflakes that had been falling in a picturesque fashion over Chelsea's well-heeled streets all evening had decided to pick up both speed and strength and were now dancing dizzily through the air, blown here and there by some decidedly icy gusts of wind. Sophie eyed a taxi longingly. Would it hurt? Just this once? Only, last time she'd checked, she had only forty pounds left in her bank account, there was still a week to go until payday and, crucially, she still hadn't bought any Christmas presents.

She'd just have to wait and hope her best friend, and fellow waitress, Ashleigh, joined her soon so that she could forget her freezing hands and sore feet in a good gossip about the evening's event. Sophie hadn't received one thank you in the three hours she had toted a laden tray around the expensively dressed party-goers, but she had experienced several jostlings, three toe-tramplings and one pat on her bottom. It was a good thing her hands had been occupied in balancing the tray or the bottom patter might have found himself wearing the stuffed prawns, which would have been momentarily satisfying but probably not the best career move.

Sophie shivered as another icy gust blew through the bus shelter and straight through her inadequate if seasonally appropriate sparkly cardigan. Why hadn't she brought a coat, a proper grown-up coat with a hood and a warm lining and a waterproof outer layer? 'Vanity, thy name is Sophie,' she muttered. Well, she was getting her just reward now; nothing shrieked high-end fashion like the 'frozen drowned rat' look.

Huddling down into the cardigan, she turned, hoping once more to see her friend, but there was still no sign of Ashleigh and Sophie's phone was out of battery—again. The snow-covered street was eerily deserted, as if she were alone in the world. She blinked, hot unwanted tears filling her eyes. It wasn't just that she was cold, or that she was tired. It was that feeling of being invisible, no more human or worthy of attention than the platters she held, less interesting than the cocktails she had been handing out.

She swallowed, resolutely blinking back the tears. *Don't be a baby*, she scolded herself. So her job was hard work? At least she had a job and she was lucky enough to work with some lovely people. So her flat was so small she couldn't offer Ashleigh even a temporary home? At least she had a flat—and, even better, an almost affordable flat right here in Chelsea. Well, 'right here' being a twenty-minute bus ride away to the unfashionable edges of Chelsea, but it was all hers.

So she was a little lonely? Far, far better to be lonely alone than lonely with someone else. She knew that all too well.

She straightened her shoulders and lifted her chin as if she could physically banish her dark thoughts, but her chest still ached with a yearning for something more than the narrow existence she had lived since moving to London just over a year and a half ago. The narrow existence she'd trapped herself in long before that. What must it be like to be a guest at one of the many glittering parties and events she worked at? To wear colour and shine, not stay demure and unnoticed in black and white?

With a sigh she looked around once more, hoping that the bright smile and can-do attitude of her old friend might help her shake this sudden and unwanted melancholy, but although the snow fell thicker and faster than ever there was still no sign of Ashleigh. Nor was there any sign of the bus. The board in the shelter was resolutely sticking to an arrival in twenty minutes' time, even though at least five long minutes had already passed…

Sophie blew on her hands and thought of the warm, inviting glow of the hotel lobby just a few metres behind her. She was staff—and temporary staff at that—but surely, after a night run off her feet catering to some of the most arrogant ignoramuses she had ever had the misfortune to waitress for, they wouldn't mind her sheltering inside for just a few minutes? Besides, a snowstorm changed the rules, everyone knew that. Even a posh hotel turned into Scrooge after the three ghosts had visited, welcoming to one and all. And it would be easier to keep a lookout for Ashleigh if she wasn't constantly blinking snow out of her eyes…

Mind made up, Sophie stepped cautiously away from the limited shelter of the bus stop and onto the increasingly snowy pavement, her feet sinking with a definite crunch in the snow as she began to walk back towards the lobby. She kept her head down against the chill, picking up speed as she neared the door, and warmth was in sight when she collided with a tall figure, her heel slipping as she did so. With a surprised yelp Sophie teetered, arms windmilling as she fought to remain upright, refusing to surrender to the inevitable crash but knowing that any millisecond now she would fall…

Just as she started to lose the battle a strong hand grasped her elbow and pulled her upright. Sophie looked up, startled, and found herself staring into a pair of the darkest brown eyes she had ever seen, framed with long thick lashes. 'Careful! It's snowing. You could hurt someone—or yourself if you don't look where you're going.'

Italian, she thought dreamily. She had been saved by an Italian man with beautiful eyes. Then his sharp tone permeated the fog in her brain and she stepped back, sharply moving away from his steadying grasp.

'Snowing? So that's what this white cold stuff is. Thank you for clearing that up.' She stopped, the anger disappearing as quickly as it came as shock flared up on his face—followed by the ghost of a smile. It was a very attractive ghost; he was probably rather gorgeous when he relaxed. *Not relevant, Sophie*. More to the point, she *had* bumped into him. 'I'm sorry, you're right, I wasn't looking where I was going. I just wanted to get inside before I turned into the little match girl. I've had to admit defeat on finding transport. It's looking like I'm going to have to walk home...' She looked ruefully down at her black heels. They were surprisingly comfortable—comfortable enough for her to wear them to work—but patent court shoes probably weren't high on most Arctic explorers' kit lists.

'Typical London, just a few flakes of snow and the taxis disappear.'

Sophie didn't want to contradict him and point out that there was a little more than a drop of snow—several inches more in fact—or that she wasn't actually looking for a taxi but for a far more prosaic bus. 'It's always the same when it snows,' she said airily, as if she were a real Londoner, blasé about everything, even the fairy-tale scene unfolding before her, but instantly ruined the effect by shivering.

'And you've come out inappropriately dressed.' The disapproval was back in his voice, but before Sophie could react, he shrugged off his expensive-looking coat and wrapped it around her. 'You'll catch pneumonia if you're not careful.'

Pride warred with her frozen limbs and lost. 'I... Thank you... Although,' she couldn't help adding, 'it wasn't actually snowing when I left home.' She snuggled into the coat. The lining felt like silk and there was a distinct scent on the collar, a fresh citrus scent, sharp and very male, rather like the smartly tailored man standing in front of her. She held out her hand, just the tips of her fingers visible, peeking out of the long coat sleeves. 'Sophie Bradshaw.'

'Marco Santoro.' He took her outstretched hand and, at his touch, a fizz of attraction shivered up Sophie's spine.

She swallowed, shocked by the sudden sensation.

It had been far too long since she'd had that kind of reaction and it unnerved her.

Unnerved her—but she couldn't deny a certain thrill of exhilaration too, and almost without meaning to she smiled up at him, holding his gaze boldly even as his eyes darkened with interest.

'I must be holding you up,' she said, searching for something interesting to say but settling on the banal, unsettled by the speculative look in his eyes. 'I should give you your coat back, thank you for coming to my rescue and let you get on your way.' But she couldn't quite bring herself to return the coat, not when she was so blissfully warm. Not when she was so very aware of every shifting expression on his rather-nice-to-look-at face with cheekbones cut like glaciers, the dark stubble a little too neat to be five o'clock shadow. She also rather approved of the suit, which enhanced, rather than hung off or strained over, his tall lean body. She did like a man who knew how to dress…

She'd given him the perfect getaway clause. One moment of chivalry could have marooned him here with this sharp-tongued girl for the rest of the evening. All he had to do was say thank you, retrieve his coat and be on his way. The words hovered on his tongue, but Marco paused. There was something he rather liked about her defiantly pointed, uptilted chin, the combative spark in her blue eyes. It was a nice contrast to the tedium that had made up his evening so far.

'Take your time and warm up. I'm in no hurry. The fresh air is just what I needed after being in there.' He gestured behind him to The Chelsea Grand. 'I was at the most overcrowded, overheated party imaginable.'

'Me too! Wasn't it awful?'

'Unbearable. What a shame I didn't see you in there. It would have brightened up a dull evening. No one ever enjoys these Export Alliance affairs, but it's necessary to show willing, don't you think?'

Her eyes flickered. 'Oh, yes, I hope the evening wasn't too much of a bore.'

Marco deliberately didn't answer straight away, running his gaze over Sophie assessingly. She was a little under average height, with silky blonde hair caught up in a neat twist. Her eyes were a clear blue, her mouth full. She wasn't as poised as his usual type, but then again he was bored of his usual type, hence the last six months' dating detox. And fate did seem to have brought them together; who was he to argue with fate? He smiled straight into her eyes. 'For a while there I thought it was. But now, maybe, it has...possibilities.'

With interest he watched her absorb his words, his meaning, colour flushing high and quick on her pale cheeks. She stepped back. 'Well, it was lovely meeting you, Mr Santoro, but I really should try to get back before I need a team of huskies to whisk me home. Thank you so much for lending me your coat. I think I'm warm enough to risk another five minutes looking for transport.'

'Or,' he suggested, 'we could wait out the storm in the comfort of a bar.' There, the gauntlet was thrown; it was up to her to take it or not.

He rather hoped she would.

Sophie opened her mouth, then closed it again. Marco could practically see the arguments running through her mind. She didn't know him. It was snowing and impossible to get home. What harm could one drink do? Was she acknowledging the sizzle of chemistry in the air? That indefinable quality that stopped him from taking his coat and walking away, that stopped her from saying a flat no. He could almost smell it, rich and ripe.

Sophie sighed, a tiny sound, a sound of capitulation. 'Thank you, a drink would be lovely.'

'*Bene*, do you know somewhere you would like to go? No? Then if I may make a suggestion, I know just the place.' He took her arm and she allowed him, as if the process of saying yes had freed her from making any more decisions. She was light under his hand, fragile as he steered her away from the hotel and down to the lights and bustle of the King's Road. Neither of them spoke, words suddenly superfluous in this winter wonderland of shadow and snow.

The bar he'd selected was just a short walk away, newly refurbished in a dazzling display of copper and light woods with long sleek tables for larger groups and hidden nooks with smaller, more intimate tables for couples. Marco steered Sophie towards the most hidden of these small areas, gesturing to the barman to bring them a bottle of Prosecco as he did so. Her eyes flickered towards his and then across their small hideaway with its low table for two, its intimate two-seater sofa, the almost hidden entrance.

'Excuse me for just a minute, I'm going to freshen up.'

'Of course, take your time.' He sat down and picked up his glass and smiled. The dull evening was suddenly alive with possibilities. Just the way he liked it.

What am I doing? What am I doing?

Sophie didn't need to look at a price list to know the bar was way out of her league—each light fitting probably cost more than every piece of furniture she owned. And she didn't need to be a mind reader to know why

Marco Santoro had selected such a small, hidden table. The whole scenario had seduction written all over it.

She'd never been the kind of girl handsome men in tailored suits wanted to seduce before. What would it be like to try that girl on for size? Just for once?

The loos were as bright and trendy as the bar, with huge mirrors running all along one wall and a counter at waist height. Sophie dumped her bag onto the counter, shrugged off the coat, hanging it onto the hat stand with care, and quickly tallied up her outfit. One dress, black. One pair of tights, nude. One pair of shoes, black. One silver shrug, wet. Hair up. Make-up minimal. She could do this.

It didn't take long; it never did. Hair taken down, shaken and brushed. That was one thing about her fine, straight blonde hair: it might be boring, but it fell into place without too much effort. A colour stick added a rich berry glow to her lips and colour to her cheeks and a sweep of mascara gave her eyes some much-needed definition. A quick sweep of powder to her nose, an unflattering scarlet after ten minutes in the snow, finished her face.

She looked at herself critically. Her face was fine, her hair would do, but even though she'd added a few stitches to the Maids in Chelsea standard black dress to improve the fit, her dress was still more suitable for church than an exclusive bar. She rummaged in her bag and pulled out a white ribbon. Two seconds later she had tied it around her waist, finishing it with a chic bow. She added oversize silver hooped earrings, looped a long, twisted silver chain around her neck and held the shrug under the dryer for a minute until it was just faintly damp. Not bad. Not bad at all. She closed her bag, slung the coat nonchalantly around her shoulders and took a deep breath. It was a drink. That was all.

An hour, maybe two, with someone who looked at her with interest. Someone who didn't know her, didn't feel sorry for her.

An hour, maybe two, of being someone different. A Chelsea girl, the kind of girl who went to glamorous parties and flirted with handsome men, not the kind of girl who stood on the sidelines with a tray of drinks.

Sophie wasn't remotely ashamed of what she did for a living. She worked hard and paid her own way—which was a lot more than many of the society women she cleaned for and waited on could say—and Clio, the owner of Maids in Chelsea, the agency Sophie worked for, had built up her successful business from scratch. Maids in Chelsea was known for supplying the best help in west London and Sophie and her colleagues were proud of their reputation. But it wasn't glamorous. And right now, she wanted just a few moments of glamour. To belong in the world she served and cleaned up after until the clock struck twelve and she turned back into a pumpkin.

Didn't she deserve this? It was nearly Christmas after all…

CHAPTER TWO

New Year's Eve

'THAT'S FANTASTIC, GRACE. No, of course I'm not mad, I'm really happy for you. So when do I get to meet him? Tonight? He's taking you to the Snowflake Ball. That's…that's really, really great. I can't wait. I'll see you there. Okay. Bye. Love you.'

Sophie put her phone down and stared across the room. If there had been room on the floor, she would have slumped in a dramatic fashion, but as every inch of the tiny sitting room/dining room/kitchenette was covered in bolts and scraps of fabric, she could only lean against the wall and swallow hard.

Did Cinderella feel resentment when she was left alone and everyone else went to the ball? No, she was quite happy to sit by the fire with the mice and Buttons and weave straw into gold before letting down her hair and eating an apple.

Okay. Maybe Sophie was muddling up her fairy tales a little.

But, crucially, Cinderella was excluded from the ball completely. How would she have felt if she had been made to attend the ball as a waitress and had to watch her stepsisters waltzing by in the arms of their handsome tycoons and earls? There would have been less singing, more teeth-gnashing then.

Not that Sophie had any inclination to gnash her teeth. She was happy for her friends, of *course* she was. It was amazing that they had all found such wonderful men and goodness knew they deserved their happiness—but did they all have to find true love at the same time? And did they have to find it just before the Snowflake Ball?

She sighed. Last year had been such fun, waitressing at the prestigious event with Emma and Grace, and she'd been looking forward to introducing Ashleigh to the glitter and sparkle that were the hallmarks of the charity gala. The ballroom always looked amazing, the organisers ensured there were plenty of breaks, tips were generous and there was a short staff event afterwards with champagne and a delicious buffet. In fact last year had been the best New Year's Eve Sophie could remember. But this year everything was different. First Emma had bumped into her estranged—and secret—husband, Jack Westwood, aka the Earl of Redminster, and after a few difficult weeks the pair had blissfully reconciled. Then Ashleigh had fallen for gorgeous Greek tycoon Lukas while house-sitting for him. Sophie had been over the moon when her old friend had phoned her on Christmas Eve to announce her whirlwind engagement—she'd never heard Ashleigh sound so happy.

But she had to admit that she had been a little relieved that Grace, like Sophie, was still single, still employed at Maids in Chelsea and would still be waitressing at the ball. There was only so much loved-upness a girl could take.

Only while Sophie had endured overcrowded trains back to Manchester on Christmas Eve to spend an uncomfortable two days back tiptoeing around her family's habitual disapproval and enduring the same old lectures on how she had messed up her life, Grace had spent *her* Christmas being swept off her feet by hotelier Finlay Armstrong. Swept off her feet and out of her waitress clothes and into a ballgown. She *would* be at the Snowflake Ball tonight, but, like Emma and Ashleigh, she'd be there as a guest, not hired help.

'You are officially a horrible person, Sophie Bradshaw,' Sophie said aloud. 'Grace of all people deserves all the happiness in the world.' She'd been alone in the world, even more alone than Sophie, so alone she'd chosen to work over Christmas rather than spend the holidays on her own. The rift in Sophie's family might seem irreparable, but at least she had them. Yes, Grace deserved every bit of luck and happiness the last week had brought her.

But didn't Sophie deserve some too?

She pushed herself off the wall and picked her way over to the sofa, resolving once again to do something about the material strewn all over every surface as well as the floor. She did deserve happiness; she knew that even if she didn't always feel it. Her ex, Harry, had done far too good a job of eroding every last bit of confidence from her for that. But happiness for her didn't lie in the arms of a man, no matter how titled or rich or handsome he was. It lay in her dreams. In her designs. In her... And if waitressing at this ball would help her achieve those dreams, then waitress she would—and she would smile and be happy for her friends even if they were divided from her by an invisible baize door.

Only...was Harry right? Was something wrong with her? Because she had had her own little romantic adventure this Christmas, but, unlike her friends, hers had ended when the clocks struck—well, not twelve but five a.m. It had been her choice to creep out of the hotel room without leaving as much as a note, let alone a glass slipper, but she couldn't imagine Jack or Lukas or Finlay leaving a stone unturned if their women simply disappeared without a trace. But although her heart gave the odd unwanted leap whenever she saw dark hair above an expensive suit—which in Chelsea was about thirty times a day on average—the last she had seen of Marco Santoro had been his naked, slumbering torso, dimly lit by the light of the bathroom as she had gathered her belongings together.

And okay, she hadn't looked for him either, not even when she'd confessed her one-night stand to her friends just a few days ago. Not only was Marco Santoro out of her league in every way, but Sophie had allowed infatuation to cloud her judgement before. She wasn't foolish enough to mistake lust for anything deeper, not again.

Although it had been an incredible night…

The sound of the buzzer interrupted her slide into reminiscences just as she was picturing the curve of Marco's mouth. Sophie shivered as she pushed the all too real picture away and picked up the answerphone. 'Yes?'

'Sophie, it's me, Ashleigh.' Her old friend's unmistakably Australian tones sang out of the intercom and Sophie's spirits immediately lifted. So all her friends would be married to insanely wealthy, influential and hot men? It wouldn't really make a difference, not where it counted most.

'Come on up.' She pressed the buzzer and looked around wildly. Was it possible to clear a space in just twenty seconds? There was a knock on the door before she had managed to do more than pick up several scraps of material and, with them still clasped in her hand, Sophie opened the door to discover not just Ashleigh but Grace and Emma as well, brandishing champagne and a thick white envelope.

'Surprise!' they sang out in chorus, surging into the room in a wave of perfume, silk and teetering heels. The dress code for the Snowflake Ball was white or silver, but blonde, tall Emma had added red shoes and accessories to her long white silk shift, Grace, glowing with happiness, was sultry in silver lace and Ashleigh had opted for a backless ivory dress, which set off the copper in her hair and the green in her eyes. They all looked gorgeous. Sophie tried not to look over at her black waitress's dress, ironed and hung on the back of the door.

'How lovely to see you all.' She narrowed her eyes at Grace. 'You must have called me from just around the corner.'

'From the taxi,' Grace confirmed, her eyes laughing.

'Congratulations again. Finlay's a lucky man and I'll tell him so when I finally meet him. I'd hug you, but I don't want to crease your dress.'

'Where are the glasses?' Emma, of course, was already at the counter optimistically known as a kitchenette looking in one of the three narrow cupboards allotted for crockery and food. 'Aha!' She brandished them triumphantly, setting them down before twisting the foil off the bottle. It was real champagne, Sophie noted, a brand well out of her price bracket. Funny to think just a few weeks ago they would have happily been drinking cheap cava from the off-licence at the end of her street. So the divide between her lifestyle and her friends' had begun. Just as it had ten years ago when she had opted for paid work and domesticity while her few friends went to university.

She pushed the thought away as the champagne cork was expertly popped. 'Not for me, Em. I can't. You know what Clio says about drinking on the job and I need to be at the hotel for staff briefing in an hour.'

'Now, that,' Ashleigh said triumphantly, 'is where you are wrong. We've asked Keisha to cover your shift and you, Miss Sophie Bradshaw, will be going to the ball! Here you are, a formal invitation.' She thrust the envelope towards Sophie, who took it mechanically.

'I've always wanted to be a fairy godmother,' Grace said, holding out her hand to accept one of the full glasses Emma was handing out.

Sophie stared at the three beaming faces, completely flabbergasted as she took in their words, the envelope still clutched unopened in her hand. 'I'm what?'

'Going to the Snowflake Ball!'

'We're taking you as our guest!'

'You didn't think we'd leave you out, did you?' Ashleigh finished, taking a glass from Emma and pressing it into Sophie's unresisting hand. 'Cheers!'

'But…but…my hair. And what will I wear?'

'Oh, I don't know,' Emma said. 'If only one of us was an aspiring fashion designer with a wardrobe crammed full of original designs. Hang on a minute…' She strode into the minuscule bedroom—so tiny Sophie could only fit in a single cabin bed—and pulled back the curtain that divided the crammed clothes rails from the rest of the room. 'Ta-dah!'

'I couldn't wear one of my designs to an event like this! Everyone else will be in dresses like, well, like yours. Expensive, designer…'

'And you will outshine us all in an original Sophie

Bradshaw.' Grace beamed at her. 'Oh, Sophie, it's going to be a magical night. I am so very happy you are coming with is. Let's get you ready...'

Why on earth did I agree to attend this ball?

More to the point, why did he agree to attend the Snowflake Ball every New Year's Eve? It was always the same, filled with the same people, the same talk, the same tedium. Marco cast a scowling look at the crowded ballroom. Oh, it was tastefully done out with abstract snowflakes suspended from the ceiling and the glitter kept to a minimum, but it was still not a patch on Venice on New Year's Eve. His was a city that knew how to celebrate and New Year was a night when the stately old city came alive.

He hadn't spent a New Year in Venice for over a decade, although there were times when the pull of the city of his birth ran through his veins like the water in the canals and he missed the alleyways and bridges, the grand old *palazzos* and the markets with an almost physical ache that no amount of excellent champagne and food could make up for. His hands folded into fists. Tomorrow he would return home, not just for a fleeting visit, some business and a duty dinner with his mother and sister. Tomorrow he would return for a fortnight, to host the Santoros' annual Epiphany Ball and then stay to walk his sister down the aisle.

Tomorrow he would step into his father's shoes, no matter that he wasn't ready. No matter that he didn't deserve to.

Marco took a deep sip of wine, barely tasting the richness. He wouldn't think about it tonight, his last night of freedom. He needed a distraction.

His eyes skimmed the room, widening with appre-

ciation as four women stopped at a table opposite. They
were talking over each other, faces lit with enthusiasm
as they took their seats. His gaze lingered on a laughing
blonde. Her silver minidress was an interesting choice
in what was a mainly conservatively dressed ballroom,
but Marco wasn't complaining, not when the wearer
possessed such excellent legs. Excellent legs, a really
nice, lithe figure and, as she turned to face him as if
she were aware of his scrutiny, a pair of familiar blue
eyes. Eyes staring straight back at him with such undisguised horror Marco almost turned and checked,
just to make sure there wasn't an axe murderer creep-
ing up behind him.

The girl from the snow. The one who had disappeared…

Marco muttered a curse, unsure whether to coolly
acknowledge her or ignore her presence; it had been
a novel experience to wake up and find himself alone
without as much as a note. Novel and not exactly pleasant; in Marco's experience women clung on long after
the relationship was over, they didn't disappear before
it had even begun.

And they certainly didn't run away before dawn.

His eyes narrowed. She owed him an explanation
at the least, apology at best. There were rules for these
kinds of encounters and Sophie Bradshaw had broken
every one. Besides, he was damned if he was going to
spend the evening marked as the big bad wolf with Little Silver Dress going all wide-eyed at the very sight of
him. He had a fortnight of difficult encounters ahead
of him; tonight was supposed to be about having fun.

Mind made up, Marco took a step in Sophie's direction, but she was already on her feet and shouldering
her way through the ballroom. Away from him. So she

liked to play, did she? He set off at an unhurried pace, following the silver dress as it darted across the crowded room and through a discreet door set in the wooden panelling. The door began to close behind her, but his long stride shortened the distance enough for him to catch it before it could close fully and he slipped inside…

To find himself inside a closet. A large closet, but a closet nonetheless, one filled with towering stacks of spare chairs, folded tables and several cleaning trolleys. Sophie was pressed against one of the tables, her hands gripping the sides, her heart-shaped face pale.

He allowed the door to close behind him, leaning against it, his arms folded, staring her down. '*Buongiorno*, Sophie.'

'Marco? Wh-what are you doing here?'

'Catching up with old friends. That's what I like about these occasions, you never know who you might bump into. Nice corner you've found here. A little crowded, lacking in decoration, but I like it.'

'I…' Her eyes were wide. Scared.

Incredulity thundered through him. He'd assumed she had hidden because she was embarrassed to see him, that maybe she hadn't told her friends—or boyfriend—about him. Or because she was playing some game and trying to lure him in. It hadn't occurred to him that she would be actually terrified at the very thought of seeing him.

Although she had fled from his bed, run away from her friends the moment she had recognised him. How many clues did he need? His mouth compressed into a thin line. 'Apologies, Sophie,' he said stiffly. 'I didn't mean to scare you. Please rest assured that I will leave you alone for the rest of the evening.' He bowed formally and turned, hand on the door handle, only to be arrested by the sound of her low voice.

'No, Marco. I should apologise. I didn't expect to see you here, I didn't expect to see you ever again actually and I overreacted. I'm not... I don't really do... You know. What we did. I have no idea how these things work.'

What we did. Marco had spent the last three weeks trying to put what they'd done out of his mind. Tried not to dwell on the satin of her skin, the taste of her, the way she laughed. The way she moaned.

Ironically he usually did know how these things worked. Temporary and discreet were the hallmarks of the perfect relationship as far as Marco was concerned. Not falling into bed with strangers he'd met on street corners. He was far too cautious. He needed to be certain that any and every prospective partner knew the rules: mutually satisfying and absolutely no strings.

But somehow that evening all his self-imposed rules had gone flying out of the window. It had been like stepping into another world; the snow deep outside, the city oddly muted, the world contracting until it was only the two of them. It seemed as if there had been no other route open to him, booking the hotel room an unsaid inevitability as they'd moved on to their second drink, walking hand in hand through the falling snow but not really touching, not yet, waiting until the room door had swung closed behind them.

And then...

Marco inhaled, the heat of that night burning through his body. He didn't know what he'd have done if she'd been there when he woke up, pulled her to him or distanced himself in the cold light of day. But he hadn't had to make that decision; like the melted snow outside, she was gone. He'd told himself it was for the best. But now that she was here, it was hard to remember why.

He turned. Sophie was still staring at him, her blue eyes huge in her pale face. 'How these things work?' he repeated, unable to stop the smile curving his mouth. 'Does there have to be a set path?'

Colour flared high on her cheekbones. 'No, I'm not looking for Mr Right, but neither am I the kind of girl who spends the night with a stranger. Usually. So I don't know what the etiquette is here.'

'Nor do I, but I'm pretty sure it doesn't require us to spend half the evening in a cleaning closet.'

'No,' she said doubtfully as if the cleaning closet were actually the perfect place to spend New Year's Eve. 'But what happens when we get out there? Do we acknowledge that we know each other or pretend that none of it ever happened?'

The latter was certainly the most sensible idea—but hadn't he decided he needed a distraction? Sophie Bradshaw in a silver minidress was the epitome of distraction. Marco stepped away from the door, leaving it a little ajar, and smiled as ruefully as he could. 'Are those my choices? They seem a little limited. How about I throw a third option in there—I ask you to dance?'

'Ask me to dance?' Her eyes were even wider than before if that was possible and she pressed even further into the table. 'But I walked out on you. Without a note! And I ran away as soon as I saw you.'

'Sì, both of these things are true, but if you dance with me, then I am willing to overlook both transgressions.'

'I did mention that I don't want a relationship, didn't I?'

'You did. Sophie, I am also not looking for anything serious and, like you, I'm not in the habit of picking up strangers in the snow. So if neither of us is interested in a relationship and neither of us indulges in one-night stands, then why not get to know each other better? Retrospectively. Unless you're here with someone else?' His hands curled into loose fists at the thought, the thrill of possession taking him by surprise. It was only because they had barely scratched the surface of their attraction, he reminded himself. Only because spending the evening with Sophie would be safe and yet satisfying. No expectations beyond fun and flirtation, although if the evening did end the same way as their past encounter, he wouldn't complain. His gaze travelled down the sixties-inspired minidress to the acres of shapely leg, lingering on the slight swell of her hips. No, he wouldn't be complaining at all.

'No. I'm here with my friends and their husbands and fiancés. They are all lovely and doing their best to include me, but they're all so madly, sickeningly in love that I can't help feeling like a spare part.'

She was wavering. Time to press his advantage. 'Then this is fate,' he said promptly. 'Every time you feel like a spare part, dance with me. We can have a code.'

Her eyebrows raised. 'A code?'

'*Sì*, you rub your nose or tug your ear and I will know you need rescuing from the tedium of romance.'

'They don't mean to be tedious.' But the wariness had disappeared from her face and she was smiling. 'What if you're not watching, when I signal?'

'Oh, I'll be watching,' he assured her. 'But just in case you forget to signal, let's make an appointment now to see the new year in together. I'll meet you...' He paused, trying to think of a landmark in the ballroom.

'Outside this closet?'

'Perfect. Yes, I'll meet you outside here at eleven.'

'But that's a whole hour before midnight.'

'You owe me half an hour of dancing for running out on me and half an hour for escaping into a closet.

I'm Italian, the hurt to my *machismo* could have been catastrophic.'

A dimple flashed in her cheek. 'Okay, eleven it is. Unless I need rescuing, in which case I'll…I'll twizzle my hair. Deal?'

'Deal.' Marco opened the door and held it, standing to one side while Sophie passed through it, brushing past him as she did so, his body exploding into awareness at each point she touched. He took her hand as he stepped out of the small room and raised it to his lips. 'Until eleven, *signorina.* I look forward to further making your acquaintance.'

Marco leaned against the door as he watched Sophie disappear back into the ballroom. Yes, she would do very nicely as a distraction, very nicely indeed. Suddenly he was looking forward to the rest of the Snowflake Ball after all.

CHAPTER THREE

'WHO IS THAT HOTTIE? What?' Emma looked round at her friends, indignation flashing in her eyes at their splutters. 'I'm married, blissfully and happily married, but I still have eyes—and, Sophie…that man is sizzling. Tell us all.'

Sophie slid into her seat uncomfortably aware that her cheeks were probably bright red under her friends' scrutiny. 'There's nothing to tell,' she said, picking up her white linen napkin, dislodging a drift of small glittery paper snowflakes as she did so. 'I didn't miss the starter, did I? I'm starving.'

'Tell me my eyes are deceiving me and I didn't just see you emerge from a closet with him.' Ashleigh leaned in to stare intently at her and Sophie's cheeks got even hotter if that was possible—she was almost combusting as it was. 'Ha! You did. Nice work, Soph. Quick work though. We've only been here for twenty minutes.'

'I didn't go *into* the closet with him.' Sophie reached for her glass of champagne and took a much-needed sip, wincing at the unexpectedly dry taste. She pushed it aside and grabbed some water instead. 'He followed me in there.'

'He did what? I take it back. He's not hot. He's

creepy. Well, kind of both. Do you want me to set Jack on him?'

'I'm sure Lukas would be only too glad to have a word,' Ashleigh chimed in with a dark look over at the corner Marco had disappeared into.

'Finlay can be very intimidating,' Grace said, smiling dreamily at her very new and very large pink diamond ring on the third finger of her left hand.

'No, thanks for the offer, but I don't need defending.' Sophie lowered her voice. 'I know him. He's the guy…'

Three faces stared at her blankly.

She sighed. It wasn't as if there had been many— or indeed any—guys since she'd moved to London. 'The guy. From a few weeks ago. The export party guy. You know, in the snow… Italian, we went to a bar…'

'Oh, the one-night-stand guy?' Ashleigh exclaimed.

'Just a little louder, Ash, I don't think he heard you over on the other side of the room, but just one more decibel should do it.'

'What's he doing here? It must be fate.'

'No, Grace, it's not fate. It's embarrassing, that's what it is. I didn't expect to see him again, that's the whole *point* of a one-night stand.'

'Ah, but the real question is are you going to see him again? Now that he's the one-night stand and the quickie-in-the-closet guy?' Emma's eyes were twinkling.

'We did not have a quickie in the closet. Your mind! Call yourself a Countess?'

'It's My Lady to you.' But Emma's smile was rueful. Her friends hadn't got tired of teasing her about her newly acquired title. Sophie wasn't sure they ever would.

'You didn't answer the question, Sophie. Are you going to see him again?'

'Look, just because the three of you are all besotted doesn't mean that I'm looking to settle down. I've been there and done that and it very much didn't agree with me. I have agreed to dance with him later. But that's all I want. Honestly.'

But the scepticism on all three faces showed that none of them believed her. And she didn't blame them because she wasn't entirely sure she believed herself. Oh, she didn't want or need what her friends had, she wasn't hankering after a diamond ring the size of Ashleigh's or Emma's, nor, beautiful as it was, did she want to wear Grace's huge pink diamond. She was quite happy with a ring-free third finger, thank you very much. In fact Sophie's ambitions were as far from domestic bliss as it was possible to get. She wanted to make something of herself. Prove to her family—prove to herself—that she hadn't thrown her life, her chances away when she'd moved in with Harry. She didn't have the time or the inclination for romance.

But shocking as it had been to see Marco, it hadn't been unpleasant. After all, Emma was right: he was smoking hot. Smoking hot and charming. Smoking hot, charming and very, very good in bed. Not that she was planning to sleep with him again. Once was an excusable lapse, twice would be something far too much like a relationship.

But a dance wouldn't hurt—would it?

Sophie had had no intention of using any of the secret signs Marco had suggested. She kept her hands firmly on her lap, on her knife and fork, or wrapped around her water glass to ensure that she didn't inadvertently summon him over. But, as the night wore on, her resolve wavered. It wasn't that her friends and their partners intentionally excluded her, but they just couldn't help themselves. They kept separating off into cosy little pairs to sway intimately on the dance floor, no matter what the music, or to indulge in some very public displays of affection over the smoked salmon starter. In some ways it was worse when they emerged from their love-struck idyll and remembered Sophie's presence, tumbling over themselves to apologise and making Sophie feel even more like a third—or seventh—wheel than ever.

Then when the men sauntered off to the bar between courses, leaving the four friends alone, the conversation turned, inevitably Sophie supposed, to Grace's and Ashleigh's forthcoming weddings.

'Definitely a church wedding,' Grace said. 'Probably in Scotland, although it would be a shame not to hold the reception at The Armstrong. After all, that's where we met. The only thing is a church can be a little limiting. Do you think it would be okay for the bridesmaids to wear short dresses in a church?'

'The bridesmaids were in minidresses at the last church wedding I attended. They were certainly effective.' So effective that Harry, Sophie's ex, hadn't been able to take his eyes off the head bridesmaid as she had paraded down the aisle all tumbled hair and bronzed, lithe legs. Nor, it had transpired just a few hours later, had he been able to keep his hands off her either. Sophie swallowed, reaching for her water blindly to try to mask the metallic taste she always noticed when she thought about that night. The taste of humiliation. Not just because Harry had treated her like that; if she was honest with herself, he'd behaved like that for far too many years. Nor was it because he had chosen to do so in front of all of their friends; after all, Sophie had spent many occasions making excuses for him or turning a well-practised blind eye. No, the scalding shame she still experienced every day was because it had taken such a blatant humiliation to force her to act, to realise that this bad boy couldn't be redeemed and he wasn't worth one more of her tears.

How had it taken seven years? Her parents had known it almost instantly, as had her few friends. And yet she'd chosen Harry over every single one of them, sure that she saw something special in him nobody else could see. Maybe if she'd been more confident, maybe if she hadn't felt so alone when she met him…

No, there were no maybes. She had only herself to blame. What a fool, young and blinded by lust and romance. Never again.

She looked over at her friends, forcing a smile. 'I have a request, no, a demand. You must promise to seat me at a table full of fabulous, fun single ladies. No set-ups with your cousin's best friend's brother's boss just because he visited Manchester once and so we'll have lots in common and no nudging me towards the best man because that's what happens at weddings. I want a party table.'

'It's a promise,' Ashleigh agreed, turning to greet Lukas with a brilliant smile as he put another champagne-filled ice bucket down on the table along with another bottle of mineral water. Maybe she was too used to cheap cava, but Sophie just couldn't drink the champagne; every sip tasted sour. Not only was she a third wheel, but she was a sober third wheel…

What was wrong with her? She *should* be having a good time; she looked okay, her dress had got several appreciative comments, which was always warming to a designer's ears, the food was really tasty, the band talented and the ballroom looked like a very tasteful winter wonderland. It was New Year's Eve and she was out with her best friends being wined and dined. Sophie straightened. She was being selfish. She shouldn't need anything more.

Except...

Sophie's gaze slid, not for the first time, over to the large round table at the other side of the room. Marco was leaning back in his chair, a glass clasped elegantly in his fingertips, apparently deeply involved in a conversation with the couple sat next to him. Only a slight inclination of the head and a tilt of the glass towards her in a light toast betrayed his awareness of her scrutiny. But he knew, she had no doubt. He'd known every time.

It was only nine o'clock. Two hours until their promised dance.

The third of the six courses had been cleared away and Emma and Jack had taken advantage of the hiatus in the meal to dance—if you called moving very slowly staring intensely at each other dancing. Grace and Finlay were sitting opposite Sophie, but there was no point trying to chat to either of them; they were looking into each other's eyes, emitting so much heat Sophie had moved the water jug closer in case they suddenly combusted. As for Ashleigh, Sophie hadn't seen her friend for several minutes, but at last sight she had been towing Lukas determinedly towards the closet Sophie had discovered earlier.

She had a choice. She could spend the next two hours sitting here feeling sorry for herself or she could allow herself some real fun. The kind of fun she'd been too busy accommodating Harry to enjoy before. The kind of fun she hadn't allowed herself since the breakup. Just looking at Marco made her stomach fall away and her breath hitch, but she was no longer a naïve teenager who couldn't tell the difference between lust and love. And that was what this was: pure and simple delicious lust. If she knew that, remembered that, then what harm could a few more hours in Marco's company do?

And as the thought crossed her mind her hand rose, almost by its own volition, and, with her eyes fixed on Marco, Sophie slowly and deliberately wound a lock of hair around her finger and smiled.

He'd been aware of her every second of the evening, from the moment she'd walked away from him to rejoin her friends. The swish of her hair, the sway of her hips, the curve of her mouth. It was as if an invisible thread stretched across the vast room connecting them; every time she moved he felt it, a deep visceral pull.

It was unlike any reaction he'd ever had towards a woman and it wasn't hard to work out why; he didn't need a degree in psychology to realise that she was probably the first woman to walk away from him and he was completely unaccustomed to not calling the shots in all his relationships, personal and professional. No wonder his interest was piqued.

Not that he wanted her to know it. Knowledge was power in every relationship, no matter how temporary.

But Marco knew every time Sophie slid a look in his direction, he felt the tension in her as if it were his, he knew she would cave in eventually and so, with a surge of triumph, he watched her as she reached up and wound a lock of silky blonde hair around her finger, a provocative smile on her full mouth—and a challenge in her eyes.

Marco's expectations of the evening had risen the second he'd caught sight of the elusive Signorina Bradshaw; at that look in her eyes they took flight. 'Excuse me,' he said, pushing his chair back and languidly getting to his feet. No need to rush. She wasn't going anywhere. 'I have some personal business to attend to.'

He held Sophie's gaze as he moved with predatory grace across the dance floor, his steps slow and easy until he came to a halt in front of her. Sophie sat alone on one side of the table, the only other occupants breaking off from an intense conversation to watch, open-mouthed, as he extended a hand. *'Signorina?'*

Sophie arched an elegant bow. 'Sir?'

He smiled at that, slow and purposeful. 'Would you do me the honour?'

'How very unexpected.' Her eyes laughed up at him. 'I don't know what to say.'

'I believe the words you are looking for are "Thank you. I would love to."'

'Are they? In that case thank you, I would love to.' And she slipped her hand into his and allowed him to lead her from her chair and onto the dance floor.

She slipped into his arms as if she had never left, every curve fitting perfectly against him, her arms resting naturally around his waist. 'Are you having a nice evening?' It was a strangely formal question considering the way her body was pressed to his.

'I am now,' Marco answered gravely and, with some satisfaction, watched the colour rise in her cheeks. 'Have you attended this ball before?'

'I was here last year.'

'No, I was here also. How on earth did I miss you? Impossible.'

She smiled, a dimple peeping out. He remembered that dimple; it had enchanted him the first time she had smiled, snowflakes tangled in her hair, slipping on the snowy ground. 'Maybe you weren't looking hard enough. So this is a regular event for you?'

He shrugged. 'Usually. One of my clients always has a table and so here I am.'

'How very convenient. Don't you want to...' But she trailed off, shaking her head. 'Never mind.'

'Don't I want to what?'

'I'm just being nosy. It's just, isn't spending New Year with clients a little, well, impersonal? What about your friends and family?'

His stomach clenched. Tomorrow would be all about family—with one glaring omission. 'My clients are my friends as well, of course. Most of the people I know in the UK I met through work. What about you? Who are the people you are here with?'

The dimple peeked out again. 'Work friends,' she admitted. 'London can be a lonely place when you first move here.'

'You're not from London?'

'Manchester, and no, I'm not spending New Year with my family either. I did Christmas and that was more than enough.' A shadow crossed her face so fleetingly he wondered if he'd imagined it. 'How about you? Whereabouts in Italy are you from?'

'Venice.'

Her eyes lit up. 'Oh, how utterly gorgeous. What an amazing place to live.'

Amazing, thrilling, beautiful, hidebound, full of rules and expectations no man could be expected to keep. 'You've been?'

'Well, no. But I've read about it, watched films, seen pictures. It's at the top of my bucket list—lying back in a gondola and watching the canals go by. Masked balls, *palazzos*, bridges…' She laughed. 'Listen to me, I sound like such a tourist.'

'No, no. It is a beautiful city. You should go.'

'One day.' She sounded wistful. 'How can you bear to live here when you could live there? London is cool and all, but Venice? There's a story, a view around every corner.'

'And a member of my family, or an old family friend, or their relative. *Sì…*' as her eyes widened in understanding '…Venice is beautiful, captivating, unique, all these things and I miss it every day, but it is also an island. A very small island.'

'Gets a little claustrophobic?'

'A little. But London? Here a man can be who he wants to be, see who he wants to see, do the work he feels fitting. Be his own man.'

'London's not that big,' she pointed out. 'After all, I've bumped into you twice—literally the first time!'

'Ah, but, *signorina…*' he leaned forward so his breath touched her ear and felt her shiver at the slight contact '…that was fate and we don't question the workings of fate.'

They were so close he could feel her heart racing against him before she pulled back. 'Still, small or not, it must be a wonderful place to live. Are your parents still there?'

'My mother,' he corrected her. 'My father died ten months ago.' He steeled himself for the usual hit of guilt, regret and anger. Guilt his father's heart had been weakened in the first place, regret they had never patched up their relationship—and anger his father would never now admit that Marco had a right to a life of his own.

'Ten months ago? That's so recent, I'm sorry.'

'Thank you.'

'She must miss you, your mother.'

He allowed a smile but knew it was wintry at best. 'Miss me? I'm not sure. Miss telling me how to live my life? Every day.'

'I know a little about that. What does your mother want that's so terrible?'

Marco shrugged. 'What every Italian mother wants for her children, especially her only son. A place in the family business under her eyes, a wife, children, the usual.'

'And you aren't hankering for *bambinos* clustered around your knee?' She didn't sound disappointed or disapproving, which made a refreshing change. So many women seemed to see Marco's lack of interest in a family as a personal affront—or, worse, a challenge. 'Sunday morning football, wet wipes in every pocket? I have two brothers and they both have kids. I know the drill.'

'I like my life the way it is. Why complicate it?'

'And I take it no interest in a wife either.' She smiled, a small dimple charming him as she did so. 'Your poor mother.'

'She only has herself to blame,' he said lightly. 'My marriage is an obsession with her. I remember going to my mother's friend's house and while the mothers talked I played with the daughter. She was a nice girl, sporty. We got on really well. When we left my *mamma* asked me if I liked her and when I said I did she said *bene* she would make a good wife for me. I was five!'

'All mothers do that. My mother was convinced I'd marry Tom next door. He played the violin and sang in the church choir, always said hello and helped shovel snow or rake leaves. Perfect husband material.'

'And yet he isn't here with you tonight?'

'Well, it turns out that Tom prefers boys to girls, so even if I had been tempted, it was never going to happen.'

'Lucky for me.' He pulled Sophie in close and swung her around. 'Tell me, *signorina*, why are we here in this beautiful room dancing to this beautiful music and discussing my mother? I can think of many more interesting topics.'

Her eyes laughed up at him. 'Such as?'

'Such as how very sexy you look in that dress. Such as how very well you dance. Such as what shall we do with all this time until midnight?'

Sophie swallowed, her eyes luminous in the bright, pulsing disco lights. His eyes were drawn to the graceful column of her neck, the lines of her throat, and he ran his thumb down her skin, feeling her pulse speed up. 'Do?' she echoed a little hoarsely. 'Why, *signor*, you asked me to dance and so far we've just swayed to the music. Less talk, more dancing. It's New Year's Eve after all.'

There was no conversation after that, just dancing, movement, an intimacy that could only be conjured by two bodies caught up in the same beat. Sophie could *move*, hair flying, eyes shining and silver minidress glittering in the disco lights as she swayed and turned. 'A childhood full of dance lessons,' she told him during a breathless break. 'I did it all, ballet, jazz, tap. I have medals and everything.'

But as the night neared midnight the music slowed and she was back in his arms. The ballroom was filled with anticipation as the seconds began to tick away, people gathering in groups ready to welcome in the new year. Marco steered Sophie to a secluded corner of the dance floor, not wanting the shared jollity, the

drunken group embraces that so often marked the new
year's first seconds. *'Felice anno nuovo.'*

'Happy New Year, Marco.' Her eyes were half shuttered, her lips full and inviting. He knew the taste of
them, the sweet plumpness of her bottom lip, knew the
way her hands wound into his hair as a kiss deepened,
how her skin slid like silk under his fingertips. Just a
dance, he'd said. Surely they'd both known that after
the night they had shared they couldn't possibly stop
at dancing. Besides, it was New Year's Eve; it was cus-
tomary to kiss.

And how he hated to be rude. Just one kiss, to round
off the evening, to round off their brief but, oh, so pleas-
ing acquaintanceship.

Sophie purred her approval as he lowered his mouth
to hers, her hands tightening on his shoulders, her body
swaying closer until he felt every curve pressed tight
against him. Marco was dimly aware that the room was
erupting with cheers as the new year dawned, could
hear bangs and pops as the balloons and streamers were
released and the first chords of 'Auld Lang Syne' began
to echo around the room, but it was as if he and Sophie
were separated from the cheerful celebration, hidden
in some alternate dimension where all he knew was her
mouth under his, her body quivering under his caress,
her touch on his neck, light enough to drive a man mad.

And then it was over as she stepped back, trembling
and wide-eyed. 'Thank you for a lovely night. I don't
think… I mean, my friends will be looking for me.'

It took a few moments for her words to penetrate his
fogged-up brain. All he wanted was to pull her back
in, take her mouth again, hold her still. Marco inhaled,
long and deep, pushing the dangerous desire deep down
where it belonged.

'It was my pleasure. I am glad I got to meet you again, *signorina*.' He took her hand, bowing formally over it, then stepped back, a final farewell. She hesitated for the briefest of seconds and then, with a quick smile, turned away.

A pleasant interlude and now it was over as all these interludes eventually were. Unless...

Tomorrow he returned home. Returned to a wedding, to play a part, to the weight of parental expectations, no less heavy with the loss of his father. Returned to guilt.

He could do with a distraction.

Sophie obviously wasn't looking for any kind of relationship; in fact this was the third time she'd walked away from him without a backwards glance. A wry smile curved his mouth; thank goodness her response to his kiss had been so all encompassing or he'd be wondering if the attraction was one-sided. And she had never seen Venice...

She would make the perfect distraction, for himself and for his family.

Marco didn't want to take any more time to think his idea through, not when Sophie was disappearing into the revelling crowd. 'Sophie?' She stopped and turned, a confused expression on her face.

He crossed the distance between them with a few long strides. 'My mother will be holding her annual party on the sixth of January, for Epiphany. I have to be there, to co-host, in place of my father. Would you like to be my guest?'

The confusion deepened. 'Me? Come to Venice? But...'

'You said yourself how much you want to go.'

'Yes.' She looked tempted for a moment, then frowned again. 'But, Marco, I hardly know you. You don't know me and I'm not really looking for anything, for anyone. I like you, I like spending time with you...'

'And I like spending time with you and I really would like to get to know you better. And that's all this is, Sophie. A couple of days in Venice, a party and then we go our separate ways. What do you say?'

'Of course you should say yes.' The ball might officially be over for another year, but the evening was far from finished yet—after all, as Emma pointed out, they hadn't properly celebrated Grace's engagement yet—and so they had all piled into taxis and gone back to The Armstrong, the hotel Finlay owned and where the newly engaged couple had met, to finish welcoming the new year in in style. It was a novel experience for Sophie to be escorted up to the exclusive suite as a guest, not a maid, and to sink onto one of the comfortable sofas, the room-service menu at her disposal and the promise of a car to take her home.

A novel experience for Sophie, but all her friends seemed to take this level of luxury almost for granted; even Grace stepped into the private lift as if it were an everyday occurrence for her. And now it was. Grace, just like Ashleigh and Emma, was marrying into some serious wealth.

This evening, lovely as it was, was exposing the very clear differences in Sophie's future and the paths her friends were headed down—and made her even more determined to shape hers the way she had always intended it to be. This year she'd put some serious effort into the website she'd recently set up and start trying to sell her designs. She clenched her hands at the familiar twist of excitement and fear. What if Harry was right? What if she was wasting her time?

Grace plumped down onto the sofa opposite, heaving her bare feet onto the glass coffee table with a sigh of relief. 'I agree. Go, have fun. It's always quiet at work at this time of year—and we've been run off our feet for months. Take some time off. You deserve it.'

'I'll lend you the fare if you need it. Consider it an early birthday present.' Ashleigh seated herself next to Sophie and nudged her. 'Venice, Soph. You've always wanted to go.'

'Marco offered to pay for my ticket. No, don't look so excited. He has loads of air miles from his work. It's not a big deal.' Actually it was. Sophie didn't want to admit how much his casual 'I'll cover all expenses, it's the least I can do, you'll be far more of a help than you realise' had touched her. Harry had not only always expected Sophie to pay her way but frequently his as well. He was a musician after all, above mundane worldly tasks like making a living. 'It's just, I hardly know him.'

Grace raised her eyebrows knowingly. 'Didn't look that way from where I was sitting tonight. The chemistry between you two…*oof*!' She fanned herself dramatically, ducking with a squeal as Sophie threw a cushion at her.

'What do you need to know?' Ashleigh asked, squeezing Sophie's hand. 'What would make you feel better about going?'

Sophie shrugged, unable to articulate the prickle of unease that ran over her when she thought about accepting Marco's casual invitation—or, more worryingly, the ripple of excitement overshadowing the unease. 'I don't know where he lives. I don't exactly know what he does for a living. I don't know if he likes music or books or walks in the country.'

'What *do* you know?' Emma curled up next to Grace. 'Tell us about him.'

'He's Italian, does something to do with art and antiques. Erm…he's lived in London for ages but really loves Venice, you can hear it in his voice. He has a gorgeous accent, dresses really well, his suits look handmade to me, beautifully designed, great fabric.'

'Focus, Sophie. We want to know about the man, not his clothes. How does he make you feel?'

How did he make her *what*? When Sophie had packed her bags, the shattered remaining pieces of her pride and her bruised heart and moved over a hundred miles away to start again, the one thing she had guarded herself against was feeling too much. It was thanks to her emotions she had fallen into such a sorry state in the first place. She picked up a cushion and cradled it close, as if it were a shield between her and the rest of the world while she thought. 'He makes me feel sexy. Wanted. Powerful.' Where had those words come from? But even as she spoke them Sophie knew that they were the truth—and that not once, in seven years, had Harry made her feel any of those things. Desperate, insecure, weak, needy, pathetic? All the above. Never powerful. Never wanted.

She straightened, turning to stare at Ashleigh half excited, half terrified. 'I should go, shouldn't I?'

'You should totally go. Who cares about his address and what exactly something in art and antiques means? As long as he isn't a drug smuggler and doesn't live with his wife and six kids, it's irrelevant. Sexy and powerful? Now, *they're* relevant.'

'Who knows where it might lead? Look at me. I went to Scotland for a bit of adventure and came back head over heels. Go for it!' Grace practically clapped in excitement, but Sophie shook her head emphatically.

'I am so happy for you, Grace, for all of you. But believe me, I'm not going to come back engaged. Marco made it very clear he's not interested in anything long-term and that suits me perfectly. There's a lot I want to achieve, that I need to achieve, and wedded bliss is very far down that list. But this will be good for me. I've been so scared of being sucked back into a relationship I've gone too far the other way. This is a big city. I should date and see people occasionally, live a little.'

'Live a lot,' Emma corrected her. 'You should, Sophie, you deserve to. And we'll be cheering you on every step of the way.'

CHAPTER FOUR

'LIVE A LOT,' Sophie reminded herself as she passed through the customs gate and into the arrivals hall. Her new mantra. She'd been repeating it throughout the flight, torn between excitement at seeing Venice—and Marco—at last and apprehension about the next few days. What if she and Marco had nothing to say to each other now she was here, or what if his mother didn't like her?

No, those negative thoughts were old Sophie, not new, improved, positive, life-grabbing Sophie. Pushing them aside, she scanned the arrivals hall, impatient to see Marco. She hadn't spoken to him since New Year's Eve as he had flown out the very next day, but he had sent an itinerary with her ticket and promised that she would be met at the airport.

Maybe he was running late…

As she scanned the waiting crowd again a sign bearing a familiar name caught her eye and, as she paused to read it again, the bearer, a slight man in his forties, formally dressed in a chauffeur's uniform and cap, caught her eye and smiled. 'Signorina Bradshaw?' he asked in heavily accented but perfect English. 'Signor Santoro asked me to meet you. He has been called away.' He handed Sophie an envelope as he deftly relieved her of her suitcase and bag.

Disappointment warred with a cowardly relief. Work had predictably been quiet over the last few days, leaving Sophie far too much time to second-guess her decision and, even though she'd tried to bury herself in her designs or wrestle with the unnecessarily complicated content management system on her still-not-live website, she often found herself sitting still staring into space, her heart thumping with panic at the prospect of stepping outside the narrow life she'd built herself.

The envelope was thick, more like an invitation than a piece of office stationery, and it took Sophie a couple of moments to open it and pull out a piece of crisp white paper. She unfolded it and scanned the brief lines.

Sophie,
Please accept my most sincere apologies but I am
unavoidably detained. Gianni will escort you to
my mother's house and I will see you at the party
this evening.
A dopo,
Marco

No kiss, she noted. What did that mean in a time when even her dentist included an X on her check-up reminder? Pocketing the note, she smiled at Gianni. 'Thank you for coming to meet me. I'm ready whenever you are.'

She'd spoken too soon. As she got her first glimpse of Venice Sophie realised that nothing could have prepared her for her first glimpse of the magnificent island city. Gianni led her out of the airport and, instead of heading to a car park, Sophie found herself at a dock.

'This way, please,' Gianni said, briskly walking her past the ferry port and the queues for the water taxis. Sophie wanted to stop and take in the strange sight of passengers embarking onto a row of boats, swaying on the gangplanks as they tried to balance their suitcases. All around her, voices exclaimed, yelled and barked in a mixture of languages, the fresh salt smell of the sea mixing with the less romantic scent of diesel.

They walked on for another few minutes until Gianni gestured her forward onto a gangplank that led onto a gleaming wooden boat. Two seats at the front were shielded from the elements by a simple screen and a further three comfortable-looking leather benches were arranged around the walls of the small glassed-in cabin. Gianni heaved her suitcase and bag onto the cabin floor, but when he gestured for Sophie to step inside she shook her head. 'Oh, please, can I sit up front, next to you? I've never been to Venice before.'

Gianni cast an assessing look at her quilted coat and the black velvet jeans she'd chosen to travel in. '*Sì*, but it gets cold on the sea. Do you have a hat?'

'And a scarf and gloves,' Sophie assured him as she took her place beside the driver's seat—or pilot's seat. She wasn't entirely sure of the correct term for a boat driver.

It took just a few moments for Gianni to cast off the ropes and expertly manoeuvre the boat out of the dock and around the fleet of ferries, water taxis and hotel boats out into the lagoon. Sophie sucked in a breath of sheer exhilaration as the boat accelerated through the clear blue water and headed towards the most beautiful place she'd ever seen. The island city rose out of the water like a stately dame.

'"Age cannot wither her, nor custom stale her infinite

variety",' Sophie quoted as the bell tower in St Mark's Square came into view. It seemed so familiar and yet so new—a picture she'd seen a thousand times and yet never really got until now. Sophie's heart squeezed and she knew she would always love this ancient city. It was in her blood already, taking further root with every breath.

She couldn't speak as Gianni steered the boat into the Grand Canal, just stared, almost overcome by the beauty all around her. Boats passed them, turning down narrow canals, bridges arched overhead and, glancing down a canal on her right, Sophie thrilled as she saw a boat piled high with a colourful variety of fruit and vegetables moored to the side, the owner twisting up produce in paper bags as he sold to eager customers.

It wasn't just the beauty of the city, it was the life thrumming through it. This was no museum, a place existing merely for the multitudes of tourists. It was a living, breathing place—and for the next two days she would be part of it. Would belong.

At that moment the boat began to turn and headed towards a small gangplank and a set of stairs leading directly to a door to an imposing cream-coloured building right on the Grand Canal. What was going on? She'd done a little research and knew that the hotels overlooking the famous canal were exorbitant. Sophie had expected a little B & B somewhere further out of the city. 'Wait, where are you going?'

Gianni looked puzzled. 'To Palazzo Santoro, of course. Signor Santoro asked me to convey you directly.'

'The *palazzo*?' Sophie's hands tightened on the side of the boat. Marco hadn't mentioned a *palazzo*—especially not one right on the Grand Canal. Her stomach twisted. Girls from the Manchester suburbs didn't belong in places like this—not unless they were serving drinks. She took a deep breath. *Palazzo* probably didn't mean anything grand. Maybe Marco's mother had a flat in this building. No one actually *owned* a building this big, no one Sophie was ever going to meet.

Before she could completely gather her thoughts the boat had stilled and Gianni was lifting her bags out of the back of the boat and extending a hand to help her disembark. Sophie climbed gingerly over the side of the boat and followed Gianni, treading carefully up the stone steps. He rapped smartly on the door and, as it opened, set Sophie's bags inside, gave her a friendly nod and ran lightly back down the steps and into the boat. She looked around wildly, hoping for a clue as to where exactly she was going, but all she could see was the open door. And her suitcase and travel bag were inside.

It fleetingly crossed Sophie's mind that no one knew exactly where she was—or who Marco was—and she could enter this house and never be seen again. But if it was a kidnap plot, it was far too elaborate a set-up for a waitress living on the outer edges of Chelsea. She took another step up the last step and entered through the ornately carved wooden door and came to an abrupt standstill.

Had she fallen down a rabbit hole? Sophie had cleaned and waitressed in some seriously swanky homes over the last year or so, but she had never seen anything quite on this scale or of this antiquity. The door led into an immense tiled hallway with a wooden-beamed ceiling and aged-looking frescos on the wall and ceiling, the only furnishings a few very old and very delicate-looking chairs. The hall ran the entire length of the building; she could see double doors at the other end, windows on either side, the sun streaming through the stained glass at the top. A gallery with intricate wrought-iron railings ran all the way around the hallway, accessed by two wide staircases, one at either end of the hall. Sophie could see several closed doors running the length of the room, discreetly hidden in the faded frescos.

What she couldn't see was any sign of life. She stepped further in, swivelling slowly as she took in every detail, jumping at the sight of the elderly woman, clad in sombre black from throat to calf, standing statue-like almost behind the open door. 'Oh, hello. I mean *buongiorno*.' All her hastily learned Italian phrases seemed to have disappeared from her head. '*Je m'appelle*... No, sorry, that's not right. Erm...*mi chiamo* Sophie. Marco is expecting me, isn't he? The driver, boatman, he seemed to think he was at the right place.'

That's right, Sophie, just keep babbling.

She was struck by a sudden thought: maybe this was a hotel and the Santoro was just a coincidence—it could be a totally common name like Smith or Brown. 'Should I check in?' she enquired hopefully. A check-in desk she could cope with. House rules, room-service menu, hopefully a fluffy white robe.

The woman didn't respond. Instead she bent slowly, so slowly Sophie could almost hear the creak of her waist, before picking up Sophie's suitcase as if it weighed less than an empty pillowcase. Sophie, who had stepped forward to stop her, froze in place as the woman stepped forward, the suitcase almost swinging from her hand. It had taken all Sophie's efforts just to heave that suitcase onto the Tube. She eyed the woman with respect and stood back out of her way as the woman strode past her with a grunted 'This way' as she did so. Sophie followed meekly behind, along the hallway, up three flights of the sweeping staircase and onto a long landing peopled with portraits of men in tights and women with fans. Sophie was panting by this point, but the woman seemed completely at ease and Sophie yet again promised herself a regular routine of Pilates, Zumba and body pump.

They came to an abrupt halt outside a wood-panelled door. The woman pushed it open and gestured for Sophie to step inside. With a wondering glance she did so, her aching legs and heaving chest instantly forgotten as she turned around in wonder.

The room was huge, easily twice the size of Sophie's entire apartment with three huge floor-to-ceiling windows overlooking the canal, shutters swung open to reveal the Juliet balconies outside each one, Venice framed like a living breathing picture within. Although the walls were painted a simple pale blue the ceiling was alive with a fresco of cherubs and angels, partying riotously across the room, edged in gilt matching the elaborate gilt headboard on the huge bed and the elegant chaise positioned before one of the windows. A huge mirror hung opposite the windows reflecting the watery light. The woman—a maid? Marco's grandmother? A complete stranger? Sophie had absolutely no idea—opened one of two matching doors on either side of the bed to reveal a dressing room, complete with dressing table and two wardrobes. The other door led into a bathroom so luxurious Sophie thought she might never be able to leave it.

'The family will gather in the reception room at six,' the lady intoned and left, shutting the door firmly behind her, leaving Sophie standing in the middle of the room torn between giddiness at the gorgeousness of her surroundings and fear at trying to find her way through this huge house to meet a set of people she didn't even have names for.

'Breathe,' she told herself. 'Live a lot, remember?' But as she sank onto the bed she was painfully conscious that all she wanted to do was hide away in this room.

Okay, here was what she knew: this was not an apartment; Marco's family appeared to own the entire, immense and very old building. Therefore the family party was unlikely to be just a few close friends, a glass of sherry and some pineapple and cheese sticks in the kitchen. The only person she knew was Marco and he wasn't even here and didn't expect to be until the party. She lay down and stared up at the cherubs, hoping they might be able to help her.

On the other hand she *was* in Venice. Sophie sat up and rolled off the bed, almost running to the window before the thought had fully formed, staring out with rapt eyes at the *palazzos* opposite, at the boats sailing below. She was in *Venice* and about to go to a party with a gorgeous man before returning to the most beautiful room she had ever set eyes on. So she was a little daunted? Time to pull on her big-girl pants—well, the nicest underwear she owned *just in case*—and try to enjoy every moment because she knew all too well that moments like this didn't come her way all too often.

'Come on, Sophie. Enjoy it. It's just a couple of days...' Two days of being someone new. Nobody here knew her, nobody here knew that she was twenty-six, had wasted the last eight years of her life, that she worked sixteen hours a day trying to pay her bills and get her own business off the ground. She wasn't Sophie Bradshaw, reliable employee of Maids in Chelsea, waitress, chambermaid and cleaner. She was Signorina

Bradshaw, the kind of woman who went to glamorous balls and got invited to stay in *palazzos*. Why not be that woman for two days? After all, she wasn't expecting to see Marco again after she went back to London. What harm could it do to live the fantasy, just for a little while?

But as she turned to look back at the ornate room fear struck her once again. How would a girl like her ever fit in a place like this? Even if it was for just a couple of days?

Marco adjusted his bow tie, painfully aware that he was running almost inexcusably late. It had been a long six days. Since his move to London Marco had kept his visits back to Venice as brief as possible—he'd been confident in his contacts in Italy; it had been the rest of the world he'd needed to concentrate on. But a decade was a long time and it was becoming painfully clear a couple of days twice a year was no longer enough. He needed to start spending some significant amounts of time here if he wanted to continue to grow his business.

His mother was also making it very clear that it was time he stepped up and assumed his role as head of the family. Only, guided by her, of course… His mouth thinned. He'd already fought that battle with one parent and he wasn't sure either of them could count a decade-long standoff as a victory. And now his father was gone it all seemed pointlessly self-destructive anyway.

But how could he complain about the burden of his name when every now and then it opened doors to homes and estates that were kept firmly shut to less exalted sons of the city? Today he had spent the day with an impoverished old Venetian family who were reluctantly selling off some of their family treasures and trusted Marco to do the job for them both lucratively and discreetly. Neither would prove to be difficult; he had a long list of potential buyers who would pay more than market value for first refusal on the beautifully carved furniture, Renaissance paintings and elaborate silverware.

A negotiation like this took time and he had been all too aware that while he was sitting drinking coffee with the Grigionis and dancing ever so politely around his commission, Sophie had arrived to an empty house with nobody to welcome her but Marta, who was a most excellent woman but not the most gregarious of people— and the chances were very high that she would run into his mother before he could warn Sophie just what he was bringing her into.

Several times over the last few days he had been on the verge of cancelling Sophie's visit. His mother had been so focussed on finding him a suitable Venetian bride he'd hoped Sophie's presence would throw her long enough to give him some space—but he'd underestimated her desire to see him wed. His father's death seemed to have intensified her hopes, and nationality no longer seemed to matter. His mother's eyes had lit up at the news he had invited a date to the party and she hadn't stopped asking him questions about his English 'friend'.

At least with Sophie by his side she wouldn't be able to introduce him to any eligible female guests with that specifically intense focus she usually employed. No, it was probably a good thing he hadn't cancelled. Sophie was here for just a couple of nights, not long enough for his mother to get too attached to her but long enough to throw her off the scent for the rest of his visit. Bringing a diversion was an excellent idea; he didn't know why he hadn't considered it earlier.

The clock had finished striking six when Marco strolled into the salon, adjusting his cuffs as he did so. Sophie was already there talking to his mother and his sister, Bianca, looking a little paler than he remembered but stunning in a pale pink beaded dress, which hung straight down to mid-thigh from two simple knotted straps. Her long blonde hair was knotted up with tendrils curling around her face, her only jewellery a pair of striking gold hoop earrings, which trembled as she moved. His blood began to pulse hot at the sight of her exposed neck. Inviting her had been an excellent idea for several reasons.

'Sophie,' he said, striding over to her and kissing her on both cheeks in welcome. 'Welcome. Did you have any trouble finding us?'

'No, no, even I would find it hard to get lost when a boat delivers me straight to the door.' Bianca and his mother laughed, but Marco's eyes narrowed. There was a tartness in her voice he hadn't heard before, the blue eyes icy and cold. Was she cross because he hadn't met her at the airport? He hoped not. Maybe a decoy was going to be as much trouble as a real girlfriend.

'Mamma, Bianca, please excuse us, I would like to make my apologies to Sophie properly for not being here when she arrived,' he said, smoothly drawing Sophie's arm through his. The pre-party drinks were being held in the reception salon, the largest sitting room on the first floor. Like most of the public rooms it overlooked the Grand Canal. Marco walked Sophie over to the furthest window, away from prying ears. 'I hope Gianni found you all right. I'm sorry I was detained.'

'No, that's fine.' But she was still staring out at the canal, her face set. 'I just wish you'd warned me, that's all.'

'I didn't realise until yesterday...'

'No! Not about being met, for goodness' sake! About this...' She looked around and he realised with a stab of compunction that her lips were quivering. 'Marco, every woman here is in a full-on ballgown. They look like they are going to a coronation, not a family party. And me? I'm wearing a little party dress I made myself. I look so underdressed.'

'You look beautiful.' And she did. Although she was right, all the other women were in floor-length, brightly coloured silk and chiffon gowns.

'And this house! Family party, you said. You forgot to mention that the family is the Borgias! I've never been anywhere like this. My bedroom is like a five-star hotel.'

'You don't like it?' Marco was struggling to understand the point she was making. So the family home was big and the party formal? Women usually loved the *palazzo*, and they loved knowing he was the future owner—owner, he supposed, not that he had any intention of setting up home here even more.

'Like it?' She made a queer noise, part gasp, part sob, part laughter. 'It's not the kind of place you like, is it? It's magnificent, beautiful, incredible, but it's not the kind of place I know as home. I don't fit in here, Marco. Not in this house, not with this kind of wealth. Your mother is wearing a diamond tiara that's probably worth more than my parents' house.' She shook her head. 'Oh, God, listen to me. I sound like the worst kind of inverted snob. I just didn't expect any of this. I'm more than a little thrown.'

Marco had never heard this kind of reaction before. True, most women who walked into the *palazzo* knew exactly who he was, briefed by their *mammas* just as he was by his. But even the wealthiest and most well-bred visitor got a covetous look in their eye when they realised the whole of the building still belonged to the family and therefore, by extension, to Marco. This kind of appalled shock was new, but it was also a relief, like a long sip of cold water after a lifetime of rich, creamy milk.

And she did have a point. He'd brought her here for his own selfish reasons; it hadn't occurred to him to warn her just what a Santoro party entailed.

'Just be yourself, Sophie. I promise you, everyone will love you—and they will adore your dress. I'm sorry, it didn't occur to me that this would all be a little overwhelming, but I promise to make it up to you. Tomorrow I'll show you Venice, not a tiara in sight. What do you say?'

She didn't answer for a long moment, indecision clear on her face. Then she turned to him, eyes big with a vulnerable expression in them that struck him hard. 'Are you sure I look all right? I'm not letting you down?'

'Not at all,' he assured her. 'In fact I predict next year most of the younger women will be glad to break with tradition and wear shorter dresses. Come, let's go and mingle and I will tell you three scandalous secrets about every person we meet. I promise you won't be intimidated by a single one by the end of the evening.'

CHAPTER FIVE

ALTHOUGH MARCO WAS true to his word and did indeed tell Sophie such scandalous secrets about every person she met—she refused to believe they could be true; *surely* that regal lady over there wasn't an international jewel thief?—she was still a little intimidated. Intimidated by the glitter and the air of self-possession displayed by every well-dressed guest, by the rapid flow of Italian all around and the familiarity with which each guest greeted each other. She felt too English, too parochial, too poor, too self-conscious, and although Marco was a charming and attentive host Sophie couldn't help thinking longingly of the city outside the old *palazzo*, ready to be explored and discovered.

But when Marco took her arm in his, when he leaned in close to whisper yet another outrageous lie, when he caught her eyes, laughter lurking in his, as his mother not so discreetly quizzed Sophie on her future plans and whether those plans involved marriage and babies, then she was pulled away from the room, away from her insecurities and into a world where all she saw was the tilt of his mouth, the warmth of his smile and the promise in his dark eyes. Anticipation flooded through her at the knowledge that when the clock struck twelve her night would only just be beginning... At least she hoped it would; she hadn't splashed out on a gorgeous new nightie in the New Year sales for nothing. The bits of silk held together with lace would hardly keep her warm after all.

She was aware of Marco's eyes on her and heat flooded through her as their gazes snagged and held, the rest of the room falling away. No, the other women in the room could do their best to attract his attention—and many of them were—but Sophie knew she wouldn't be sleeping alone that night.

After drinks and appetisers and a formal, beautifully presented meal for fifty, the party moved into an even grander and bigger room. Here yet more guests joined them, the numbers swelling into the hundreds as a band played at one end and immaculately dressed waiters circled with trays of drinks. Marco's mother had 'borrowed' him to greet an elderly relative and Sophie hovered by the window, unsure where to go or who to speak to—if she could make herself understood, that was. It was all too reminiscent of standing at the back of one of Harry's gigs, not quite knowing what to say or whether she was welcome in any of the close-knit, self-possessed groups.

'I'm sorry, it must all be a little too much for you. We are bad enough when it's just the family, but when all of Venice is here? I wish I could run and hide, so I have no idea how horrifying you must find tonight.'

Sophie turned to see Marco's sister, Bianca, standing beside her, a sympathetic smile on her heart-shaped face. She was very beautiful in a classically Italian way with masses of dark wavy hair and huge brown eyes fringed with lashes so long they made Sophie gasp with envy, tall and shapely with a generous bosom spilling out of the top of her low-cut strapless dress.

'It's a little more than I was expecting. Marco didn't quite communicate the full scale of the evening. I didn't expect to meet so many people. As you can see I'm not really dressed appropriately...' She gestured towards her dress self-consciously, aware that the hand-sewn beads and cheap fabric paled beside Bianca's ravishing emerald silk gown.

'Your dress is *bellissima*,' Bianca reassured her. 'I have heard many envious comments. Of course, you have such lovely ivory skin. That pale pink would make me far too sallow. I predict next year half the younger women will break with convention and wear something a little more fun and fashionable.' Bianca echoed her brother's prediction.

'Thank you.' Sophie didn't think her skin looked lovely or ivory, more the pale blue an English winter turned her naturally pale complexion. She'd much rather be blessed with Bianca's gorgeous olive skin and generous curves.

'And the cut, I love how it is so modern and yet looks so vintage. Who's the designer?'

'Oh, well, I am.' Sophie always felt absurdly diffident when admitting to designing or making her clothes. Her friends were supportive, asking for commissions and nagging her into starting a website to sell to a wider audience, but they were her friends—it was their job to tell her to follow her heart and aim high. Showing her work to other people was exposing. Harry had always told her that she was wasting her time and the problem was she didn't only believe him then, she still half believed him now.

'You made this? But, Sophie, it is incredible. No wonder it fits you so well. You are so talented.'

'Thank you, but it's not that hard...'

'Of course it is! I can barely thread a needle. Do you make all your clothes?'

'Most of them,' Sophie admitted. 'Some from scratch, with new material, but many of my clothes are do-overs. I buy them from charity shops or in sales, tear them apart and put them back together again.'

'How creative.' Bianca sighed. 'I tried for years to find my talent, but no matter how many private lessons I had I remained tone deaf, turned into a plank of wood on stage, and I'm still incapable of drawing better than a five-year-old. Antonio tells me not to worry, that handling spreadsheets is a talent in itself, but I'd much rather be a dancer than an accountant.'

'You're an accountant?' Sophie always thought of accountants as faded and grey—not vibrant and full of life like the woman in front of her.

'Head of Finance at Antonio's company. It's how we met. He says marrying me will stop me being head-hunted—I let him think that. I don't want to shatter his illusions! But I'd like to work for an international company if I get the opportunity. All those complicated tax laws would be really interesting.'

'Quite.' Sophie had no idea what to say, all her preconceptions tumbling down. It had been too easy to look at Bianca and see nothing but the beautifully dressed daughter of an obviously wealthy family—but there was clearly a lot more to her than that. 'As someone who can dance and sew but gets a cold sweat at the thought of a budget I have to say I think you got the better end of the deal.'

'Maybe. So where did you and Marco meet?'

Here it was. The interrogation. Sophie had already been through something similar from Marco's mother, an aunt and his godmother. 'At a party. Actually after the party, it was snowing and we sort of...collided.'

'How romantic.' The dark eyes were keen and focussed very intently on Sophie. 'Snow and an unexpected encounter. And you've seen much of each other since?'

'I wouldn't say much.' She forced a laugh. 'How friendly everyone is and they all want to know about me.'

'You must think we're all very nosy. But this is the first time in a long time that Marco has ever willingly brought a date to any occasion—and definitely the first time he brought someone Mamma hasn't set him up with. So you see, we are all consumed with curiosity to find out more about the mysterious English girl who has captured my brother's heart.'

Who had *what*? What exactly had Marco intimated? 'I wouldn't go that far. We are still getting to know each other. It's very early days...'

The two women had drifted over to one of the uncomfortable formal-looking sofas and Bianca sat down with a relieved 'Oomph, my feet are so swollen. How I am going to manage a whole wedding in heels, I don't know. I usually wear flats, I'm so tall. But Mamma insisted I wear heels on my wedding day. Luckily Antonio is tall too, so I won't tower over him!'

'You're getting married soon?' Really, it was absurd how ill prepared she was to meet this family. Next time a gorgeous stranger suggested a spontaneous trip to a family party she would insist on crib sheets and a written exam first.

'Next week.' Bianca sighed. 'Only, I think I ate too much over Christmas and I'm really scared my dress won't do up. The shame! But look at the size of my breasts! I'm going to be falling out of it, I know it.'

'But you must have a final fitting booked, surely? There will be something they can do. Let out a seam or fit a false back. I wouldn't worry, a good designer is always prepared for some fluctuation in weight.'

'But she's not here. She's gone to New Zealand for the whole month and won't be back until after the wedding. I didn't think it would be a problem. My weight doesn't usually change...' Bianca's voice trailed off and she looked so woebegone Sophie couldn't help sympathising.

'I could take a look,' she suggested. 'Make a few suggestions. Obviously it depends on the fabric and cut, but I might be able to help.' As soon as she said the words she wanted to snatch them back. What was she thinking? A wedding dress? A designer wedding dress no doubt, costing thousands and made of the best silks and laces. As if she were qualified to do as much as tack a hem on that kind of gown, let alone attempt some kind of alteration, but, Sophie realised with a sinking heart, it was too late to backtrack. Bianca was clutching at her arm, gratitude beaming out of her eyes.

'Really? You'd do that?'

'Well... I...'

'Oh, Sophie, that's so wonderful. *Grazie.* It's such a relief to know that you're right here. Wait, when are you going back to London?'

'The day after tomorrow, but I'm sure I can find time to look at it before I go, make some suggestions.'

'The day after tomorrow? But the wedding isn't for another week! What if something else changes?'

Sophie's smile froze. She'd heard tales of bridezillas but had never had to deal with one before, not even at work. In fact Emma's vow renewal was the first time she'd been directly involved with the bridal party, not a duty invite or a plus-one on the guest list—somehow she'd let her few school friends slip away through the Harry years and had never really connected with his friends' ever-changing parade of girlfriends.

'I'm sure it will be fine...'

But Bianca was shaking her head. 'So much could go wrong—a button could loosen or a hem fray or my veil need adjusting. What was I thinking to choose a designer who isn't here for the wedding? It has to be perfect. But if you were here, I wouldn't have to worry.'

'Bianca, no one would notice if a button was loose, I promise.'

'And what if I get bigger? Or smaller? With all the stress, I don't know if I'll lose my appetite or eat chocolate for the next seven days. Everything is very unpredictable at the moment.' To Sophie's horror Bianca's voice began to waver. She wasn't going to cry on her, was she?

'It's only a week. I'm sure it won't make any difference if you eat nothing but chocolate, not at this stage.'

'And this is your first time in Venice, no? You can't possibly see the city in just one day. Marco should have known better. You must stay, see the city properly and then come to the wedding. I would love to have you.' She turned to Sophie, her smile wide again, all traces of tears miraculously disappeared. 'There, now we are all happy, me, you and Marco. Perfect.'

'What will make me happy?'

Sophie's stomach turned as Marco strode up beside them. He'd think she'd been plotting with his sister, think the *palazzo* had turned her head and she wanted to stay, to inveigle her way into his family.

'Nothing. Bianca is panicking a little about her wedding, but I'm telling her not to worry,' she said quickly.

He raised an eyebrow. 'Don't tell me, the flowers are out of season and so you need to call the whole wedding off? She used to be quite sensible,' he added to Sophie, 'until this wedding nonsense.'

'It's not nonsense. Wait until it's your turn,' Bianca said indignantly. 'But, Marco, wait. I have a wonderful idea. Sophie should stay here with us until the wedding and come as your date. What do you think?'

Sophie should *what*? Marco froze to the spot, eyes narrowed at his beaming sister. Had she been consulting with their mother? Was this some elaborate plot? Was Sophie in on it? He cast her a quick glance. No, her cheeks were red and eyes lowered in mortification.

'What do I think?' he repeated.

'He thinks it's impossible.' Sophie reached up and took his hand, giving it a reassuring squeeze. 'I have to get back and he doesn't need a date anyway. I don't want to cramp his style.'

'Nonsense,' Bianca said. 'He would love to have you there.'

Amusing as it was to hear the two women politely disagree about what he did or didn't want, it was time to take control. 'Of course I would love to have you attend the wedding with me, Sophie, but if you have to get back, then there is no more to say. Besides, I have a lot to do over the next few days and I would hate you to be bored here alone.'

Bianca shot to her feet and glared at him. 'It's my wedding and I want her there. I need her, Marco.'

'But…' He wasn't often at a loss for words, but seeing his usually sensible, logical sister so het up robbed him of all coherent speech. 'Bianca, Sophie's said she needs to get back. You can't force her to stay.'

But as he said the words he began to consider just what would happen if Sophie *did* stay. He'd warned her he had to work so there would be no expectation for him to be responsible for her—and then when they returned to England he'd give it a few weeks before casually telling his mother they had parted company. In the meantime... He laced his fingers through hers, enjoying the smoothness of her skin against his. In the meantime it had been too long since he had enjoyed one of his discreet affairs. Two nights and a day wasn't long enough, not when every time she moved the beads on her dress shimmered, showcasing the outline of her breasts, the shapeliness of her calves.

And she'd made it very clear to him she wasn't interested in anything long-term...

'Of course, if there was some way you could arrange things so that you could spend a few more days with us, then you would be very welcome, Sophie.' He smiled at her. 'Besides, bitter experience has taught me that Bianca usually gets her way, so it saves time if you just agree with her at the start.'

'But...you don't want, I mean, this is a family occasion.'

'Three hundred guests, at least a hundred of whom are my parents' business associates and another hundred Bianca and Antonio's clients. I wouldn't worry about gatecrashing.'

Her mouth opened and she stared at Bianca incredulously. 'Three hundred guests?'

'You see why it has to be perfect? Please, Sophie, say yes. I'll be in your debt for ever.'

Marco knew not many people were able to resist

Bianca when she turned the full force of her charm on them and Sophie was no different. 'I suppose I could take a few more days off work. I have a lot of holidays saved up. I'm not a miracle worker,' she warned his sister, 'but I'll do my best. Okay, if you really want me to, I'll stay, but, honestly, you might be better off consulting a professional.'

'I am so happy.' Bianca clapped her hands. 'When can you take a look? Tomorrow?'

It was time to intervene. 'Tomorrow, Bianca, Sophie belongs to me. You can have her the rest of the week. No…' as she tried to interrupt '…you need to practice patience, my child. Sophie, there's someone over here I would like to introduce you to. Bianca has been monopolising you long enough.' He pulled Sophie to her feet, giving his pouting sister a mock bow. '*Arrivederci*, Bianca.'

'Who are you introducing me to?' Sophie asked as he walked her away from the party, opening a door hidden in the ballroom panelling and ushering her into the small adjoining salon, lit only by a few low lamps. 'I hate to break it to you, but the party is that way and there's no one here. Unless it's some ancestor of yours,' she added, looking up at the huge portraits hanging over the mantelpiece. 'He doesn't look overly impressed with your choice of date.'

'That's my great, great, many more greats grandfather Lorenzo Santoro. He didn't approve of anyone or anything by all accounts, a problem in pleasure-loving Venice.'

'I won't take it personally, then.' She turned and faced him, her hair gleaming gold in the low lights, the dress swaying seductively around her thighs. 'So if you don't want to introduce me to Lorenzo, then who am I here to meet?'

'Me. I haven't seen you since New Year's Eve, almost a week ago, and I've neglected you shamefully since you got here. I think it's time I made amends.' He noted with some satisfaction how her colour rose at his words, tinging her cheeks, throat and décolletage a delicate rose pink.

'Oh…' She looked up at him then, the blue eyes earnest. 'Marco, it was really nice of you to ask me here in the first place. I'd really hate for you to think I was trying to force you into extending my invitation. Your sister seems so worried about her dress, I offered to help and the next thing I knew…'

'Sophie, I know exactly what my sister is like, please don't worry. If you wish to stay for the wedding, then I would love for you to do so, but if she railroaded you…'

'She did, but it's not exactly a hardship to stay here and explore Venice a bit more.'

'Then it's settled, you stay. And, Sophie?'

'Yes?'

He took a step closer. 'Let's get one thing straight. I wasn't being nice when I asked you here.'

'You weren't?'

'Not at all. I wanted to see you again.' His gaze dropped to her full mouth. 'I wanted to renew our acquaintance.'

'To renew our acquaintance?' she echoed. 'So that's what they call it nowadays.'

Another step. 'Do you know what this room is?'

That elusive, kissable dimple peeked out at the corner of her mouth. 'Another room for unsuspecting guests to get lost in?'

'Did you see how the door was almost hidden in the panelling? It's an assignation room. Ancestors would slip away in the middle of a ball to meet their lovers here discreetly.'

'Not Grandfather Lorenzo surely?'

'Probably not him. But the rest of the Santoros. We're a degenerate lot.'

'Consider me warned. So, Signor Santoro, did you bring me here for nefarious purposes?'

His voice was soft but full of intent and satisfaction ran through him as he saw her shiver, her eyes dilating at his words. 'I wanted to say hello to you properly.'

'And how were you planning to do that?'

She was teasing him, leading him exactly where she wanted him to go, exactly where he wanted to be. Here, now, no need to plan or think ahead. Just two people enjoying all the benefits of mutual attraction. He took another step and then another, backing her up until she hit the wall, her breath coming in short pants. Slowly but with absolute intent Marco put one arm on the wall and leaned in so she had to look up at him, her body guarded by his, surrounded by his. It took all his strength not to pull her in close, crush her against him, not to lose himself in that mouth, that small perfect body, her sweet-smelling hair. 'Hello.'

'Hi yourself.'

Her mouth curved, the dimple provoking him, daring him, tempting him and, with a groan, he succumbed, dipping his tongue into the small hollow, her answering shiver pushing the last restraints away. With a smothered growl he swung her up in his arms, capturing her mouth with his, inhaling, demanding, needing, taking as he carried her over to the chaise, discreet in the corner of the room. Her kiss was equally fierce, her hands twisted in his hair as he lowered her onto the green brocade. Sophie lay, hair fanned out around her, eyes half closed, chest heaving. Marco stared down at her, trying to regain some vestiges of control. She extended a hand, her eyes wicked in the lamplight. 'Come on, then, *signor*, show me just how a Santoro conducts an illicit liaison.'

CHAPTER SIX

'GOOD MORNING, SLEEPYHEAD.' Marco looked up as Sophie entered the ridiculously huge breakfast room. He looked completely at home—not surprising, she reminded herself. This *was* his home. He sat back in a comfortable-looking chair, newspaper spread open before him on the polished table, coffee in one hand. It was all quite normal—or at least it would be if the table weren't large enough to seat thirty, every chair an antique and the view out of the line of shuttered windows not one she had seen in a hundred iconic photos.

'It's only eight a.m.—and considering I'm still on London time and got lost three times finding the breakfast room…' Was this whole room seriously just to eat breakfast in? It was plausible. The *palazzo* was big enough to have a brunch room, afternoon-tea room, supper room and midnight-snack room if the owners wished. 'I think I'm pretty bright and early.'

Especially as the man lounging opposite with a wicked grin in his eyes had kept her up half the night, leaving her room sometime in the early hours. It was better to be discreet, he'd said; his mother would be calling the banns if she found him in there—but Sophie hadn't minded. Sex was one thing, it was just intense chemistry, but sleeping together? That was real intimacy.

Marco smiled, the slow, sexy grin that made the breath leave her lungs and her knees weaken. 'I thought we'd get breakfast out, the Venetian way. Are you ready to go or do you need more time?'

'Ready? I've been ready since you mentioned this trip, ready since I got a passport, since I first saw Indiana Jones. I mean, we have canals in Manchester, but it's not quite the same. And the sun's shining. In January! What else could I possibly need?' Sophie had dressed with care for a day's sightseeing in a grey wool dress she had bought from a Chelsea charity shop and then redesigned, taking it in, shortening it and adding pink and purple flower buttons in two vertical rows to the flared skirt. A pair of black-and-grey-striped tights, her comfiest black patent brogues, her thick black jacket and a bright pink hat and gloves completed her outfit. She bounced on her toes. 'Let's go.'

Marco took a last, deliberate swig of his coffee before pushing his chair back and languidly getting to his feet. 'In that case, *signorina*, I'm at your service. I thought we'd start the day on foot and head onto the water later. Does that sound agreeable?'

'On foot. By boat, or even on a donkey. I'm happy any way you choose.'

Sophie had been too anxious the day before to really take Venice in. She had clear flashes of the city like snapshots of memory: the first glimpse of the Grand Canal, the flaking pastel paint on the canal-side *palazzos*, a gondola, boats crammed with people pulling in at a stop as nonchalantly as a red London bus stopping outside her flat. The greengrocer boat bartering and trading just like a market stall at the Portobello Market and yet strange and exotic. But the whole had escaped her and she was at fever pitch as Marco guided her along the gallery and down the stately staircase back into the vast hallway. It was almost an anticlimax when Marco ushered her out of the *palazzo's* grand double doors, at the other end of the hallway from the water door she had entered by, to find herself on a street, no water to be seen.

Okay, it was as far from her busy, traffic-filled, bustling London home as a street could be. Narrow and flagstoned, almost an alley, with aged buildings rising on either side. Doors lined up on both sides, some preceded by a step, others opening directly onto the street, and shuttered windows punctuated the plaster and stone of the graceful buildings. Voices floated from open windows, the Italian fast and incomprehensible. The air throbbed with vibrancy and life.

She hadn't expected this somehow. Venice was a fairy-tale setting, a film backdrop, a picture; she had forgotten it was a home too. How could Marco bear to live away from this unique beauty?

'This way,' he said, slipping on a pair of sunglasses against the sun's glare. He was more casually dressed than she had seen him so far in a pair of faded jeans, which clung perfectly in all the right places, a thin grey woollen jumper and a double-breasted black jacket. Somehow he managed to look both relaxed and elegant, a combination few British men could pull off. 'Hungry?'

'A little,' she admitted. 'Actually a lot. I could barely eat anything last night.' Nor had she managed much in the day, her stomach twisting with nerves.

'We don't usually have much for breakfast in Venice,' he said to her dismay. 'A coffee, maybe a brioche or small pastry standing up at the bar. But on a special occasion we visit a *pasticceria* for something a little more substantial. You do have a sweet tooth, don't you?'

Obviously it was far more sophisticated to say no, actually she only liked to nibble on raw cacao and a few olives were more than enough to satisfy her snack cravings, but honesty won out. 'Like a child in a sweet shop.'

'*Bene*, then I think you'll be more than happy.'

The next few hours slipped by like a dream. First Marco took her to a little neighbourhood *pasticceria*, which showcased a breathtaking array of little pastries and cakes in the display cabinets under the glass and wood counters. People dressed for work queued at the long polished wooden bar, where they quickly tossed back a small, bitter-looking coffee and maybe ate a pastry before ducking back out into the street, another caffeine seeker seamlessly moving into their place. Breakfast almost on the go. Marco and Sophie elected to take a little more time and sat at one of the elegant round tables, where Marco introduced Sophie to *frittelle*, round, doughnut-style pastries stuffed with pine nuts and raisins. 'They are usually eaten during *carnivale*,' he explained as Sophie uttered a moan of sheer delight at the taste. 'But some places make them all year round.'

'I'd love to see *carnivale*,' she said, licking her fingers, not wanting to waste even the tiniest crumb. 'It sounds so exotic.'

'It's crowded, noisy—and utterly magical. I have missed the last few, thanks to work, and every year I wish I'd been able to make the time to be here. There's nothing like it.'

Her curiosity was piqued by the longing in his voice. 'But you could live here if you wanted, couldn't you? You were working yesterday. Couldn't your business be based here?'

'Like I said in London, Venice is a village on an

island. There's no escape. Besides, it's good to try somewhere new, you know that. Where are you from? Manchester, didn't you say? You moved cities too.'

He was eyeing her keenly and Sophie shifted, not comfortable with the conversation turning to her and her decision to move to London. 'I think every home town can feel like a village at times. So, what else are we going to do today and will it involve more cake?'

After their brief but sugar-filled breakfast Marco led her along some more twisty streets. At the end of every junction she could see water, her throat swelling with excitement every time she heard the swish of waves lapping against stone, until finally she was walking along a pavement bordering not a road, but a broad canal complete with boats; private boats, taxis, even a police boat serenely cruising along. Sophie had to stop and photograph everything, much to Marco's amusement—especially the fat ginger cat sunning himself on one of the wooden jetties.

She was especially charmed when their route brought them out at a *traghetto* pier and Marco, after a quick conversation and handshake, gestured for her to get in and stand in the long, narrow boat. Two more passengers joined them before the two oarsmen—one at the front and one at the rear—pushed off and began to steer the boat across the Grand Canal.

'These are the traditional way to cross the Grand Canal.' Marco was standing just behind her, one hand on her shoulder, steadying her as the boat rocked in the slight swell of the water. 'There are seven crossings, although there were many more when my parents were small. The businesses have often been in families for generations, passed on from father to son.'

'Why are there two prices? Is one a return?'

'One for tourists and one for residents, but Angelo here considered you a resident this time.'

'Because I'm with you?'

'And because he said you have beautiful eyes.'

Sophie could feel her cheeks heat up and she was glad Angelo was too busy rowing to notice her reaction—and that Marco couldn't see her face at all.

After disembarking from the *traghetto* they headed to the tourist mecca of St Mark's square. It was still too early for many visitors to be out and about—and now that the Christmas holidays were finished Venice was entering its quiet season—but they were far from alone in the vast space. People were taking photos of the ubiquitous pigeons and the imposing tower or were sitting outside one of the many cafés that lined the famous *piazza*. Sophie's camera was in her hand instantly, every view, every angle needing capturing whether it was the blue of the canal and the lagoon beyond or the old palace, dominating the other end of the square.

Three hours later Sophie was light-headed and slightly nauseous. They had toured the Doge's Palace, crossed the infamous Bridge of Sighs and, thanks to an old school friend of Marco's, got a chance to see some of the hidden parts of the palace including the *pozzi*, tiny, dank, dark cells where Casanova had once been imprisoned. When Marco suggested a walk down to the Rialto Bridge she gave him a pleading smile. 'Can I have some lunch first? I know it's early, but I'm hungry and my legs don't seem to want to walk anywhere without sustenance and a sit down.'

'*Sì*, of course.' He didn't seem at all put out that she hadn't fallen in with his suggestion. It was so refreshing; she'd never been able to make off-the-cuff suggestions to Harry. At the merest hint that his itinerary didn't suit her he would fall into a monumental sulk, which would need all her best cajoling and coaxing to pull him out of. Her heart clenched at the thought. What had she been thinking of? To allow such a spoilt brat to dictate her life for so long? Of all the ways to choose to assert her independence. If she could only go back in time and talk sense into her eighteen-year-old self, then…eighteen-year-old Sophie would probably have ignored her as she'd ignored everyone else. Too giddy with lust, with independence, too convinced it was love. Too foolish.

But no, she wasn't going to sully one moment of this perfect day thinking about her past, indulging in regrets. She was in Venice with a gorgeous, attentive man and he was about to provide lunch. Life really didn't get much better than that.

Marco knew the perfect place for lunch. Close enough to St Mark's for his hungry companion, far enough away to avoid tourist prices and menus. A locals' café, with fresh food, a menu that changed daily depending on what was in at the markets and a bustling, friendly atmosphere. He used to eat there with his father, but when long, conversational lunches had turned into lectures with food he had stopped coming. He couldn't wipe out the last ten years of cold civility, couldn't repair his father's heart—but maybe he could reclaim some of the spaces they used to inhabit.

They had barely set foot over the threshold when he saw her, straight-backed, elegant and as lethal as a tiger eyeing her prey. His chest tightened. She hadn't come in here to wait for them, had she? Surely even his mother wasn't that conniving. But it was barely noon and she usually ate a little later than this. And that was an unusually triumphant look in her eyes.

'Marco, *vita mia*, how lovely to see you and your *bella* friend.' She leant in and embraced Sophie, who returned the traditional two kisses with a dumbstruck look Marco was sure must be mirrored on his own face.

'Mamma,' he said drily. 'What a coincidence.'

'*Sì,*' she agreed, but even though her eyes were wide and candid, Marco knew better. 'But a lovely one, no? I barely got to talk to Sophie yesterday. I hear you are staying for Bianca's wedding? We are delighted to have you with us for longer and, Sophie, *cara*, please consider the *palazzo* your home the whole time you are in Venice.'

There was no way out. Half amused, half annoyed, Marco accepted his mother's invitation to join her and they were soon seated at an intimate table for three so his mother could begin her interrogation. At least the food would be good, he thought as he ordered a *vermicelli al nero di seppia* for himself, a dish he refused to eat anywhere other than Venice, and advised Sophie, who still looked a little pale, to try the risotto. He then poured them all a glass of the local Soave and sat back to watch the show.

'So, Sophie, what is it you do in London?' And she was off… If Sophie had any secrets, they would be expertly extracted before the bread and oil reached the table.

Or not. By the end of the meal Marco knew very little more than he had at the start. Maybe she was secret-service trained because Sophie Bradshaw had avoided every one of his mother's expertly laid traps like a professional—and what was more, she had done it in such a way Marco doubted his mother had noticed. She had mentioned two brothers and nieces and nephews—and then, while his mother had gone misty-eyed at the very thought of babies and grandchildren, had turned the tables and asked his mother so many questions about Bianca's forthcoming wedding his mother had been quite disarmed. Very clever.

Marco leaned back in his chair and eyed Sophie thoughtfully. It hadn't mattered that he knew little more than her name when she had been due to spend less than forty-eight hours with him, but now she was staying with his dangerously excitable family for over a week he found himself a little more curious. Who was Sophie Bradshaw and what did she really want? Was she really as happy with a casual relationship as she'd made out? She liked fashion and designing—although she had told his mother that she took other jobs while she worked to get her business off the ground. What other jobs? She came from Manchester but at some unspecified point had moved to London. She had two brothers and five nieces and nephews. That was it. All he knew.

He didn't need to know more. Why would he? After next week he would probably never see her again. But he'd never met a woman less willing to share—and there was a shadow behind those blue eyes that made him suspect there was a reason she was so reticent.

Whatever the reason, it was her business; he didn't need to get involved. Once you got involved, then expectations got raised, then things got messy. He knew that all too well.

It was with some amusement that Marco watched his mother kiss Sophie on both cheeks and embrace her warmly as they left the restaurant—and even more amusement that he heard Sophie suck in a huge sigh of relief. 'Well done, you held her off beautifully.'

'I thought I was going to crack any minute.'

'It was a good move to bring up Bianca's wedding. That's been her sole focus for the last year and the only thing guaranteed to distract her.'

'It nearly backfired though.' Sophie pulled on her gloves as they emerged into the bright, sunny but cold street. 'She managed to bring every question back to me. Would I prefer an A-line or a fitted dress, didn't I agree that an heirloom tiara was classier than a newly bought one, what colour scheme did I like, would I prefer a princess cut or a pear shape or maybe I wanted sapphires to match my eyes? I got the impression if I gave a straight answer to any question I'd have a ring on my finger and find myself frogmarched down an aisle whether I wanted to be or not.'

Her tone was light, but her words still struck him. He'd expected his mother to take an overactive interest in Sophie, but it was frustrating to have it confirmed that nothing had really changed, that ten years of exile, all the drama and anger had been for nothing. His mother had no intention of respecting his decisions. He tried to keep his own voice equally light, not to let his anger show. 'You can see why I asked you here. Mamma is obsessed with weddings. While she thinks there's a chance we might end up together she won't be busy matchmaking. It's perfect. I owe you, Sophie. Thank you.'

There was just the most infinitesimal pause before Sophie echoed, 'Yes, perfect. As long as I don't crack. Don't leave me alone with her, that's all I'm saying. I'm not sure I'd win in a straight duel. Has she always been this way?'

Marco began to stroll down towards the Rialto Bridge. He planned for them to cross over the famous bridge and then head back to the *palazzo* to collect his boat for the afternoon. 'As long as I can remember.'

'But why? It's usually the other way round, isn't it? Pressure on the daughter to marry? I'm sure you're a catch and all…' The dimple was out again and he couldn't stop smiling back in response even though his mother's obsession with his future was his least favourite topic. And it wasn't easy to put into words.

'It's not about me, not really. She's obsessed with the past, the future, the *palazzo*. Venice is changing, has been for the last fifty years. More and more real estate is owned by foreigners, many of whom don't live here, which means more and more families moving onto the mainland. Both my parents came from ancient Venetian families, together they owned a lot of real estate, a lot of businesses around the city.' He allowed himself a brief smile. 'We're a city of traders, of merchants. Even I, though I wanted to set out on my own, trade goods back and forth. It's in my blood, like the sea.'

'What does that have to do with marriage?'

'It's about not letting the old bloodlines die out, with keeping a Santoro in the *palazzo*, running the family business, sons at his knees, just like the old days. Now Bianca is getting married—and to another scion of an ancient family—her attentions can be fully focussed on me. London might not be far enough. I may try Mars.'

'Would it be so bad? Marriage?' She held her hands up, laughing as he turned to look at her. 'That's not a proposal, by the way, not even a leading question. Just plain curiosity.'

'I'm the Santoro heir,' he said. 'It's a position that comes with privilege, sure, but also with expectations.

I'm the only son. And from the moment I was born I was reminded that I had a duty to the family, to the name, to Venice. That what I want doesn't matter, that to pursue my dreams is a selfishness unbefitting a Santoro.' He could hear his father shouting the words as he spoke them. 'Marriage is part of that responsibility. So to me it isn't something natural, something healthy, something good. It's a heavy expectation I'm expected to bear. And now my father is gone...' He swallowed as he said the words. It still didn't seem possible. Venice seemed emptier without him, the *palazzo* hollower. 'Now I'm not just the only son, I'm the only remaining male, it's become even more imperative to my mother that I marry and soon. But the more she pushes, the less ready I feel. And I love my city, my family, of course I do. But I won't sacrifice myself, my integrity to tradition.'

'Have you told her?' Sophie asked softly. 'Told her how you feel. That you're not ready.'

His mouth quirked into a smile; if only it were that easy. 'Many times. But she only listens when she wants to. Hears what she wants to hear.'

'It's not good to let misunderstandings grow, let resentments fester.' There was a quiet certainty in Sophie's voice.

'I think we understand Mamma too well, Bianca and I. She was orphaned young, raised alone by her grandparents in an old *palazzo*. They had a title, an illustrious ancestry but no wealth. When she married my father she wanted security and a large family. Together they built up an empire to rival that of the early Santoros, but they had to settle for a small family. After Bianca she just couldn't conceive again. So she turned her attentions to grandchildren, to building the dynasty she always dreamed of. She thinks she knows best what will make us happy. I don't hurt her on purpose, but we have such different ideas on the way I should live.'

Hurt was inevitable. Every time he said 'no'. Every time he chose his own path. But if he didn't, then what had it all been for? The hard-fought-for independence, the ten years of estrangement, the knowledge he would never make it up with his father.

The knowledge that his father might even yet have been here, still alive, if Marco had been a different kind of man. More pliable, obedient.

'So you live in a different country and seldom come home?' Sophie was shaking her head. 'I don't know, Marco, it's a solution, but it doesn't sound like a good one. Not at all.'

And the worst thing was, Marco knew she was right. But what other choice did he have?

CHAPTER SEVEN

'DID YOU AND Marco have a good day yesterday?' Bianca's eyes were sly as she looked at Sophie in the mirror. 'Mamma was disappointed you didn't come back for supper. She was so looking forward to getting to know you better.'

Sophie circled Bianca, checking every seam and every hem. The dress was gorgeous, far bigger and more ornate than she would have chosen personally but perfect for a wedding as imposing as Bianca's promised to be. But Bianca's new curves spilled out of the silk ballgown's sweetheart neckline, turning it from daring to borderline indecent, and it was a struggle to get the zip up at the low back—in fact Sophie had decided against forcing it, not wanting to snag the delicate fabric.

'Lovely, thanks. We spent the morning at the palace, and then we had lunch with your mother, so I hope she wasn't too disappointed we missed supper, and then Marco took me out onto the lagoon for the afternoon.' He'd pointed out some of the more notable islands, promising to bring her back to visit one or two before the end of their trip, and then he had taken her to dine at an island hotel. Sailing in through the private water gate to be escorted up to the glassed-in terrace with views across to Venice itself had been the most romantic thing

Sophie had ever experienced. If only she hadn't felt so tired and her appetite hadn't been so capricious. And if only she hadn't replayed Marco's words over and over in her mind. *You can see why I asked you here.*

She wasn't sure why those words had pricked her. She had been under no illusions about his sudden invitation; Marco hadn't brought her here because he'd been struck down with instalove—and she'd accepted for that very reason. But to have him spell out so baldly that she was a mere ploy to keep his mother happy was a little bruising to her pride.

But then again, after one lunch with his mother she fully accepted his reasons, sympathised with them even. Only, it would be nice to be more than convenient, to really matter to someone... She stopped still, staring down at Bianca's elaborate train. Where had that thought come from? She was happy on her own, remember? Not at all interested in a relationship.

But maybe one day. If she chose better, found someone who valued and cherished her the way her friends were loved and cherished, then maybe she could take that risk. Because if she did spend her life hiding from the possibility of love, did spend her life thinking she wasn't good enough, then Harry won after all, didn't he?

'Right.' Sophie blinked back unexpected, hot tears. What on earth was wrong with her? It was time to remember why she was here and not on a plane back to London. 'There's no way this dress is going to fit the way it is. Luckily your hips and waist have only increased by the smallest amount, so it's a reasonably easy fix, no major restructuring needed, but we do need to do something about the neckline.' She hesitated, searching for the right words. 'I could re-bone the bodice, but I still think you'll look more top-heavy than you intended. So what I'm proposing is that in addition to letting out the seams and adjusting the zip I make you a lace overdress. It's up to you if you just want it for your top or to cover the skirt as well. Look, I'll show you.' She picked up a gossamer-thin scarf and deftly twisted it around Bianca, pinning it in place.

'You need to imagine this is lace,' she warned Bianca. 'This is just to give us an idea.'

Sophie stepped back and pursed her lips as she fixed her design in her head. 'The beading on your skirt is lovely. It would be a real shame to cover it up with lace,' she decided. 'Let's go with a lace bodice. I'll find buttons to match your beads, tiny ones, and it can button up your back.' She shot Bianca a reassuring smile. 'I'll sew those on at the very last minute to make absolutely sure it fits.'

Bianca stared at herself in the mirror, hope flaring in her expressive dark eyes. 'Will it really work?'

'Absolutely.' In fact the more Sophie thought about it, the surer she was. 'I think it will be stunning. I can give you capped sleeves, little straps just off the shoulder— or we could go really regal with full-length sleeves, so decide what you'd prefer. The most important thing is making sure the lace matches the exact colour of the dress. Not all ivories are created equal. Do you have a swatch I can use?'

Bianca nodded, her eyes bright with tears. 'Thank you, Sophie. I can't begin to tell you how much I appreciate this, how much it means that you haven't just fixed my problem but made my dress even better.' She caught a tear with her finger, wiping it away, pulling a watery smile as she did so. 'If there is anything I can do to repay you...'

'No repayment necessary, I promise. I'm happy to

do it. Let's get you out of the dress before you spoil the silk with your tears and I'll take a look at the zip. It only needs a few millimetres, I think, to be comfortable. I might not even need to add an insert. Unpicking the stitches and redoing it might be enough.'

It took a few minutes to manoeuvre Bianca out of the many folds of the dress, but eventually Sophie hung the layers of net and tulle and silk back up, smoothing the silk out with careful hands as she figured out the best way to deal with it. 'I wonder if I could get my hands on a tailor's dummy,' she pondered. 'If I put a dummy on a dais, I would find it easier. There must be some-where I could source that from. I'll draw up a list of all we need: lace, silk, thread, buttons.'

'Si, none of that should be a problem. The best place for lace is Burano, one of the islands. I'll ask Marco to take you. It's very pretty. I think you'll like it.'

'Sounds perfect.' Sophie turned to look at Bianca. The Italian girl sat on her unmade bed, a robe loosely drawn around her, the magnificent mane of hair spilling around her shoulders, tears still shimmering in her eyes.

'I'm sorry, Sophie, I'm not usually such a mess. The thing is...' she took a deep breath '...I didn't eat too much over Christmas, nor am I that stressed about the wedding, not really. It's just that...I'm having a baby and I haven't told anyone yet.'

'You're what? But that's wonderful. No wonder you've gone up over two cup sizes and barely gained a centimetre around your waist! How far along are you?'

'The doctor says ten weeks. I only realised at the end of last week. I've always been irregular, so I didn't no-tice any changes there, but I was always crying, or sud-denly really hungry and then really nauseous. I've been so tired, light-headed. And I can't even cope with the smell of coffee, let alone the taste. Honestly, for some-one with so many qualifications I can be very stupid, but I just didn't realise what was wrong. It wasn't like we were trying.'

Sophie perched onto the bed next to Bianca and pat-ted her arm a little awkwardly. 'But this is good news, surely? After all, you're about to get married.'

'*Sì*, it is, at least, it will be, when I get used to it. I just thought we'd have time to *be* married before start-ing a family.'

'So,' Sophie asked gently, 'why the secrecy?'

'Antonio is stressed about the wedding, it's so big, I just don't want to give him anything else to worry about. I will tell him,' she said defensively as Sophie raised her eyebrows. 'I was planning to tonight—telling you was the first time I've said it out loud. It wasn't as hard as I expected.'

'And your mother will be over the moon.'

Bianca's mouth twisted. 'Oh, *sì*, Mamma will be de-lighted. But I won't be telling her until after the honey-moon. She can be a little overpowering.' She giggled. 'Okay, a lot overpowering. She already tried to take over the planning of the wedding, make it into her dream wedding, not mine. I'm not ready for her to take over the baby as well, not until I know how I feel about it all.'

'That makes sense.' But Sophie's mind had wandered back to something Bianca had said earlier. Something about not noticing that she was pregnant because she was irregular. Sophie was the complete opposite. In fact she was like clockwork, every twenty-eight days. Usually…

Frantically she counted back. Almost five weeks had passed since she had spent the night with Marco.

Over five weeks without her period. Her regular-as-clockwork period...

'That's all great, Bianca, I mean congratulations again and I can't wait to get started. I just remembered, I didn't pack for a week-long stay and there's a few things I need, so I'm just going to go out and grab them...' She collected her bag and backed out of the door still babbling inanely. 'When I get back we'll talk lace, okay? I won't be long.' The last thing she saw as the door swung shut behind her was Bianca, upright and staring at her in complete surprise.

Smoothly done, Sophie.

But she couldn't wait, not another second, not while this big *what if* was thundering through her body, beating its question with every thud of her heart.

Although she found her way out of the *palazzo* easily enough, having earmarked enough landmarks to find her way to the main hallway and back up to her room, as soon as she set foot outside it was a different matter. Sophie plunged into the alleyways and back streets searching for the green cross that meant pharmacy in a dozen different languages. But each road seemed to lead her nowhere, a dead end with water rippling gently at the end, round in a gently curving circle back to the same square over and over.

And what would happen when she reached a pharmacy? She could barely order a pizza in Italian let alone a pregnancy test and she doubted her mime skills were up to scratch.

You're being ridiculous, she told herself. *You used protection, you were careful, he was careful.*

But the rest of Bianca's words came back, almost visible, floating around her in the still, cold air. Emotional? Check, look at the pity party she'd held for herself on

New Year's Eve, the tears just now. Light-headed and tired? For a couple of weeks now. Nauseous? Yes, a low level, almost constant feeling of sickness. All kinds of things set it off. She hadn't been able to stomach even the smell of wine for ages; it had been an oddly teetotal Christmas and New Year's Eve.

Sophie stopped dead in the middle of the street. Of course she was pregnant. How could she not have known—and what on earth was she going to do now?

'Sophie, Bianca mentioned you wanted to visit Burano. Would this afternoon be convenient?'

Sophie skidded to a stop outside the salon and fought an urge to hide her handbag behind her back as if Marco might see through the leather, to the paper bag within. It had been a mortifying experience, but thanks to the Internet, her phone, some overly helpful shoppers and a very patient pharmacist she had finally got what she needed.

Well, two of what she needed. She hadn't paid that much attention in Science, but she was pretty sure all experiments could go wrong.

'Marco! Hi! Yes, Burano, this afternoon, sounds wonderful, great.'

One eyebrow rose. 'Are you okay?' He sauntered over to the salon door and she had to fight the urge to step away.

'Fine, I've been out. I got a little lost, that's all.'

'The best way to learn Venice is to get lost in her,' he said, but there was a quizzical gleam in his dark eyes as he looked at her.

'In that case we'll soon be the best of friends.' Sophie knew she was acting oddly, but she needed to get out of this hallway and up into the safety of her room and find out for once and for all. 'What time do you want to leave?'

'If we leave here just after noon, we could stop for lunch along the way.'

'That sounds wonderful. I just need to talk to Bianca then, take another look at the dress and get a swatch of material. Shall I meet you back here in an hour? Great. See you then.'

She barely registered his response as she walked as fast as she could up the stairs, slowing a little as she tackled the second and then the third staircase until finally she was twisting open the door to her room, throwing her bag onto the bed, grabbing the paper bag and rushing into the bathroom, tearing open the plastic on the box as she did so...

She was pregnant. Two tests' worth of pregnant.

Sophie sank onto the bed with a strangled sob, throwing her hand across her mouth to try to keep the noise in. Idiot. Fool. Stupid, stupid girl. It was different for Bianca. She was engaged to a man she loved, she had a great career, a life ready and waiting for a baby. What did Sophie have? A fling with a commitment-shy man she barely knew, a shoebox of a flat, an un-fulfilled dream and a job scrubbing toilets and serving drinks. How was she going to fit a baby into her flat, let alone her life?

She slumped down on the bed and stared up at the ceiling, every fat cherub leg, every beaming cherub grin on the fresco an unneeded reminder. The thing was she *did* want children. Had planned to have them with Harry—although she had never got him to admit the time was right. Thank goodness. She shuddered; if she had had his baby, would she ever have got out? Ever freed herself or would she still be there now? Holding down a job, taking care of the house, looking after the kids while Harry lied and cheated and manipulated...

But Marco wasn't like Harry. He was, well, he was... 'Face it,' Sophie said aloud. 'You know nothing about him except he doesn't want to get married. He's rich. He's handsome. He's good in bed. He seems kind, when it suits him to be...' Added together it didn't seem an awful lot to know about the father of her baby.

Father. Baby. She swallowed a hysterical sob.

She had to tell him; it was the right, the fair, thing to do.

And then what? He might walk away although, she conceded, he didn't seem the type. Sophie wrapped her arms around herself, trying to hug some warmth into her suddenly chilled body. He might accuse her of entrapment. Think this was done on purpose...

He didn't want to get married, she knew that, and that was okay. After all, they didn't really know each other. But what about when his mother found out? She wanted grandchildren, heirs, and here Sophie was carrying a Santoro heir as a good little wife should.

She shivered again, nausea rolling in her stomach. She'd been free for one year and six months, independent for such a short while. No placating, no begging, no reassuring, no abasing, no making herself less so someone else could be more. No eggshells. She was pretty sure Marco wasn't another Harry, she knew his mother had all the best intentions, but if they knew she was pregnant, she would have every choice stripped away, be suffocated with kindness and concern and responsibility until every bit of that hard-won independence shrivelled away and she belonged to them. Just as she had belonged to Harry. Besides, Bianca was getting married in a week. This was her time. It wouldn't be fair to spoil her wedding with the inevitable drama Sophie's news would cause.

I won't tell him yet, she decided. *I need to know him first, know who the real Marco is. Know if I can trust him. I'll get to know him over this week and then I'll tell him. After the wedding.*

Marco manoeuvred his boat out of the Grand Canal with practised ease. It came more naturally than driving, even after a decade in London. Sometimes he thought he felt truly alive only when he was here on the water, the sun dancing on the waves around him, Venice at his back, the open lagoon his for the taking.

'Warm enough?' He'd elected not to take the traditional, bigger family boat with its polished wood and spacious covered seating area. Instead they were in his own small but speedy white runabout, which didn't have any shelter beyond the splash screen at the front. He'd reminded Sophie to wrap up warmly for the journey over, but she was so pale and silent maybe she'd underestimated the bite of the January wind out in the lagoon.

'Hmm? No, thanks, honestly I'm toasty.' He could see her visibly push away whatever was occupying her thoughts as she turned to him and smiled. 'Bianca says Burano is beautiful. I'm really looking forward to seeing it.'

'It is,' he assured her. 'Very different from Venice, but equally stunning in a quieter way.'

'Did you visit the islands a lot when you were younger? What about the rest of Italy? It's such a beautiful country. It must have been wonderful to have had it all on your doorstep,' she added quickly as he raised an eyebrow at her series of questions.

'It is beautiful and, yes, most of our childhood holidays were spent in Italy. Venice gets so hot and busy in the summer and we have a villa by Lake Como, so every summer we would spend a month there. And I don't remember a time when I didn't explore the islands. Every Venice child grows up able to handle a boat before they learn to ride a bike.'

'And swim?'

'*Sì*, and swim.'

'I still can't imagine what it was like, actually living here, crossing water to get to school. It just seems impossibly exotic.'

'Not when it's your normal. To me, your childhood in Manchester would have seemed equally exotic. What was your route to school? A bus?'

'I doubt it. Suburbia is suburbia, nothing exciting there. But a school boat? Now, that's fun.' And once again she turned his question aside effortlessly. Was there some dark secret there or did she really think her past was of so little interest? 'What else did you do when you were little? Were you a football player or addicted to video games or a bookworm?'

'None of the above. If I wasn't messing around on a boat, I was always trying to find a way to do some kind of deal.' He grinned at her surprised expression. 'I told you, we're an island of merchants, sailors, traders. Oh, it's been several hundred years since we had any influence, since we controlled the waves, but it's still there in any true Venetian's veins.'

'What did your parents say?'

'Oh, they were proud,' he assured her. 'So many families forgot their roots, watched the *palazzos* crumble around them as the money ran out. My mother is a big believer in a good day's work, no matter who you are.' Proud right until she realised his independent entrepreneurial streak wasn't just a phase.

It was as if Sophie had read his mind. 'Was she disappointed when you set up for yourself? Left Venice?' She leaned against the windscreen, half turned to face him, eyes intent on him as if the answers really mattered.

'Yes. She's convinced one day I'll get over my little rebellion and come home, settle down and take over the family affairs.' He paused as he navigated the boat around a buoy. 'Of course, since my father died she's been keener than ever and at some point I need to make a decision about where my future lies. But right now she's not ready to give up the reins no matter what she says—she'll spend every second of her retirement second-guessing every decision I make. I have a while yet. Besides...' Marco had always known the day would come when he would have to step in, but he wanted to see how big his own business could grow first. He already turned over several million euros annually, and there was plenty of room to expand, new territories to trade in.

'Besides what?'

'Bianca. Maybe she could take over the Santoro holdings. She's an extremely talented businesswoman, she's got exactly the same heritage as me and I know she wants a family, so she could hand the business on, just as my parents wanted.'

'That makes sense. Hasn't your mother ever considered it?'

'Neither of my parents have. In many ways they were very old-fashioned. Bianca's a woman, so in their eyes when she marries she'll no longer be a true Santoro. But it's just a name...' And if Bianca did take over the business, the *palazzo* and provide the heirs, then he would be free.

Was it the perfect solution—or was he merely fulfilling his father's prophecies and eluding his responsibilities? Marco had no idea. It all seemed so clear, so simple in London, but the second he set foot back in Venice he got tangled up in all the threads of loyalty, duty and family he'd spent most of his life struggling to free himself from.

They had reached the open waters of the lagoon and Marco let out the throttle, allowing the boat to zoom ahead. 'I miss this,' he admitted. 'This freedom.'

'I can imagine. I know there's a harbour in Chelsea, but sailing up and down the Thames must be a little sedate after living here. What do you like to do in London for fun? Apart from attending parties, that is.'

Marco eased off on the throttle and let the boat slow as Burano came into view. 'Is this an interview?' He was teasing but noted the high colour that rose over her cheeks with interest. 'An interrogation? Will you lock me up in the Doge's palace if I answer wrongly?'

'Yes, right next to Casanova. No, no interrogation, I'm just interested. We're spending all this time together and I know nothing about you. I need to be prepared if you want your mother to think we're a real couple. What if she gets me alone? Imagine how suspicious she would be if I don't know your favourite football team, or how you take your coffee.'

'Black, strong, no sugar and of course I support Venezia despite our current ranking. Thank goodness our national team is a little more inspiring.' Sophie was right, he realised. If they were acting the couple, it made sense to know more about each other. Besides, she was fun company, insightful with a dry wit he appreciated. 'How about you? City or United?'

'Me?' She blinked. 'My family is City, so I am by default, but to be honest I'm not really bothered. We were a bit divided on gender lines when I was a child. My father would take my brothers to matches, but I was eight years younger and so I was always left behind with my mother, who was definitely *not* interested. I think she thought sport was invented to ruin her weekends.'

'Did that annoy you? Being left out by your brothers?'

She wrinkled her nose. 'No one likes being the baby of the family, do they? But my mother encouraged it, I think. By the time I was born my brothers' lives revolved around sport. Footie, cricket, rugby—it's all they talked about, watched, did. She always said she was delighted to have a daughter, an ally at last.' She sounded wistful, her eyes fixed on the sea.

'You weren't into sport, then?'

Sophie shrugged. 'I didn't really have the option. Like I said, Dad would take the boys to matches or whatever and Mum and I would be left behind. Besides, she was determined not to lose me to their side. She had me in classes of her choosing as soon as I could walk. Dance,' she confirmed at his enquiring look. 'I wasn't kidding when I told you at the Snowflake Ball that I'd done every kind of dancing.'

'A dancer? Professionally?' It made sense. She had the build, petite as she was, strong and lithe, and he dimly remembered her mentioning it on New Year's Eve.

'Could have been. Mum thought I'd be a ballerina. She wanted me to train properly at sixteen, dance at Covent Garden one day.'

'But you didn't want to?'

She shook her head. 'It's not just about talent, it's luck, build, you know, having the right body, discipline but most of all drive. I was good, but good enough? Probably not. I didn't want it enough. I stopped just before I turned sixteen. It broke her heart.'

She looked down at her hands and he didn't pursue it—he knew all about breaking parental hearts, was a gold medallist in it. 'What did you want to do instead?' It wasn't just about polite conversation; he was actually interested. His hands tightened on the wheel as the realisation dawned.

Sophie smiled, slow and nostalgic. 'The thing I did really like about ballet, about performing, was the costumes. Every show involves a lot of net and tulle and gluing sequins—I loved that part. I was always much happier with a needle than a pointe shoe. So I guess I'm lucky, trying to make a go of the thing I love. If I'd become a ballet dancer, I'd be over halfway through my career by now. Not that I can imagine I'd have had much of one. Like I say, I was never driven enough.' She stopped and stared as they neared the pretty harbour and the brightly coloured fishermen's cottages came into view. 'Oh, my goodness, how beautiful. Where's my camera?' She turned away, grabbing her camera and exclaiming over the colours, the boats, the sea, the sky.

As he guided the boat into the harbour, mooring it at a convenient stop, Marco's thoughts were preoccupied with Sophie, still chattering excitedly and snapping away. Why was he so intrigued by her? Sure, she was fun, they had chemistry and she was proving extremely helpful in calming Bianca's ever more volatile nerves and keeping his mother off his back. But next week she would return to London and their brief relationship would be over. There was no point in prolonging it when they both knew they weren't heading anywhere. Short, sweet and to the point just as all perfect liaisons should be.

But what would it be like not to feel as if every relationship was ticking towards an expiration date, not to worry about getting in too deep, about not raising expectations he had no intention of fulfilling? For every new woman to be an adventure, a world to be explored, not a potential trap? He'd never cared before, happy with the limits he set upon himself, upon his time, upon his heart. But, for the first time in a really long time, as he helped Sophie ashore, felt the warm clasp of her hand, watched her face alight with sheer happiness as she took in every detail on the colourful island, Marco was aware that maybe, just maybe, he was missing some colour in his perfectly organised, privileged, grey life.

CHAPTER EIGHT

IT WAS THE MOST beautiful commute in the world. How many people travelled to their office by boat? Marco took a deep breath, his lungs glad of the fresh salty air, a much-needed contrast to the polluted London air he usually breathed in on his way to work. No, he thought as he steered his boat across the lagoon towards the dock at the mainland Venetian district of Mestre, this was a much better way to spend his early mornings.

Marco hadn't intended to work from the Santoro Azienda offices, but he found it easier to concentrate away from the *palazzo*. Bianca was staying at home until her wedding and every room was full of tulle or confetti or wedding favours—it was like living in a five-year-old girl's dream doll's house. Besides, working at the *palazzo* meant working in close proximity to Sophie and that, he was discovering, was distracting. And if his mother and sister were at home, then they kept interrupting him to ask his opinion on everything from how the napkins should be folded to where Gia Ana should be seated, given that she had fallen out with every other member of the family.

And when they *weren't* at home, then it was almost impossible for him not to seek Sophie out on some barely disguised pretext—or for her to casually wander

by him—knowing that within seconds their eyes would
meet, hold, and, like teenagers taking advantage of an
empty house, they would drag each other into the nearest
bedroom... There was something particularly thrilling
about the illicitness of it all, the sneaking down corridors, the stolen kisses, the hurried pulling off clothes
or pulling them back on again. Not that his mother or
Bianca were fooled for a moment, but that wasn't the
point. It was all about appearances. His mother would
only countenance an engaged couple sleeping together
under her roof. Or not sleeping...

Yes, working at the *palazzo* certainly had its benefits,
but he had far too much to do to allow himself to be
continuously distracted, so, for the last couple of days,
knowing his mother was so busy with the final details
for the wedding she was unlikely to be at work, he had
taken to heading off to the office early, returning home
during the long lunch break to meet up with Sophie,
who was spending most of her mornings working on
Bianca's dress. He didn't have to come home, she'd assured him, she was happy to explore Venice on her own
if he was too busy, but he was enjoying rediscovering
his city, seeing it through her eyes as she absorbed the
sights and smells of the city.

The Santoro Azienda offices were a short walk away
from the dock. As his parents' real estate and other business interests had expanded and they had taken on more
and more staff it had become increasingly clear they
needed professional offices out of the *palazzo*. The decision to base the offices on the mainland hadn't been
taken lightly, but for the sake of their staff, many of
whom no longer lived on the islands, it had made sense
and twenty years ago they had moved into the light,

modern, purpose-built building. All glass and chrome, it was as different from the *palazzo* as a building could be.

Until last week Marco hadn't set foot in the offices in ten years. It was one of the many things he'd regretted since he'd shouldered his father's coffin to walk it down the aisle towards the altar—and yet he still couldn't see any other way, how he could have played things differently. It took two to compromise and he hadn't been the only one at fault.

Marco strode through the sliding glass doors and, with a nod at the security guard and the receptionists, headed straight for the lifts and the top floor, exiting into the plush corridors that marked the Santoro Azienda's Executive Floor. Left led to his parents' offices, right to the suite of rooms he was using. He hadn't turned left once since he'd returned to the building.

He stood and hesitated, then, with a muffled curse, turned left.

His parents had had adjoining offices on opposite corners of the building, sharing a PA, a bathroom and a small kitchen and seating area. He'd been in his teens when they'd relocated here, spending many days in one office or the other being put to work, being trained up to manage the huge portfolio of properties and companies they owned. No one had ever asked him if it was what he wanted. If they had noticed that he was happier rolling his sleeves up and engaging on the ground level, they ignored it. He was destined to take over and his interest in art and antiques, in dealing directly with people, was a quirk, a hobby.

'A multimillion-euro hobby, Papà,' he said softly. Not that it would have made any difference.

His father's name was still on his office door and Marco stood there for a long moment staring at the letters before twisting the handle and, with a deep breath, entering the room. It was a shock to see that nothing had changed, as if his father could walk in any moment, espresso in hand. The desk still heaped with papers, the carafe of water filled on the oak sideboard, the comfy chair by the window, where his father had liked to sit after lunch and face the city while he took his siesta. Photographs covered the walls, views of Venice, of buildings they owned, goods they made, food prepared in restaurants they owned. There were no photographs of Marco or Bianca. 'The office is for work,' his father used to say. And work he had, in early, out late, deals and successes and annoyances his favourite topic of conversation over the evening meal.

Marco picked up a piece of paper and stared at it, not taking in the typed words. Was his mother coping, doing the work of two people? She hated delegating as much as his father had, didn't like handing too much power to people not part of their family.

They were as stubborn as each other.

He barely registered her footsteps, but he knew she was there before she spoke.

'Marco.'

He closed his eyes briefly. 'Hello, Mamma.'

He turned, forced a smile. In the bright artificial office light he could see the lines on her forehead, the hollows in her cheeks. She was working too hard, still grieving for his father.

'You've been home for two weeks and yet I barely see you.' Her voice might be full of reproach, but her eyes were shrewd, assessing his every expression.

'I've been busy. As have you.'

'*Sì*, weddings don't organise themselves. Maybe you'll find that out one day.' She linked her arm through his and gave a small tug. 'Come, Marco, take coffee with me. Let's have a proper catch-up.'

Words guaranteed to strike a chill through any dutiful child's heart. 'No coffee for me, Mamma. I have a lot to do.'

She stepped back and looked up at him. It was many years since she had topped him yet he still had the urge to look up—she carried herself as if she were seven feet tall. 'You work too hard, Marco. A young man like you should be out, enjoying himself. Sophie must be feeling sadly neglected.'

'I doubt it. She's making herself a dress for Bianca's wedding. I'm not sure I would be of much help.'

'Clever girl. She's so creative.' Her eyes flickered over his face and Marco stayed as expressionless as possible. 'We lack that in our family. We're all good at facts, at figures, at making money, but none of us has any creativity. It would be nice...' Her voice trailed off, but he knew exactly what she meant. Nice to breed that creativity in. 'She has such lovely colouring as well, the peaches-and-cream English complexion.' As if Sophie were a brood mare, waiting to be mated with a prize stallion.

The old feelings of being imprisoned, stifled, descended like physical bars, enclosing him in, trying to strip all choice away. His mouth narrowed as he fought to keep his cool. 'Yes, she's very pretty.'

'Oh, Marco, she's beautiful. And so sweet. Bianca adores her, says she is just like a sister. We'll all miss her when she returns to London. We'll miss you as well. It's been lovely having you home.'

'Luckily for Bianca they have invented these marvellous little devices which make it possible to communicate over large distances. In fact she usually has one glued to her hand. I'm sure she can speak to Sophie as much as she would like to.'

His mother walked over to the desk and picked up the fountain pen his father had always used. 'My own mother always said one of her greatest joys was watching you and Bianca grow up.'

This was a new one. 'Nonna was a very special person. I miss her.'

'She was in her early twenties when I was born, and I, of course, was very young when I had you. She was still only in her forties when she became a grandmother. Young enough to be active, to be able to play with you. Of course, her dearest wish was to see you marry, have a family of your own.'

'She was taken from us too early.'

'I will be sixty next year, Marco. Sixty.'

He was impressed; she didn't usually admit to her age. 'And you don't look a day over forty-five. Are you sure you have the right year?'

But she wasn't in the mood for gallantry, barely raising a smile at the compliment. 'I want to see my grandchildren, Marco. I want to know them, watch them grow up, not be an old lady, too tired and ill to be able to play when they finally arrive.'

Marco sighed. 'Mamma…'

'I want you back home, back here, where you belong, heading up the Santoro family. I want you settled down and married with children of your own.'

'I know you do. It's all you've ever wanted.'

'I just want you to be happy, Marco.'

He fought to keep his voice even. 'I know. But you have to accept that happiness comes in many different forms, in many different ways. I like what I do. I like London.'

'And what of me? Of the business?'

'There are other options. Bianca, for instance. Come on, Mamma, you must have considered it. Bianca is more than fit to take over from you. She's the best of us all when it comes to figures, she's ambitious and she's a Santoro to her fingernails, no matter who she marries and what her last name is. Don't overlook her. You'll be doing all of us a disservice.'

His mother only smiled. 'You think I haven't considered her? That your father didn't? Of course we have. You're right, in many ways she's the cleverest of us all and when it comes to the finances there's no one I would rather have in charge. But she doesn't have what your father had—what you have—she doesn't have the flair, the inspired spark.'

Guilt flared as she compared him to his father and Marco's hands curled into fists involuntarily. 'I don't know what you mean.'

'Yes, you do,' she said, staring at him as if she could imprint her words into him. 'Bianca and I can manage, we can audit, we can run—but you and your father can build. Can take an idea and make it grow, see where opportunity lies and grab it with both hands. I'm not discounting Bianca because she's a woman and getting married, I'm discounting her because she won't grow the company like you will. Because you are the heir your father wanted.'

Bitterness coated his mouth. 'Papà didn't want me to be inspired. He didn't want me to be anything but an obedient clone. He sat in this room, at this desk, and told me if I went to England, continued to mess around with antiques, we were finished.'

'They were just words. You know what he was like. Words came too easily and he never meant them—it was what he did which counted. And he was proud of you, Marco. He followed your every move. People would tell him of you, people you worked with in Venice, further afield, would seek him out to talk of you and he would drink in every word.'

The ache in Marco's chest eased, just a little. 'He never said, never showed that he even knew what I was doing...'

'You didn't give him the opportunity. Besides...' she shrugged '...he was too proud to make the first move. He was proud, you are proud and here you are.'

'He sat there and disowned me and when I disobeyed him he...' But he couldn't say the words.

'He had a heart attack,' she finished calmly. 'It wasn't your fault, Marco.'

Easy for her to say. He knew better; he'd always known. 'Of course it was. If I had settled to be what he wanted...'

'Then you wouldn't be you. He knew that. But it hurt him that you barely returned. That from the moment you went to London you never again spent a night under our roof.'

Misunderstandings, pride, stubbornness. Family traits passed on from father to son. 'I couldn't. I didn't dare. I couldn't let his health blackmail me into compliance, nor could I let him work himself into one of his passions. It was better to stay away.' He stopped, bleak. 'He died anyway.'

'*Sì*. But not because of anything you said or didn't say but because he didn't listen to his doctor, didn't listen to me, didn't exercise or take his pills or cut down on red meat. Stubborn. But it's not your fault, Marco. That first heart attack would have happened anyway, you must know that. We're lucky we had him for another ten years.'

But Marco hadn't had him; he'd lost his father long before. 'And now it's too late, he's gone and he didn't even know I said goodbye.'

Her eyes were soft with understanding, with love. 'He knew. You came straight away. He was conscious enough to know you were there. Forgive yourself, Marco. Nobody else blames you for any of it, nobody ever did. But I would like you to come home, at least to be here more often. To advise me even if you won't take over. I just want to see my son more than a couple of hours once or twice a year.'

'Yes.' His mind was whirling. Why had his father never told him that he was proud of him, never said he hadn't meant a word of the bitter denunciation that had left him in the hospital and Marco in exile? But his mother was right. Marco hadn't stayed away just out of fear he would trigger another heart attack, he'd stayed away out of pride. Just as bad as his father. Maybe it was time to let some of that pride go.

'Yes,' he said again. 'I can be here more often. And I can't promise you I'll take over, but I can advise—and make sure you have the right people in place to help you. You need to delegate more, Mamma, and accept that people who aren't Santoros can still care about the company.'

'It's a deal.'

Relief flooded through him. They had compromised and, for the first time, he didn't feel that she had tried to manipulate him; she had respected his decision. He would, should spend more time in Venice. It was only right that he at least took a board role in his family company.

He bent, kissed his mother's cheek and turned to leave but stopped as she called his name softly. 'Marco?'

'Yes?'

'Ten years wasted, Marco, out of pride, out of anger...' She paused. 'Don't make that mistake again. I know you say you aren't ready to marry and I know you are angry with me, with your father, for what happened ten years ago. But don't let that pride, that anger, push Sophie away. She's a lovely girl, Marco. But I don't think there will be second chances with that one. You need to get it right.'

'Mamma, we've only just met.'

'I know, and I am staying out of it.' Despite his prickle of annoyance he couldn't help an incredulous laugh at her words. 'Just think about it. That's all I'm asking. Just take care with her.'

'Okay.' He could promise that with an easy mind. Taking care came easily to him; he knew how to tread for an easy relationship and an easier exit. 'I'll take care. Now I really have to get on.' But as he walked away her words echoed in his mind. *No more second chances.* He didn't need a second chance. He liked Sophie, he liked her a lot, enough to know that she deserved a lot better than anything a man like him could offer. He should thank her though, for all her help. He might not be able to offer her happy ever after—and she probably wouldn't take it if he did—but he could offer her one perfect day. It was the least he could do. It had to be; it was all that he had.

CHAPTER NINE

To Sophie's amazement Marco was still in the breakfast room when she came down, having overslept again. She stopped and hovered at the door, stupidly shy.

How she could feel shy when he'd left her bedroom just four short hours ago, how she could still feel shy after the things they'd done in that bedroom, eluded her and yet her stomach swooped at the sight of him and her tongue was suddenly too large for her mouth, like a teenager seeing her crush across the hallway.

They hadn't eaten breakfast together since that first morning. He was usually already out working when she came downstairs, their first communication of the day at lunch. Lunch was civilised, easy to navigate, but breakfast? Breakfast was an intimate meal. She wasn't ready for breakfast…

His presence wasn't the only thing that had changed. The atmosphere in the *palazzo* seemed lighter somehow, less fraught. Less weighted with the air of things left unsaid, when the silences were more eloquent than words. For the first time since the party she and Marco had stayed at the *palazzo* for dinner last night and Marco hadn't tensed up too much when his mother had quizzed Sophie once more about her future plans and shot him meaningful glances every time she did so. Marco's mother was very charming, but over the space of the evening she'd ramped up the inquisitional levels to almost overbearing, her hints so broad Sophie hadn't known where to look half the time. She'd aimed for obliviousness, but it was difficult to look unknowing when she was invited to try on Marco's dead grandmother's engagement ring, asked about her perfect honeymoon plans or how many children she wanted and didn't she think her eyes with Marco's colouring would look cute in a baby?

She might, possibly, have been able to laugh the whole thing off if it weren't for the pregnancy. Guilt, embarrassment and fear mingled in a toxic concoction every time Marco's mother opened her mouth. Every time Signora Santoro mentioned children guilt shot through Sophie, like a physical pain. It took everything she had to sit and pretend everything was okay, not to jump up and announce her pregnancy in a rush of tears. She still thought it was fair to wait until after the wedding, it was just a week's delay after all, but she knew in her heart she was deceiving Marco, lying to him by omission.

And part of her knew it wasn't Bianca's welfare really driving her, it was fear. She'd spent so long living her mother's dreams, only to crush them when she'd walked away, the rift still no way near repaired. Then she'd allowed Harry to set her course, making him the sole focus of her life. This family was so certain, so overbearing, so grand and overwhelming—what if they tried to take control as soon as they knew about the baby? Had the last year and a half given her enough strength to hold firm and make her own choices?

Time would tell, but she needed these days to prepare. To try to work out exactly what she, Sophie

Bradshaw, wanted, before the Santoro expectations descended onto her.

She took a deep breath and walked into the room, hooking a chair and sitting down, swiping a piece of brioche off Marco's plate as she did so. The key to fighting off both the tiredness and nausea, she'd realised, was carbs and plenty of them. The way she was eating she'd be sporting plenty of bumps long before the baby actually started to show.

'Good morning. All on your own?'

Marco folded his newspaper up and pushed it to one side. Sophie really liked the way he focussed his full attention on the people he was with, apologising if he checked his phone or took a call. He never kept his phone on the table when they were out, never scrolled through it when she was speaking. Harry had never made any secret of the fact every contact in his phone, every game, every meme, every football result came before her. 'You just missed Mamma and Bianca. They told me to remind you that you can join them at any time. Apparently the twenty times they asked you last night wasn't a pressing enough invitation. Are you sure you don't want to go with them?'

Sophie grinned. 'Your mother, Bianca's future mother-in-law, all five of her future sisters-in-law and her three best friends all alternately talking in Italian so I sit there gaping like a goldfish before switching to English to quiz me on your intentions and my potential wedding plans? There's not a spa luxurious enough to tempt me.' She realised how ungrateful that sounded and backtracked quickly. 'I like them all well enough, in fact I love Bianca and your mother individually...'

'But together they strike fear into the heart of the bravest warrior?'

'They really do. Besides, the day after tomorrow it's the wedding and I fly back to London the morning after that. I'm making final adjustments to Bianca's and the bridesmaids' dresses tomorrow, which makes this my last free day here. I want to make the most of it. Explore Venice one final time.'

'Do you want some company?'

Happiness fizzed up at the casual words. 'Of course, but don't you need to work? Don't worry about me if so...'

Giuliana, one of the maids, set a cup, a small tea-pot and a plate laden with sweet bread, slices of fruit, cheese and a couple of pastries in front of Sophie. Her preference for herbal tea first thing had caused some consternation in the caffeinated household at first, but the staff had eventually adjusted to both tea and her very un-Venetian need for a breakfast more substantial than a few bites of something quick. Sophie nodded her thanks, grateful as the familiar ginger aroma wafted up, displacing the bitter scent of coffee and settling her queasy stomach.

'A few days off seems like the perfect plan right now,' Marco said as Sophie started to tuck in. 'I need time to think about where my business is headed, how I can continue to grow and still meet my obligations to the family business.' His mouth twisted into a rueful smile. 'I realised yesterday that even if I don't want to take over I still need to be involved. Besides, when I started out I used my contacts here to source antiques, but it was important for me to be in London to build contacts for the other side of the business, the people I would sell to. I've been based there ten years, own a house in Chelsea. In many ways it's my home.'

Right there and then the chasm between them widened even further. Sophie rented a shoebox on the top floor of a building on a busy road. Buses thundered past at all hours of the day and night, streetlights lit up her room, casting an orange glow over her dreams, and the bass from the flat below provided a thudding soundtrack to everything she did. Half her pay went straight to her landlord. Owning a home of her own was a distant enough dream, her city shoebox well out of her range. A whole house? In Chelsea? Not for the likes of her.

It was all going to make telling him about the baby even harder. If only they were equals financially... She pushed the thought away, adding it to her ever-lengthening list of things to worry about in the future. 'But now?'

'I still need an office and a base in London, but those contacts are secure. I have a whole global network of dealers, buyers, designers who know and trust me. I'm having to work a little harder on the Italian side now. There's a new generation of suppliers coming along and I don't have the same links with them, the same trust. It means I'm no longer the automatic first choice and that could impact my future stock.'

'So, you need to spend more time here?' Her heart twisted. She had no idea what her future held, but she hadn't expected to have a baby with a man she wasn't committed to, a man who spent half his life out of the country.

Suck it up, she told herself fiercely. *This will be your reality. Deal with it.*

'I do. But these are thoughts for another day. I'm very much aware how much we owe you, Sophie. Bianca would have imploded if you hadn't stayed. Let me make it up to you. Anything you want. How do you want to spend the day? A trip to the lakes? To Roma? Buy out the whole of the lace shops on Burano?'

Guilt twisted again. She'd had her own selfish reasons for staying, for getting close to Marco's family. But she couldn't pass up this opportunity to spend a day with the father of her child—and she didn't want to. She wanted to spend the day with him, to get to know him a little better, to have one last carefree day before she shattered his world. 'Nothing so elaborate. Show me your Venice, Marco, the things you love most about the city. That's what I'd like to do today. If you're okay with that.'

'Really? That's what you want to do? You're willing to take the risk?' He looked surprised, but he was smiling. 'In that case I'll meet you back here in half an hour. Wear comfy shoes and wrap up warm. We may be out for some time.'

CHAPTER TEN

SOPHIE INSTANTLY FELL in love with the Dorsoduro. Although there were plenty of tourists around, exclaiming over the views and taking selfies with the canals and bridges as backdrops, it had a more relaxed air than the streets around the Rialto Bridge and Saint Mark's square, a sense of home and belonging, especially once they reached the quieter back streets and small tree-lined squares. Amongst the grocery and souvenir shops, the cafés and restaurants, she spotted some gorgeous boutiques, specialising in stationery, in paints, in textiles as well as enticing pastry and confectionery shops that made her mouth water and she itched to explore further. 'Can I go shopping before lunch and then explore this afternoon? I'd really like to look at those textiles if I could.'

'Of course. I'm not sure how we've managed to miss this area out of our tours,' Marco said. 'We spent some time in the east of the *sestieri*, but somehow we haven't wandered here.'

'That's because we were meant to come here today. It's been waiting for me all week, an old friend I haven't met yet.'

'That's exactly what this area is, an old friend. If I ever lived back in Venice full-time, I wouldn't want to live in the *palazzo*. I'd prefer a little house tucked away in the back streets here. Something smaller than the London house, overlooking a canal.'

No one Sophie had ever met who lived in London had ever wanted something smaller. Curiosity got the better of her manners. 'How big *is* your house in London?'

Marco shrugged. 'Four bedrooms. It's just a terrace, round the back of the King's Road. Three floors and a basement, courtyard garden.'

Sophie managed to keep walking somehow. *Just* a terrace. *Just* round the back of the King's Road. She often walked those streets, picking out her favourites from the ivy-covered, white and pastel painted houses, knowing that houses like that, lifestyles like that, were as beyond her dreams as living on Mars.

She'd known that Marco's family was rich, knew he had enough money to buy handmade suits and frequent expensive bars, but somehow she hadn't realised that Marco was rich—really rich, not merely well off—in his own right.

It made everything infinitely worse.

It took two to make a baby, she reminded herself. This wasn't her fault. She wasn't trying to trap him, to enrich herself at his expense. But it was what people would think. It might be what he would think and she couldn't blame him. It would all be so much easier if he were a little more normal, if his family hadn't made the idea of fatherhood, marriage and settling down into his worst nightmare. If she thought he'd be happy with her news, not horrified…

Preoccupied, she hadn't noticed where they were walking, barely taking in that Marco had turned out of the narrow road to lead her through an arched gate and onto a rough floor made of wooden slats, leading down to the canal. Wooden, balconied buildings took up two sides of the square, the open canals the other two, and upturned gondolas lined up on the floor in neat rows.

'Marco!' A man dressed in overalls, wiping his hands on a rag, just as if this were a normal garage in a normal town, straightened and strode over, embracing Marco in a warm hug. Marco returned the embrace and the two men began to talk in loud, voluble Italian. Sophie didn't even try to follow the conversation, even when she heard her name mentioned; instead she pulled out her camera and began to take pictures of two young men bending over a gondola, faces intent as they applied varnish to the curved hull. It was the closest she'd got to a gondola in all the time she'd been here; Marco owned his own boat, of course, and had made it clear that gondola rides were only for tourists. She'd not argued but couldn't help feeling a little cheated out of the quintessential Venetian experience.

'Sì...sì, grazie.' Marco embraced the man again and Sophie whipped the camera round to capture the moment, his body completely relaxed, his smile open and wide in a way it never was at the *palazzo*. His family were only a small part of his world here. He had his business contacts, yes, family obligations and friends—but also this whole other life. His own friends and interests, left behind when he started a new life in London, and yet still obviously important. This was what he would be returning to when he started to spend more time here. Leaving behind the network of business friends he spent his time with in London for people who really knew him. Sophie swallowed. She could go back to Manchester tomorrow and not meet one person who would make her smile the way Marco was smiling now.

'Ready?' He stepped over an oar and re-joined Sophie.

'For what?'

'I thought you wanted to go shopping and I have a few things I need to buy. *Arrivederci*,' he called over his shoulder as they exited the yard as speedily as they had entered it.

Sophie looked back, wishing they'd had more time for her to take in every detail. 'Is that where gondolas go to die?'

His mouth curved into the rare genuine smile she loved to see, the smile she liked to draw out of him. 'No, it's where they go to get better. Tonio's family have been fixing them for generations. When we were boys he swore it wouldn't be for him, swore that he would travel the world, be his own man...'

'What happened?'

Marco shrugged. 'He travelled the world and realised that all he wanted was to come home and run the yard. Now he's the most respected gondola maker and fixer in all of Venice.'

It didn't take long to reach the shops Sophie had noted when they'd first entered the Dorsoduro and she was immediately torn between a textile shop specialising in hand-woven materials and a traditional mask maker. She hadn't had to dip too far into her carefully hoarded money so far; a few ingredients for the meal she'd cooked Marco, material from a warehouse for her dress and for Bianca's wedding gift, but she wanted to buy presents for her friends if possible.

'I have a few errands to run,' Marco said as she wavered between the two. 'See you back here in an hour? I know the perfect place for lunch.' And before she could respond he was gone. Sophie checked her watch. She had just under an hour and streets of tempting little shops to explore; there was no time to waste. With a deep breath and a feeling of impending bankruptcy she opted for the mask shop.

It was like stepping into another world, a world of velvet and lace, of secrecy and whispers, seductive and terrifying in equal measure. Sophie turned slowly, marvelling at the artistry in every detail, her eyes drawn to a half-face cat mask, one side gold, the other a green brocade, sequins highlighting the slanted eye slits and the perfect feline nose. She picked it up and held it against her face, immediately transformed into someone— something—dangerous and unknown. She replaced it with a sigh of longing. The gorgeous carnival masks, all made and painted by hand, were definitely beyond her means and having seen the real thing she didn't want to waste her money on the cheaper, mass-produced masks displayed on souvenir stalls throughout the city. Likewise she soon realised that the colourful fabrics, still produced on traditional wooden looms, would bankrupt her.

Three quarters of an hour later she was done, choosing beautiful handmade paper journals, one for each of her friends. Turning as she exited the shop, she saw Marco sauntering towards her, a secretive, pleased smile on his face. 'Done already?' he asked as he reached her side. 'I usually have to drag Bianca and Mamma out of these shops kicking and screaming.'

'I could just look at the colours and the workmanship for hours,' Sophie admitted. 'I very nearly came home with a cat mask. But options for wearing such a thing in London are sadly limited. Not that I can imagine actually wearing it. It's a work of art.'

'You should see the city at *carnivale*. It's not just the masks, the costumes are out of this world— hats, dominoes, elaborate gowns. You would go crazy for the colours and designs. My mother has five different outfits and six different masks, so each year she changes her look completely.'

'What about you? What do you wear?'

'I go for the simple black domino and a half-mask, but it's many years since I've been here during *carnivale*. The city gets a little fevered. It's easy to get carried away.'

After a light lunch at a pretty café overlooking a narrow back-street canal they explored the rest of the vibrant district, wandering down to the university, visiting churches and museums as they went. The afternoon flew by and it was a surprise when Sophie realised it was late afternoon and their wandering no longer had an aimless quality to it. Marco was walking with intent as they retraced their steps back to the gondola yard they had visited earlier. The gates were closed now, but Marco knocked loudly on the wooden door and almost immediately one large gate swung open. Sophie didn't recognise the owner at first. He'd changed out of his overalls and into the striped top and straw hat of a gondolier, although, in a nod to the season, he had put a smart black jacket over the top.

'This way,' Marco said and steered her towards the jetty. A gondola was moored there, gleaming black in the fading light. Warm velvety throws were placed over the black leather seats, several more were folded on the two stools that provided the only other seating. 'It gets cold,' Marco said briefly as he took her hand and helped her step into the gently rocking boat. 'Welcome aboard, *signorina*.'

The rug was soft and warm as Sophie wriggled into one of the two main seats, placed side by side along the middle of the long narrow boat. Marco picked up another

blanket and draped it across her knees and Sophie folded
her hands into the fabric, glad of the extra coverings.
Her tights and wool jacket were good enough protection
against the chill while she was moving and the sun was
out, but, sitting still as the evening began to reach dark
fingers along the sky, she was suddenly very aware it
was winter. Marco set a basket on the small table in the
middle of the seating area before gracefully stepping
aboard and taking his seat next to hers. It was a narrow
space and she could feel the hard length of his thigh
next to hers, his body heat as he slipped an arm around
her shoulders and shouted something unintelligible to
his friend. The next moment the moorings were untied
and the boat began to glide away from the dock, moving smoothly down the canal.

Marco leaned forward and, with a flourish, took two
champagne glasses and a bottle out of the basket, and
set them in front of her, followed by a selection of small
fruit and custard tarts, beautifully presented in a lav-
ishly decorated box.

'It's far too early for dinner,' he explained. 'But I
thought you might enjoy a picnic. And don't worry, I've
remembered your 'no drinking in January' rule. The
bottle is actually lightly sparkling grape juice, although
it really should be Prosecco.'

Sophie didn't need Prosecco, the unexpected sweetness of the surprise he had so carefully planned more
intoxicating than any drink could possibly be. The
grape juice wasn't too sweet, the tartness a welcome
relief against the flaky pastry and sugared fruit of the
delicious tarts. Replete, she snuggled back against
Marco's arm and watched Venice go by. She'd spent
many hours on the canals, but the city felt closer, more

magical from the gondola, as if she were in a dream, part of the city's very fabric.

Marco had obviously planned the route with his friend in advance and the gondola took them into several hidden corners of the city, going through water gates into some of the *palazzos* and even slipping beneath churches into secret passages. Their route took them through the back waters and quieter canals and at times it was as if they were the only people in the city, even their gondolier fading into the background as, with a final burst of orange and pink, the sun finally began to sink into the water and the velvety dusk fell.

'I don't know why you said a gondola was a tourist trap. It is the most romantic thing that has ever happened to me,' Sophie said as the last of the day disappeared, their way now lit by the soft gold of the lamps, their reflections glowing in the murky water.

'More romantic than you knocking me over in the snow?'

She pretended to think about it. 'Almost. Even more romantic than you chasing me into a cupboard on New Year's Eve.'

'I have fond memories of that cupboard,' he said and she elbowed him.

'Nothing happened in that cupboard, unless you're mixing me up with someone else that night.'

'Oh, no, you are definitely one of a kind,' Marco said softly. 'The first girl who ever ran away from me.'

'I find that hard to believe.' But she didn't. She found it hard to believe that she ever had run away, that she had had the strength of will to walk away that first night and again on New Year's Eve. 'Is that why you asked me here, because I walked away?'

'Ran,' he corrected her. 'One sight of me and you

were tearing through that ballroom like an Olympic medallist in heels. And maybe that's why. I was intrigued for sure, wanted to spend more time with you.'

And now? She wanted to ask, but she didn't quite dare. The carefully orchestrated romance of the evening was perfect but could so easily be a farewell gesture. 'You didn't bargain for quite so much time,' she said instead. 'Thank you, Marco, I know you were blindsided by your sister, but thank you for making me feel welcome, for making me feel wanted...'

He leaned over then, pulling her close, his mouth on hers, harder than his usual sweet kisses, more demanding. He kissed her as if they were the only two people in the whole of Venice, as if the world might stop if she didn't acquiesce, fall into it, fall into him. The world fell away, the heat of his mouth, his hands holding her still, holding her close all she knew, all she wanted to know. Her own arms encircled him as she buried one hand in his hair, the other clutching at his shoulder as if she were drowning and he all that stood between her and a watery grave.

It was the first time he'd kissed her for kissing's sake, she realised in some dim part of her mind. That first night they didn't lay a hand on each other until they were in the hotel room, New Year's Eve she had walked away from his touch—but if she hadn't, she knew full well they would have ended up in that same hotel room, the kiss a precursor, a promise of things yet to come. It would have been another hotel, not his house; close as it must have been, that was too intimate for Marco, not her flat, too intimate for her.

Even here in Venice they were curiously separate... Oh, he kissed her cheek in greeting, held her arm to guide her, but there were no gestures of intimacy; no holding hands, no caresses as they passed each other, no cuddles or embraces. No kisses on bridges or boats. Kisses, caresses, embraces—they were saved for under cover of darkness, saved for passion and escape. But there could be no passion or escape here in the middle of a canal, visible to anyone and everyone walking by. This was kissing for kissing's sake. Touching for touching's sake. This was togetherness.

Her heart might burst—or it might break—but all she could do was kiss him back and let all her yearning, her need, her want pour out of her and into him. Savour each second—because if this was it, if this was a farewell gesture, she wanted to remember every single moment, remember what was good before she blew his world apart.

Sophie hadn't expected the evening to continue after the gondola ride, but after they reluctantly disembarked Marco took her to a few of his favourite *bàcaro*, small bars serving wine and *cicchetti*, little tapas-type snacks. In one *bàcaro* Sophie was enchanted by the selection of *francobollo*, teeny little sandwiches filled with a selection of meats or roasted vegetables. 'They're so tiny it's like I'm not eating anything at all,' she explained to a fascinated Marco as she consumed her tenth—or was it eleventh? 'Less than a mouthful doesn't count, everyone knows that.' In another she tried the tastiest meatballs she had ever eaten and a third offered a selection of seafood that rivalled the fanciest of restaurants. One day, she promised herself, she would return when the smell of the different house wines didn't make her wrinkle her nose in disgust and she could sample the excellent coffee without wanting to throw up.

She had no idea how long they spent in the friendly,

noisy bars as early evening turned into evening. Marco seemed to know people everywhere they went and introduced her to all of them until she had completely lost track of who was a school friend, who a college friend and who had got who into the most trouble in their teens. Everyone was very welcoming and made an effort to speak in English, but Sophie was very conscious of their curious glances, a confirmation that Marco seldom, if ever, brought girlfriends back to Venice.

'Okay,' Marco announced as Sophie was wondering if she could possibly manage just one more *francobollo*. 'Time to go.' She glanced up, surprised; she'd assumed that this was the purpose of the evening, that they didn't have anywhere else to go.

'Go?' she echoed.

He nodded, his face solemn but his eyes gleaming with suppressed mischief.

Sophie got to her feet. They couldn't possibly be going out for dinner, not after the almost constant snacking starting with the pastries in the gondola and ending with that last small sandwich, and it was too dark to head back out on the water. She was relieved that she'd dressed smartly that morning, and some bright lipstick and mascara had been enough to make her look bar ready; she just hoped it would work for whatever Marco had planned next. 'Okay, I'm ready. Lead on, MacDuff.'

It didn't take them more than five minutes to reach their mystery destination, a grand-looking *palazzo*, just off St Mark's Square. The main door was ajar, guarded by a broad, suited man, and to Sophie's surprise Marco produced two tickets and handed them over. The man examined them and then with a nod of his head opened the door and bade them enter. They were ushered through a grand hallway, beautifully furnished in the formal Venetian style, up the sweeping staircase and into a grand salon, where around sixty people were milling around, all smartly dressed. In the corner a string quartet were tuning their instruments.

One end of the room was empty, furniture carefully placed in a way that reminded Sophie of a stage set; chairs had been placed in semicircles facing the empty area. 'Is this a recital?'

'Not quite. Have you been to the opera before?'

'The opera? No, never. Is that what this is? In a house?'

'*La Traviata,*' Marco confirmed. 'Each act takes place in a different room in the *palazzo* so that the audience is both spectator and part of the scene. It's one of my favourite things to do when I'm home. I thought you might enjoy it.'

'Oh, I'm sure I will.' Sophie knew nothing about opera, had no idea if she would like the music, but it didn't matter—what mattered was the effort Marco had put into her last free evening here. The effort he had put in to show her the parts of Venice that meant something to him, show her the city he loved and missed. 'Thank you, Marco. This is the loveliest thing anyone has ever, ever done for me.'

He smiled, but before he could reply they were asked to take their seats.

The next couple of hours passed by in a blur of music, of song, of spectacle, of tears. Sophie was so engrossed she didn't notice the tears rolling down her face as Violetta sang her swansong, not until Marco pressed a handkerchief into her trembling hand. It wasn't just the music, moving as it was, it was the setting, it was the night as a whole, it was the realisation that these were the last innocent hours she and Marco would spend together, that whatever happened after this would be heavy with expectation. She wanted to freeze every second, frame them, remember it all.

'Did you enjoy that?'

She nodded, wrapping her scarf a little tighter as they exited the *palazzo* and turned into St Mark's Square. The moon was low and round, casting an enchantment on the ancient buildings, lit up and golden by the street-lights. 'I loved every bit of it,' she said. 'The whole evening, Marco. Thank you.'

He caught her hand, a boyish carefree gesture, and as he did so realisation rocketed through her, sudden and painful in its clarity. She was in love with him. Deeply, relentlessly, irrevocably in love with him. How had this happened? Maybe it was hormones, her version of mood swings, an emotion that would drain away when she hit the magic twelve-week mark. Maybe it was fear, fear of raising the baby alone in a tiny flat on a busy main road. Maybe it was simply the novelty of being treated as if she mattered, as if she was worth something by a man worth everything.

Or maybe it was real, that elusive alchemy of desire and compatibility and friendship.

She rose onto her tiptoes, pressing a soft kiss to his bristled cheek in thanks. He moved as she did so, catching her in his arms, capturing her mouth under his so that her light embrace was turned into something more powerful. She allowed him to take control, leaning into him, into his warmth and strength. Allowed him to claim her as his. Because she was, his. But that was almost irrelevant. How could she tell him when he was already burdened by his family's heavy expectations? How could she tell him she loved him when she still had to tell him about the baby? Her love would be one more load for him to bear, one more expectation for him to manage and she couldn't do it to him. She had this night, this kiss. They had to be enough.

CHAPTER ELEVEN

BIANCA QUIVERED AS the music struck up and she clutched his arm even more tightly.

'Hold on in there,' Marco said. 'Not long to go.'

'I'm not nervous, I'm excited. I love Antonio and I can't wait to marry him, to start our life together, I just…' She faltered, her dark eyes tearing up, and he squeezed her hand.

'I know, you wish Papà was here. I do too.'

'He liked Antonio. I'm glad about that. Glad he got to know him, that they respected each other. He'd have liked Sophie too.'

'Bianca, Sophie and I aren't…'

She turned and looked straight at him, beautiful, glowing with her hair caught up behind the heirloom tiara, her veil arranged in foamy folds down her back. 'Not yet, but you could be. I see the way you look at her when you think nobody's watching you.'

'And how's that?'

'You look the way I feel about Antonio, that's how.'

'I think you're seeing what you want to see. I like her, of course I do, I admire her…'

'Fancy the pants off her?' Bianca's mouth curved into a wide grin and she waggled her perfectly plucked eyebrows at him.

'The mouth on you. And a bride at that! Yes, I find her attractive too, but that's not...' He stopped, unable to find the right words.

'That's not what? What falling in love is? I never had you down as the stars and flowers type, Marco. Falling in love might be instantaneous, strike-me-down, can't-live-without-this person, all-consuming lust when you are sixteen, when you're twenty. It's meant to be like that when you're young. But when you grow up, when you're an adult, then love is something slower but stronger. You start off with like and admire and attract and over time it grows and becomes all the more powerful for that. But you have to let it grow, not run away the first chance you get.'

Marco stared down into his little sister's face. 'When did you get so wise?'

She smirked. 'I always was. Now stand up straight and get ready to support me down this aisle. These heels are ridiculous and I have no intention of tripping and prostrating myself at Antonio's feet!'

The music swelled, their cue. He bent slightly and kissed Bianca's cheek. 'Ready, *sorellina*?'

She inhaled slowly, her hand shaking as she did so. 'Ready. Let's go get me married.'

Bianca had chosen to marry in the gorgeous Church of Santa Maria dei Miracoli, partly because of the sumptuous décor and partly, Marco suspected, because she'd liked the idea of standing at the top of the marble staircase to make her vows. There weren't quite enough seats for all the guests and people were standing at the back and along the sides, all three hundred pairs of eyes staring right at Marco and Bianca. Marco barely noticed them; he was searching for the one person he wanted to see, Bianca's words hammering through his brain with every step they took.

Like, admire, attract.

Was she right? Was it that simple? If so, why did the very thought of it feel so terrifying? So insurmountable? And yet…he inhaled, his heart hammering fast, louder than the organ music filling the great church. And yet in some ways it made perfect sense.

As they neared the front of the church he caught sight of Sophie, elegant and poised, standing next to his mother. If he hadn't known that she had whipped her dress up in just two days, he would never have believed it; she looked as if she were wearing the most exclusive designer fashion. She'd opted for a silvery grey damask material, which shimmered faintly under the chandelier lights. It was a seemingly conservative design, wide straps at her neck with the neckline cut high, almost to her throat—a stark contrast to the deep vee at her back, exposing creamy skin down to the mid-point of her spine. The bodice fitted tightly right to her waist and then the material flared out into a full knee-length skirt. The look was deceptively demure—but the dress fitted the contours of her body perfectly, the material lovingly caressing every slight curve. She'd twisted her hair up into a loose chignon confined by a silver band showing off the graceful lines of her neck. She was elegant and sophisticated, easily outshining the more elaborate and colourful dresses crowding the pews of the ornate church.

She looked right at him and smiled, a soft intimate smile, and his chest tightened. Two days ago he had promised her a perfect day. It hadn't been altogether altruistic; payment for all the work she had put in on the wedding, work that had ended up going way beyond altering one dress; distraction for him as he mulled over the momentous decision to step back into the family business, to spend more time at home; seduction, he'd wanted the kind of day that would make her boneless with desire because sex with her was out of this world and they had so little time left. No, his reasons hadn't been altogether altruistic.

But she hadn't demanded fine wines and five-star restaurants, she'd asked him to show her his world. He hadn't realised it at the time, but the price of her day was far higher than the most expensive restaurant in Italy. He'd paid her in intimacy, in revealing parts of his soul he kept hidden from the whole world.

Like, admire, attract.

Surely, despite the short amount of time he'd known her they had gone way beyond those three words and he'd no idea how it had happened, how he'd let his guard down. He'd kept himself so safe, most of the women he'd met over the last decade or so had as little interest in his inner life as he had in theirs. They cared about his name, his family, his prospects, his money. They made superficiality all too easy, all too attractive.

But Sophie wasn't like that. She was visibly shocked by his wealth, unimpressed by his name. And still he hid. Because if she found him wanting, it would matter; this time it could hurt.

Marco escorted Bianca up the stairs towards the altar and her waiting groom. She'd forgotten about him, about the church full of people waiting to see her get married, all her attention on Antonio, her eyes shining and luminous. He crossed himself as they neared the altar and, as if in a dream, waited to play his small part, before descending the steps to join Sophie and his mother, leaving Bianca making her vows, readying herself for a life in the family she chose, not the one she was born to.

The church hushed, the only sound the voices of the priest, Bianca and her new husband as they repeated vows with heartbreaking sincerity and emotion. All his sister's usual theatrics had disappeared as she gazed at the man she was promising to love in sickness and in health.

'I couldn't understand a word, but that was beautiful.' Sophie gulped as the crowd burst into enthusiastic applause as Bianca and Antonio embraced for the first time as husband and wife. 'She looks so gorgeous. Like the perfect bride. And they look so happy...' Her voice wavered. Next to her one of Marco's aunts was sobbing, on his other side his mother was still applying her handkerchief. Marco looked around wildly, but he was trapped; there was no escape from wet-eyed, sniffing females.

At least no escape until he was crushed into the narrow pew as his mother elbowed her way past him. 'Oh, Sophie, *grazie, cara*. You performed miracles. Hey, Chesca, this is Sophie, Marco's *ragazza*. Did you see how she transformed Bianca's dress? *Sì, bellissima*.'

His mother kept up her chatter as they made their way down the aisle. She was obviously buzzing from the wedding and wanted everyone to know how Sophie had helped—binding the English girl ever closer to the family, he thought wryly. 'Yes, she and Marco are very close, he's quite besotted,' he heard her confide more than once. 'We expect an announcement any day now.'

Her whispered predictions didn't surprise him, his lack of anger did. But she was wrong; there would be no announcement. Things had moved too fast, so fast he'd barely noticed that they were out of the shallows and heading towards the deep water. Sophie was going home tomorrow and perhaps it was for the best. Enjoy the short time they had left, then put a stop to it before he let her down. He might not mean to, but he would. It was his hallmark after all.

Sophie had been aware of the stares before the wedding started. It was worse than the party at Epiphany. Then, she had been new to the city, unaware of the subtext. Today she knew all too well that everyone was looking at her and wondering if she would be the next Santoro bride. She had been the subject of more than a few cool, assessing once-overs from expensively clad and groomed women, the contemptuous flicker of their eyes judging her and finding her wanting.

But the stares intensified once the ceremony was over. Marco's mother was making it very clear that she considered Sophie one of the family, introducing her to what seemed like every single one of the three hundred guests. Even worse, she told everyone she could about how Sophie had 'saved' Bianca's dress. Sophie knew that if Ashleigh were here she'd be telling her to milk the situation for all she was worth, think of future commissions and suck it up, but she felt guilty taking all the credit—she'd only adapted what was already there after all.

The whole wedding party walked the short distance between the church and the *palazzo* where Bianca and Antonio were hosting their wedding reception. There had, Sophie gathered, been some heated family debate on the venue, the Santoros wanting to hold it at the family home, but Bianca preferring a neutral venue—and for she and Antonio to pick up the tab. 'Mamma wants to control every little detail as it is,' she'd explained to

Sophie. 'The only way I can guarantee having things the way I want them is to pay for it myself.'

And goodness knew what she had paid. The couple had taken over one of the most illustrious hotels in Venice for the evening, demanding sole use of the fourteenth-century *palazzo* for their guests. Sophie had been intimidated by the faded glory of the Santoro home, but this fully restored *palazzo* took her breath away, from the bright frescos adorning every wall and ceiling to the marble staircase, the huge terrace overlooking the Grand Canal, furnished with tables, chairs and throws to wrap around the hardier wedding guests venturing out in the January chill, to the ballroom in which the reception was being held. This was an immense room, decorated with elaborate, huge gold frescos, the ceiling high above adding to the feeling of grandeur and space. She had waitressed at some glitzy events over the last eighteen months, had seen some fabulous occasions, but nothing came close to the sheer grandeur of this wedding, this room, this family.

What on earth was she doing here?

'Signorina Bradshaw?' She jumped at a gentle tap on her elbow, turning to see a petite brunette with a wide smile, conservatively dressed in a smart, dark blue suit. 'Hello. I am Flavia, fashion reporter for *Marchesa* magazine.'

That was another unexpected facet to today's wedding. She had known the Santoros were rich, had known that the family was old Venetian blue blood, but it simply hadn't occurred to her that there would be outside interest in the wedding. It came as a shock when she realised several newspapers and magazines had been waiting outside the church and the high society *Marchesa* magazine had permission to cover the early part of the reception. Sophie resisted the urge to smooth down her dress and did her best to smile. 'Hi, yes, I'm Sophie Bradshaw.'

'You are here with Signor Santoro?'

'Erm…yes.' That wasn't exactly privileged information and Marco's mother had already announced it to pretty much the whole of Venice. The reporter looked at her expectantly and Sophie struggled to find something else to say. 'It was very kind of him to ask me along to such a beautiful occasion.'

There, she knew her role was to act as a buffer between Marco and his family's expectations, but at least she wasn't publicly staking her claim. The journalist didn't look convinced, raising a sceptical eyebrow before plastering on her smile. 'The big news is, of course, the wedding dress. Everyone has been raving over it and I hear you are responsible for making some big last-minute changes?'

Sophie paused. She didn't want to say that Bianca had put on weight and she certainly wasn't going to mention the pregnancy. 'I…'

'Sophie saved me.' The bride swooped down upon them, kissing Sophie exuberantly. 'My dress was beautiful, yes, but too plain for such an occasion, not entirely appropriate for a church wedding. And she took this beautiful dress and made it unique and special.' She twirled round, allowing the accompanying photographer to take pictures. 'Look at the stitching, and these beautiful buttons, and how she took it in here and here. She made the dress she's wearing too. Don't be fooled by how simple it looks. It is truly *elegante*.'

To Sophie's relief, once her photo had been taken, one with the bride and one posing self-consciously by herself by one of the three huge windows, the journalist moved away. Sophie scanned the crowds but couldn't see Marco anywhere and she couldn't face another round of being introduced as the new member of the family. It was probably a little futile checking her hair and make-up after the magazine had taken her photo, but she knew she needed a few moments to ready herself for the rest of the event.

She'd always found large social events intimidating, much preferring quiet evenings to a big crowd. Make the crowd larger, wealthier and effortlessly chic, add in a language she didn't speak and she was officially way out of her depth.

Luckily it didn't take her long to find the ladies' room. The door led into a large sitting area, filled with inviting-looking seats and sofas and several dressing tables, each piled high with cotton wool, hair spray and even straighteners for maximum primping. A door at the other end led to toilets and sinks and, as another guest came through, Sophie noted the opulence of the marble sinks and the gilt fittings. She suspected the individual toilet stalls might be bigger than her own shower room back in London—not that difficult: most cupboards were bigger than her shower room.

Sinking onto one of the sofas with a sigh of relief, Sophie told herself sternly she had five minutes to get herself together before heading back in. Things were coming to a head, that was all. She was leaving first thing tomorrow—really going this time—and she had to tell Marco about the baby before she did so. He hadn't mentioned anything about seeing each other in London, so she couldn't assume that there would be an easy opportunity to tell him once she was back.

She closed her eyes and wished, just for a moment, that things were different. That she and Marco really were as together as his mother assumed, that she would be joining this loud, overbearing, terrifyingly opinionated, loving, inclusive family. Not once had Sophie felt not good enough. Not when she hadn't known how to address the maid. Not when she couldn't follow the conversation, not when she admitted she made most of her clothes, not when Marco had realised she was worrying about money.

She'd never once felt good enough for Harry. Which was ironic because now she could see she was far, far too good for him.

If she weren't pregnant, would she act any differently? Be more honest about how she felt? It was too difficult to know; she *was* pregnant and although that made everything infinitely more complicated she couldn't be sorry. Besides, Marco's mother was right: she and Marco probably would make a beautiful baby.

Opening her eyes, Sophie jumped. Three terrifyingly elegant women had sat opposite her and were all staring at her in undisguised curiosity. She managed to raise a smile and said, 'Weddings are tiring, aren't they?'

They nodded as if one. All three were wearing their glossy, expensively cut hair down in the kind of swishy style Sophie always envied and were all dressed exquisitely in labels Sophie wasn't sure she'd ever seen outside glossy magazines.

The woman in the middle leaned forward, her eyes bright. 'May I ask you something?' she asked in heavily accented but perfect English.

'I suppose so,' Sophie said warily.

'How did you do it?'

'Do what? Bianca's dress? It was...'

'No,' the woman on the left interrupted her. 'Although that is very impressive. No, how did you tie Marco down?'

'How did I...? I haven't... I mean, we're not engaged.'

'Yet.' With a heavy emphasis. 'I dated him for three years. Mamma was planning my dress, Papà was ready to buy us our own house, and then *poof...*' the woman on the right clicked her fingers '...he was gone. He told me I had trapped him, that he didn't want to be tied down.'

Sophie's stomach lurched. Would he feel the same way when she told him she was pregnant? Trapped?

'I'm sorry to hear that.'

'I was humiliated, heartbroken, and he never told me why. Just left, went to England. Left me to pick up the pieces alone. I should hate him...' Her voice softened. 'I tell myself I hate him...'

'But you...' one of her friends chimed in.

'Everyone is talking about it...'

'Living at the *palazzo*, friends with his sister...'

'What's your secret?'

'I don't know whether to pity or admire you.'

'Or envy you.'

Sophie swallowed. Marco had been completely up front from the very beginning. He'd told her this was temporary, fun, a one-time thing, but at some point she'd allowed herself to hope for more. There was no point deceiving herself any longer. It wouldn't change anything. She was having his baby; he had to know. Those were the inescapable facts.

'I'm sorry,' she said. 'But I really have to go. If you'll excuse me?'

With a deep breath she got to her feet. It was time to find Marco—whatever happened next was entirely up to him.

CHAPTER TWELVE

MARCO SCANNED THE ROOM. One minute Sophie had been with his sister, the next she had completely disappeared. He was pretty sure she could take care of herself, but in a room that seemed to be comprised solely of his extended family and women he used to date, even the most hardened party-goer would need backup.

Hell, *he* needed backup. That was why she was here, wasn't it?

'Marco.' He jumped as she came up behind him, laying one pale hand on his sleeve.

'There you are. I was thinking you must have been cornered by my great-aunt Annunciata.'

'No, not yet. Look, could I have a word? In private?'

Her hand wasn't the only part of her that was pale. Her cheeks were almost white, her lips bloodless. Anger rose, hot and hungry. Had someone said something to hurt her? 'Is everything okay?'

'Yes, I just need to talk to you about something.'

Marco looked around. The door to the terrace was ajar and it looked as if nobody else was braving the sharp winter air. He took her hand, her fingers sliding into his as if they belonged there, and led her outside. Trees in pots lined the walls and vines twisted around the railings. He selected a table at the far end of the terrace and pulled out a chair for Sophie, tucking one of the blankets left out for the purpose around her shoulders as she sat.

'I was talking to some of the other guests just now. They all knew you.'

'Did they?' He raised his eyebrows. She sounded solemn. Solemn at weddings wasn't usually good.

'One of them was an ex-girlfriend of yours. She's a little bitter. Apparently you practically left her at the altar.'

Understanding dawned. 'You were talking to Celia, which I expect means she was flanked by Beatrice and Elena. They usually work as a team.'

'I didn't get their names.'

Something was off here and he couldn't work out what. 'It's a bit of an exaggeration to say I left her at the altar. We were never formally engaged.'

'So what happened? I deserve to know,' she added. 'If looks could kill, I'd currently be laid out on the floor of the women's bathroom and wedding guests would have to step over my corpse to get to the sinks.'

Marco rubbed his eyes wearily. Celia was so intrinsically mixed up with the events that had led to him leaving Venice, to the row with his father, that he'd done his best to not think of her at all over the last decade. He should have known he couldn't return home without the whole sorry business being dredged up again. 'It sounds like a bigger deal than it was,' he said, staring out at the Grand Canal, following a small open boat with his eyes as it cruised slowly opposite. 'Celia and I started seeing each other after I finished university. We were together for about three years.'

'She said you just disappeared.'

'It wasn't quite like that. She was pretty, a little crazy,

fun, all the things a man in his early twenties finds attractive. I guess I thought I was in love, thought she loved me, not that I had any idea what love was.' Bianca's words floated back to him. She was right; it had been infatuation, not love. He sighed. 'She was a welcome distraction from home. I was just starting out, collecting and reselling, developing a client list, building up a reputation, but my father thought I was wasting my time—and told me every chance he got.'

'That must have been difficult.'

'It was challenging,' he admitted. 'But I was young and driven and wanted my own path. I thought Celia agreed with me, but gradually I realised she wanted very different things. She didn't love the Marco Santoro who was passionate about his business and happy to start from scratch if he had to. She loved the Santoro heir with all the privileges that entailed and she kept pushing me to listen to my father. To give in.'

'But you didn't.'

'I didn't. So we'd argue, she'd cry, I'd feel guilty, we'd make up. It was an exhausting cycle mirrored by the constant battles with my father. Soon I realised she spent more time at the *palazzo* than I did, that she was shopping with Mamma and going out with Bianca, that she was already considered part of the family. Hints were dropped, more than hints, that a proposal would be nice. Her father took me aside and made noises about buying us a house as a wedding gift. Nonna presented me with her engagement ring and told me how proud I made her.'

Sophie put a cold hand on his. 'That must have been difficult.'

He'd been trapped. Each way he'd turned, an impossible choice. Give in and live a life he didn't want or stand firm and disappoint everyone who loved him. 'My life was just beginning. It should have been full of possibilities. Instead everyone I knew, everyone I loved, everyone I respected was trying to narrow it down, to cage me in. The girl I thought I was falling for had been replaced with a woman I didn't recognise, a woman who didn't want me as I was but wanted to change me, mould me.'

'But she didn't succeed. You walked away.'

Celia had succeeded in one way: she *had* changed him. All that youthful optimism and hope had been replaced with wariness; his home had become a prison.

'I decided I had to leave Venice. I couldn't carry on being scrutinised and criticised at every turn. I told Celia, gave her the option to come with me. She laughed at first, thought I was joking. When she realised I was serious...' He shook his head. 'The contempt in her eyes. I realised then that it was the package she wanted, not the man.'

'She was a fool.'

'She was ambitious. Oh, don't think I spent the next ten years weeping over my lost love. I was relieved more than heartbroken. Besides, it just confirmed what I already knew. That what I was mattered more than who I was and I was tired of it, tired of Venice, tired of all their expectations. So I went to see my father and told him I was done.'

'How did he take it?'

'Not well. He got so angry he collapsed with a suspected heart attack.'

'Oh, Marco.'

'And I went anyway. He was in the hospital and I packed my bags and left. I knew if I stayed the guilt would suck me in and I would never be free, so as soon as the doctors said he should make a full recovery I was out of Venice and starting again. I barely saw him after that, a couple of times a year of guarded pleasantries and then it was too late. For both of us.'

'I'm sure he knew you loved him. I'm sure he was proud of you.'

'Maybe.' Suddenly he was tired of it all. Of the guilt, of the uncertainty. 'All I knew was that I wasn't good enough. Not as a son, as an heir, as a partner. It's been easier—safer—not to get involved. Not to allow anyone to let me down. Allow anyone to look at me and tell me I'm not enough as I am.' Safer but ultimately unsatisfying. Short-term relationships, friendships based on business not deep-rooted companionship, family kept at arm's length. No wonder he'd worked eighteen hours a day, seven days a week. He'd had very little else.

He looked at Sophie as she stared out onto the Grand Canal, her profile sad and thoughtful, and for a moment he wondered what would happen if she told him he did matter, he mattered to her. Would he be able to believe her—or would he brush her off, turn away?

Time stood still, the air shimmering over the water while he waited an eternity for her to speak. She swallowed, a convulsive shudder, and her hand pressed on his, icy now in the winter chill.

'I don't believe you're not enough, Marco, at least I hope you are, more than enough. Not for me, I know that's not what you want, but for your child. I'm pregnant, Marco. I'm having a baby, your baby.'

CHAPTER THIRTEEN

SHE COULDN'T LOOK him straight in the eye. Instead Sophie stared at her hand, still covering his, gleaming pale white in the moonlight, and waited. Marco had stilled under her touch, turning to marble the second the words left her mouth.

'Pregnant?'

'Yes.' She waited for him to ask the obvious questions. *Are you sure? How do I know it's mine?* But they didn't come. Relief flooded over her as he nodded slowly.

Only to recede as he looked straight over at her, eyes hooded. 'Then we had better get married.'

It wasn't a question.

It was an assumption. Sophie's heart sped up.

'Married?'

'London would be best. Three weeks from now. We'll tell everyone we wanted to keep it quiet. We don't want this kind of fuss.' He shrugged in a way that encompassed all of Bianca's wedding.

No, Sophie didn't need three hundred guests, had no desire to book out an exclusive old *palazzo*, say her vows in a world-famous church. But when—if—she got married she would want her friends, her family there. She would want it to be a celebration of love, just as

Bianca was so clearly celebrating her love for Antonio today. Not a clandestine affair hidden from the world as if she were ashamed.

And if—when—she got married she wanted to be asked. She didn't need an extravagant proposal, but she would hope that any future husband wouldn't just *assume*...

'Marco, I...'

'Then we'll return here. You can live at the *palazzo*. You'll need family around you and you don't want to go back to Manchester. Besides, I need to be either here or London, so it has to be Venice. I can sell the London house, get a flat for when I'm there. I will have to travel a great deal, another reason why you'll need my family close by.'

That was how he saw her future, was it? Here in Venice, safely tucked away with his family, the family he'd spent over ten years avoiding as much as possible, while he stayed in London.

She opened her mouth, but he ploughed on. 'I don't think we should tell anyone anything yet. You can go back to London as planned tomorrow. I'll be back in a week. I'll arrange for somebody to move your things into my house this week.'

It was obviously all decided. All taken care of in less than a minute's decision-making. It didn't matter what she thought, what she wanted. She was a problem to be taken care of. A problem he had solved in record time.

It wasn't that she didn't love Venice, that she couldn't imagine living here, although she wasn't sure she would ever feel at home in the huge, ancient *palazzo*. It wasn't that she didn't adore Marco's family, overbearing as they were, because she did. But it had taken Sophie far too long to get to the point where *she* made the decisions about her life. She wasn't about to hand over control to someone else. Just go along meekly with his plans like an obedient little wife.

'Marco, stop. We don't need to decide all this now.' She couldn't help the slight emphasis on the 'we'. 'Let's take a few days to think about it and talk about it then, when you've had time to digest everything.'

He got to his feet, body half turned away, the message clear; this conversation was over. 'There's nothing to decide. Look, Sophie, you might not like it. You don't have to like it. This doesn't fit my plans either.' Hurt lanced through her at his cold tones, at each distinct word. 'But what's done is done and we need to act like adults, put our own preferences aside.' He smiled then, a wintry half-smile that left her colder than his earlier bleakness. 'We get on well enough. We have chemistry. There are worse foundations for marriage.'

'Yes, but there are better foundations too.' She looked up at him, putting every ounce of conviction she had into her voice. 'Marco, it's the twenty-first century. We can both be involved, be good parents without needing to be married. We don't need to live together, or even *be* together. We just need to respect each other and work together. I need you to listen to me, to consult me, not to make pronouncements that affect my entire life and expect me to jump to.' Sophie could hear the quiver in her voice and swallowed, holding back the threatened tears. 'I know you don't want to get married and so thank you for suggesting it. But I don't think a reluctant marriage is the best thing for me or for the baby.'

She stood up, the blanket slipping off her shoulders as she did so. 'I am heading back to the *palazzo*. Please make my apologies to Bianca. I'm going to get my plane tomorrow and I'm asking you to give me some space.

Please don't come to my room tonight or offer to drop me off in the morning—I think we both need some time to think. Think about what's best for *all* of us.'

Head held high, she touched him lightly on the cheek before turning and walking away. She'd been expecting anger or denial. Not this cold acceptance. But secretly, buried so deep down she'd hardly been aware of it, she'd been hoping for more. Maybe not love, she wasn't that much of a fool, but liking. An indication he wanted to be with her. Not cold, hard duty.

But it looked as if cold, hard duty was all he had to offer—and it wasn't enough. She deserved more—even if her heart was breaking as she turned and walked away. But better a cracked heart now than a lifetime with someone who didn't want or respect her. Better a cracked heart than allowing someone to dictate her life. Because she'd allowed that to happen twice, and she'd had to fight to be free twice. Last time she'd vowed never again and she'd meant it. She meant it now. No matter how much it hurt.

CHAPTER FOURTEEN

'I CAN'T BELIEVE there are so many photos of you. It's like Marco and his family are famous!' Ashleigh was once again searching through Italian gossip sites on Sophie's laptop.

'Not famous exactly, it's just they're a really old family. A really old rich family. A bit like minor royalty.' Sophie turned her head, not wanting to catch a glimpse of Marco, even on screen. He hadn't texted, hadn't called. A week of radio silence. She'd asked for time, asked for space, but this was beginning to feel a lot like punishment. 'Marco and Bianca are gossip-column staples. Her wedding was a big deal. Not that I knew that when I offered to fix her dress. I'd have been far too terrified.'

'So that makes you the mother-to-be of minor royalty,' Grace said.

'I can't believe you're pregnant.' Emma was staring at Sophie's stomach. 'You haven't put on an ounce.'

'I have, many ounces, but half of it is Italian food,' Sophie pointed out, but Emma's words brought her situation home. It was too easy, back in the safety of her flat, of her routine, to hide from her future. But that future was growing rapidly and she couldn't hide it for much longer. 'And I can't believe it either. There are moments when I'm thrilled—and then I start panicking again. I don't know how to be a mother. It's not like I have the best relationship with mine.'

'Sure you know how,' Ashleigh said with a soft smile. 'You know how to be an awesome friend. You're over halfway there.'

'Besides...' Emma jumped to her feet and stepped over to give her a hug. Sophie leaned gratefully on her shoulder, glad of the support. 'You have us. We're going to be the best team of aunties-stroke-fairy-godmothers any child ever had. You're not alone, Soph. Don't ever think it.'

'And I wouldn't worry about your future. I predict amazing things,' Grace said, wrestling the laptop away from Ashleigh. 'Not only is the whole of Italy wild about the alterations you made to Bianca's dress, but they love the going-away outfit you made her too. I've seen dozens of blogs and articles raving about it. Now your website is finally going live...' she shot a mock stern look at Sophie '...and people can actually *order* your clothes, success can't be far away.'

'Long-deserved success,' Ashleigh chimed in, holding up her cup of tea in a toast.

Sophie blinked back tears. Not only had her friends collected her from the airport, smothered her with affection, tea and cake, waited patiently until she had been able to find the words to tell them about the baby—and about Marco and her feelings for him—but they had also gently encouraged her to capitalise on her new-found design fame, helping her put the finishing touches to her website and testing it for her so when it went live—any second now—she could be confident it worked. Ashleigh had also helped her organise her space in the tiny flat so that finished designs could be photographed in a clutter-free space and her material was neatly stacked, giving her more room to work. Potential customers could either choose from her small collection of existing stock or order by design, choosing the material they liked best from her assortment of vintage prints or sending their own for her to make up.

One day she would like to have a larger collection of ready-to-buy stock—but for that she would need a studio and storage, possibly a couple of seamstresses. No, tiny steps were best. If she could just make enough to keep herself and the baby afloat, then she would have options; she didn't want to need Marco's money. She *would* like his emotional support though.

Which was ironic—he had money to spare but support, real support, was much harder for him. Maybe too hard.

'Right, we have to get off.' Ashleigh hauled herself to her feet. 'Are you sure you don't want to come, Sophie?' Grace's fiancé was hosting a glamorous fundraising event at his hotel and all three of her friends were attending. Funny to think that just a few months ago they would probably have all been waitressing for it.

Which reminded her, she needed to discuss hours and jobs with Clio. Heavy cleaning and too much standing around were probably out, but Sophie wanted to ensure she had some steady income while the first orders came in. Her waitressing days weren't behind her yet.

'I'm sure. I'm exhausted by nine at the moment. Besides, I want to stalk my inbox and wait for an order.'

'It won't be long,' Grace said loyally, dropping a kiss onto her cheek. 'If you need a hand, well, I can't sew. Or cut out. But I am very good at parcels—and making tea.'

'You'll be my first port of call,' Sophie promised, kissing her back and then embracing Emma and Ashleigh in turn.

The flat felt larger without her friends—a little larger—and a lot emptier. Sophie put her laptop on the kitchen counter and refreshed her email. Nothing. Maybe her friends were wrong, maybe the publicity and excitement over Bianca's wedding dress and the two-piece, sixties-inspired going-away outfit she had gifted the bride were just a storm in a teacup and wouldn't translate into sales.

But she couldn't believe that, wouldn't believe it. After all, photos of Bianca were everywhere and not just in the Italian press; a few British sites had picked up the chatter about the 'London-based designer' and had run short pieces extolling her as one to watch. Every piece used the same photo, taken at the wedding, Sophie in her grey dress smiling up at Marco, handsome in his tuxedo. Her heart turned over at the picture. They looked so happy, so together—to a casual observer as if they were head over heels in love. But she wasn't a casual observer.

Impatient to shake her bad mood, Sophie grabbed her pad and pencil. The success of Bianca's wedding dress made her wonder if there might be more bridal commissions in her future and she wanted to be prepared...

Stretching, she realised she'd lost track of time. Over two hours had passed while she'd sketched her first attempts at twenties-, fifties- and sixties-inspired bridal gowns. Not too bad, she decided, standing back and taking a fresh look. She'd like to get some samples started soon, a heavy silk for the twenties dress, lace and chiffon for the fifties dress and embroidered velvet for the sixties-inspired design.

As she moved the pad further away her hand knocked

the keyboard and her laptop screen blared into life, opening onto her brand-new inbox. Only, it wasn't empty as it had been when she last looked; no, there were four unopened emails sitting there and they didn't look like spam… With a trembling hand she clicked on one and scanned the message; would she be able to design a wedding dress and what were her fees?

Sophie took a deep breath; she'd been right to turn her attentions to bridal. The second was from a boutique here in Chelsea asking if they could discuss stocking some of her designs, the third another enquiry, this time for an evening gown. So far so good. No actual money but the possibility of work. The fourth, however, came from the automated payment system she had set up. She took a deep breath and clicked. 'Yes!' she shouted. 'Yes!' An order, a real order for two of her dresses, a shift dress in a polka-dot pink and a copy of the dress she'd worn to Bianca's wedding in a gorgeous green flowered cotton. She had done it! She was a real designer with real sales to people she didn't know.

She looked round, wanting to jump up and down, to babble her excitement into someone else's ear, to have someone else to confirm that, yes, the emails said exactly what she thought they said. But there was nobody there; her shoebox had never felt so spacious, never felt so lonely. She could text her friends, of course. They would be delighted. But, she realised, sinking back onto her stool, the euphoria draining away, she didn't want to impress them. She didn't need to witness their reactions.

She wanted Marco there, celebrating alongside her. She wanted to see him look impressed, to tell her how proud he was. But he was a long, long way away. Emotionally, physically, in every way that mattered. She'd thought she'd been lonely in the past, but it didn't compare to how she felt now. Completely and utterly alone. She couldn't let that stop her. She'd pulled herself back from the brink before, she could do it again. Besides, it wasn't all about her, not any more. She had to be strong for the baby—she simply had no other option.

Marco took another look at the address. He hadn't thought too much about where Sophie lived, but he'd assumed it would be in a flat in one of Chelsea's leafy streets, possibly sharing with a couple of friends. Not on this noisy, busy road, cars honking horns impatiently as they queued three abreast, fumes acrid in the damp air.

'Number one eight one,' he muttered, coming to a stop outside the right building. There was a takeaway on the ground floor and Marco grimaced as the scent of greasy fried chicken assailed him. The door to the flats was a dingy green, the doorstop covered in thrown-away boxes and discarded chicken bones. No way was any child of his growing up here, he vowed.

He scanned the names, almost illegible against the long list of buzzers, but before he found Sophie's name, the door opened and a young woman barged out, leaving the door ajar. Marco added security to the list of undesirables and shouldered it open. He needed Flat Ten. He looked at the door at the end of the ground floor—number one. It looked like he was going up...and up and up. Another item for his list: too many stairs. How on earth did she think she would cart a baby up here?

It was easier to list all the reasons for Sophie to move than it was to face the other list, the list that had brought him to the door. The list that started with how big, how lonely his bed felt every night, the list that included how much he missed her. The list that concluded that he didn't want to live in the Chelsea house or Venice on his own. The list that told him he had reacted badly to the news of her pregnancy, that he might be a little too convinced of his own eligibility, possibly bordering on arrogant where his marriage prospects were concerned. He patted Nonna's ring, secure in his top pocket. He would do better this time. He had to.

Finally he made his way to the top floor. Sophie's door was the same dull navy as all the other flat doors, but the handle was polished and two terracotta pots filled with lush greenery brightened the narrow landing. Marco shifted, nervous for the first time since he had boarded the plane this morning fired up with purpose. Before he could start listing why this was a bad idea he raised his hand and knocked firmly at the door.

'Mr Kowaski, have you forgotten your keys again? It's okay, I... Oh.' The door was fully open and Sophie stood there, shock mingling with something Marco couldn't define but hoped might be pleasure. 'How did you get in?'

'A neighbour.'

'They're not supposed to just let people... Not that it matters. Come on in.'

She stepped back and Marco entered her flat. There wasn't much of it, a small attic room, a large dormer window to the right the only natural light. A sofa ran along the wall to his left, opposite him a narrow counter defined the small kitchen, a high table barely big enough for two by the window. He'd been on larger boats.

The furniture was old and battered, but the room was scrupulously clean, the cream walls covered in bright prints and swathes of material, the sofa heaped with inviting throws and cushions. Along the wall adjoining the window a clothing rail lined up, dresses hanging on it in a neat row and drawings and patterns were pinned up on a huge easel.

There was no door between the living space and her bedroom, just a narrow archway. Through it he could see a single bed and two more rails bulging with brightly patterned dresses and skirts.

He walked over to the nearest rail and pulled out the first dress. Just like the outfit she'd worn to Bianca's wedding—just like everything he'd seen her in—it was deceptively simple. She obviously took her inspiration from the past, each outfit having a vintage vibe, but the detailing and cut gave it a modern twist.

'So this is what you do.' She'd said she wanted to be a designer, he'd seen her work first-hand, but he hadn't appreciated just how talented—just how motivated—she was, not until he stood in the tiny flat, more work-space than home. He'd met so many Chelsea girls over the last few years, women with family money who pottered around playing at being designers or artists or jewellers. He'd assumed Sophie belonged to their tribe, although looking back the signs were there: how careful she was with money, how little she spoke about her family. It was painfully clear how much he'd misjudged her, how little he knew about her.

'This is what I do. It's taken me a long time to get even this far. I don't make a living from it yet. In fact…' she took a deep breath '…I owe you an apology. I didn't mean to mislead you…'

'About what?'

'When we met, that first night. I was at the party but not as a guest. You didn't see me because I was invisible—I was waitressing there. I was supposed to be waitressing at the Snowflake Ball as well. Only, my friends played fairy godmother and bought me a ticket.

That's how I make ends meet, have done since I moved to London. I work for Maids in Chelsea, cleaning, shopping, bar work—whatever is needed.'

Her blue eyes were defiant, her chin tilted, hands bunched on her hips. 'You worked and produced all this? When did you find time to sleep? To eat?'

The defiance dimmed, replaced with relief. 'Sleep's overrated.'

'You didn't lie. You told me you were a designer. Looking at all this, I'd say that's exactly what you are. These are incredible.'

'Thank you.' She twisted her hands together. 'But you didn't come here to pay me compliments. I know we need to talk, but it's late and I'm really tired. Could we meet tomorrow and do this then?'

She did look exhausted, he realised with a pang of guilt. Purple shadows darkened her eyes, her hair, twisted up into a loose ponytail was duller than usual, her lips pale. She looked more vulnerable than he'd ever seen her and he ached for the right to take care of her. She was carrying his child. *His.* It was almost impossible to imagine, her body still slender, seemingly unchanged, and yet his blood thrilled at the realisation. He'd been running from this commitment for so long yet now he was confronted with the actuality he was filled with a primal joy. A determination to do better, be a better father than he had been a son, to not make the same mistakes his own father had made but to love his child no matter what their aspirations, who they wanted to be.

'We can, but I just need to say one thing. I'm sorry for how I reacted, when you told me about the pregnancy. It was such a shock, so unexpected. I needed to fix it, solve it. That's what I do.'

'I understand.'

'I made assumptions about you, about us. That was wrong. But I've missed you, Sophie. All this week I keep turning to speak to you, to see your reaction, and you're not there. That's my fault, I know, and it's up to me to make things right.' It was his turn to take a deep breath. He had never thought he would ever reach this point, but now he was here it made sense as nothing had ever made sense before. Maybe this was destined, the meeting in the snow, the baby, bringing him to this point.

Reaching into his top pocket, he pulled out the small black box. Sophie's eyes widened and she retreated back a step, but he took her hand in his, sinking to one knee like an actor playing his part. 'Sophie, it would make me very happy if you would do me the very great honour of becoming my wife.'

He smiled up at her, waiting for her agreement.

'No. I'm sorry, Marco, but I can't.'

CHAPTER FIFTEEN

SOPHIE STEPPED BACK one more step, pulling her hand free of his. A chill of loneliness shivered through her and she had to fight the urge to tell him she'd changed her mind, of course she would marry him. But he wasn't here for her, not for Sophie Bradshaw, he was here for the mother of his child. Here because it was the right thing to do. And she appreciated that, she really did. But she couldn't stake the rest of her life on it. 'I'm sorry,' she repeated.

Marco slowly straightened, regret mingled with anger and embarrassment clear on his face. 'I see.'

Ten minutes ago all Sophie had wanted was the coolness of her newly washed sheets, to burrow under her duvet and fall into the kind of heavy, dreamless, all-encompassing sleep her body demanded. She'd asked him to wait until tomorrow, told him she was tired and yet he'd still overridden her wishes. The only difference from last week's conversation was that this time Marco had couched his demand for marriage as a request.

A request he clearly expected her to acquiesce to.

No, nothing had changed. 'I appreciate that you think getting married is the right thing to do, especially knowing how you feel about marriage, but I can't.'

Eyes grim, mouth narrowed, he nodded once. 'Then

there's nothing else to say.' Marco turned, clearly heading for the door, out of her flat and potentially out of her life. Out of their child's life.

Sophie wavered, torn. She wanted him involved, but he expected so much, too much. But, dammit, she knew she owed him an explanation; after all, it wasn't his fault it wasn't enough for her. At least a dozen women at the wedding would have leapt at his first decisive statement; they'd have swooned at a ring and a bended knee—after saying yes, of course. 'Would you like a drink? I think I have a beer in the fridge.'

He stilled, stopped. 'That would be nice, but you're tired.'

'I am, but you're here now. Sit down.' She nodded at the sofa. 'I'll bring you a beer.'

Sophie busied herself for a few minutes, opening the beer, making herself a peppermint tea and pouring some crisps into a bowl and setting it on the tiny portable all-purpose table, before sinking into the sofa next to him. Next to him but not touching. She pulled her legs up before her, propping her chin on her knees, her arms hugging her legs, wanting the warmth, the support. Neither spoke, the silence neither hostile nor comfortable, more a cautious truce.

'I owe you an honest explanation, at the very least,' she said after a while. 'It's not easy for me to talk about, even to think about. I'm not very proud of my past.'

His eyes flickered at that, but he didn't say anything. Instead he took a long drink from the bottle of beer and settled back against the sofa, his gaze steady as he watched her. Sophie stared past him, her eyes fixed on the wall behind him, tracing the colours in the material hanging there, following the pattern round and round. 'For most of my life I thought my only value was in how happy I made others. My parents weren't cruel, not at all. I had everything. Private school, lovely clothes, everything I needed except for freedom, except for autonomy. My mother liked a project, you see. She's very determined, very focussed.' She smiled. 'I often wonder what will happen when she meets your mother. They'll be the definition of the unstoppable force versus the immoveable object. Scientists should study them under test conditions.'

She sipped her tea, her gaze still fixed on the material. It was hard to untangle her feelings about her mother; they were so complicated. She'd been so loved, Sophie knew that. But the burden of expectation had been crushing and Sophie wasn't sure she'd ever stop being resentful, stop wishing for a more carefree childhood. A childhood that had prepared her for adulthood instead of leaving her wide open and vulnerable.

'I think I mentioned before that I was born quite a long time after my brothers. It was like being an only child in many ways and I was quite isolated. My mum liked to pick out my friends, my clothes, my activities, and I soon learned that my role in the family was to make her happy—and she was happy when I did exactly what she wanted. It's dangerous, linking love to approval, making a child feel that it's conditional. And that was very much how I felt. I didn't dare complain, I didn't dare disagree because when I had her approval I knew I was loved. But I wasn't happy. My school was quite a long way away from my home and I was dancing most evenings from a young age, so I didn't have many friends. Ashleigh was my closest friend, but I only knew her for a short while and then her family moved back to Australia. By the time I hit my mid-teens I was a bit of a loner and really naïve.

'My mother had planned for me to apply for professional training when I was sixteen—but I think I told you in Venice that my heart wasn't in it. It was the first time I had said no, first time I'd let her down and she didn't hide her disappointment in me. But I felt free for the first time. I started to go out, to gigs to see local bands, to make my own clothes and find my own look. The more I started to work out who I wanted to be, the harder she tried to hold on. We had such terrible, horrible rows, said nasty, vicious things.'

They had both been guilty, she knew that. But Sophie had still been a child in many ways and her mother had left her in no doubt that she wasn't good enough, not any more. That Sophie's own style, her own wishes, her own hobbies were wrong and behind her bravado her fledgling self-confidence had begun to crumble.

'That was a long time ago. How are things now?'

'Fragile,' she admitted. 'Uncomfortable. That's why I rarely go back to Manchester.' She found a smile. 'See, we do have some things in common.' But their solutions to their family problems had been drastically different. Marco had taken control of his life, made a huge success out of his passions, his business. Sophie? She had run from one controlling situation to another.

She took another sip of the comforting tea and tried to order her thoughts. She hadn't spoken about Harry since the day she had finally come to her senses and walked out of the door. If she told Marco, it would be like probing a wound to see if it had really healed or still bubbled with infection.

'Like I said, I was a bit of a loner and really naïve. Ripe to be exploited. I met Harry at one of his gigs. He was the singer—all brash confidence and raw sexuality. I had never seen or spoken to anybody like him before and I was besotted before we even spoke. When he singled me out I thought I was the luckiest girl alive. It was every teen cliché come true. My parents hated him, of course. He was older than me for a start, arrogant, entitled. Looking back, he was just really rude, but I thought he was authentic and being true to himself. The more they tried to stop me seeing him, the more attractive he got.'

'How old were you?'

'Seventeen, a really young seventeen. I thought I was Juliet, of course, brimful of forbidden love.' Her mouth twisted into a wry smile. 'There is nothing more guaranteed to drive your hormonal teenaged daughter into the arms of a complete sod than to try to stop her seeing him. If they'd relaxed and made him welcome, or at least pretended to, maybe I'd have seen the truth a lot sooner.'

Maybe.

'Things were tense for a year. Home was like a battlefield, every sentence an ambush. My parents couldn't cope. Their sweet, biddable daughter had been replaced by a foul-mouthed hellion. I drank, stayed out all night, ditched school—and of course Harry encouraged me all the way. It shouldn't be an excuse, but, remember, I needed approval to feel loved and Harry's approval was intoxicating. I lived for it—and he knew it. Eventually my dad put his foot down in a "not in my house, young lady, you live in these walls you obey my rules" kind of way and I said "fine". Packed my bags and walked out the day I turned eighteen.'

He echoed her thoughts. 'We're both runaways, then. You're right, we do have something in common.'

'Only, you moved to a new city and started a successful business. I moved into a squat three miles away and became a cook, cleaner, cheerleader and paid heavily for the privilege. Harry had me exactly where he wanted me. My original plan had been to go to college and study art and textiles while living with him, but he persuaded me I'd be wasting my time. That I wasn't that talented, that original.' To her horror she could feel the tears gathering in her eyes and swiped her sleeve angrily against them. 'He said I'd be of more use getting a job so we could get a flat—obviously he was too busy being a musician to dirty his hands with real work. So instead of college I worked in a greasy spoon café. I was there for six years. I paid for our flat and our food. I cleaned our flat. I cooked our food. I soon learned not to ask Harry to do anything, not to expect anything from him. Including fidelity.'

She swiped her eyes again. 'I know what you're thinking because I'm thinking it too. Why did I put up with it? Why did I let him treat me that way? I think it every day. He made me feel like I was completely worthless, that I couldn't do anything, be anyone without him. That I was lucky to have him. And I believed him. The worst part is that every now and then he'd do something sweet, remind me why I fell in love with him in the first place. I lived for those moments, craved them, would lie there every night he didn't come home and relive every one of them.'

His hands had curled into fists and a primal part of him welcomed his anger. 'He didn't deserve you. You know that, right? You left, you got away.'

'Eventually. We were at a wedding and when he saw the head bridesmaid his tongue was practically hanging out. I'd turned a blind eye to his flings before, but when he kissed her on the dance floor—in front of his friends and family—I knew I had to get out before he destroyed me completely. I called a taxi, packed my things and went straight to the train station. I didn't trust myself not to waver if I saw him.'

'That was very brave.'

'I was running on adrenaline,' she admitted. 'If I'd thought about what I was doing, moving on my own to a city I didn't know, to a place where I knew no one, I would have just given up.'

But he was shaking his head. 'You're stronger than you think, Sophie. When I look at you I don't see a victim or weakness. I see a survivor. I see resilience. I see strength.'

Warmth flooded through her, not just because of his words but because of the respect she saw in his eyes. 'It's been a slow journey, Marco. I don't feel strong, not all the time. I've worked really hard to get to this place. My flat is tiny and horribly overpriced, but *I* pay the rent for me. It's my home, my sanctuary. I've finally put my designs out in the world. I have friends here, good friends. I'm my own person.'

'You'd still be your own person if you married me. I wouldn't stand in your way.'

She would give anything to believe him—but she didn't. 'When I told you about the baby you went into decision-making overdrive. We would do this, I would do that, this is how it would be. I know you were thinking of me and the baby, but I can't live like that, Marco, not again.'

He had paled, his eyes hard. 'You think I'm like your ex? That I would control you? Put you down?'

'No, no…' She reached a hand out to him. 'You're nothing like Harry. Your kindness was one of the first things I lo…liked about you. But you do like things your own way. That's why you moved to London in the first place. You're used to being in charge and I won't risk losing myself. I won't be the peacemaker, the compromiser again. I can't.'

She needed him to understand, desperately hoped that he did, but his mouth was grim.

'I understand, Sophie, I really do. But this isn't just about you, not any more. You might not like it, but my role now is to take care of you and our baby and I won't let you push me aside. You've come a long way, but you need to learn to let go, to trust me not to hurt you.'

She opened her mouth to tell him she did, but she couldn't say the words. He sighed. 'There's a difference between protecting you and controlling you. I have to do the first, but I can promise you I'll never do the second. I'm here, Sophie, for you and for our baby and I'm not going anywhere. The sooner you accept that, the better. Thanks for the drink. I'll see myself out.'

She sat frozen as he got to his feet. Two seconds later the door clicked behind him and he was gone. Part of her was relieved he still wanted to be involved, that she wouldn't have to bring the baby up alone, but his parting words rang in her ears. *The sooner you accept that, the better.* He was wrong; she wasn't accepting anything and no man would ever tell her what she could or could not do ever again. 'Damn you, Marco,' she whispered as she got wearily to her feet, the cold bone deep inside her. 'Why didn't you ask me what I want rather than telling me what you think I need?'

He said he respected her, now she needed him to show it. It was a poor substitute for love, but Sophie suspected it was all she was going to get. The question was, would it be enough?

CHAPTER SIXTEEN

'ARE YOU SURE you don't want me to come with you? Hold your hand?'

Sophie smiled, touched at the concern in Ashleigh's voice. 'It's a scan. I don't think it hurts.'

'That's not the point,' her friend said firmly. 'It's a huge moment, and on Valentine's Day too. You're going to need someone to hold the tissues.'

'I'm not dragging you away from Lukas on your first Valentine's Day. What kind of best friend do you think I am? Besides, it's different for you loved-up types, but I've never made a fuss about the fourteenth of February. It's just a day.'

Ashleigh's voice took on the dreamy tinge she always used when talking about Lukas. 'I think Lukas is planning dinner in Paris from all the not so subtle hints, but we can get a later train. I don't mind at all.'

'No, go to Paris, be happy and in love. I'll email you a picture of the scan, okay?'

'Only if you're sure.'

'More than sure. Now go and get ready to look surprised. *Au revoir.*'

'Email me straight away, love you.'

'I love you too.' Sophie clicked her phone off and suppressed a sigh. It would have been lovely to have her oldest and best friend with her when she met her baby for the first time, but there was no way she would butt in on Ashleigh's first Valentine's Day with Lukas.

She turned her phone over and over in her hand. She didn't *have* to go alone. After all, there was someone else who was probably just as keen to meet his baby. Their baby.

She hadn't met up with Marco at all over the last few weeks, partly because he was travelling and partly because he seemed to be respecting her request for space and time. It hadn't stopped him sending details through for potential flats and houses he 'wondered' if she might find more suitable or arranging a delivery service to supply her with home-cooked meals she just needed to heat up. She told herself that she should be mad at his officiousness, but she was so busy and tired the meals were a godsend and she couldn't help but concede he had a point about the flat. Hers was too small, too noisy and up too many flights of stairs.

The only problem was that every property he sent her was way, way out of her price range. She was pretty sure he was expecting to pay for wherever she moved to and knew that unless she suddenly sold every outfit she had made she was going to have to accept in the short-term at least. Necessity didn't make it easy though. 'For goodness' sake,' she told herself. 'At least he's not expecting you to support him. That's a huge improvement, right?' But much as it made sense it still felt like the first step on a very slippery slope.

She sighed. They did need to talk and a scan was a good, positive place to start. Before she could change her mind she called up his name and pressed Send. It was the right thing to do.

* * *

'Buongiorno.'

Marco scanned Sophie with a critical eye, nodding with satisfaction as he noted the shadows had disappeared from under her eyes and her cheeks had colour once more. Her hair was freshly washed and full of its usual bounce and her eyes no longer had the sad, defeated look he'd taken away with him when he'd left her a few weeks ago. 'You look beautiful.'

'Hi.' She smiled shyly at him and his heart squeezed. It had taken every single ounce of self-control he possessed not to call her or pop round over the last few weeks, but he had promised her, promised himself, that he would give her the control she needed, the time she needed. It had seemed like an eternity.

He'd thought he'd missed her when she left Italy, but that was nothing to the way he'd felt over the last few weeks. He'd thrown himself into work, but it had been almost impossible to concentrate when all he could think about was how he had blown it, how he had destroyed the best thing that had ever happened to him. Through arrogance, through ignorance.

Marco wasn't sure when he had fallen in love with Sophie, but he did know that this pain in his chest, the ache in his heart, the constant knowledge that something fundamental was missing, was love. He suspected he had fallen for her at some point in Venice. He was sure he loved her when he'd walked away from her flat, when he knew he'd let her down and had no idea how to fix it. When he'd decided that he had to respect her decisions, her choices, no matter how much it hurt him to do so.

He'd hoped that it would simplify things, but, looking at her nervous smile, he realised it complicated everything. If he told her how he felt, he suspected she would feel manipulated, think that he was saying what she wanted to hear, not what he felt, and after the last few weeks he wouldn't blame her.

He usually had all the answers, but today he had nothing. 'Thank you, for asking me here today.'

'I should have given you more notice. It's lucky you were in London.'

He hadn't left London, although he'd given her the impression he was away. He couldn't have left her if his business depended on it. What if she needed him and he was nowhere to be found? He'd let down one family member through pride. That was more than enough.

'I'd have found a way to get here. What do we do now?'

'We go in there, register, I have to drink lots of water and then we meet our baby. Ready?'

Our baby. The words hit him with full force. He, Marco Santoro, was going to be a father. Excitement mingled with pride filled him and he vowed he would do anything and everything to keep his child safe and secure. To make him or her happy. For the first time he understood why his mother fretted and planned and pressured him. Why his father had insisted he knew best no matter what Marco said or felt. They too felt this way; misguided as they might have been, they had just wanted to protect him. He just needed to remember that his version of happiness might not be the same as his child's. He took a deep breath. Yes, he was ready for fatherhood and all it entailed. '*Sì*, let's do this.'

'I can't believe this is our child.' Marco took another look at the black-and-white picture in disbelief.

'I know, it does look a little like an alien, doesn't it?

Do you think I got beamed up onto a spaceship and just didn't realise it?'

'Shh, the *bambino* will hear you. An alien indeed.' He snorted. 'With that nose? This is a Venetian baby for sure.'

'The next scan we can get in colour, you can properly see features and everything. Did you mind that they didn't tell us the sex? We could go for a private scan if you wanted to find out.'

Hope flared at her casual use of 'we'. 'I don't mind either way. Do you want to know?'

'Yes and no,' she admitted. 'It would be handy for names, but I'm not really a pink for a girl, blue for a boy type. I just want it to be healthy and happy.'

'It will be.' He knew he sounded serious, but he would lay his life down for that little alien without even blinking.

They'd reached the hospital doors and Sophie paused. 'I know you're busy, but do you have to get back? I'm really grateful you've given me some time, but there's a lot of things we need to talk about. It's all feeling very real at the moment.'

'I can clear my diary.' He already had, but she didn't need to know that. 'Where do you want to go?'

'Anywhere outside. It's so nice to have a dry day after two weeks of rain, I want to take advantage of it.'

Marco agreed. The torrential downpours of the last two weeks had added to his impatience as he'd waited for Sophie to get in touch.

'I could eat though,' she added. 'Before I kept eating to stop me feeling sick. Now I just want to eat all the time because I am ravenous. The books tell me I need to be really healthy, but my body just wants carbs, the greasier and unhealthier, the better. You can tell the baby is half Italian the amount of pasta and pizza it demands.'

'I think I know just the place.' He hesitated. 'Unless you have somewhere in mind?'

'No, go ahead. And while we're talking about food, thank you for arranging for those meals. There have been times when I was too tired to even make toast. They have been brilliant.'

Marco exhaled. Bianca had announced her pregnancy shortly after he'd last seen Sophie and had mentioned how tired she was in the evening and what an effort making dinner was. The difference was she had Mamma taking around dishes of pasta and Antonio to cook for her; he'd hated to think of Sophie exhausted and hungry all alone. 'So the meals come under protective and not controlling?'

She nodded. 'They do. They also come under thoughtful and sweet. I really appreciate it.'

It was a start. If he had his way, she'd be living with him and wouldn't need to cope on her own. But he had agreed to respect her wishes—it didn't mean he couldn't make things a little easier for her though.

Marco hailed a cab the second they left the hospital and gave directions as he opened the door for Sophie. Neither of them spoke as the taxi crawled along. It was barely three miles to their destination, but in London traffic that could mean an eternity. As they sat there Marco was assailed by homesickness for the city of his birth. Yes, Venice could be insanely crowded, but just five minutes on a boat and he could be in a deserted spot the tourists would never discover. London had been a wonderful adventure, the place where he had grown up, established himself, become a man in his own right, not just the Santoro heir, but he was ready to move on.

Except Sophie was here—and so his child would be here. Which meant London was his home too for the foreseeable future.

'I don't know this area at all.' Sophie was looking around as the taxi inched its way around Hyde Park heading north. 'I spent my first few nights in London at a cheap hotel near Euston while I looked for work and, once I had the job, rented a flat as close by the office as I could afford. Luckily I had a small savings account I'd kept from Harry—if he'd known, he'd have spent it on guitars or booze or a lads' holiday. I was saving up for a wedding or a baby. Luckily I came to my senses before either of those chained me to him, but it did mean I could afford the first six months' rent while I started to make a life for myself here. But I'm ashamed to say I haven't explored London much at all in the year and a half I've been here. I'm usually working for Clio or working for myself at home.'

She sounded so matter of fact, Marco couldn't imagine how hard it must have been starting afresh in a new city where she knew no one, had nothing. He had already had some contacts when he'd made the move over, a fledgling business and money enough to make the move easy and comfortable. Being his own man was so important to him, but, he acknowledged ruefully, it was easier to start from a position of privilege with a network of contacts than it was completely alone and from scratch. He might have the more successful business, the expensive house, the influential network, but Sophie had a grit and determination he could only hope to emulate and learn from.

He'd thought she was beautiful the first time he'd met her, shivering in the snow, enjoyed her company over the first couple of glasses of wine. He'd been intrigued by her lack of interest in pursuing a relationship with him, a refreshing attitude to his jaded soul, and been taken aback by her horrified response to his family's wealth and influence. There was a grounded realness to Sophie he hadn't come across before. Her experiences could so easily have made her bitter, but instead, although she maintained a guard over her emotions, she was willing and ready to embrace life, to try new things whether it was a small challenge like driving his boat or a huge one like motherhood. He wanted to be with her every step of the way. He just had no idea how to make her believe he meant it.

Marco was quieter than usual. Partly because, like her, he was overwhelmed by the scan bringing the baby to life before their eyes and partly, she suspected, because he was trying his best to show her that he had taken her wishes on board. How long he would manage to consult her before taking any step, from hailing a taxi to opening the door for her, she wasn't sure, but she was touched to see the effort he was making with such sincerity.

The taxi had dropped them off just north of Paddington by a canal filled, to Sophie's delight, with colourful narrowboats. 'They call this area Little Venice,' Marco explained. 'It isn't a patch on the real thing, naturally, but it has a real beauty of its own.'

'I love narrowboats,' Sophie said, staring around her with fascination. 'I've always wanted to live on one and travel from place to place, you know, with pots of herbs and flowers on the roof and maybe a dog.'

'Lovely in summer,' he said doubtfully. 'Probably less romantic in late November when it's been raining for weeks and you can't dry your clothes.'

'It's always sunny in my imagination.' They began walking along the towpath, Sophie peeking in at each boat they passed, squeaking in excitement when she spotted something novel whether it was a cat curled up in the sun or a riotous selection of flowers and vegetables covering the entirety of the boat.

He didn't say that the *palazzo* overlooked a canal on one side, that the terrace and courtyard were big enough to grow all the herbs and flowers she desired, that the heating kept it toasty warm in the colder months and the shuttered windows and thick walls provided shade and coolness in the summer. He didn't need to; she knew it as well as he did.

She knew there were plenty of empty salons just waiting to be put to use, rooms she could line with rails filled with her designs, a drawing board set up by the window, her sewing machine in one corner, a cutting-out table in the other. All that could be hers, she only had to say the word.

But space and money weren't enough. All she wanted, all she'd ever wanted was unconditional love. And for that she'd have gladly lived on a narrowboat through the fiercest of storms.

'There are several cafés on boats, one of which is an Italian deli run by a Venetian man. I can vouch for the quality of both his pasta and his bread. How hungry are you?'

Sophie considered. She could always eat, but was she actually hungry? 'You know, I think if I get a snack to sustain me I would rather walk first, eat afterwards. Is that okay?'

'Of course, it's still early. Why don't we walk up to Regent's Park and decide what to do next from there?'

After a black coffee for Marco and a bottle of sparkling water and a toasted ciabatta filled with mozzarella and tomatoes for Sophie at what was, she conceded, the best Italian café she had been to in London, they headed north towards Maida Vale and Regent's Park. The sun was warm, a gorgeous contrast to the dampness that had characterised most of February and added to the almost holiday atmosphere along the canal side. A family passed them, a baby snug in a sling against its mother's chest, a curly-haired toddler swung high on his father's shoulders. Sophie and Marco paused on the towpath to let them walk by and then stood looking after them as the couple chattered and laughed as they pointed things out to their small son.

Sophie's heart ached. Would she and Marco ever walk along with their baby in such compatible ease or would it be the polite handovers and lonely nights of a civilised joint custody?

'They look happy,' he said softly as if reading her mind.

'Yes.'

He put a hand on her shoulder and she looked up, surprised, to see a serious expression darkening his eyes. 'Sophie, I just want you to know that I am here for you, whatever you decide to do, however you decide to do it. I know how important your independence is to you. I admire...' he paused, a smile twisting his mouth '...I really admire how hard you've fought for it, fought for everything you've achieved. You should be so proud. I am. I just want you to know that.'

Sophie's heart began to speed up, her throat constricting as she listened to him.

'It's yours, whatever you need, my house in London or the *palazzo* in Venice or somewhere new. For me they are just places, but I want to help you find a home, the right home for you and the baby. If you'll let me. I don't have much else to offer, I realise that now. Strip away my name, strip away my family and there's not much there. I told myself that I didn't need them, that I was enough by myself, yet at the same time I coasted along comfortably on all they brought me. I admit, I didn't think I needed to ask whether you wanted to marry me or not. I'd spent so long running from marriage it didn't occur to me that you might turn me down, want something different for your life. I was an arrogant fool.'

His eyes, still steady on hers, were heavy with sadness and she impulsively lifted a hand to his cheek. 'No, you had good reason to feel that way. I was with you, at that wedding. I saw how people looked at you. I heard what they said. And if I was someone else, if I hadn't been so broken, then maybe I would have said yes. Maybe respect and chemistry would have been enough.'

He shook his head. 'No, you were right. Love is the only basis for marriage. It should be. It's hard enough to succeed at something so huge without starting out short. I didn't think I was the kind of man who could love, but you've taught me differently.'

Her pulse began to hammer so loudly the rest of the world was drowned out. Was he saying what she thought he was saying?

'I thought of love as selfish, as needy, as constrictive. I thought love meant giving up who you are, what you are. But now I know it means wanting the best for someone else regardless of the cost to you. Tell me what you need from me and I'll do it. Anything. All I want is to be the best father I can be to our child, to make you as proud of me as I am of you.'

All the surety had been wiped away, replaced with

a heartfelt expression and the kind of tenderness Sophie hadn't believed could exist in the world, not for her. Scarcely believing, she stared into his face and saw the truth blazing out. He loved her, not because of what she could do, nor because of how she made him feel, but because of who she was.

'Anything?' She couldn't believe her voice was so steady.

'Anything,' he confirmed.

'Then marry me.' She hadn't even known that was what she was going to say, but as soon as she said the words she knew they were right. That they were perfect. 'Marry me three weeks from now in a small ceremony here in London. Just like you wanted, only with the people we love and the people who love us celebrating with us because a wedding should be a celebration, always.'

'It should. I was a fool to think any differently. Sophie, are you sure? You don't have to do this.'

'Surer than I have ever been about anything. I love you, Marco. Saying no to you was the hardest thing I've ever done, but I couldn't be with someone who didn't love me again, not even for the baby.'

'You won't need to,' he vowed. 'Because I love you more than I ever thought possible.' He grinned. 'See how far I've come? My *machismo* is not even slightly dented by your proposal.'

'You did propose to me twice first,' she pointed out. 'Although the first time was more of a fait accompli than an actual proposal.'

Marco caught both her hands in his. 'Not only do I accept your proposal, but I'll make you a promise, here and now, as binding as any wedding vow. We're a team. I'll always remember that. I won't ever try to control you, try to stop you from fulfilling your dreams, from being the person you want to be.'

'That's all I need.' She laced her fingers through his; now she could hold on to him she didn't want to ever let go. 'That's all I ever needed. Your promise and you.'

And as he bent his head to hers to seal their bargain with a kiss Sophie knew she was home at last. London, Venice, a narrowboat cruising the country, wherever Marco was she would be too. She finally had a place of her own.

* * * * *

THE SHERIFF'S NINE-MONTH SURPRISE

BRENDA HARLEN

To #professionalromancefans—avid readers
and tireless ambassadors of the genre.

With sincere appreciation.

Chapter One

Twenty-eight months

Katelyn Gilmore fell back onto the king-size mattress and drew in a long, deep breath as she stared up at the textured ceiling of the Courtland Hotel-Boulder City.

Twenty-eight months devoted exclusively to the establishment of her law practice, working long hours every day, including evenings and weekends, to prove herself to her clients and colleagues. Now, after twenty-eight months, she'd finally allowed herself to venture away from the office for a few days.

Okay, a conference wasn't actually a vacation, but the opportunity to hone her legal skills and enjoy a change of scenery was one that she couldn't refuse. And she was determined to enjoy the weekend—to get out of the hotel when the workshops had ended and breathe in some fresh air. Maybe she'd even take the time to see some sights, have a drink or two at a local bar, maybe flirt with a hand-some cowboy—if she remembered how.

She enjoyed the company of men, and her sexual experiences—though limited—had been pleasant enough. Maybe not earth-shattering, but she didn't really believe that earth-shattering sex existed outside of books and movies. The truth was, she felt more anticipation when she was prepping for a trial than thinking about getting naked with a man.

"Which only proves you're getting naked with the wrong men," her sister had told her as she tucked a box of condoms in the suitcase Kate had packed for her trip.

Though Skylar was younger by five years, she had a much better understanding of the way a man's brain worked—and a lot more experience with other parts of the male anatomy.

Kate had removed the box and given it back to her sister. "I'm going to a legal conference at a five-star hotel, not an open house at a brothel."

"Still, you might luck out and meet a guy who is something more than a stuffed shirt," Sky had said, and returned the box to the niche she'd created between Kate's makeup bag and her underwear. "And even if you don't, it's better to be safe than sorry."

Because she agreed with her sister's last point, she'd left the condoms in her suitcase.

She also believed in careful planning and deliberation and wasn't the type of woman to act on impulse. Hooking up with a guy she met at a conference would be exactly that—and a little tawdry, too.

So when she hung up her suits and unpacked her other essentials, she left the condoms in her luggage, certain she'd have no need for them.

Certain...and maybe just a little disappointed.

* * *

Reid Davidson was sitting with his back to the wall and his eyes on the door when she walked into the conference room.

From a young age, he'd learned to be aware of his surroundings and the people around him—it was easier to dodge a backhand if he saw it coming—and the habit had served him well as the Sheriff of Echo Ridge, Texas.

But even if he hadn't seen her arrive, even if his head had momentarily been turned away, Reid would have been aware of her presence. She was the type of woman who snagged a man's full and complete attention and didn't let go.

She had bold blue eyes and sharp cheekbones in a heart-shaped face that was saved from looking prim by a lushly shaped mouth that promised the fulfillment of his wickedest fantasies. Her dark hair, shining with hints of gold and copper, was caught up in some kind of fancy twist that made him want to take out the pins and slide his fingers through it.

After pausing for a brief moment in the doorway, her gaze searching for an empty chair, she moved to the other side of the room with a brisk, confident stride that suggested she was a woman with important places to go and people to see.

Her body—long and lean with curves in all the right places—was buttoned up in a slim-fitting blue suit. The color was both lighter and brighter than navy and brought to mind the fancy glass his grandmother had collected. The skirt hugged her hips, and the matching jacket was fastened below her breasts with a single square button, above which peeked a hint of black silk.

He'd resigned himself to spending the weekend surrounded by lawyers and judges and other legal types. It wouldn't have been his first choice on how to spend three days, but the Echo Ridge town council strongly advocated continuing education for all its employees and, since that council was footing the bill for the weekend, he hadn't balked at the request.

He'd chosen to attend Sentencing Considerations in the Criminal Courts, believing it would be held in Boulder, Colorado, less than a two-hour flight from Echo Ridge. It turned out the conference was in Boulder *City*, which was in Nevada, adding another hour and another time zone to his travel. Although a potentially fortuitous error on his part, as he'd recently decided to move away from Echo Ridge and had, in fact, already applied to fill a vacancy in the Sheriff's Office in Haven, Nevada.

So he'd flown in a day early and made a quick trip to the northern part of the state to meet with the hiring committee before the conference. He'd been advised that a decision would be made before 4:00 p.m. Monday, and he figured the conference would distract him from counting the hours until then. As he watched the stunning brunette settle into her chair, almost directly across from him, he couldn't help but think that she would be an even better distraction.

She unzipped the top of her briefcase and removed a bottle of water, her cell phone and her iPad. If he'd been a betting man, he would have put money on her having been a straight-A student in school—the type who willingly sat at the front of the class to ensure she didn't miss a single word the teacher said.

The good girl had never been his type, and if he really wanted the distraction of a willing female to help get him through the weekend, he'd be better off hitting a club or the hotel bar when five o'clock rolled around. But his gaze lingered on the brunette, because it was a shame that a good girl should have a mouth that suggested it was capable of doing wonderfully bad things.

Now that she was set up, she turned to the balding man in the ill-fitting brown suit who was seated on her left. Making friends with her neighbors, he realized, when she said something, smiled and shook the man's hand. Then she turned to the woman on her other side, a skinny redhead with sharp eyes, and repeated the process.

Having finished with the introductions, she sat back in her chair. As more stragglers found their way to the room and filled the last few seats, she let her gaze move around the table. Then her eyes locked on his, and his stomach clenched as it absorbed the punch of sexual awareness.

He hadn't experienced anything like that in a long while, and he knew then that he wasn't going to walk away from her so quickly when the hour-long session was over.

Most of the seats were taken by the time Kate found the conference room where tables were set up around the perimeter to facilitate discussion. But she found a space between Lyle, a victims' rights advocate from Carson City, and Marcia, a former prosecutor-turned-defense-attorney from Fresno, California.

When she was settled in her chair, she let her gaze scan the room as last-minute arrivals squeezed into vacant seats. Her lazy perusal came to an abrupt halt when she saw him.

He was wearing a light gray micro-check shirt that stretched across mouth-wateringly broad shoulders with a loosely knotted plum-colored tie at his throat. His hair was brown, a few shades lighter than her own, and cut short. His forehead was high, his brows thick, his eyes—green? Brown? She couldn't quite tell from across the distance that separated them, but they were focused and intense. The bronze skin suggested that he spent a lot of time working or playing outdoors. The strong jaw, square and dark with stubble, gave him a slightly dangerous and yet somehow appealing edge.

There was no ring on the third finger of his left hand, resting casually on top of the table, but she knew that wasn't always proof of unmarried status. Then he caught her eye and winked boldly, and she felt heat spread up her neck and across her cheeks as she tore her gaze away. She was embarrassed to have been caught staring. She was also—unexpectedly and undeniably—aware of him on a purely visceral level.

It had been a long time since she'd been attracted to a man and even longer since she'd shared any kind of physical intimacy with one. She didn't know precisely how long, but it had been at least twenty-eight months because she hadn't been away from Haven in that period of time—and she definitely hadn't hooked up with anyone in her hometown. Heck, she couldn't even have coffee with a male colleague during morning recess from court without her sister texting to ask for details before her cup was empty.

So maybe it was the extended duration of her most recent dating hiatus that was responsible for her reaction to him. Or maybe it was his shoulders. Apparently she had a weakness for guys with great shoulders and strong jawlines and—

And somehow her errant gaze had drifted back to him again. Chiding herself for her reaction, she folded back the cover of her tablet and swiped to unlock the screen.

The moderator closed the door, effectively silencing the quiet murmur of conversation and focusing attention in his direction. After a brief introduction, he handed out some case studies for the participants to review and discuss.

As the debate evolved, Kate found herself arguing against the position taken by the broad-shouldered stranger who'd caught her eye. He insisted that adult crimes deserved adult punishment; she maintained that children didn't have experience making decisions or controlling their impulses and shouldn't be held to the same standards as their adult counterparts.

When the moderator finally called time on the session, neither of them had given an inch. And yet Kate found herself invigorated rather than frustrated, because while she didn't agree with her opponent's position, she had to admit that he'd made some good points and he presented his arguments in a rational and respectful manner.

As most of the other attendees funneled toward the door, he moved the other way—toward her. She took her time putting her materials away, pleased to note that her hands were steady despite the pounding of her heart. She uncapped her water bottle and tipped it to her lips to moisten her suddenly dry throat.

He wore jeans with his shirt and tie, and well-worn cowboy boots on his feet. Six feet two inches, she decided when she had to tip her head back to meet his gaze. And his eyes weren't green *or* brown but an intriguing combination of both. Hazel, she decided, though the word failed to describe the magnetism of his gaze. Tiny lines crinkled at the corners of his eyes and bracketed his mouth, and a thin scar slashed through his right eyebrow.

"Reid Davidson," he said.

She took the proffered hand—wide-palmed and strong—and felt a tingle of something dangerously tempting shoot up her arm and arrow toward her center. "Katelyn Gilmore."

"Defense attorney?" he guessed.

She nodded. "Among other things."

"Six months out of law school?"

She narrowed her gaze, not sure if his question was a legitimate guess or a subtle insult. "Four years."

He seemed surprised by that revelation. "Four years and you're not completely disillusioned yet?"

"My determination to fight for justice doesn't blind me to the flaws in our system."

"That's…admirable," he decided.

She slid the strap of her briefcase onto her shoulder. "You're a prosecutor," she guessed.

"No," he said quickly. Vehemently. "I'm not a lawyer."

"So what *do* you do, Not-a-Lawyer Reid Davidson?"

"I'm a sheriff."

She nodded, easily able to picture a shiny badge pinned to that wide chest. "And you throw the book at anyone who doesn't toe the line in your jurisdiction."

He didn't deny it. "It's my job to uphold the law."

"The law doesn't exist in a vacuum," she argued. "It requires context."

"Apparently you have some strong opinions on the subject," he noted. "Why don't we continue this discussion elsewhere, and you can enlighten me?"

She absolutely wanted to continue this discussion—or any discussion—if it meant spending more time with the broad-shouldered sheriff with the mesmerizing eyes and sexy smile.

"What did you have in mind?" she asked, determined to play it cool despite the anticipation racing through her veins.

"I could buy you a drink," he suggested.

She considered herself a smart woman—too smart to hook up with a stranger. But while she didn't know even the first page of Reid's life story, she knew that he set her blood humming in a way that it hadn't done in a very long time. And after more than two years without a man even registering a blip in her pulse, she was too curious to walk away without determining if the attraction she felt was reciprocated.

She wasn't looking for love. She wasn't even looking for sex. But she couldn't deny that she enjoyed looking at Sheriff Reid Davidson.

Sometimes you don't know what you want until it's right in front of you.

With the echo of her sister's voice in her ears, she made her decision. "A drink sounds good."

Reid had never been afraid to admit when he was wrong, and he'd realized—less than halfway through the workshop discussion—that he'd been wrong about her.

Katelyn.

The name struck him as a unique combination of the classic and contemporary, and as intriguing as the woman herself. Because while she might look prim and cool, there was a lot of heat beneath the surface. She argued not just eloquently but passionately, making him suspect that a woman who was so animated in her discussion of a hypothetical situation would be even more interesting up close and personal. Now he was about to find out.

There were two bars in the hotel—the first was an open lounge area that saw a lot of traffic as guests made their way around the hotel; the second, adjacent to the restaurant, was more remote and private. He opted for the second, where patrons could be seated at pub-style tables with high-back leather stools or narrow booths that afforded a degree of intimacy.

He guided her to a vacant booth. When the waitress came to take their drink order, Katelyn requested a Napa Valley cabernet sauvignon and he opted for a locally brewed IPA, signing the check to his room when the drinks were delivered.

After the server had gone, he raised his glass. "To stimulating discourse."

Though she lifted her brows at his deliberately suggestive word choice, she tapped the rim of her glass against the neck of his bottle.

"Where are you from, Sheriff Reid Davidson?" she asked, after sipping her wine.

"Echo Ridge, Texas."

"You're a long way from home," she noted.

"So it would seem," he agreed. "How about you?"

"Northern Nevada, so not quite such a long way."

"Humboldt, Haven or Elko County?"

"You must have aced geography in school," she remarked.

"I didn't ace anything in school," he confessed. "But I recently visited the town of Haven."

"Why were you there?" she asked, then held up a hand before he could respond. "No, don't tell me. I don't want to know."

"Why don't you want to know?"

"Because almost everyone in Haven knows everyone else—or at least knows someone who knows that someone else, and if it turns out that you hooked up with someone I know, this—" she gestured from her own chest to his and back again "—isn't going to happen."

"Is this—" he copied her gesture "—going to happen?"

She sipped her wine. "I'm thinking about it."

"While you're thinking, let me reassure you that I've never hooked up with anyone from Haven." His lips curved as he lifted his bottle. "Yet."

She set her glass on the table, her fingers trailing slowly down the stem. "You're pretty confident, aren't you?"

"Optimistic," he told her. "But I do need to ask you something."

"What's that?"

"Is there anyone waiting for you at home in Haven?"

"Aside from my father, grandparents, sister, two brothers, several aunts, uncles and cousins, you mean?"

"Aside from them," he confirmed.

"No, there's no one waiting for me." She traced the base of her wineglass with a neatly shaped but unpainted fingernail. "What about you, Sheriff Davidson—are you married?"

He shook his head. "Divorced."

"Girlfriend?"

"No," he said again. "Any more questions?"

"Just one," she said.

He held her gaze, waiting, hoping.

"Do you want to take these drinks back to my room?"

Chapter Two

Five weeks later

"I can't believe you're leaving." Trish Stilton pouted as she rubbed a hand over the curve of her hugely pregnant belly. "Especially now, only a few weeks before the baby's due to be born."

Reid dumped the entire contents of his cutlery drawer into a box. Though he didn't dare say it aloud, considering the imminent delivery of his ex-wife's baby, he'd decided that his timing was almost perfect.

"Just last week, I told Jonah that we should ask you to be the godfather, but now that you're moving to Nevada, that's out of the question."

Which further convinced Reid that he'd made the right choice in accepting the offer to take over the sheriff's position in Haven. Though he and Trish had been divorced for more than four years and she'd been remarried for almost three, they'd remained close. Maybe too close.

When she'd walked down the aisle to exchange vows with her current husband, Reid had been the man to give her away. Yeah, it had seemed an odd request to him, but he didn't see how he could refuse. When she'd found out that she was pregnant, she'd stopped at the Sheriff's Office to share the news with Reid even before she'd told her husband. And when she'd cried—tears of joy, because she was going to be a mother, mingled with grief, because her child would never know his grandfather—he'd held her and comforted her.

If she'd asked him to be her baby's godfather—as Jonah Stilton had warned him she intended to do—Reid wouldn't have been able to refuse. How could he refuse any request from the daughter of the man who'd saved his life?

Reid had been an orphaned teenager running with a bad crowd when the local sheriff took him under his wing. He didn't just turn Reid's life around, he saved it, and Reid knew there was no way he could ever repay the man who had been his mentor, father figure and friend. So when Hank realized he wasn't going to beat the cancer that had invaded his body and he'd confided to Reid that he was worried about his daughter, Reid had promised to take care of her. The news of their engagement had been a balm to the older man's battered spirits, and he'd managed to hold on long enough to see Reid and Trish exchange their vows.

"I'm honored that you thought of me," he said to his ex-wife now. "But I'm sure your baby's father would prefer to have his brother fill that role."

"Jonah understands how important you are to me," she said, without denying his claim.

"You're important to me, too, but I think this move is going to be the best thing for all of us."

"But why do you have to go so far away?" she demanded.

"Nevada's not all that far," he said soothingly.

"But Haven?" she pressed. "I looked it up—it might as well be called Nowhere, Nevada, because that's where it is."

"Then I won't expect you to visit," he said mildly.

"Of course, I'll visit," she promised. "Because you don't have any friends or family in that town."

"Actually, I do have a…friend…in Haven."

"A female friend?" she guessed.

He nodded.

"I *knew* there had to be another reason that you suddenly decided to leave Echo Ridge—something more than a temporary job."

"She's not the reason I'm leaving," he said truthfully. "But I am looking forward to seeing her again."

"What's her name?"

Reid shook his head. "None of your business."

Trish smiled. "Afraid I'll track her down and ask about her intentions?"

"Yes," he admitted.

Not that he was really worried. He had no doubt that Katelyn Gilmore could handle his ex-wife. But the attorney had no idea that he was moving to Haven, because they hadn't exchanged any contact information before they went their separate ways after the conference. And with the perspective that came with time and distance, he couldn't help but wonder if he'd made the weekend they'd spent together into more than it really was.

"Well, it would only be fair," Trish said now. "You wouldn't let me go out on a second date with Jonah until you'd done a complete background check on him."

"Because your father asked me to take care of you," he reminded her.

"He wanted us to take care of each other," she said.

And for a while, they'd done just that. But Trish had wanted more than he'd been willing or able to give her—an *irreconcilable difference* that led to the end of their marriage. When that happened, he felt as if he'd let down Hank as much as Trish, but he knew his old friend would be pleased to see his daughter in a committed relationship with a man who could give her everything Reid couldn't.

He was sincerely happy for her, because she was happy. For himself, he'd decided a long time ago that he wasn't cut out to be a dad. A kid who'd been knocked around by his mother's various boyfriends for the first six years of his life, then raised by his widowed grandmother for the next eight before being kicked into and around the system didn't know anything about being a father. He'd lucked out when he'd met Hank. Trish's father had given him an idea of the type of man a dad should be, but Reid suspected it was too little too late, that the scars from his earlier years were too numerous and deep to ever truly heal.

"Now you've got Jonah," he reminded her.

"Yes, I do," Trish said, smiling through the tears that filled her eyes again.

"Jeez, will you stop with the waterworks?" he demanded, passing her a box of tissues.

She plucked one out and dabbed at her eyes. "I can't help it—it's pregnancy hormones."

"Well, let your husband deal with your blubbering—he's the one who knocked you up."

"Yes, he did," she said proudly, rubbing a hand over the enormous swell of her belly. "And those hormones have also led to doing a lot more of what got me into this condition."

He lifted his hands to cover his ears. "Way too much information, Trish."

She laughed through her tears. Then she reached out

a hand to touch his arm. "Can I give you one piece of advice?"

"Can I stop you?" he countered drily.

She ignored his question. "Before you get involved with this woman—before *she* gets involved with you—be honest about what you want and don't want from a relationship."

"I never meant to be dishonest with you," he said quietly.

"I know," she admitted. "The problem was, we rushed into marriage without ever talking about all the things we should have talked about."

He nodded. "But now you have everything you wanted."

"Soon," she amended, rubbing a hand over her baby bump again. Then with her other hand, she grabbed his and drew it to the curve of her belly. "Do you feel that? He's kicking."

He did feel it, little nudges against his palm. He wondered if it hurt her, to have a tiny human being moving around inside of her, but that seemed like too personal a question to ask. Not that his ex-wife seemed to care about boundaries, which was why Reid was moving out of state in an effort to establish some. Instead he asked, "He?"

Trish smiled and nodded. "It's a boy. We're going name him Henry—for my dad."

Reid had to clear the tightness from his own throat before he could respond. "That's a great name."

She watched him tape the flaps of the box shut. "I really wish you weren't going."

He hadn't expected that his ex-wife would make this easy for him, but he hadn't expected that it would be so hard, either. But he didn't—couldn't—waver. He needed to move on with his life, and as long as he was living a stone's throw away from her, he knew that wouldn't happen.

"You're going to be okay, Trish. You don't need me anymore."

She sniffed and knuckled away a tear that spilled onto her cheeks. "But what if you still need me?"

She'd been his family—his only family—for seven years now. But it didn't matter if he still needed her—it was time for him to move on.

Kate thanked the clerk as she slid the judge's signed order into her client's file, tucked the file into her briefcase and turned away from the desk. She exited the courthouse, pausing outside the doors to perch her sunglasses on her nose in defense against the bright afternoon sun, then continued on her way. She'd been told that she moved purposefully, like a woman on a mission, and she usually was.

Today her mission was to get away from the courthouse before she threw up. She crossed the street and ducked into the shade of the trees that lined the perimeter of Shearing Park. The greenspace was usually quiet at this time of day, offering the privacy she needed. She lowered herself onto the wooden slats of a bench and reached into her briefcase for the sleeve of saltine crackers she'd been carrying for the past few days.

She inhaled, taking three long deep breaths. Then she nibbled on a cracker and sipped some water. When she felt a little steadier, she pulled out her cell phone and dialed her office.

"I've got the custody order for Debby Hansen," she said when her assistant answered the phone. "If you want to print up the cover letter and final account so everything's ready to go, that would be great. I'm heading to a settlement conference in Winnemucca this afternoon, but I'll be back in the office in the morning."

She could picture Beth frowning at Kate's schedule on

her computer screen. "I don't have anything about a settlement conference."

"I set it up myself—a favor for a friend," she explained.
Lied.

If she was looking in a mirror, she would see flags of color on her cheeks. Thankfully, Beth wasn't able to see the telltale proof of her deception.

"Okay," the other woman said agreeably. "I'll leave your docket and the files for tomorrow morning on your desk before I lock up."

"Thanks, Beth."

She disconnected the call and nibbled on another cracker. She'd never felt good about lying, but lately she'd been doing a lot of it.

Lying to her assistant, to explain her absences from the office. To her dad, when he said she looked peaked. To her sister, when Sky asked what was wrong. To her grandmother, when she hinted that Kate was working too hard.

To herself, when she suggested that the first home pregnancy test was faulty and there was no reason to panic.

It was only when a second, and then a third, test showed the same obviously inaccurate result that she'd decided to see an ob-gyn.

She tucked her crackers back into her briefcase, walked to her car and headed toward Battle Mountain. Because she would rather drive thirty-five miles out of town than risk the inevitable speculation that would follow a visit to a local doctor.

"Good afternoon, Ms. Gilmore—I'm Camila Amaro."

Kate accepted the proffered hand of the woman who entered the exam room. "Thank you for squeezing me in."

"You sounded a little panicked on the phone."

"I'm feeling a little panicked," she admitted.

The doctor didn't go behind her desk to sit down but

leaned back against it, facing her patient. "Is this your first pregnancy?"

She managed a weak smile. "So much for thinking the results of three home pregnancy tests might be wrong."

"False results do happen," the doctor acknowledged. "But a false positive is extremely rare, and the test we ran here confirms the presence of hCG—the pregnancy hormone—in your system."

"I'm really pregnant? I'm going to have a baby?"

"You're really pregnant," the doctor confirmed.

She'd dreaded receiving this confirmation. How could she possibly juggle her professional responsibilities with the demands of a baby? And yet, something surprising happened when the doctor said those three words. She felt a loosening of the knots in her stomach and unexpected joy in her heart.

A baby.

And she knew then that it didn't matter that she hadn't planned for this—she would figure out a way to make it work.

"Do you want to set up a sonogram so we can establish how far along you are and discuss the options that are available to you?" Dr. Amaro asked.

"Five weeks and six days," Kate told her.

"You're sure?"

She nodded. "Broken condom."

The doctor opened the folder she carried and made a note in the file. "Are you in an exclusive relationship with the father?"

The question was matter-of-fact and without any hint of censure, but Kate felt her cheeks flush with embarrassment that she'd been so foolish and careless. A weekend fling had seemed like a good idea at the time—some harmless fun to break the monotony of her everyday life. She'd never anticipated that a few unforgettable nights would give her a lasting reminder of those nights with the handsome sheriff from Texas.

"No," she admitted. "In fact...I haven't seen him since the weekend that we were...together."

"Then maybe we should run some other tests?" the doctor suggested gently.

She wouldn't have thought it was possible, but her already burning cheeks flamed even hotter. She'd been so off-kilter about the possibility of a pregnancy that she hadn't given a thought to any other potential consequences of unprotected sex.

Of course, when the condom broke, she and Reid had talked about their respective sexual histories to reassure one another that there was no cause for alarm. But she nodded her assent to the doctor now. "Yes, please. Whatever you need to do—I want to know that my baby's going to be okay."

"Then you do want to have the baby?" Dr. Amaro asked in the same neutral tone.

Kate nodded again. While she appreciated the woman's professional manner and obvious determination not to influence her decision, there had never been any question in Kate's mind. Even when she'd still been firmly in denial about the possibility of a pregnancy, she'd known that—if she was pregnant—there was no other choice for her but to have the baby.

She'd always wanted to have a family...someday. Of course, she'd expected to be more established in her career—and preferably married—before that dream became a reality, but she was going to play the hand that had been dealt and be the best mother she could be to her baby.

She had no intention of making any claims on Sheriff Reid Davidson of Echo Ridge, Texas. She'd gone to bed with him not just willingly but eagerly, and even if the possibility of a pregnancy had never entered her mind, she alone had chosen to have this baby and she alone would be the responsible for that choice.

And while she had no idea how he would respond to the news that he was going to be a father, she knew that she had to tell him.

Soon.

Chapter Three

Reid stared at the modest pile of boxes in the middle of his new kitchen. He suspected that most people, by thirty-four years of age, had acquired more stuff, but when he and Trish had separated, he'd moved into a fully furnished apartment and let her keep the house and almost everything in it.

While looking at the housing options in Haven, he'd found an in-law suite available to rent only a few blocks from the Sheriff's Office—furnishings available—and decided that was again the easy option. Glancing around his new home, he acknowledged that he should have asked for photos.

Whether or not his decision to move to Haven, Nevada, would prove to be the right one had yet to be determined. But he'd needed a fresh start, he'd liked what he'd seen of the town on his first visit and he'd been assured by Jed Traynor, the former sheriff who had been forced into early retirement by some health concerns—and his wife—that Haven was populated by mostly good people.

And then, of course, there was the Katelyn factor.

He wasn't foolish enough to let his career decisions be influenced by a weekend fling, no matter how spectacular and unforgettable the sex had been. But he'd been thinking about her a lot and he was looking forward to the opportunity to see her again.

Seeing her naked again would be even better.

She was a woman of intriguing contrasts. When she'd walked into the conference room, she'd been the picture of cool professionalism, but it hadn't taken long for him to realize how much heat simmered beneath the surface. The passion she'd displayed in advocating her position in the conference room was just as evident in the bedroom.

She'd made the first move—not just when she'd invited him back to her room, but when she'd kissed him. There had been nothing tentative about that first kiss. No questions or doubts about what either of them wanted. Their mouths had come together eagerly, almost desperately.

They'd both been enthusiastic participants in their lovemaking. Tearing at their own clothes while simultaneously trying to undress each other, laughing when limbs got tangled in uncooperative fabric.

When she'd been stripped down to a tiny pair of black bikini panties and a low-cut bra, he'd stopped laughing.

Hell, his heart had almost stopped beating.

She was so incredibly hot.

So wonderfully agile.

So totally willing.

And even six weeks after only two nights together, he hadn't forgotten any of the details of the time he'd spent in her bed. Not the way her eyes went dark when she was aroused or the soft, sexy sounds that emanated from deep in her throat. Not the rosy pink buds of her nipples or the tiny brown mole beside her belly button. Not the way her hair looked fanned out on the soft pillow behind her head, or the erotic brush of those long tresses as her lips leisurely explored his body. Not the way her thighs quivered when he stroked deep inside her or the way her inner muscles clenched around him when she finally succumbed to her climax.

Yeah, he was definitely looking forward to seeing her again.

With that thought in mind, he decided to abandon his unpacking for a while and wander the neighborhood—to get his bearings. At least that would be the justification if anyone asked. The truth was, he'd already located the most important places: Sheriff's Office; courthouse; Diggers', the neighborhood bar and grill; Jo's, a local pizza place; The Trading Post, the general store; and, a few blocks down from the courthouse, The Law Office of Katelyn T. Gilmore.

Her practice was set up in a beautiful old building with a cornerstone that established the date of its erection as 1885. Maybe the old library, he speculated, since Jed had pointed out the new community center, which included a swimming pool, gymnasium, "the new library," several multipurpose rooms and administrative offices.

"Are you in need of legal counsel?"

Reid turned to face a woman who appeared to be in her mid- to late-sixties, about five-four with shoulder-length dark hair liberally streaked with gray, wearing a plaid shirt with faded jeans and well-worn boots.

"No, ma'am," he said. "Just admiring the building."

"The old library," she said, confirming his supposition. "It was built in 1885, as were most of the buildings on this stretch of Main Street, but the doors didn't open until 1887.

It's rumored that sixteen-year-old Elena Sanchez hid out in the basement of this very building for three weeks in the fall of 1904 to avoid being forced to marry."

"Did she succeed?"

The woman nodded. "With the help of the librarian, Edward Jurczyk, who sneaked in blankets and food for her. Two years later, they were married. Nine years after that, Edward was killed fighting in The Great War in Europe."

"Haven has quite an interesting history," he mused, his gaze returning to the wide front window where Katelyn T. Gilmore was painted in bold black letters outlined in gold and Attorney at Law was spelled out below in slightly smaller letters.

"Katie opened her office here almost two-and-a-half years ago," the woman continued. "If you're ever in need of an attorney, you couldn't do better. She sometimes has office hours on weekends, but she's out of town right now."

"You seem to know a lot about Ms. Gilmore's schedule," he noted.

And sharing more information than you should with a stranger, he wanted to caution. Of course, he kept that admonition to himself, as he was eager to hear anything about Katelyn that she was willing to tell him.

"Of course, I do," she replied. "Katie's my granddaughter."

"I'm beginning to believe that everyone in town knows— or is—a Gilmore." He offered his hand. "I'm Reid Davidson, the—"

"The new sheriff," she finished for him, as she gripped his hand in a surprisingly firm shake. "I know who you are. And I'm Evelyn Gilmore, not some dotty old woman who would spill personal information about my family to a stranger on the street."

Then her gaze narrowed speculatively. "So you apparently know that Haven was founded by the Gilmore family," she acknowledged, "but what do you know about the Blakes?"

He forced his expression to remain blank. "Who?"

She laughed. "It might turn out that you're exactly what this town needs, Sheriff Reid Davidson. You plan on staying beyond the completion of your current term?"

"Maybe you should table that question until after I've actually started my job," he suggested.

"Maybe I will," she decided. "Until then, if you've got time for a cup of coffee, I can introduce you to Donna Bradley. She's been working the counter at The Daily Grind for longer than it's been The Daily Grind.

"Cal's Coffee Shop, it used to be called," she continued. "But Cal died nearly a dozen years ago now and when his granddaughter took it over, she gave it a face-lift and a new name. She was smart enough to keep Donna, though, and if there's any news in town, she's usually the first to know it."

"I've always got time for a cup of coffee," Reid said, looking forward to her commentary on the community and its residents—and hopeful that she'd share more information about Katelyn.

Though Kate had been feeling tired for a couple of weeks, having the doctor explain that fatigue was normal in the first trimester, because her body was expending lots of energy helping to grow a baby, seemed to exacerbate the situation. By the end of the following week, she was really dragging.

Thankfully, she didn't have court Friday morning, but she did have an appointment at the community center in the afternoon to talk to a group of seniors about wills and estate planning. After the session was finished, she decided to call it a day.

Her cell phone rang just as she pulled into the parking lot behind the old library, which housed not only her law office but her apartment above it. Shifting her vehicle into Park, she glanced longingly at the second-floor windows. If she ignored the ringing, she could have her shoes off and her feet up in less than three minutes.

She answered the call, anyway.

"Hey, Kate—it's Liam," her brother said, as if she wouldn't recognize his voice or the number on the display.

"What's up?" It was unusual for him to contact her in the middle of the day, so she knew his call had a specific purpose.

"Do you remember my friend, Chase, from school?"

"Of course," she said.

"Well, I just got off the phone with his brother, Gage, who called me because Chase told him that my sister is an attorney."

"Are you getting to a point anytime soon?"

"Yeah," he said. "Gage's son, Aiden, has been arrested."

Now *that* was a surprise.

Aiden wasn't just a good kid, he was unfailingly honest. The type of kid who wouldn't swipe a pack of chewing gum from The Trading Post. In fact, Kate remembered a time when he'd paid a dollar for ten gummy worms but Samantha Allen, who was working behind the counter, miscounted. When Aiden realized he'd been given eleven candies, he tried to give one back.

"What did he allegedly do?"

"I don't know," Liam admitted. "I didn't think to ask, but Gage is panicking because he's still half an hour out of town and he wanted to know if there was anything you could do to help."

"Okay," Kate decided. "Tell him to bring Aiden in to see me tomorrow morning. I have a couple of later appointments but I should be able to squeeze them in around eleven."

"This can't wait until tomorrow. Aiden's being held for a bail hearing—that's why Gage is so frantic."

"He's a juvenile with no prior record," Kate said, thinking aloud.

"Can you find out what's going on?" Liam asked.

"I'm on my way to the Sheriff's Office right now," she promised.

She parked her vehicle then walked the few blocks to the Sheriff's Office. Judy Talon, the administrative assistant, was seated behind the front desk.

"Hey, Katie—are you here about Aiden Hampton?"

She nodded. "But I don't have any of the details," she admitted. "Can you fill me in?"

Judy glanced at the sheriff's closed door but still dropped her voice when she said, "He was arrested with Trent Marshall."

Under normal circumstances, they both knew that Aiden Hampton didn't keep company with kids like Trent Marshall—and he definitely didn't get in trouble with the law. Unfortunately, nothing had been normal for Aiden since his grandmother had died a few weeks earlier.

"What did they do?"

"Found a car with the keys in the ignition and decided to take it for a spin."

"Joyriding," she realized.

"Some would say," Judy agreed. "The new sheriff is saying grand larceny of a motor vehicle."

"You've got to be kidding."

The other woman shook her head. "I wish I was."

"Grand larceny is a felony."

"Which is why he's being held over for a bail hearing," Judy explained.

"Obviously, Jed didn't tell his replacement how things work around here." Kate glanced at her watch. "What time is the hearing?"

"Ten a.m. Monday morning."

"Oh, no." She shook her head. "I'm not letting Aiden spend the weekend in lockup."

"I hope he doesn't have to," the other woman agreed, though her tone was skeptical.

Kate looked toward the office. When Jed had run the department, the door was almost always open. Now it was closed, and she hoped that status wasn't a reflection of the sheriff's mind. "Can you let the new sheriff know that I need a few minutes of his time?"

Judy picked up the phone to connect with the sheriff, but first whispered, "Good luck."

She didn't let the woman's words unnerve her. After giving a perfunctory knock on the door, she turned the knob.

Be confident. Be convincing. Don't back down.

She repeated the refrain inside her head as she stepped into the office.

Be confident. Be convincing. Don't—

The rest of the words slipped from her mind as familiar hazel eyes lifted to meet her gaze.

And she found herself face-to-face with her baby's daddy.

Reid had been looking forward to the day when he would see Katelyn Gilmore again. He didn't anticipate that it would happen as soon as his third day behind the desk in the Sheriff's Office.

He'd been writing a report when she walked in, and he automatically glanced up—and was immediately sucker punched by her presence.

If the sudden widening of her eyes and the sharp intake of her breath were any indication, Katelyn was just as surprised to see him. Maybe even more so, because while he'd known their paths would cross and had eagerly anticipated that eventuality, it appeared that she'd been unaware of the identity of Haven's new sheriff.

"Reid?"

"Hello, Katelyn." He thought he'd remembered how beautiful she was, but seeing her again proved his memories inadequate.

She was wearing another one of those lawyer suits, this one a deep purple color with a pale pink shell under the jacket, which made him wonder what color lace she might be wearing beneath that. Her hair was pinned up as it had been the day of their first meeting, but he knew now how it felt when he slid his fingers through it as he kissed her. And maybe that wasn't a memory he should linger on while he was wearing his official sheriff's uniform, because the mental image was causing his body to stir in a very unprofessional way.

She opened her delectably shaped and incredibly talented mouth, then closed it again without saying another word.

"You're Aiden Hampton's attorney?" he prompted.

She nodded. "And you're the new sheriff."

"I am," he confirmed.

"But…I thought you lived in Texas. I even—" Now she shook her head. "It doesn't matter."

"What doesn't matter?"

She ignored his question to ask her own. "Why are you here?"

"I applied for the job before I met you," he said, wanting to dispel any concern she might have about his motivation. "In fact, I interviewed with the hiring committee the day before the conference in Boulder City."

Her cheeks flushed as she cast a quick glance at his open office door.

He nodded to the phone on his desk, indicating the light that revealed his assistant was occupied with a call.

"When I told you that I was from Haven, why didn't you mention that you'd applied for a job here?"

"Because you didn't want to know," he reminded her.

Her brows drew together as she recalled that earlier conversation and finally admitted, "I guess I did."

"And when I got the call offering me the job, well, I figured our paths would cross soon enough."

"They're going to cross frequently if you insist on locking up juveniles who should be released on their own recognizances."

He leaned back in his chair. Though he was disappointed that she'd so quickly refocused on her client, he could appreciate that she had a job to do. Any personal business could wait until after-hours. "Grand larceny of a motor vehicle is a felony."

"Grand larceny of a motor vehicle is a ridiculously trumped-up charge."

"Tell that to Rebecca Blake—it was her brand-new S-Class Mercedes, worth close to two hundred thousand dollars."

That revelation gave her pause, but just for a second. "Was the vehicle damaged?"

"Thankfully, no," he acknowledged.

She nodded, and he could almost see her switching mental gears from confrontation to persuasion. "He's a good kid, Reid—a straight-A student grieving for his grandmother."

He wouldn't—couldn't—let sympathy for the kid interfere with his responsibilities. "There are lots of kids who lose family members and don't act out by stealing a car."

"Elsie Hampton helped raise Aiden from birth, after his mother walked out of the hospital without her baby, leaving him in the custody of his seventeen-year-old father. But of course, you didn't know that, did you?"

"How could I?" he countered.

"You could have asked someone," she told him. "Everyone in Haven knows his family and his history. In fact, his dad works with Jed's son at Blake Mining."

He gave a short nod. "Point taken."

"So I can take my client home now?"

"No," he said.

"Why not?" she demanded.

"Because I've already gone on the record stating that he's to be held over for a bail hearing."

She sighed. "Then you're going to have to call Judge Calvert and ADA Dustin Perry and tell them you want to have a bail hearing."

"While I appreciate your passionate advocacy, Katelyn, you don't make the rules around here—I do."

"I get that you're new," she said. "Not just new to this office but new in town, and you might think I'm trying to manipulate you for the sake of my client, but I'm not."

"Well, okay, then," he said, making no effort to disguise his sarcasm. "I'm sure the judge and the prosecutor will both be thrilled to be called out to a bail hearing at four thirty on a Friday afternoon."

"I'm sure they won't be," she countered. "But they'd be even less happy to find out, on Monday morning, that you made Aiden Hampton spend the weekend in a cell."

"If I agree to do this, it will look like your client got preferential treatment," he warned.

"No, it will look like the new sheriff finally took his head out of his butt for a few minutes."

Though her blatant disrespect irked him, Reid couldn't help but admire her passion and conviction.

"Your client was processed by the book," he told her.

"Maybe," she allowed. "*If* he'd actually committed grand larceny of a motor vehicle, but the reality is that he went for a joyride—and joyriding is a misdemeanor offense."

"A gross misdemeanor," he clarified.

"Are you going to make those calls or should I, Sheriff?"

"Are you really trying to put my badge between us now, Katelyn?"

"Seems like you were the one who did that," she said. "And it's Kate. Everyone here calls me Kate."

"Or Katie," he noted.

She frowned. "Only my family calls me Katie."

"I like Katelyn better, anyway."

She huffed out a breath. "The judge and ADA?" she prompted.

He picked up the phone.

Thirty minutes later, all parties were assembled at the courthouse. Less than half that time had passed again before Aiden Hampton was released into the care of his grateful and relieved father.

The assistant district attorney didn't stick around any longer than was necessary to sign the papers. The judge didn't even wait that long. After enumerating the usual conditions for release, he gave the new sheriff a brief but pointed speech about the value of the court's time and suggested that he familiarize himself with the way things were done in Haven, because apparently it was different than what he was used to.

Kate didn't let herself feel sorry for Reid. But she did appreciate that he'd called the hearing, albeit reluctantly, and she said so as they walked side by side out of the courthouse. "Thank you."

"The next time I put your client in a cell, he's going to stay there a lot longer," Reid warned.

"There won't be a next time," she said. "Aiden really is a good kid who chose the wrong way to work through some stuff."

"By hanging out with a friend already on probation?"

"I don't know what he was doing with Trent Marshall," she admitted. "They don't usually run in the same circles."

"I'm guessing you represent the Marshall kid, too?"

She nodded. "And I'm curious as to how the kid already on probation walked away with a summons to court and the kid who's never been cited for jaywalking ends up locked in a cell."

"If you really want to know, I'll tell you—over dinner."

Chapter Four

Kate's mind was reeling. Not just because she was once again in close proximity to the sheriff, with whom she'd had the Best. Sex. Ever. a few weeks earlier, but because she now had to accept that the father of her baby wasn't fifteen hundred miles away but living in the same town.

"Dinner?" she echoed, and realized it could be the perfect opportunity to share her big—and growing—news.

"Traditionally the third and biggest meal of the day," he explained, amusement dancing in those hazel eyes.

"I understand the term," she assured him. "I was just… surprised…by your invitation."

"Surprised is okay," he decided. "But are you hungry?"

She realized that she was. The queasiness that left her feeling unsettled through most of the morning usually disappeared by lunch, and lunch had been a long time ago.

"I could eat," she finally responded to his question, determined not to allow the sexy sheriff's nearness stir other appetites.

"Good," he said. "I'd like to buy you dinner, but I'm going to ask you to decide where since I'm still finding my way around town."

"There are only three places in this town where you can get a decent meal," she told him. "The Sunnyside Diner, which does a great all-day breakfast but isn't so great with other menu options, Jo's Pizza, which makes the best thin crust pizza I've ever had—and their wings are pretty good, too—but eating in means nabbing one of only half a dozen tables crammed into a tiny space and no hope of a private conversation, and Diggers'."

"I've been to Diggers'," he told her. "The food was great."

"It is," she confirmed. "But we can't go there."

"Why not?"

"Because Diggers' is second only to The Daily Grind for gossip in Haven."

"You're worried people will talk about us sharing a meal?"

"I don't want to have to answer questions about how I'm acquainted with the new sheriff," she admitted.

"What's wrong with the truth?"

She shook her head. Now more than ever, she didn't want anyone to know that she'd met Reid in Boulder City, because when her pregnancy became apparent and people started counting backward, they'd suspect the baby had been conceived while she was out of town and she'd rather they didn't know that Haven's new sheriff had been there, too.

"Actually, I was referring to the other truth," he said. "That our paths crossed when you came to my office."

Which was a perfectly reasonable explanation. As an attorney, it made sense that she'd want to cultivate a good relationship with the new sheriff. But she also knew that

if she was seen in public with him, it would be all the excuse anyone else wanted or needed to interrupt their conversation to wrangle their own introductions.

"Except that it's Friday."

"And?" he prompted, obviously seeking clarification.

"And my sister, Skylar, works at Diggers' on the weekend," she admitted.

"We could pick up pizza and take it back to my place,"
he suggested as an alternative.

She hesitated. "Look, Sheriff, despite what happened
between us in Boulder City, I'm really not that kind of
girl."

"You're not the kind of girl who likes pizza?"

She managed a smile. "I'm not the kind of girl who
goes back to a guy's place—or invites him back to hers."

"I wasn't expecting to share anything more than pizza,"
he said, then shrugged. "Hoping, maybe, but not expecting."

The honest response undermined her resolve. "Why
don't I make something for dinner instead?" she impulsively offered.

"I'd never say no to a home-cooked meal."

"I'm not promising anything fancy," she warned. "But
you'll be able to eat and we'll be able to talk without a
thousand interruptions."

"That works for me," he agreed.

She glanced at her watch, then mentally calculated the
time she needed to make a quick trip to The Trading Post
before she could start cooking. "Seven o'clock?"

"Sure," he agreed.

"Okay, I'll see you then."

He caught her arm as she started to turn away. "Only
if you give me your address."

"Do you know where my office is?"

"You live at your office?"

"Above the office. Apartment 2B."

"I'll see you at seven."

Inviting Reid to have dinner at her place seemed like a good idea at the time—or, if not a good idea, at least a necessary compromise. They needed to talk and she didn't want to have the conversation where anyone might overhear it. But now that he was here, Kate realized she'd made a tactical error.

She loved her apartment—the ultramodern kitchen and open-concept living area with tall windows looking down on Main Street, two spacious bedrooms and a luxurious bathroom. Certainly, it had never seemed small—until Reid Davidson stepped inside. He wasn't a man whose presence was in any way, shape or form subtle, and it was as if he filled every square inch of space with his potent masculinity.

Being near him had her hormones clamoring so loudly she could barely hear herself think. And while her mind was desperately trying to focus on certain facts that needed to be discussed, her body was stirring, aching, wanting.

She took the bottle of wine he offered, and as her fingertips brushed against his, she was suddenly reminded of the way those fingers had touched her—the bold confidence of his hands as they stroked over her body, taking her to heights of pleasure she'd never even imagined.

He'd changed out of his sheriff's uniform and into a navy polo shirt that stretched across his broad shoulders. The hem of the shirt was tucked into a pair of softly faded jeans that hugged his lean hips and strong thighs, as her legs had hugged those hips and thighs, their naked limbs tangled and their bodies moving together.

She set the bottle of wine on the counter and turned to

dump the pasta in the pot of boiling water on the stove, hoping the steam would explain the sudden flush in her cheeks.

"Did you want wine or beer or something else?"

"I'd love a beer if you've got one handy," he said.

She stirred the pasta, then moved to the refrigerator to retrieve a bottle of Icky IPA. "Bottle or glass?" she asked as she pried off the cap.

"Bottle's fine."

Instead of taking the bottle she offered, he wrapped his hand around hers.

"What are you doing?" she asked warily.

"Trying to figure out why you invited me to dinner but haven't made eye contact since I walked through the door."

She lifted her gaze to meet his. "I'm just trying to get dinner finished up."

"Tell me what I can do to help," he suggested.

Go back to Echo Ridge.

The response immediately sprang to mind, but of course, she couldn't say the words aloud without then explaining why his sudden and unexpected appearance in Haven complicated her life.

Instead, she only said, "For starters, you could give me back my hand."

He loosened his grip so that she could pull her hand away without dropping the bottle. "What else?"

She gestured to the living area. "Go sit down."

"You don't trust me to help?"

"There's really nothing you can do," she told him.

"Do you want me to open the wine?"

She shook her head. "I'm going to stick with water—I've got work to do tonight." Which was true, if not the whole truth.

He took his beer and moved around to the other side

of the island. But instead of retreating to the living area and relaxing on the sofa, he chose one of the stools at the counter.

"So what do you think of Haven so far?" she asked, resigned to making small talk for eight minutes while the pasta cooked.

"I like it," he said. "It's a little smaller than Echo Ridge, but there's a strong sense of community here."

"There is," she confirmed, lowering the heat on the burner beneath the sauce. "Even when I was away at school, I knew I'd come back here after graduation."

"Summa cum laude from UCLA Law."

She frowned. "How'd you know that?"

"I met your grandmother," he confided.

"How? When?"

"Last weekend. I was walking down Main Street, trying to get a feel for the town, and our paths crossed. We had coffee together."

"You had coffee with my grandmother?"

He nodded. "She introduced me to Donna Bradley at The Daily Grind."

"You had coffee with my grandmother," she said again.

He studied her as he tipped his bottle to his lips, swallowed. "Why does that bother you?"

"It doesn't bother me," she denied. "But it's a little weird."

"Why?"

"Because she's my grandmother and you're…"

"The guy you had lots of naked sweaty sex with?"

"Okay, yes," she allowed.

"I didn't tell her about the naked sweaty sex," he promised.

"Thank you for that," she said drily.

He just grinned.

And that smile did strange things to her pulse…or maybe it was the heat from standing so close to the stove.

"But I haven't stopped thinking about it—or you," he continued. "I applied for the job before I met you, but you were definitely a factor in my decision to accept it."

"We weren't ever supposed to see one another again," she reminded him of the agreement they'd made in Boulder City.

"And yet, you went to Echo Ridge last weekend." The surprise must have shown on her face because he explained, "You left a message with Deputy Ryker."

She nodded. "A friend of mine from law school lives in Texas. Since I was there, I thought I'd stop by to say hi."

"Texas is a pretty big state."

"Chloe lives just outside of Dallas, so a side-trip to Echo Ridge wasn't really out of my way."

"Oh," he said, sounding disappointed. "I was kind of hoping you'd made the trip to see me."

The timer on the stove buzzed, granting her a temporary reprieve from the increasingly awkward conversation.

"Dinner's ready."

There was something on her mind.

Something more than concern about the client who'd brought her into his office a few hours earlier. When Luke Ryker told him that she'd shown up at the Sheriff's Office, he'd hoped it was memories of the nights they'd spent together that inspired Katelyn to track him down. But she certainly wasn't giving the impression of a woman motivated by carnal desires.

And though she kept up her end of the conversation while they ate, her thoughts were obviously elsewhere.

"Is it convenient or tiresome to live above your office?" he asked, attempting to engage her attention.

Katelyn twirled her fork in her pasta. "It's convenient," she said. "Certainly a lot more convenient than driving twenty miles into town from the Circle G Ranch every day."

He'd heard of the Circle G—reputedly the biggest and most prosperous cattle ranch in all of Haven County. It was also, if he remembered the story correctly, half of the property that was the original source of friction between the Gilmore and Blake families when they settled in the area more than one hundred and fifty years before.

According to local folklore, back in the spring of 1855, a developer sold a 100,000-acre parcel of land in Nevada to Everett Gilmore, a struggling farmer from Plattsmouth, Nebraska. The same developer also sold 100,000 acres to Samuel Blake, a down-on-his-luck businessman from Omaha. Both men subsequently packed up their families and their worldly possessions and headed west for a fresh start.

Everett Gilmore arrived first, and it was only when Samuel Blake showed up with his deed in hand that the two men realized they'd been sold the exact same parcel of land. Since both title deeds were stamped with the same date, there was no way of knowing who was the legitimate owner of the land. Distrustful of the local magistrate's ability to resolve the situation to anyone's satisfaction—and not wanting to publicly admit that they'd been duped—the two men agreed to share the property between them, using the natural divide of Eighteen-Mile Creek as the boundary between their lands.

Because the Gilmores had already started to build their home in the valley—on the west side of the creek—the Blakes were relegated to the higher elevation on the east, where the land was mostly comprised of rocky hills and ridges. The Gilmores' cattle immediately benefitted from grazing on more hospitable terrain, while the Blakes struggled for a lot of years to keep their herd viable—until silver and gold were found in the hills on their side of the creek and they gave up ranching in favor of mining.

"Is there any truth to that story about the ancestors of the Gilmore and Blake families coming to Nevada to settle the same piece of land?" he asked her now.

"It's all true," she assured him. "The Gilmores still own the fifty thousand acres on the west side of the creek and the Blakes own the fifty thousand acres, including all the gold and silver, on the east."

She put her fork down and picked up her glass of water. "You were going to tell me why Trent was given a court date and Aiden was locked up," she reminded him.

"Because Trent was a passenger in the car that Aiden was driving."

"Where'd they find the car?" she asked.

"Parked, with the key in the cup holder, in the driveway of the owner's house on Mountainview Road."

Katelyn shook her head. "Anyone who leaves, in plain view, the key to a fancy car deserves to have it stolen."

"I'll pretend I didn't hear you say that."

"How mad was Rebecca Blake when she realized her car had been taken?"

"Beyond mad," he admitted. "And more than a little embarrassed, because she knew that she'd left the key in it."

"She was at Elsie Hampton's funeral—and she's known Aiden since he was in diapers," Katelyn told him. "As mad and embarrassed as she was, I'm a little surprised that she wanted to press charges."

"It wasn't her choice," he said.

"You do know you'll never get a conviction on grand larceny, don't you? It would be a waste of time and resources to even take it to trial."

"That's an argument better saved for your discussions with the prosecutor," he suggested.

"Maybe it's different in Echo Ridge, but here the prosecutor doesn't usually make decisions about the disposition of charges without first consulting the Sheriff's Office."

"I investigated the complaint of a stolen vehicle and made the appropriate arrests," he said. "Now it's up to your pal in the ADA's office to decide what to do with the defendants."

"Dustin Perry's not my pal," she told him.

"I saw the two of you chatting while waiting for the judge. He seemed...favorably inclined toward you."

"You know, for a guy who was quick to point out that he's not a lawyer, you sound an awful lot like one at times."

He frowned. "Are you trying to spoil my appetite?"

She looked at his almost empty plate. "Not much chance of that."

"What can I say? This is great pasta," he said.

And it was. The red sauce had chunks of tomato, pepper and onion and was just a little bit spicy. But while he'd been mopping up sauce with a second slice of crusty bread, he noticed that she'd hardly touched her meal. She had her fork in hand and was pushing the pasta around on her plate, but she'd rarely lifted the utensil to her mouth.

"I didn't make anything for dessert, but I do have ice cream," she told him.

"What kind?"

She pushed her chair away from the table and went to open the freezer drawer below the refrigerator. Her appliances were all top of the line—as was everything else that he could see. Whoever had renovated the building had spared no expense in the dark walnut cupboards, natural granite countertops, marble tile and hardwood floors.

"Chocolate, chocolate 'n' peanut butter or chocolate chip cookie dough," she offered.

"Nothing with chocolate?" he asked drily.

A smile tugged at the corners of her mouth as she shrugged. "Sorry."

"Do you have cones?"

"No, but I have waffle bowls," she told him.

"Even better," he decided.

"What kind do you want?"

"Cookie dough."

She took the container out of the freezer and set it on the counter, then opened the cupboard and stood on her toes. "If they were more easily accessible, I'd indulge all the time," she explained, as she stretched toward the top shelf.

"If you didn't want to indulge, you wouldn't buy them," he commented, easily reaching over her head for the box.

She pulled open a drawer to retrieve an ice-cream scoop. "That's just the kind of logic I'd expect from a man."

He set the box on the corner, then lifted his hand to tuck an errant strand of hair behind her ear, his fingertip slowly tracing the outer shell.

The scoop slipped from her grasp, bounced on the counter.

"I don't remember you being skittish," he said.

She swallowed. "I'm not usually."

"So what has you strung so tight now?" he wondered aloud. "Are you worried that I'm going to make a move?" He stepped closer, so that she was trapped between the counter at her back and him at her front. "Or that I'm not?"

The pulse at the base of her jaw was racing, and her slightly parted lips—so tempting and soft—were mere inches from his own. Her gaze went to his mouth, lingered, as if she wanted his kiss as much as he wanted to kiss her.

Then she turned her head away and shifted to the left, sidestepping both him and his question.

"What's going on, Katelyn?" he pressed, because it was obvious that *something* was.

She nibbled on her bottom lip as she pried the lid off the ice-cream container.

"Katelyn?" he prompted, ignoring the caution lights that were flashing in his head.

Finally, she looked at him, her big blue eyes filled with wariness and worry. "I'm pregnant."

Chapter Five

She hadn't intended to blurt it out like that, but now that the words had been spoken, Kate actually felt relieved. It was no longer this big secret that she was keeping bottled up inside; she'd done the right thing and told Reid about the baby.

Now she just had to deal with his reaction, whatever that might be.

He reached behind him, his hands curling over the edge of the island countertop, as if he needed the support to remain standing. She understood how he felt—she was more than a little unsteady herself.

She moistened her lips with the tip of her tongue, waiting for him to say something, anything.

"You're sure?" he asked, after a long minute had passed.

She nodded. "I took one of those over-the-counter tests. Actually, I took three," she admitted. "And I got official confirmation from the doctor last week."

He went back to the table for his beer, tipped the bottle to his lips. "That's why you were in Echo Ridge," he realized. "Because you think it's mine."

Her cheeks burned with embarrassment, but she couldn't fault him for asking. She'd jumped into bed with him only a few hours after their first meeting—why wouldn't he assume that was normal behavior for her?

"I know it's yours," she told him. "You're the only man I've been with in…a long time. But considering how quickly everything happened between us, I can understand why you'd ask, why you'd want proof."

He fell silent again, and she found herself babbling in an effort to fill the silence.

"We can have a DNA test as soon as the baby's born. It's possible to do paternity testing before birth, through amniocentesis, but it also increases the risk of miscarriage and I'd rather not take the chance when there are no other factors that warrant it."

He nodded, but whether it was in agreement or understanding, she had no idea.

"I'm not asking anything of you," she hastened to reassure him. "I made the decision to have this baby on my own, and I intend to raise the baby on my own."

That, finally, got a response from him.

"You didn't make the baby on your own," he pointed out.

"Well, no," she agreed, her body humming in remembrance of the pleasures she'd experienced in his arms.

"And I don't shirk my responsibilities," he said with grim resolve.

"I appreciate that, Reid, but—"

He shook his head. "No buts, Katelyn."

She didn't know him well enough to have anticipated his response to the news—whether he'd be shocked or angry or disbelieving, but she'd tried to prepare for all those possibilities. So far, he hadn't responded with any recognizable emotion.

"I think we both need to take some time to think about what this means and where we want to go from here," she suggested cautiously.

Finally, he nodded. "That's probably a good idea."

She exhaled a quiet sigh of relief as she followed him to the door.

He paused with his hand on the knob. "If you need anything, give me a call."

"I will."

Then he leaned down and touched his lips to the top of her head. "Thanks for dinner, Katelyn."

The sweet gesture made her throat tighten. She closed her eyes against the sudden sting of tears as she shut the door behind him and flipped the lock.

Only eight days had passed since Dr. Amaro had confirmed her pregnancy, after which her first thought had been to track down Reid and let him know that she was going to have his baby. Traveling all the way to Echo Ridge only to discover that he wasn't there had been another emotional upheaval. She'd been filled with disappointment and frustration and, yes, relief.

It was as if she'd been given a reprieve, an opportunity to figure out what she wanted to do without having to factor her baby's father into the equation. Finding him in the Sheriff's Office in Haven was just one more surprise she hadn't been anticipating.

Working in family law had shown her that co-parenting could make things a lot easier—or a lot harder. She also knew that if Reid wanted to acknowledge paternity and be a father to their child, there was nothing she could do to stop him.

Was it any wonder that she was feeling exhausted and overwhelmed and terrified?

Because if he didn't want to be involved, she'd have to struggle through every step on her own. Not just pregnancy and childbirth, but midnight feedings, diaper rashes and teething woes. Then skinned knees and long division and, in later years, first dates and broken hearts and various other disappointments.

But she was equally terrified that he'd embrace fatherhood and she'd have to interact with him on an almost daily basis for the next eighteen years and beyond. The recent trend toward shared custody meant that he could be entitled to equal time with the baby who was right now nestled in the warm comfort of her womb. He would have an equal say in where their child went to school and what sports or activities he or she participated in.

And maybe they'd be in complete agreement about all those things—but what if they weren't?

She touched a hand to her still-flat stomach, awed and amazed to think that there was a tiny life growing inside her. A tiny life that would someday call her mama, then mommy and mom and eventually mother, accompanied by a preteen eye-roll.

She had no experience of her own to draw on after that. Theresa Gilmore had died when Kate was twelve, forcing her to negotiate the awkward teen years and all major transitions after that without her guidance. There were so many milestones that she'd marked without her mother's presence: graduation from high school, acceptance to law school, the unveiling of her name stenciled on her office window.

There were so many times over the years that she'd missed having her mom around, but never had she missed her support more than she did upon realizing that she was going to be a mother herself. And now, she was going to have to go through all the phases of pregnancy and child-birth without her, too.

Still, Kate knew she was lucky. Though her father wouldn't be happy to learn that his unmarried daughter was going to have a baby, she didn't doubt that he'd be supportive—or that he'd love his grandchild. Her grand-parents and sister and brothers would also be there any time she needed anything. And her best friend, Emerson, a recent new mother, would be able to offer advice and insights.

Despite all the support available to her, she was scared to death that she'd somehow screw this up.

And because her baby had been conceived with a man she barely knew, she'd have to work with him to figure out what was best for their child.

Oh, what a mess I've made of my life.

Except that she didn't really regret anything that had happened, because she already loved her baby more than she'd ever thought possible.

Returning to the kitchen to tidy up the dishes, she no-ticed the forgotten chocolate chip cookie dough on the counter. She dropped the unused scoop back in the cutlery drawer and took out a spoon. Then she sat down on the cold tile floor and dipped her spoon into the tub.

Because melting ice cream was at least one problem she knew how to solve.

Reid left her apartment with no concept of where he was going or what he was going to do.

Katelyn Gilmore was pregnant—with his child—and he was completely unprepared to be a father.

It wasn't just bad timing. He wasn't one of those guys who always thought he'd be a father "someday" but had to accept that the day would come sooner than anticipated. No, years earlier Reid had consciously decided that he wouldn't ever have a child. He'd even considered having surgery to ensure it couldn't happen, except that the prospect of going under the knife was daunting and condoms were readily available.

But fate had apparently decided to kick that conscious decision to the curb. It was as if all the stars had aligned to screw him over with a broken condom.

Not that he'd ever put much stock in fate or the alignment of stars, but when his ex-wife had met her current husband, she told Reid that fate had put Jonah in her path. He'd countered with skepticism, pointing out that the hand of destiny—if there was such a thing—had better things to do than muck around in the computers at 4evermatch.com. Trish would no doubt get a huge kick out of his current predicament, claiming it was karma because he'd disrespected the higher powers of the universe.

Not that he intended to tell Trish—or anyone else. At least not until he and Katelyn had figured out what they were going to do.

For now, he just started walking. He didn't want to go home. He didn't want to be alone, because then he'd have to think about the news Katelyn had dropped in his lap. He'd have to acknowledge that, all conscious decision-making and careful planning aside, he was going to be a father.

He walked with no clear destination in mind, past the shops and businesses that lined Main Street. He lifted his hand in greeting when Reggie Mann—owner and operator of Mann's Movie Theater—called out to him, but he didn't pause. He didn't want to make conversation; he didn't want to make friends.

What he wanted, he realized as he approached Diggers' Bar & Grill, was to get so rip-roaring drunk he could no longer hear the words that continued to echo in his head. Of course, he'd never let the residents of Haven see their sheriff in such a state, but he was off duty and out of uniform, so he figured it was okay to have a drink or two.

The double doors opened into an enclosed foyer that housed two entrances. The one on the left was clearly marked Bar and the one on the right designated Grill. Once inside it was easy enough to move from one side to the other, as both were under the same roof with only a partial wall dividing them, but it allowed families to take their kids for a meal without having to walk through a bar to get to a table.

The interior was deliberately rustic, with floors of unpainted, weathered wood slats, scuffed and scarred from the steady traffic of boot heels. Framed newspaper headlines proclaiming the discovery of gold and silver in the nearby hills hung on the walls along with miners' helmets, metal pans, buckets, coils of rope, pickaxes and a few other items that he had no idea what they were but hoped were securely fastened, because some of them had the potential to be lethal weapons otherwise.

Reid's first day on the job, Jed Traynor had taken him through the door on the right to Diggers' Grill for lunch. Tonight, he went through the door on the left.

There were several patrons already seated at the bar—some of them watching the baseball game on the two big screens, a young couple snuggled close together sharing a plate heaped with cheesy nachos, a trio of older men focused on their drinks.

He straddled a vacant stool and surveyed the labels on the taps in front of him. Not that it really mattered which one he chose—after a few, they all tasted pretty much the same. And his only purpose in being here right now was to drink until his brain was fuzzy enough to let him forget he was going to be a dad.

The irony of the situation was not lost on him. His marriage had fallen apart because he didn't want to have a child with his wife. Now he was going to have a child with a woman he barely knew. And while the situation wasn't what he would have chosen, Katelyn's pregnancy took choice out of the equation.

Maybe it's not mine.

The thought sneaked into his mind, seductively tempting.

But over the years, he'd gotten adept at reading people, and nothing Katelyn had said or done had given him reason to suspect she wasn't being honest with him.

I know it's yours. You're the only man I've been with in...a long time.

And if he needed any more evidence that he could plausibly be the father of her baby, there was the broken condom.

That had created a moment of panic for both of them, but they'd managed to convince themselves that the odds of a faulty bit of latex coinciding with her fertile time were negligible. And they'd put the broken condom out of their minds and made love several more times after that, without any further mishaps, unable to get enough of one another. He hadn't been so hot for any female since he was a teenager and the sight of Lana Doucet in skintight jeans and a clingy sweater was enough to give him a hard-on.

But there was something about Katelyn—from the minute she'd walked through the door of that conference room, he'd wanted her. He'd been sure it was his lucky day when she agreed to have a drink with him. When she invited him back to her room, he'd felt like the luckiest man in the world.

Apparently his luck had run out.

One of the bartenders, an attractive blonde with blue eyes and an easy—almost familiar—smile, made her way down the bar. Reid studied her for a minute, wondering if he'd already met her in town. If he had, he couldn't remember when or where.

"What can I get for you?" she asked.

"I'll have a pint of the Sierra Nevada Pale Ale."

She grabbed a glass from the shelf but paused before setting it under the tap. "Are you sure you don't want something stronger?"

"What?"

"You've got the look of a man who needs a shot—or two dozen—of strong whiskey."

He'd never been the type to turn to the bottle, but he'd never been faced with a situation of such magnitude. "Maybe you're right," he acknowledged. "What do you recommend?"

She replaced the glass and selected a bottle, holding it up for his approval.

Reid nodded and she poured a generous two fingers of Maker's Mark into a whiskey glass, then set the drink on a paper coaster in front of him. "Anything you want to talk about?"

He shook his head. He not only wasn't ready to talk about Katclyn's disclosure, he didn't want to think about it. But even if he wanted to talk, he knew better than to say a word to anyone in this town where everyone seemed to know the Gilmore family.

"I've been told that I'm a good listener," the bartender said to him, her smile encouraging.

"By anyone who wasn't drunk?"

She laughed. "As a matter of fact, yes."

"Well, I have a confession… I've never been told that I'm a good talker."

"Maybe this will help," she said, and poured him another drink.

He stared at the amber liquid in his glass, tempted to throw it back. Then another and another. Until he finally managed to drown out the echo of Katelyn's voice in his head.

I'm pregnant. I'm pregnant. I'm pregnant.

"Do you have a name? Or should I just call you Mister-Not-A-Good-Talker?" the bartender asked.

"Reid," he said.

"Are you new in town, Reid, or just passing through?"

"New in town," he said.

"From…Texas?" she guessed.

He nodded.

"Which would make you the new sheriff."

He nodded again.

"Well, you're a definite upgrade from the old sheriff," she remarked. "I mean, Jed's a nice guy and all, but when women sigh over a man in uniform, they aren't sighing over men like Jed. But you, on the other hand—yeah, women would sigh over you."

He looked up from his drink. "Are you flirting with me?"

"Me?" She seemed genuinely surprised by the question. "No." Then, more emphatically. "God, no."

He lifted a brow.

"Sorry," she said. "I didn't mean to sound quite so vehement, I just didn't realize that you would assume… Although now that I'm replaying the words in my mind, of course you assumed I was flirting with you. But the truth is, I was thinking about someone who hasn't sighed over a man in a long time." She shook her head. "Now it sounds like I'm covering up for my own fumbling attempts at flirting with you, and I'm not, and I'm sorry if I've made you uncomfortable."

"You haven't," he assured her.

"But now I have a question that might," she warned. "What's your relationship status?"

"My relationship status?"

She nodded. "Are you married, engaged or otherwise involved?"

"If you're not flirting with me, how is my relationship status at all relevant?" he wondered.

"I'll tell you the relevance if you tell me your status."

"Are you sure you're not flirting with me?"

"You're cute, Sheriff, but you're not my type. You are, however, the type of guy I can imagine my sister totally going for."

"Thank you, I think. As for my relationship status… there might be a wedding in my not-too-distant future."

"That sucks," she said. "Oh—not for you, of course. It's great for you. But it's not easy to meet guys in this town, especially when your last name is Gilmore, and Katie hasn't had a date in… I don't even know how long."

"Wait a minute." Reid held up a hand. "Did you say your last name is Gilmore?"

She nodded.

"And your sister's name is Katie—or Katelyn?"

She nodded again, confirming his suspicion that everyone in town knew the Gilmores—or *was* a Gilmore.

"Then you must be Skylar."

Her gaze narrowed suspiciously. "How would you know that?"

"Because I know your sister."

"You do?"

"In fact—" he lifted his glass of whiskey, as if making a toast "—she's the woman I'm going to marry."

Chapter Six

Kate was already in her pajamas when her cell phone chimed to announce a text message. She wanted to ignore it. She wanted to burrow under the covers and fall into a deep and dreamless sleep to forget—for at least a few hours—that her entire life was about to change.

Of course, she couldn't do that—at least not without checking the message first to ensure it wasn't a family emergency or a client crisis or anything else that required an immediate response. She paused the baseball game on TV and picked up her phone.

She felt a quick spurt of panic when she read the message and keyed a quick response. Then, after exchanging her pajama bottoms for a pair of yoga pants and tugging a hoody over her T-shirt, she headed out.

Eight minutes after leaving her apartment, she was walking into Diggers'.

Haven was only one of three cities in the whole state of

Nevada where gambling was prohibited, which meant that weekends saw a regular exodus of residents who sought more exciting opportunities than those available within city limits. For those who opted to stay, Diggers' was a popular destination.

Tonight, the local watering hole was doing a brisk business, with most of the seats at the bar occupied. Right now, Kate's sister was simultaneously pouring drinks, taking cash and flirting with several customers. A lot of people knew Dave Gilmore's youngest daughter worked weekends as a bartender at Diggers'—only a handful knew that she was a masters candidate who tended bar not just for tips and fun but to observe human behavior.

Kate spotted Reid right away, sitting between Oscar Weston, a local mechanic who was sipping his usual Budweiser straight from the bottle, and a couple of younger guys sipping scotch, neat, and arguing over the validity of the umpire's call in the same baseball game she'd been watching at home. Despite the presence of other patrons around him, it was apparent that Reid was alone and wanted to be that way.

She squeezed herself between the stools and leaned an elbow on the bar. "Hey, Sheriff."

"Katelyn?" He blinked at her, as if he was having trouble focusing. "What are you doing here?"

"I got a text from my sister, asking me why a drunk guy at the bar believed he was going to marry me." She kept her voice low to ensure their conversation wouldn't be overheard.

"Because I am," he asserted. "And I'm not drunk."

She looked at the empty whiskey glass on the coaster in front of him. "How many of those have you had?"

"Three?" He nodded his thanks to Skylar when she set a mug of coffee in front of him. "I was celebrating."

"What were you celebrating?"

"My impending nuptials," he said, the relatively co-herent pronunciation suggesting that he wasn't as inebri-ated as she'd feared. On the other hand, his brain had to be addled by alcohol if he was thinking a wedding was anywhere in their future. "Not only am I getting married, but I'm going to be—"

She pressed a hand to his mouth, anticipating and si-lencing the rest of his words.

"It's a secret?"

She nodded and let her hand drop away.

He lifted the mug to his mouth, watching her over the rim as he sipped his coffee. "You are so incredibly beauti-ful. I thought I remembered what you looked like, but when you walked into my office… Was that today? Yesterday?"

"Today," she confirmed.

"When you walked into my office today, you took my breath away."

"Are you sure you've only had three whiskeys?"

He swallowed another mouthful of coffee. "Pretty sure," he said. "And though I wouldn't attempt to operate a motor vehicle right now, I promise I haven't had enough alcohol to impair my vision."

"Finish your coffee," she suggested. "And I'll take you home."

He dutifully picked up the cup again. "I've been think-ing about you for weeks," he confided. "Dreaming about you."

She shot a quick glance to the left and then the right, but no one seemed to be paying any attention to their con-versation.

"In fact, I haven't stopped thinking about you since you walked into that conference room in Boulder," he continued. Then he shook his head. "No, it was Boulder City, wasn't it?"

She rolled her eyes. "And now you're in Haven, and I need to know where you live so I can get you home."

"133 Chicory Drive."

She was familiar with the street and mentally placed the number. "Norm and Beverly Clayton's place?"

He nodded. "I'm renting the basement apartment."

Which Kate knew had been an in-law suite where Beverly's mom had lived for a lot of years. After she broke her hip and needed to go into a long-term care facility, Norm and Beverly had periodically offered the space for rent.

"Let's get you back there and into bed," Kate suggested.

"If you want me in bed, you only need to ask."

She shook her head, but she couldn't hold back the smile that curved her lips. "Even drunk you can't turn off the charm, can you?"

"Am I charming the pants off you?"

"You already did," she reminded him. "That's why you were trying to drink yourself into oblivion."

Reid didn't tell her again that he wasn't drunk. He just paid his tab, adding a generous tip for the bartender, and let Kate lead him away.

She automatically turned south when they stepped out of the bar. "Where'd you park?"

"I didn't drive, I walked."

He stopped in the middle of the sidewalk. "You're not walking me to my apartment, then walking back, alone, to yours."

"Reid, I've lived in Haven my whole life—I have no concerns about being out on my own after dark."

"But you thought I needed an escort home?"

"Sky's message led me to believe that you were more intoxicated than you apparently are."

"Now that you know I'm not, I'll walk you home," he decided, turning in the opposite direction.

"Fine," she agreed, falling into step beside him. "We'll walk back to my apartment and then I'll drive you to yours."

She turned at the corner of Page Street, then again into the parking lot behind her building. She hit the button on her key fob to unlock the doors, then climbed behind the wheel as he went around to the passenger side of the SUV.

"Why'd you come to the bar?" he asked.

"Because if you get stumbling-down drunk, people are going to gossip and speculate, and I'll feel responsible."

"Why would you feel responsible?" he asked.

She started the car and pulled out of her parking space. "Because I turned your world upside down tonight."

"Yeah, you did," he acknowledged. "And I turned yours upside down by launching super swimmers into your fallopian tubes."

She laughed softly as she turned onto Second Street. "I have to admit, I've never heard the fertilization process described in quite that way."

"I'm just trying to point out that we're both responsible for what happened—and the consequences."

"You're right," she said. "But I can't help wondering if you might have made a different decision about coming to Haven if you'd known I was pregnant."

He shook his head. "I wouldn't have made a different decision," he assured her. "I wouldn't—I don't—want to be anywhere else.

"Well, except maybe a different apartment," he acknowledged as she pulled into his driveway.

"What's wrong with the apartment?" she asked.

He just shook his head. "You have to see it to believe it."

Her gaze narrowed suspiciously. "If you're trying to get me into your bedroom…"

He shook his head. "It's the living room—and the kitchen—you have to see."

She turned off the ignition.

He led her to the side of the house, where there was a separate entrance to his apartment, and unlocked the door.

Kate was still wary, but she followed him inside.

"It's very open," she noted. "Lots of space and natural light. And the decor is…interesting."

"I was looking for a place that was furnished," he explained. "And although I'm not actually allergic to flowers, I want to sneeze every time I walk in here."

She nodded. "There are a lot of flowers."

It wasn't just that the sofa and chairs were covered in bold floral fabrics, but the coffee table, end tables, desk, filing cabinet and lamps were all painted with cabbage roses and daisies and tulips.

"I heard that Beverly took a tole painting class a few years back," Katelyn told him. "I didn't realize how much she obviously enjoyed it."

"There are flowers everywhere," he said. "The kitchen table is covered—I thought it was one of those doily things and figured I could fold it up and put it in the linen closet. But it's painted right on."

She went through the living area to the kitchen to examine the table.

"It's really very well done," she noted, tracing a finger along the delicate edge of the "lace."

"I don't know how long I can live like this," he confided.

"Some women like a man who's in touch with his feminine side."

"I'd rather be in touch with a woman's feminine side."

His response was so predictably defensive, she couldn't help but smile. "Why does that not surprise me?"

"You have a really great smile," he told her. "Every time you smile at me…even when you're not smiling, every time I see you… I don't know how to describe what happens inside me, but I look at you, and I want you."

"You're definitely feeling the effects of that whiskey now," she said, unwilling to admit—even to herself—the powerfully seductive effect his words had on her.

"Why are you so determined to deny what's between us?"

"The only thing between us is the baby that resulted from a broken condom."

"Do you really believe that?"

There was something in his tone, just the slightest hint of an edge that should have set off warning bells in her head, but she was so determined to prove her point, she ignored the signs. "It's true, Reid, what happened in—"

That was as far as she got before his mouth came down on hers.

And if he was under the influence of the alcohol he'd drunk, it certainly didn't affect his aim or impact his skill.

The first time they'd kissed, she'd discovered that Reid was a patient and thorough man. Kissing wasn't just foreplay to him but an incredibly sensual experience that turned her on more than she'd ever thought a kiss could do.

The same focus and skill that had seduced her then was seducing her now. The rational part of her brain told her that this shouldn't be happening, but all rationality was drowned out by the clamoring needs of her body.

She hadn't consciously parted her lips, but suddenly his tongue was dancing with hers, leading it in a sensual rhythm that promised more, so much more. Liquid warmth began to spread through her body, pool between her thighs.

His hands slid under her hoody and skimmed up her

sides. She could feel the heat of his touch through the thin fabric of her T-shirt. His palms brushed the sides of her breasts, and paused when he realized she wasn't wearing a bra.

She held her breath, waiting to see what he would do next. She knew what she *should* do—push him away, say good-night and walk out the door. But her brain and her body clearly wanted different things, and it had only taken one kiss to remind her of the pleasures she'd experienced in his arms. Pleasures she wanted to experience again.

Suddenly his hands were stroking boldly over her bare skin, stoking the fire that was already burning inside her. His callused thumbs scraped over her nipples, making her gasp as arrows of pleasure shot to her core.

He tore his mouth from hers only long enough to yank her hoody and T-shirt up and over her head and toss them aside. Then he was kissing and touching her again, and it was all she wanted, but somehow not enough.

Desperate to touch him as he was touching her, she tugged his shirt out of his jeans and let her hands explore the rippling muscles of his stomach, chest and shoulders. There was just something about those shoulders that made her crazy.

His lips eased away from hers to rain kisses along her jawline…down her throat…across her collarbone…over the curve of her breast. Then they fastened around her peaked nipple and drew it into his mouth, and her knees almost buckled. But Reid's arm was around her back, holding her close. Her fingers dug into his broad, strong shoulders so hard her nails had to be scoring his skin. He merely shifted his attention to the other breast.

"Reid."

It was all she said, all she could manage with so many wants and needs battering at her from all directions.

He lifted his head from her breast, but his hands immediately took over where his mouth had left off, teasing and tweaking the hard buds. In the past few weeks, she'd noticed that her breasts were a little more sensitive than usual—a not uncommon effect of early pregnancy. Apparently they were even more sensitive than she'd realized, because Reid's touch had pushed her almost to the point of climax.

"Do you have any idea how much I want you?" he asked.

She could feel the press of his erection against her belly, and the answering heat spread through her veins, making her eyes cross. "I hope it's half as much as I want you."

His eyes, hot and dark, locked on hers.

"If you're going to tell me to stop, you better say it now," he warned.

She could only shake her head. "I don't want you to stop." She slid a hand between their bodies, stroking him through denim. "I want you."

He sucked in a breath. "You're killing me here, Katelyn."

"Don't tell the sheriff." She tugged on his belt. "He'll lock me up."

"That scenario does hold some appeal," he admitted.

She nibbled on his bottom lip. "Let's get you out of these clothes," she suggested, carefully working the straining zipper over the bulge of his erection.

"And you out of yours," he agreed.

Of course, she was just wearing yoga pants, so he had the easier task. He hooked his thumbs in the waistband and slid them over her hips and down her legs.

"You said you didn't want to go near my bedroom," he reminded her.

"And I wouldn't want to be accused of lying," she said, tumbling with him onto the sofa.

There was laughter and frustration as he tried to wriggle out of his clothes with her body draped over his, but eventually they were both naked and panting, desperate for one another.

"Katelyn—"

She didn't know what else he was going to say, but she suspected she didn't want to hear it, so she took a page out of his book and silenced his words with her mouth. She kissed him long and slow and deep, and while she was kissing him, she positioned her knees on either side of his hips, then eased her lips from his and pulled back so that his erection was poised at the juncture of her thighs.

She was hot and wet for him, her insides trembling with the anticipation of taking his hard length deep inside her, but apparently she still had a few working brain cells because she hesitated. "I know there's no point in worrying about birth control but—"

"I haven't been with anyone else since we were together," he told her. "I haven't wanted anyone but you. But I do have condoms in the—"

He stopped talking when she tilted her hips. She took the tip of him inside her...then a little bit more. Deliberately drawing out his pleasure...and her own. Until he was finally...completely...deeply inside her.

She closed her eyes, relishing the sensations that were zinging through her system like a thousand tiny little balls inside an out-of-control pinball machine.

Reid gave her a minute to adjust to his size and presence, then he lifted his hips, moving inside her. Slowly at first, establishing an even and steady rhythm...then faster...harder. And those erotic sensations continued to build and multiply until...it was too much.

And everything inside her shattered.

Chapter Seven

Reid woke up naked and alone.

He was sprawled on the flowered sofa with his clothes strewn around the floor, proof that his recollection of the previous evening was more than a dream.

If he'd had any doubts that his memories were hotter than the reality of getting naked with Katelyn, last night's sofa sex had laid them to rest.

Unfortunately, waking up and finding her gone suggested that they still had some issues to resolve. Remembering that she was pregnant multiplied those issues and amplified the importance of finding a resolution.

He made his way to the bathroom, cranking up the hot water in the shower in the hope that it would help clear some of the cobwebs from his brain. He braced his forearms on the ceramic tile as the spray pounded against his back, and he acknowledged that nothing could change the simple and basic facts:

Katelyn was pregnant.

And he was the father of her baby.

Since the idea of drinking himself into oblivion hadn't succeeded, he needed a plan B.

Unfortunately, the only possible fix he could see for this impossible situation was marriage. He vaguely recalled mentioning the idea to Katelyn last night— and that she'd responded with little enthusiasm.

He wasn't exactly thrilled by the prospect, either, but he didn't see any other choice. He'd been taught to take responsibility for his actions, even—and especially—when the consequences were uncomfortable. And marrying the mother of his child was the right thing to do.

He was still freaked out about the idea of being a father—a job for which he had no skills and even less experience—but he could see only one path forward. Maybe it was old-fashioned to want his son or daughter to grow up with two parents, but that was what Reid wanted for his child. The very thing he himself had been denied.

Which meant that he had a major task ahead: convincing Katelyn to marry him.

Kate woke up in her own bed and wanting coffee— desperately.

Dr. Amaro had assured her that she didn't need to give up caffeine completely but had suggested that she cut back to twelve ounces a day. Kate honestly didn't know how much she usually drank—she'd never worried about keeping track before. Her first cup was always at home in the morning, to help kick her brain into gear as she got ready for work, and throughout the day, there was usually a cup within arm's reach on her desk. If she was in court, recess meant a quick trip to the courthouse café for a vanilla latte.

But since she'd vowed to reduce her caffeine intake,

she'd been starting her mornings with a cup of herbal tea instead. She had yet to find a flavor that put her in a good mood to start the day. Today's pick—lemon ginger—was supposed to help combat nausea, but it had a distinctly medicinal taste that wasn't at all appealing. She took another sip and made a mental note to pick up some decaf coffee later. She'd never understood why anyone would drink decaf—what was the point of coffee without caffeine?—but under the circumstances, she thought she might give it a try.

In the meantime, she was going to have to sort out the mess she'd made of her life without the boost of caffeine.

Every decision she made from now on had to take into account not only what she wanted but what was best for the baby she was carrying. She had no idea how sex with Reid fit into that equation. Obviously getting naked with him had been a mistake, even if it had felt really good at the time.

Which wasn't something she should be thinking about right now, so when Sky walked in, Kate was so grateful for the distraction that she didn't think to wonder what her sister was doing in town on a Saturday morning.

Completely at home in Kate's apartment, Sky took a mug from the cupboard and set it under the spout of the coffee maker, then selected a coffee pod and dropped it into the machine. "Is he here?" she asked.

"Is who here?" Kate wondered.

Her sister grinned. "Sheriff Hottie."

She shook her head. "No. Of course he's not here."

"I don't know if I'm relieved or disappointed," her sister admitted.

"Relieved," Kate decided for her.

"There are times when I wish I could be more like you—every aspect of my life ordered and compartmentalized," Sky said. "But there are other times that I worry because your life is so ordered and compartmentalized."

Maybe that had been true before, but her impulsive actions in Boulder City had changed everything. "It's too early in the morning for deep philosophical musings," she protested.

"You need a guy who will shake up your life."

Reid Davidson had undeniably done that, but she still felt compelled to take issue with her sister's phraseology. "I don't need a guy at all."

"You're right." Sky nodded in acknowledgment even as her lips curved. "But you want him."

Since her sister would see right through any effort to deny it, she didn't even try. "Only because I always want what isn't good for me—like Sweet Caroline's caramel fudge brownie cheesecake."

"Mmm," Sky agreed, stirring sugar into her mug. "And why isn't that good for you?"

Kate breathed in deeply, as if the scent of her sister's coffee might be enough to jolt her sluggish brain. "Because one little slice has about a gazillion calories."

"Calories you could burn off with Sheriff Hottie," Sky suggested, taking a seat at the island.

Kate just shook her head. "Not going to happen."

Not again.

Of course, she hadn't intended for it to happen last night, either, but something happened whenever Reid touched her. A hormonal surge that short-circuited her brain, making her body spark like a live wire, humming and crackling with the electricity zipping through it.

She reached into the bread bag, retrieved two slices and slid them into the toaster, focusing intently on the task so she didn't have to look at her sister. Because just the memory of Reid's touch caused her blood to heat and pulse in her veins, and she could feel the warmth spread into her cheeks. "Do you want toast?"

"No, thanks, I ate at home. Martina made huevos rancheros this morning," she said, referring to the Circle G's longtime housekeeper.

"Lucky you." Though just the thought of eggs and chorizo sausage smothered in spicy salsa was enough to make Kate's stomach pitch.

"So," Sky said, when she realized her sister was watching her bread crisp, "are you going to explain to me what that whole 'I'm going to marry your sister' thing was about?"

Kate reached into the cupboard for a plate as the toast popped up. "It was clearly the rambling of a drunk man."

Sky seemed to consider the explanation as she sipped her coffee. "I can believe that alcohol was a factor in causing him to blurt out the declaration, but I suspect he had a reason to be hearing wedding bells. Which leads me to believe that either the new sheriff doesn't always live in the land of sane people or he's the guy you got naked with at that conference in Boulder City."

One of the best things about having a sister was that she could tell her anything. One of the worst things about having a sister was that she told her—and her best friend, Emerson—everything. And they forgot nothing.

"He's the guy I got naked with in Boulder City," she admitted, nibbling on the edge of a piece of toast.

And last night.

But there was no way she was going to share *that* information. It was one thing to confide that she'd had earth-moving sex with a guy her sister didn't know and was never expected to meet, and something entirely different to admit she'd done the deed with the man who was the new sheriff in town.

"And he immediately fell so head over heels in love with you that he decided to apply for Jed Traynor's job so that he could convince you to marry him?" Sky suggested dubiously.

"No. He applied for the position before we met. And I didn't know he was the new sheriff until I went to his office yesterday to discuss a case."

"How's Aiden doing?" Sky asked, proving that Kate's efforts to honor her client's confidentiality were for naught in a town where everyone knew everyone else's business.

"You know I can't talk to you about a client—or even confirm the identity of a client."

"You don't need to confirm it—his dad was overheard talking to Glenn Davis at the hardware store, and he said that you're the reason his son isn't stuck in a jail cell this weekend."

She sighed. "How am I supposed to maintain solicitor-client privilege if my clients—or clients' parents—don't keep their own mouths shut?"

"Okay, I won't ask any more questions about Aiden," Sky promised. "Which brings us back to the new sheriff, his proposal and your baby."

Kate sucked in a breath, then sputtered and coughed on the toast crumbs lodged in her throat.

Sky started to rise, but Kate held up a hand—holding her sister off—and swallowed a mouthful of lukewarm tea.

"Are you okay?" Sky asked.

She cleared her throat and nodded. "Yeah, you just… Where did that that idea about a baby come from?"

"It comes from knowing you, Kate. You're not drinking coffee, you're nibbling on dry toast—and you look like you're having trouble even keeping that down. Not to mention that most guys don't propose after a single weekend with a woman, so I figured Sheriff Hottie had to have a pretty good reason for doing so."

"Okay, you're right," she finally acknowledged. "I'm pregnant."

"You're going to be a mom," Sky said quietly, almost reverently. Then she grinned. "And I'm going to be an auntie." She hopped off her seat and embraced her sister. "I'm going to be the best auntie in the world—I promise."

"You can start by not telling anyone else about my pregnancy," Kate told her.

"I won't tell anyone," Sky assured her. "But how long do you think you can keep it a secret?"

"I don't know, but I just found out myself last week," she admitted.

"And told the sheriff last night—before he wandered into Diggers'," her sister guessed.

She nodded.

"Are you going to say yes?"

"He didn't actually ask me to marry him, Sky."

"But he will."

"How can you possibly know something like that?" Kate challenged.

"I study human behavior," Sky reminded her. "And the new sheriff is the type of man who truly believes it's his duty to serve and protect, and that sense of responsibility extends not just to the residents of his town but even more so to the people he cares about. He's honorable, upstanding and just traditional enough to believe that marrying the mother of his child is the right thing to do."

"No one rushes to the altar because of an unplanned pregnancy in this day and age," Kate reasoned.

"I'm going to offer you a piece of advice, anyway."

"What's that?" she asked warily.

"If you decide to marry him, let Dad walk you down

the aisle—don't run off to Vegas like Caleb and Brielle did," Sky cautioned.

Their brother's impulsive and short-lived marriage was rarely discussed—and never within earshot of their father.

"Dad wasn't mad that they went to Vegas to get married—he was furious that his son had knocked up a Blake." Although technically Brielle was a Channing, her mother was a Blake, which meant, for all intents and purposes, she was a Blake, too—and, therefore, an enemy of the Gilmores.

"But I promise that I won't run off to Vegas to get married," Kate said to her sister now. "Because I have no intention of getting married."

"Maybe you don't," Sky acknowledged. "But I wouldn't bet against Sheriff Hottie on anything."

Reid wanted to respect Katelyn's request for space, but considering that she'd asked for time before he'd left her apartment Friday night—and before they'd gotten naked together again, he figured that action wiped the slate clean.

Recalling her grandmother's mention of Saturday appointments, he tried her office first.

He walked in just as Katelyn was escorting a client to the door. There was no one else waiting in the reception area and the desk that he assumed belonged to a secretary or assistant was vacant.

Still, she didn't acknowledge him until her client had gone. "Did we have a meeting scheduled, Sheriff Davidson?"

"Nothing definite, Lawyer Gilmore."

She smiled at that, just a little.

He held up the manila envelope in his hand. "I have the discovery documents in the Johansen case for you."

She frowned as she took the envelope and lifted the flap.

"The Johansen case?" She pulled out the sheaf of blank papers, then looked at him.

He shrugged. "I figured I should have a pretext to justify my presence at your office."

"Very clever," she said.

"Was that your last appointment?" he asked.

"It was," she confirmed.

"Do you want to grab some lunch?"

"I appreciate the invitation," she said. "But I thought you were going to take some time to think about the situation."

"I've done nothing else since you told me that you're having my baby," he said.

"Why are you suddenly so willing to believe the baby's yours?"

"I wasn't disbelieving so much as stunned," he told her. "When you invited me to your place for dinner, the last thing I expected was for you to say that you were pregnant. And we weren't careless. I've *never* been careless."

"Neither have I," she said.

"I guess it's true that condoms are only ninety-eight percent effective."

"I could have lived a happy and fulfilling life without ever being proof of that statistic."

"And yet, here we are," he said.

"Here we are," she agreed. "And while I appreciate your willingness to charge full speed ahead, I'm not sure the revelation of my pregnancy has fully registered. I only told you about the baby—" she glanced at the watch on her wrist, did a quick mental calculation "—eighteen hours ago, and you were drunk for several of those."

His lips curved in a slow smile as his gaze skimmed over her. "We both know I wasn't drunk last night, Katelyn."

She turned away from him and slid the "documents" he'd given her into the paper tray of the printer beside the reception desk.

"But you're right," he acknowledged. "I didn't take the news well at first. On the other hand, it was the first time a woman's ever told me that she was going to have my baby, so I'm sorry I didn't know the right thing to say or do."

"It was the first time I've ever told a man he was the father of my child, so I might not have handled it the best way, either."

"But when I woke up this morning—alone and naked," he said, with another pointed look at her, "I was resolved."

"Resolved?" she echoed warily.

"To do the right thing."

She shook her head. "We can't get married, Reid—we hardly know each other."

"Living together as husband and wife will change that quickly enough," he told her.

She huffed out a breath. "I told you about the baby because I thought you had a right to know, but I don't want anything from you. As far as I'm concerned, no one else ever needs to know you're the father."

"Which proves your point that we don't know each other," he said. "Because if you knew me, you'd know that I'm not going to walk away from my child—or the child's mother."

Kate lowered herself into Beth's chair and pressed her fingers to her temples, as if that might alleviate the pounding inside her head. She hadn't expected that it would be easy to tell Reid about her pregnancy. She'd been prepared for him to question the paternity of her baby, and she'd expected that he'd need some time to accept the truth of what she was saying. She hadn't been prepared for him to jump from questioning to acceptance in the blink of an eye—and she hadn't expected him to jump from acceptance to marriage at all.

She felt his hands come down on her shoulders, and she jumped.

"Relax, Katelyn," he said, and began to massage gently.

It was easy for him to say—not so easy for her to do. He'd called her skittish the night before, and she couldn't disagree. She was certainly excitable whenever he was near.

And when he touched her, as he was touching her now, she melted. Which was precisely why she shouldn't let him touch her.

But she couldn't bring herself to ask him to stop. She didn't want him to stop. She wanted—

She abruptly severed the thought, unwilling to acknowledge her latent erotic desires.

"I know this isn't what either of us planned, but we're in it together now," he said, as he continued to loosen her muscles.

She wanted to believe it was true. Since the doctor confirmed her pregnancy, she'd felt alone and overwhelmed.

But it wasn't just her baby, it was his baby, too. And if he really wanted to be a *we*, there was part of her that couldn't help but think it would be easier than *me*.

But co-parenting suggested a level of relationship she wasn't ready for, and marriage was several levels beyond that.

"Why aren't you running away as far and fast as you can?" she wondered aloud.

"Because I don't shirk my responsibilities."

She turned the chair so that she was facing him, forcing his hands to drop away. "If you were one of my clients, I'd tell you to demand a paternity test."

"Why would I do that when you told me there's zero chance anyone else could be the father?" he asked.

"Because you shouldn't take my word for it," she protested. "I could be manipulating you for financial gain— or attempting to finagle a marriage proposal."

"I do have some savings and investments, which I'd willingly give to support our child, and I've already suggested marriage, but you're resistant to the idea."

She shook her head. "Do you have no sense of self-preservation?"

"Maybe I haven't known you very long," he acknowledged. "And there are undoubtedly a lot of things I don't know about you, but I know you're not lying about the paternity of the baby you're carrying."

"You seem to be handling the news a lot better than I did," she admitted.

"Believe me, I'm in full-scale panic mode on the inside," he told her.

"I'm familiar with panic. Although when I realized I was late, my initial reaction was denial. Because there are a lot of different things that can mess up a woman's cycle, and whatever had messed up mine, it couldn't possibly be a baby.

"But then a few days turned into a week, then two weeks. So when I was in Elko for a custody hearing, I went to a pharmacy to buy a home pregnancy test."

"It was positive?" he guessed.

She nodded. "But I still didn't believe it. I was sure that the test must have been faulty, or I'd somehow done it wrong."

"There's a wrong way to pee on a stick?"

She managed a smile. "It was easier to believe that than trust the result. So I bought a second test, but it was faulty, too."

"I'm sensing a pattern."

"I just couldn't wrap my head around the possibility that there was a tiny life growing inside of me," she admitted. "Maybe I'd always thought I'd be a mother someday, but someday was supposed to be a lot of years down the road."

"Then you bought a third test?"

"From a different pharmacy, because clearly the entire shipment at the first store was defective. When that test gave me the same result, I finally went to see Dr. Amaro."

"Have you told anyone else?"

She shook her head. "My sister knows, but I didn't tell her. In fact, it was your mention of marriage that tipped her off."

"I was thinking out loud," he admitted.

"Believe me, I know what a shock it is to discover that, after a casual hookup, you're going to be a parent."

"I never would have said, 'Hey, let's have unprotected sex and see what happens,'" he acknowledged, "but the reality of a baby changes everything."

She instinctively touched a hand to her belly. "The reality is only about the size of a lentil right now."

"A lentil? Is that like a bean?"

"Close enough," she said.

"That's pretty small."

She nodded. "But he or she will do a lot of growing over the next seven months."

"Still, a little bean would benefit from having both a mom and a dad looking out for him or her, don't you think?"

Chapter Eight

Kate had never understood why expectant parents referred to an unborn child by cute nicknames, but she couldn't deny there was something about the way Reid said *little bean* that was endearing. She also appreciated that he'd used both gender pronouns rather than defaulting to the masculine as so many people—especially men—tended to do.

Except that, despite his warm tone and conciliatory demeanor, he was doing exactly what Sky had warned her he would do—trying to push her toward marriage so that he could feel better about doing "the right thing."

Thankfully, she knew how to push back.

"Reid, I only found out about the baby a few days before you did, and I'm not ready to think about all the ways my life is going to change. I know it's going to change," she acknowledged, "but getting married is definitely not a change that ever crossed my mind."

"Think about it now," he suggested.

She sighed. "Don't you already have one divorce behind you?"

"Yeah," he admitted.

"So why would you want to rush into another marriage, especially one that would be doomed from the start?"

"Why do you think our marriage would be doomed?"

"Because we'd only be getting married for the sake of our baby," she pointed out to him.

"I can't think of a better reason."

"What about love?" she challenged.

"Is that what you're holding out for?"

"I'm not holding out for anything," she denied. "But whenever I thought about getting married, I assumed it would happen because I was in love with the man I was planning to spend my life with."

"I'm sorry this situation is forcing you to deviate from your plan," he said. "But I'm not going to pretend to be in love with you so you can feel better about marrying me."

"I don't want you to pretend anything, and I don't want to marry you," she told him.

Except that she did want to give her baby a real family—the kind that she'd known for the first twelve years of her life. Since the death of her mother, a crucial piece of their family had been missing, and Kate couldn't help but worry that her child might feel the same emptiness growing up without a full-time father.

"But I appreciate your willingness to do the right thing," she said to Reid now. "Even if we're not in agreement as to what that is."

"Your pregnancy is one of those curveballs life likes to throw at us to see how we'll respond," he told her. "I'm ready to step up to the plate and hit that ball out of the park."

She rolled her eyes. "I'm guessing you're a baseball fan."

"My Rangers tickets were the only thing I was sorry to leave in Texas," he admitted.

"Just one more thing I didn't know about you—because I don't know you," she said again.

"Just one of the many things we have yet to discover about one another," he countered, putting a different spin on the point.

"Well, there's something you should know about me," she told him. "I hate the Rangers."

He winced. "Despite that blasphemous statement, I'm willing to trust that your failure to appreciate America's pastime isn't indicative of greater character flaws."

"I don't hate baseball," she said, eager to clarify her previous statement. "I hate the Rangers because I'm an Angels fan."

"Now that might be indicative of greater character flaws," he said, shaking his head sadly.

"You won't find many Rangers fans in Nevada, and in this part of the state, they're mostly Dodgers or Athletics fans with a handful of Angels and Giants supporters in the mix."

"How'd you end up cheering for the Angels?"

"Three years at UCLA," she reminded him.

"Okay, let's put aside our differences with respect to baseball for the moment and focus on what's best for our baby."

Our baby.

The words spilled out of his mouth easily, as if they didn't twist his stomach into painful knots. And maybe they didn't. Maybe he'd accepted the reality of their situation a lot more easily than Kate had done, because as much as she loved her unborn child already, there were moments when her doubts and fears seemed stronger than anything else.

Her biggest concerns were based on not knowing how she would manage to juggle her career and the demands of a child. And, of course, long before the baby was born, she was going to have to tell her father about her pregnancy.

He'd be supportive, but he'd also be disappointed to learn she would be a mother before she was a wife. And he'd probably wonder if the death of her own mother so many years earlier had somehow caused her to fall into bed with a man she barely knew.

A ring on her finger would reassure her father that, although she'd made a mistake, she'd be taken care of. Because while David Gilmore was open-minded enough to encourage his daughters to be anything they wanted to be, he was also old-fashioned enough to believe a woman needed a man to take care of her.

Yes, as difficult as it would be to tell him she was pregnant, she knew he'd accept the news more easily if it was followed by *and I'm going to marry the father of my baby*.

But she wasn't going to take what looked like the easy path now, because it would only be that much harder later on when the relationship fell apart and their child was caught in the middle of a messy divorce.

"Can we please just take some time before making any life-altering decisions?" she asked him now.

"How much time do you think you need?"

"Eight months?" she suggested, aware that their baby would be born before that period of time had passed.

He folded his arms over his chest and looked at her as if she was a recalcitrant child. Maybe he was practicing his stern father facade and, if so, he was doing a good job—which made her want to both laugh and cry, because her emotions were a complete mess.

"More than a day," she told him.

"Okay," he relented.

"And, in the meantime, can we keep this…news…between us?"

"I'm already an outsider—and not in any hurry to face the judgment that will follow when people find out I got Katelyn Gilmore pregnant."

"I'm willing to keep the paternity of my baby a secret," she reminded him.

But Reid shook his head stubbornly. "I'm not."

He gave her a week.

And every day that passed during that week, he waited for his phone to ring or for Katelyn to show up at his office. But it never happened, and Reid was beginning to suspect that it never would.

So he took the initiative—and a pizza—and crossed his fingers that she wouldn't toss the box back in his face when he showed up at her door.

After buzzing him in, she eyed him with suspicion—and the pizza box with interest. "What are you doing here, Reid?"

"Well, you made dinner for me last week, so I figured it was my turn," he explained. "But I'm not much of a cook, so this seemed like a safer option."

"What's on the pizza?"

"Pepperoni, black olives and hot peppers."

"Since it would be too much of a coincidence to discover that those are your favorite toppings, I'm guessing you asked my sister what I like."

"Guilty."

With a sigh of resignation, she stepped away from the door so he could enter.

He could tell she was wary, so he deliberately kept the

conversation focused on neutral topics while they ate, and they chatted about local news, current events and baseball scores of their rival teams. They didn't discuss Aiden Hampton, although Reid knew that she'd talked to the ADA about a local diversion program that would allow Aiden to take responsibility for his actions and perform community service in exchange for a withdrawal of the charges.

"Let's go to a movie," he suggested, when the pizza box was empty.

"Why?"

"Because it's Friday night and there's nothing good on TV."

"I have a brief to research and write."

"Come on, Katelyn—it's Friday night. Play hooky with me."

She bent down to scoop up a napkin that had fallen onto the floor. "There are only two screens at the local theater— it's quite possible there's nothing good at the movies, either."

"You can choose between the latest Marvel movie and some artsy-sounding film that I've never heard of," he told her, making it clear what his choice would be.

She grinned. "Who doesn't love superheroes in spandex?"

They found seats inside the theater, then Reid went to get snacks while Katelyn thumbed through the messages on her phone, just so that she had something to focus her eyes on while her mind wandered. She wished she'd had the opportunity to get to know Reid better without the specter of her pregnancy hanging over them. But, of course, the tiny life growing inside her changed everything. Even if no one else knew about the baby right now, there would be speculation about the relationship—and more so when her condition became evident.

Reid came back carrying a tray with two soft drinks, a big bag of popcorn, a package of licorice and box of Milk Duds.

"If I didn't know otherwise, I'd think you'd skipped dinner," she commented.

"Those aren't for me." He put the drinks in their respective cup holders, then set the tray of snacks in her lap. "They're for you."

"For me?"

"I didn't know what you liked."

"I like everything," she admitted, keeping her voice quiet to ensure that no one seated around them would overhear their conversation. "But I'm not actually eating for two, you know."

"Then you could share with me," he suggested.

"Hmm…that was your plan all along, wasn't it?"

He winked as he settled into the seat beside her. "Maybe."

It was almost like a real date, and it made Kate wonder how things might have played out if a condom hadn't failed. How would she have responded to discovering that he was the new sheriff of Haven?

She would have been pleased to see him. Because even before she'd begun to suspect that there were consequences of her trip to Boulder City, she hadn't stopped thinking about those two blissful nights. But she also would have been wary of any kind of personal relationship, because he was now wearing a badge in the town where she was building her law practice. It wasn't a direct conflict of interest, but Kate would have wanted to steer clear of the slightest appearance of impropriety.

Of course, being pregnant with the new sheriff's baby

took away that option. And even if no one else knew the truth about their relationship, being seen with him at the local movie theater would generate a fair amount of talk. And maybe, since Reid was prepared to acknowledge paternity of the baby, she was subconsciously hoping that people wouldn't later count the number of weeks between his arrival in town and the arrival of her baby and realize she was pregnant before he showed up in Haven.

The lights in the theater dimmed, and she settled deeper into her seat to focus on the coming attractions. But if she'd hoped the movie might provide a distraction from thinking about her pregnancy, she hadn't anticipated that sitting beside Reid in the dark theater distracted her from everything else. Everything but her awareness of the man.

An awareness that intensified with every brush of his leg and every bump of his arm. And when he leaned close to whisper in her ear, the scent of him—clean, simple and masculine—tempted her more than the buttery popcorn.

Determined to ignore the hunger stirring in her veins, she tore open the box of Milk Duds and popped a chocolate-coated caramel into her mouth, letting it sit on her tongue until it began to melt. And she continued to pop candy into her mouth, one at a time, until the box was empty.

"Licorice?" Reid offered the bag to her.

She shook her head. "No, thanks."

Because she'd already consumed an overload of sugar and it had done nothing to curb her appetite for what she really wanted but couldn't have.

He set the licorice and the half-empty bag of popcorn aside and reached for her hand, linking their fingers together. At first, she felt self-conscious and wondered if the overture was intended as some kind of statement about their relationship. But the theater was dark, making it unlikely that anyone could see their hands.

So they watched the rest of the movie like that, their fingers entwined in the dark. And when she stopped trying to read any deeper meaning into the gesture, she could admit that it felt surprisingly nice.

But she also suspected this was part of his campaign to convince her to do "the right thing," and she wasn't convinced that marriage was the right thing.

She knew that relationships didn't come with guarantees, but getting married because of an unplanned pregnancy seemed like a guarantee of heartache. And yet, she was tempted to accept his offer, because heartache at some distant time in the future seemed preferable to the doubts and insecurities about being a single mother that plagued her now.

Of course, the characters in the movie were battling much bigger problems, so she put aside her own thoughts and concerns and let herself be drawn into the action on the screen.

When the credits began to roll and spectators started to exit the theater, Reid gave her hand a subtle squeeze and released it, preserving the illusion that they were acquaintances simply enjoying a movie together. It was a perfectly legitimate and believable explanation for them being together, but Kate decided that if people were going to talk, she might as well give them something to talk about.

She led the way out of the theater and, after dropping her empty Milk Duds box and drink cup into the garbage, reached for his hand again.

"Thank you," she said, as they exited onto the sidewalk and the crowd began to disperse in various directions.

"For what?"

"For tonight—the pizza, the movie, the snacks. But especially for helping me forget about everything for a couple of hours."

"It was my pleasure," he told her.

"You might feel differently when you're fielding questions from everyone who saw us together tonight."

"There were questions before we hit the ticket counter," he confided.

"From who?" she asked.

"Jolene Landry," he said, naming the owner of Jo's Pizza. "Apparently the pepperoni, hot peppers and black olives combo is known to be your particular favorite."

"I didn't think about that," she admitted.

"Well, Jolene now believes—at least, I think I managed to convince her—that those are my favorite toppings, too."

"But the pizza combined with being seen together at the movie is going to be grist for the gossip mill."

"There is one way we could nip it in the bud," he said.

"What's that?"

"We could announce our engagement."

She sighed. "I should have known you couldn't let it go for ten minutes."

"I let it go for more than three hours," he countered. "But I'll make you a deal."

"What kind of deal?" she asked warily.

"I'll stop bringing up the subject if you promise to give serious consideration to the idea and let me know when you've made up your mind."

"I have made up my mind," she told him.

"*Serious* consideration," he said again.

"Okay," she relented, withdrawing her keys from her pocket as they approached her building.

"Promise?"

"I promise." She unlocked the door. "Good night, Reid."

He held the door. "I'll see you up."

"It's really not necessary," she protested.

"It is," he insisted. "Unless you want me to kiss you good-night right here, where we're illuminated under the security light for anyone who might be passing by."

"Maybe I don't want you to kiss me good-night." Of course, she did, but kissing Reid tended to lead to other intimacies, and she was determined to ignore the sexual attraction between them. Or at least try.

"I still want to see you safely inside," he told her.

Because she suspected it was true, she let him follow her up the stairs to the second floor, where she unlocked the interior door to her apartment and turned on the lights.

He did a quick visual scan of the open area, as if to be sure that everything was as they'd left it, then moved to the windows, checked that the latches were all fastened, and nodded.

"Do you want to look for monsters under my bed, too?" she asked.

"Lead the way."

She shook her head. "I'm *not* showing you my bedroom."

His lips curved in a slow and blatantly sensual smile. "Well, the sofa worked just fine at my place."

She didn't need the reminder. She remembered, in very clear and vivid detail, every kiss and touch they'd shared that night—and the two nights they'd spent together in Boulder City. And that was why it was a bad idea to let him touch her again.

"We have to be smart about this," she told him. "We have to think not just about what we want but what's best for our baby."

"What's best for our baby is to have two parents who are together."

"That's not always true," she said. Being a family law

attorney, she'd had a front-row seat to the drama that ensued when marriages—and families—fell apart, and she had no desire to add a failed union of her own to the statistics.

"You're right," he admitted. "But I know we could make it work, because we're both too stubborn to accept anything less than success—and because the sizzling chemistry between us would go a long way toward smoothing any bumps in the road."

"Just like a guy to think that sex is the answer to everything."

"Not everything," he denied. "But—"

Whatever else he'd intended to say was cut off by the abrupt ring of his cell phone.

Reid cursed under his breath as he pulled the device out of his pocket and glanced at the screen.

"Aren't you going to answer that?" she asked, when he made no move to do so.

"I'd rather not," he admitted.

"It's almost midnight, and no one calls at midnight unless it's important." She lifted her brows as another thought occurred to her. "Or a booty call."

"It's not a booty call," he assured her.

But he touched the keypad to connect the call, and Kate wandered into the kitchen to give him some privacy.

"Sorry about that," Reid said, after he'd finished with the call and tucked his phone away again.

"Was it something urgent?" she asked.

"Everything's urgent to Trish."

"Trish?" she queried, before she could stop herself.

"My ex-wife," he told her. "She called to tell me that she's in labor."

Chapter Nine

Reid didn't think about how his words might be interpreted until Katelyn's eyes went wide.

"You're going to be a father?"

"What? *No!*" His emphatic response was followed by a short laugh. "Well, yes, but only to your baby."

Her brow furrowed, as if she couldn't make sense of what he was saying. "Your ex-wife is having another man's baby?"

"Yes," he confirmed.

"You don't seem too upset by that," she noted.

"Why would I be? The other man's her husband."

"Her husband?"

"We've been divorced for four years," he explained. "And Trish has been remarried for three of those."

She opened her mouth to speak, then closed it again without saying a word.

"You're wondering why she called to tell me about a baby that isn't mine?" he guessed.

"Maybe. Yeah," she admitted.

"Because my ex-wife has no concept of boundaries."

She considered his response before asking, "How long were you married?"

"Two-and-a-half years. But we were friends for a long time before we got married, and we continued to be friends after our marriage fell apart."

"That's...surprising."

"And possibly a mistake," he acknowledged. "I can't imagine ever completely cutting ties with her, but I recently accepted that those ties were a little too close, which is one of the reasons I decided to move away from Echo Ridge."

"And ended up in Haven—having to deal with another woman who's going to have a baby," she noted.

He nodded.

"You know, it's probably not too late for you to get out," she said. "Isn't there a probationary period during which you can decide that the job isn't working out—or that Haven isn't what you were looking for?"

"Whether or not any of this is what I wanted, it's what we've got," he said.

And though the idea of fatherhood was no less terrifying now than when he'd first learned of her pregnancy, he remained committed to doing the right thing. He just had to convince Katelyn to let him.

"Well, if you're determined to stick around, I have a favor to ask," she said.

"Anything," he immediately replied.

"You might want to wait until you know what I want," she suggested.

"Anything," he said again.

"I'd like you to come with me to the Circle G for a barbecue Sunday afternoon."

"You want me to meet your family?"

"You've already met my grandmother and my sister," she reminded him. "But yes, I'd like to introduce you to everyone else, too, so that when I get around to telling them I'm pregnant, they will have met the baby's father."

He was surprised by the invitation, because he suspected that showing up at the ranch with Katelyn would create a lot more speculation than going to a movie in town. But he only asked, "What time should I pick you up?"

After Kate closed the office door behind her last client Saturday afternoon, she sent a quick text to Emerson Kellner—her best friend since kindergarten. Kate had been the maid of honor when Emerson got married three years earlier, and the godmother of her first child at Keegan's baptism six months ago.

Her message, asking if Emerson was up for some company, received an immediate reply: YES! PLEASE!

Aware of her friend's fondness for white chocolate macadamia nut cookies, Kate stopped at Sweet Caroline's Sweets on the way and picked up a dozen of the treats.

"I'm still carrying eight pounds of baby fat," Emerson protested, eyeing the white bakery box in her friend's hands.

"You look fabulous," Kate told her sincerely. "But it's really my godson I want to see."

She'd first held the baby only a few hours after his birth. He'd had wispy blond hair, a pert little nose, a rosebud mouth and tiny hands curled into tiny fists. And when he'd opened his eyes, she'd fallen head over heels in love. Ten months later, she loved him even more.

"He'll be waking up from his nap soon," Emerson promised, moving toward the back of the house. "In the meantime, I've got a pitcher of lemonade out by the pool, where you can tell me about the sexy new sheriff."

Kate stretched out in the lounger beside her friend. "Why are you asking me about him?"

"Because I heard you had a date with him last night."

"I did not," she denied.

"Really?" Emerson said skeptically. "Because Lacey Bolton heard from Deanna Nardone that Megan Carmichael saw you snuggled up with an—" she made air quotes with her fingers "—'unknown hottie' at the movies last night."

"I hate this town," Kate muttered, tipping her head back and closing her eyes.

"Were you at the movies or not?"

"Yes," she admitted.

"And?" her friend prompted.

"It's definitely worth the price of a ticket. If you and Mark want to see it, I'd be happy to watch Keegan."

"I wasn't asking about the movie," her friend chided. "And don't think I didn't notice your failure to comment, positively or negatively, on my description of the sheriff as sexy, which suggests to me—and remember, I know you better than anyone else—that he's got you all churned up inside."

He did, of course, although not only for the reasons her friend was thinking. "His name is Reid Davidson and yes, he's tall, dark and handsome."

Emerson shook her head. "No skimping on details."

"Approximately six-two, short brown hair, hazel eyes, strong jaw, broad shoulders."

"You've always had a thing for guys with great shoulders," her friend noted.

"Is that description adequate?"

"It's helping me put together a mental picture," Emerson confirmed. "But I need a number."

"Seriously, Em, we're not in high school anymore."

"I know. I'm an old married woman stuck at home with a baby now—I need to get my thrills vicariously."

"You're twenty-eight years old, married to the love of your life and Keegan is the most adorable baby in the world."

"It's all true," she admitted. "But I still want a number."

The number system they'd established in high school for rating the guys they liked was hardly unique. Emerson had never dated anyone who was less than an eight-point-five and Kate had never dated anyone at all.

After watching *Erin Brockovich* with her mother, Kate had announced that she was going to be a lawyer someday. Her mother had been both proud and supportive of her goal, and when Tessa died, Kate had been more determined than ever to follow through with her plan. And while her best friend was dating all the cute boys at their high school, Kate was focused on getting into college and then law school. She had no intention of letting any guy—even a ten-plus—derail her plans.

"Assigning a number is insensitive and objectifying," she protested.

"He's a ten-plus, isn't he?" Emerson guessed.

Kate answered with reluctant honesty. "Yeah, he's a ten-plus."

"And they're in short supply in this town," her friend noted. "You better snap him up before someone else does."

"I'm at the building-my-career phase of my life," she said, conveniently ignoring—at least for the minute—that she was also at the growing-a-life phase way ahead of schedule.

"Things don't always go according to plan," Emerson

warned. "You can't predict when you'll meet the right guy and you shouldn't pretend he isn't the right guy just because the timing is wrong."

"But if it's the wrong time, is he really the right guy?" Kate countered, attempting to divert her friend's focus.

"Would you sleep with him?" Emerson pressed, proving the effort ineffective.

She hesitated, just a fraction of a second, before responding, "Actually...I already did."

"Oh. My. God. I should have realized...when you mentioned the shoulders—he's the sheriff you knocked boots with in Boulder City."

Kate rolled her eyes. "Yes, he's the one."

"You told me the sex was spectacular," her friend recalled. "Off-the-charts spectacular, in fact."

"With the proviso that I'd been celibate for a long time prior to that weekend, so my assessment might have been a little bit skewed."

"And now he's Haven's new sheriff." Emerson picked up her lemonade, sipped. "Was that a coincidence or is he stalking you?"

"Coincidence," Kate assured her. "He actually interviewed for Jed's job before the conference started."

"Maybe fate then," her friend suggested.

"Please don't make this into something that it isn't. And please don't tell anyone—even Mark—that I hooked up with Haven's new sheriff."

"I can't lie to my husband," Emerson protested.

"You won't have to lie because it's not going to come up in conversation if you don't bring it up," she said, lifting her hand to cover a yawn.

"Fine—but it's not like he'd tell anyone else."

"Too many people know already."

"Who else knows besides me, you and the sheriff?"

"My sister," Kate confided.

"You told Sky before you told me?"

Admitting that Reid had told Sky—more or less—would create more questions, so she only said, "I saw Sky before I saw you."

"Still." Emerson pretended to pout. "I'm your best friend. I'm supposed to hear all the important stuff first."

"You were the first person I told when I came back from Boulder City," she said soothingly.

That revelation didn't appease her friend, who was studying her through narrowed eyes. "You're still holding something back."

Thankfully, before Emerson could press her further, a cheery babble sounded through the baby monitor on the table.

Kate immediately pushed herself up off the lounger. "Keegan's awake."

"Awake but not fussing," her friend noted.

"That's my favorite kind of baby," she said, opening the sliding door.

"Wait until you have one of your own," Emerson warned, following her into the house. "Believe me, after the first few months of constant demands, you won't be in such a hurry to pick him up every time he makes a sound."

Which was going to happen a lot sooner than her friend suspected—and a lot sooner than Kate ever would have predicted. But now that she'd had a couple weeks to get used to the idea, she could confidently say that the prospect of impending motherhood filled her with more joy than trepidation. She still had fears and concerns, but the happiness that filled her heart when she thought about holding her baby in her arms was so all encompassing, it managed to hold those fears and concerns at bay.

Or it had until today when a client's child-from-hell had

screamed like a banshee for the whole forty minutes she was in Kate's office.

She followed the familiar path up the stairs and down the hall to the nursery, peeking in to see that Keegan had pulled himself up on the bars and was gnawing on the rail, drool dripping off his chin.

He looked up and grinned when he recognized his godmother.

"Oh, my goodness," Kate said. "Look at all those teeth."

He smiled again, showing them off.

"Aren't you such a big boy now?"

He released his grip on the rail and lifted his arms toward her, a silent request to be picked up. But without the support of the rail, he lost his balance and immediately fell down onto his bottom. His little brow furrowed.

"Oopsie daisy," she said, and he giggled. She reached into the crib and lifted him out. "Kiss?"

He puckered up and touched his lips to her cheek.

"A little sloppy, Keeg," she said. "Hopefully you'll fix that before adolescence." She patted a hand against his bottom. "And give some consideration to potty training, too."

"Do you want me to change him?" Emerson offered.

"I can handle a wet diaper," Kate assured her.

Emerson settled into the rocking chair in the corner of the room, content to let her friend handle the diaper duties. "Remember—he's a boy."

Kate nodded. The first time she'd ever changed Keegan, she hadn't thought to cover him when she pulled the wet diaper away and he'd sprinkled like a fountain. "I don't think I'll ever forget."

Clean diapers and wipes were within easy reach, and she had everything ready before she unsnapped the fasteners of his romper. He immediately twisted, trying to roll away from her.

"Get over here, Mr. Wiggly Worm," she chastised, splaying her hand across his belly to hold him in position.

"He certainly is that," Emerson agreed. "I remember how thrilled I was when he finally rolled over at five months—now I just wish he would hold still every once in a while."

"My grandmother says that new parents spend the first year of a child's life eager for him to walk and talk—and the next sixteen wishing he'd sit down and shut up."

Emerson laughed. "I'm sure there's some truth in that."

When Keegan tried to roll over again, Kate reached for one of his favorite teething toys. She jingled the plastic keys, immediately snagging his attention. He kicked his chubby legs and stretched his arms out for the toy.

She jingled the keys again, then let him take them from her so she could secure the tabs of his diaper and fasten the snaps of his romper. When that was done, she dropped the dirty diaper into the bin beside the table and picked up the baby, propping him against her hip.

"I've figured it out," Emerson said, when they were once again reclining in the loungers by the pool, Keegan sitting in Kate's lap. "What you've been holding back."

The baby tossed the keys to the ground, and Kate reached to scoop them up—a familiar game between them. "What do you think I've been holding back?"

"You're pregnant."

This time the plastic keys slipped out of *her* hand.

"I'll take that as a yes," Emerson said, retrieving the toy for her son.

It wasn't just the words but the absolute conviction in her friend's voice that warned Kate any effort to deny the truth would be in vain. And maybe she'd come here for this—to talk to somebody who knew her better than anyone else and who knew what it meant to be a mother.

"Am I wearing a sign?" she wondered aloud, a little unnerved that first her sister and now her best friend had so readily uncovered her secret.

Emerson smiled. "There are all kinds of signs if someone knows you—especially if that someone has recent experience with pregnancy."

"What kind of signs?"

"You're pale and fatigued and your boobs are practically spilling out of your bra."

Kate's gaze immediately dropped to her chest. "Apparently you know me even better than I realized," she remarked.

"But does *he* know?" Emerson asked.

She nodded.

"How'd he respond?"

"He thinks we should get married."

Her friend's brows lifted. "What do you think?"

"I don't think a broken condom is the first stop on the road to wedded bliss." Kate rubbed Keegan's back. "If and when I get married, I want it to be because I've fallen in love. Maybe that's selfish under the circumstances, but I want what you and Mark have," she said, imploring Emerson to understand.

"Anyone would have reservations in your situation," her friend acknowledged. "But you wouldn't be pregnant if you and the sheriff didn't have some powerful chemistry."

"And if that was a valid reason for a legal union, the traditional wedding vows would forgo mention of love, honor and cherish in favor of lots of really hot sex."

"The love, honor and cherish stuff is easier to do when there's lots of really hot sex added to the mix," Emerson said.

Which wasn't all that different from the argument Reid had made but still didn't hold much sway for Kate.

"I had a client—a young, single mom—come in today with a six-month-old. She wants an order to compel a DNA test so she can get financial support from the baby's father. She also said she wouldn't mind if Dad wanted to take the baby off her hands some of the time.

"Which seemed an odd comment to me, at first," Kate noted. "Until the baby, suddenly and inexplicably, started screaming. The mom checked her diaper, offered a drink and a snack, but nothing soothed the kid. The baby kept screaming until even the mom was crying, and…I'm terrified that's going to be me in the future."

"I've been there," Emerson confided. "There are times when it seems nothing I do will soothe Keegan, then I start to doubt everything I'm doing and feel like a total failure as a mother.

"I can only imagine how much harder it would be if I didn't have Mark to help out, so if you came here for reassurance, I'm not sure I can give it," her friend said. "Don't get me wrong—I love Keegan with my whole heart and I love being a mom, but there are days I'm so overwhelmed, I don't realize until Mark gets home that it's dinnertime and the breakfast and lunch dishes are still in the sink because I haven't had a chance to empty the dishwasher. And I'm still in my pajamas because I didn't have time to get dressed—or even notice that I wasn't.

"It's even worse when Mark's out of town on business. Last week, he was gone for three days. When he finally got back, as soon as he walked through the front door, I handed him the baby and walked out. I just needed some space, just five minutes by myself, so that I could hear myself think."

"Thanks," Kate said drily. "I feel so much better now."

"I wouldn't be a true friend if I told you it was all smiles and giggles," Emerson said. "Although those smiles and giggles do have a way of making you forget about poopy diapers and projectile vomit—at least in the moment.

"Still, I know how much you've always wanted a real family of your own," her friend continued in a gentler tone. "So before you make any final decisions, you need to consider all your options—including saying 'I do' to the sexy sheriff."

Chapter Ten

Katelyn wanted to be at the Circle G around four o'clock. Reid had mapped the route on his phone and discovered it was about a thirty-minute drive from her apartment, so he was at her door promptly at 3:30.

She was ready when he arrived and immediately came out rather than buzzing him in. She was wearing a sleeveless white V-neck top printed with tiny blue flowers over a pair of slim-fitting navy capri pants with white leather slip-on sandals. Her hair tumbled in loose waves over her shoulders, the ends dancing in the light summer breeze.

She looked cool and casual and far too sexy for his peace of mind. Certainly no one looking at her would ever suspect that she was pregnant.

"Boy or girl?" Katelyn asked, fastening her seat belt.

"Huh?" he said.

She smiled as she slid a pair of dark sunglasses over her eyes. "I assume your ex-wife had the baby by now—I was wondering if it was a boy or a girl."

"Oh. Yes, she did. A boy," he told her. "Henry."

"Are you hoping our baby is a boy or a girl?" she asked.

He pulled out of the parking lot and turned onto Page Street. "I can't honestly say that I've given the matter any thought."

"Think about it now," she suggested.

Thinking about her pregnancy was scary enough without imagining the baby that would come at the end. Reid didn't have a lot of experience with kids, but he knew infants were completely dependent on their parents for everything—food, clothing, shelter, attention and affection.

"Or is it too soon to be thinking about the sex?" she wondered.

"I'm always ready to think about sex," he told her.

A smile tugged at her lips as she shook her head. "I meant the sex of our baby."

"Oh. Yeah, it's too soon to be thinking about that," he agreed.

Definitely too soon.

He wasn't ready to be a father, and he didn't imagine himself being any more ready in seven months.

Maybe seven years.

Yes, that might work.

Or, better yet—never.

Unfortunately, that wasn't really an option.

"I've thought about it," she admitted. "I don't have a preference, but it's fun to imagine what our son or daughter will look like."

He considered for a moment, then shook his head. "I don't want to imagine what our daughter would look like."

"Why not?"

"Because now I'm picturing her with dark hair and

blue eyes like her mom, so breathtakingly beautiful that my badge and gun will be my only hope of keeping the boys at a distance."

"And then she'll sneak off for a weekend, somewhere away from the watchful eye of her overprotective father, and get knocked up," Katelyn warned.

He slid her a look. "Not *my* daughter."

"I'm sure that's what my father would have said, too," she agreed. "If anyone had suggested the possibility to him."

His fingers tightened on the steering wheel. "He's going to want to kill me, isn't he?"

"Wanting and doing are completely different things," she said, as if to reassure him. "And I'm not planning to tell him today."

"What are you going to tell him?" Reid wondered. "Will you be introducing me as the new sheriff or your boyfriend?"

The way she nibbled on her bottom lip before responding suggested that she hadn't considered any of the details. "I guess it wouldn't hurt to give them the impression that we're dating," she admitted. "It would certainly make it easier to explain a baby later on—but no PDAs."

"What about sneaking up to the hayloft?" he asked, only half teasing.

"That would be another no," she said firmly.

He wasn't surprised by her response, but he was disappointed. "Anything else I should know before I meet your family?"

"Just don't mention the name Blake and everything should be fine."

"Are the Gilmores and the Blakes still feuding?"

"The Hatfields and McCoys of Nevada," she told him.

"I'll have to remember not to get on your bad side," he mused. "Apparently Gilmores know how to hold a grudge."

"Only as well as Blakes," she retorted.

"And all because one guy got the prime land and the other ended up with some precious metals."

"Wars have been fought over less," she remarked. "And then there was the ill-fated love affair between Everett Gilmore's daughter, Maggie, and Samuel Blake's youngest son, James."

"I haven't heard that part of the story," he admitted.

"It's not unlike so many other forbidden love stories. Boy meets girl, their families disapprove, they run away together. Then the families come together, at least temporarily, to track down their missing offspring and drag them home again."

"Something must have happened to widen the rift again after that," Reid guessed.

She nodded. "Eight months later, Maggie died pushing her stillborn son into the world and James, overwhelmed by grief and guilt, set off on horseback and was never seen again. That story has been retold to each successive generation of Gilmores—and probably Blakes, too—as a warning of the kind of tragedy that results whenever the families forget that they're enemies."

"Just don't tell it to the little bean as a bedtime story," Reid suggested. "It's kind of dark."

"It is," she agreed. "And yet, my brother Caleb managed to forget the ending for a while."

"He fell in love with the daughter of your father's archenemy?" he guessed.

"I don't know if he loved her," she said. "But for a few weeks, he was married to her."

"Now that sounds like an interesting story."

"It's not even a unique one. They were young, they

screwed around, Brielle got pregnant and Caleb took her to Las Vegas for a quickie wedding. She lost the baby, they got a quickie divorce—end of story."

"Really?" he said dubiously. "That's it?"

"That's it," she confirmed. "After that, Brielle went away to school in New York City, and I don't think she's been back more than once or twice since."

"Maybe she's still in love with your brother," he suggested.

"Or maybe she's happy in New York," she countered.

"What about your brother—is he happy?"

"He's never given any indication that he's not," she said. "Liam, on the other hand, makes no secret of the fact that he has ambitions other than waking up at the Circle G every morning for the rest of his life."

"What does he want to do?"

"Renovate the old Stagecoach Inn and reopen it as a boutique hotel and spa."

"That doesn't sound like a bad idea," he said. "Aside from the Dusty Boots Motel out by the highway, Haven doesn't have a hotel."

"I don't disagree that a hotel is a good idea—if somebody else wanted to tackle the project, but 'Gilmores are ranchers,'" she said, deepening her voice in what was clearly intended as an imitation of her father.

"Did he object when you decided to go to law school?"

She shook her head. "My dad might have strong opinions about—well, he has strong opinions about everything," she acknowledged. "But he appreciates that everyone, even ranchers, need lawyers."

Reid turned where she indicated, passing through the open gates under an arched metalwork sign announcing Circle G Ranch.

The paved highway gave way to a gravel road and

stones kicked up under his tires, pinging against the undercarriage. He trusted that she knew how to get to the ranch, but the road he was on seemed to go nowhere. Every direction he looked, there was nothing but open fields dotted with cattle and, in the distance, the Silver Ridge Mountains speared into the cloudless blue sky. It was a full three minutes after he'd pulled off the highway before the house—two impressive stories of timber frame and cut stone—came into view.

He parked his truck, noting that there were five pickups, three SUVs and two ATVs ahead of his vehicle in the driveway.

"Good," Katelyn said, already reaching for the handle of her door. "It looks like everyone's here."

"You told me that you had a sister and two brothers," he reminded her, as he unhooked his belt.

"That's right," she confirmed, exiting the truck.

He followed suit, albeit less eagerly. "So who do all these vehicles belong to?"

She laughed at the obvious trepidation in his tone. "The gray truck is my dad's, the red one belongs to my grandparents, the pimped-up Jeep is Caleb's, Liam usually drives the green truck and Sky the blue SUV. The others belong to my uncle and cousins and the ranch foreman."

"This is a usual family dinner?"

"Pretty much," she confirmed, then nudged him with her shoulder. "Come on—I'll introduce you."

She did so, and though she'd given Reid a brief heads-up with respect to everyone else in attendance, it was apparent that Katelyn's family had received no advance warning that she'd be bringing a date.

"Trust me," she said later, when they moved toward the paddock to check out the foal born a few days earlier. "It's better that they didn't know you were coming, because they didn't have a chance to prepare an interrogation."

"Thank you, I think." Then, as he looked around the property, he had to admit, "This place is impressive."

"Six generations of Gilmores have worked to make it a success."

"It must have been quite an experience to grow up here, surrounded by all of this."

"It was," she agreed.

"And a big adjustment—moving from one of the biggest ranches in Haven to an apartment in town."

"It was," she said again.

"You don't miss this?"

She shook her head. "I miss my family sometimes, although it seems as if someone always has an excuse to make a trip into town to check up on me, but I don't miss the ranch."

There was something in her voice, a hint of defiance that he suspected was a deliberate cover of a deeper pain.

"You didn't grow up wanting to be a cowgirl?"

"No," she said. "Not since I was twelve, anyway."

"What happened when you were twelve?"

She was quiet for a moment. "My mom died."

He winced. "I'm sorry, Katelyn."

She just nodded and continued walking. After a few minutes, she stopped beneath a Jeffrey pine, her gaze fixed somewhere in the distance. "My mom loved everything about the ranch," she told him. "And she worked as hard as any of the hands. But sometimes, early in the mornings, she would saddle up her favorite horse and just ride. And sometimes she'd let me go with her. I loved those early morning rides when it was just the two of us."

Reid could see where the story was going now and regretted that he'd asked.

"We were out by the eastern border near the creek that morning. I saw something moving on the ground, but before I could say anything, Honey spotted it, too, and instinctively reared up. My mom was a good rider—skilled and experienced—but she'd been pointing to something in the distance and was unprepared for the abrupt movement.

"She was thrown off the back of the horse," she continued, her voice flat now and all the more heartbreaking for the lack of emotion in it. "And broke her neck when she fell.

"I didn't know what to do," Kate admitted. "She probably had a cell phone, but I didn't think about that at the time. Instead, I raced back to the house, to get help. My dad called 911, then he went after her. By the time he got to her, it was too late."

"I'm so sorry," Reid said.

"I didn't ride for a long time after that," she confided, as they made their way back to the paddock. "I hated Honey, I hated all the horses and the chores and everything about the ranch.

"I don't hate it anymore, but I don't think I'll ever love it the way I used to."

"Losing someone you love has a way of changing things," he acknowledged, reflecting briefly on his abandonment by his mother, his grandmother's death, and then the loss of Hank, too. Each of those events had played a part in making him the man that he was today—and his determination to be a father to the baby Katelyn was carrying.

"I miss her every single day, but now…now that I'm going to be a mother myself, the wound is somehow fresher and deeper again," she told him.

"I didn't tell anyone, when I first suspected that I might be pregnant, but I would have told her. I'm not saying she would have been overjoyed to hear that her unmarried daughter was having a stranger's baby, but she would have listened without judging...and she would have loved our baby."

He slid an arm across her shoulders and drew her to his side, a silent gesture of support. She let her head fall against his shoulder, for just a minute before she said, "Is this a PDA?"

"Nope—there's no one else around, so it's strictly a DA."

She laughed softly. "You know, under other circumstances, I could really like you, Sheriff."

"Why can't you like me under current circumstances?"

"Because current circumstances are complicated."

"Life is complicated."

"And although we're having a simple meal tonight, I should see if Martina and Grams need a hand in the kitchen."

"Very smooth segue, counselor."

She responded with a sassy smile. "Do you want to come back to the house with me?"

"I'll hang out here for a while," he decided.

Ten minutes later, when he was flanked by her brothers and cousins, he was wishing he'd opted to return to the house with Katelyn.

"Are you on duty or off?" Caleb asked, offering a beer to him.

"Off," he said, nodding his thanks as he accepted the bottle.

"I have to make a trip into town later and I wouldn't want to run afoul of the law," Liam said, explaining the soda can in his hand.

"Heather again?" One of the cousins—Mitchell—asked.

Liam grinned. "Yep."

"This is going on what—three weeks now?" the other

cousin—Michael—asked. "That's a long-term relationship for you."

"As much as I enjoy roasting my brother," Caleb interjected. "We're getting sidetracked from the real issue here."

And they all turned, as if on cue, to look at Reid.

He tipped the bottle to his lips, sipped. "Am I an issue?"

"That's what we're trying to figure out," Caleb told him.

"Katie doesn't usually bring a date to family events," Liam commented.

"Katie doesn't *ever* bring a date to family events," Mitchell clarified.

"Then I'm doubly honored to have been invited," Reid said.

"Of course, as a defense attorney, she'd understand the importance of establishing a positive relationship with local law enforcement," Liam noted.

"Which might be why she included you," Caleb suggested.

"I know better than to question a woman's motives," Reid told them.

"We want to know if the two of you are dating," Michael said, cutting to the chase.

"I'm enjoying spending time with her," he said, since he wasn't sure that one date actually qualified as dating.

"You can't have spent much time with her yet," Liam said. "You've only been in town a few weeks."

"Actually, I knew Katelyn before I moved to Haven."

The brothers and cousins exchanged a look, clearly not pleased by this revelation.

"From where and for how long?" Caleb asked.

"From 'none of your business' and as long as 'none of your business,'" Katelyn responded from behind them.

The five men turned to face her.

"You're our sister," Liam reminded her.

"And our cousin," Mitchell piped in.

"That makes it our business," Caleb finished.

"While I acknowledge and appreciate that the name carries a certain weight and status in this town, being born a Gilmore doesn't automatically imply the forfeiture of any expectation of privacy."

Michael slanted a look at Caleb. "Now you've done it."

"When she's really annoyed, she starts with the lawyer-speak," Liam explained to Reid. "And since I've got horses to feed before dinner, I'm going to go do that before she really gets on a roll."

"We'll help you," Michael said.

They all moved away from the paddock together.

Kate folded her arms and leaned them on the rail, her gaze fixed on the foal that was prancing on spindly legs beside its mother.

"I'm sorry," she said. "I knew my family would have questions when we showed up together, but I thought they'd exercise some discretion."

"They're just looking out for you," he noted.

"Maybe," she allowed. "Although sometimes I think they harass people just for sport."

"They did seem to have a good rhythm going with their interrogation, as if they'd had a lot of practice."

"No doubt they have," she agreed, then hastened to clarify. "Interrogating Skylar's numerous boyfriends in high school, I mean."

"What about your boyfriends?"

She shook her head. "I didn't date in high school."

"Not much or not at all?"

"Not at all," she admitted. "I was more interested in studying than boys."

"So when did you have your first boyfriend?" he asked.

"My first year of college, but even he didn't get an invitation home to meet my family."

"Who was the first guy who did?"

"I, uh...actually, I can't remember."

His gaze narrowed. "You remember—you just don't want to tell me."

"It's really not important," she told him.

"Your refusal to share the name suggests otherwise."

She sighed. "If I tell you, you're going to wish you'd let this go," she warned.

"Maybe," he acknowledged. "But I still want to know."

"You," she said.

He waited for her to finish her thought, but that single word was all she said.

"What about me?" he prompted.

"You, Sheriff Reid Davidson, recent transplant from Echo Ridge, Texas, are the first man I've ever brought home to meet my family."

She had to be joking. There was no way he was the first. Except that the flags of color high on her cheeks gave credence to her claim.

"How old are you?" he blurted out.

She laughed. "Twenty-eight." Then, after a tiny hesitation, she added, "Today."

And the surprises kept coming. "It's your birthday today?"

She nodded.

"Happy Birthday."

"Thanks."

His mind was still reeling over the first revelation—that she'd never introduced a man to her family. She must have had boyfriends—because she wasn't a virgin when they were together. But he was beginning to realize he'd misjudged her experience. "So what happened between us in Boulder City…"

"My first ever one-night stand," she admitted.

"And not technically a one-night stand."

She nodded.

"I turned thirty-four in March," he told her.

"Happy belated birthday?"

He managed a smile. "I just wanted you to know that there's a six-year age gap between us."

"Does that bother you?"

"Are you kidding? Guys always want to be with hot young chicks."

She laughed. "Is that what I am—a hot young chick?"

"Very hot—and younger than I realized," he admitted.

"But we're not really together," she reminded him.

"Are you sure? Because I'd guess your family is thinking that we're not only together but that our relationship is pretty serious, since I'm the first guy you've ever brought home to meet them."

"You know why I wanted them to meet you."

"So it doesn't come as a shock when you tell them we're getting married?" he asked hopefully.

Chapter Eleven

Kate shook her head, exasperated by his unwillingness to give up on the idea—and increasingly tempted to take what he was offering. But for the moment, she held firm. "We're *not* getting married."

"I haven't stopped thinking about you since the weekend we spent together in Boulder City," he told her.

"I'm flattered," she said. "But that's no reason to start planning a wedding."

"You're right," he agreed. "But what about a baby? Do you think having a baby is a good reason?"

"I'd say it depends on the preexisting relationship between the expectant parents," she said. "If there was no preexisting relationship, then I'd have to say no—a baby is not a good reason to get married."

"What if those two people, despite having no preexisting relationship, somehow just click whenever they're together?"

"I'm not sure 'click' is either a valid or relevant factor," she said dubiously.

"It's both," he insisted.

"Sometimes an attraction just confuses the issue," she pointed out.

"I'll admit to being confused about a lot of things, but wanting to marry you isn't one of them."

And when he said it like that, with unwavering conviction, she almost believed it was true. But she knew he didn't really *want* to marry her, he just wanted to do the right thing. And she definitely didn't want to have the same arguments with him again.

"We should get back," she said instead. "Dinner will be ready soon."

It was almost dark by the time they'd said their goodbyes to everyone and drove away from the ranch. Though Reid knew her family still had a lot of questions about his relationship with Katelyn, he considered the afternoon a success. Of course, everything would likely change when they found out she was pregnant, so he was grateful she didn't seem to be in a hurry to share that news.

"Your family sure knows how to put on a barbecue," he commented, fondly recalling the platters of ribs and burgers and sausages, heaping bowls of potato salad, coleslaw and macaroni and cheese, the enormous pot filled with homemade baked beans and baskets with thick slices of corn bread. It had seemed like a mountain of food, but the mountain was soon conquered by the Gilmores and their guests.

"My family doesn't believe in doing anything by half measures," she told him.

"I enjoyed meeting them," he said as he turned onto

the highway to head back into town. "Thank you for inviting me today."

"I'm glad you survived," she said, a smile playing at the corners of her mouth. "I know they can be a little... overwhelming at times."

A little overwhelming was something of an understatement. On the other hand, he'd enjoyed watching Katelyn with her relatives—the teasing and shorthand communications that develop through close relationships. The way one person would start a story only to have someone else pick up the narrative of the shared experience without missing a beat.

"You were lucky to grow up in such a close family."

"I know," she acknowledged. "Even if I didn't always think so at the time."

He'd been on his own for so long, he'd forgotten what it meant to be connected to someone else. Being with Katelyn's family today had given him a glimpse, and he was glad their baby was going to be part of that family.

"I realized something else today," she told him.

"What's that?" he asked.

"That you don't talk about your family."

"There's not much to talk about," he said. "For a long time, it was just me and my grandmother. Then I spent some time in foster care, living with other people's families, until Hank took me in."

"Who's Hank?"

"Hank Mahoney was the Sheriff of Echo Ridge when I was growing up there."

"He's the reason you went into law enforcement?" she guessed. "To follow in the footsteps of a man you admired?"

"Yeah," he admitted. "Although it was a little more complicated than that."

"It's a long drive back to town," she reminded him.

She was right, and even if there were parts of his history that he wasn't proud of, she deserved to know his background.

"I first met Hank when I was seventeen," he told her. "Young and dumb enough to attempt to hot-wire the sheriff's truck."

Her brows lifted. "You can really do that? I thought that was just something that happened in the movies."

"I can really do it, but I'm not very good at it—which is why Hank caught me in the act. I'd just been bumped from yet another foster home and, thankfully, he recognized that I was acting out of anger and frustration more than I was looking for trouble, and he gave me a chance."

"Like you did with Aiden, once you knew the whole story."

He kept his gaze focused on the road. "What makes you think I did anything?"

"Haven't you learned yet that it's next to impossible to keep a secret in Haven?" she chided. "When I went to see the ADA about the charges against Aiden, he said Rebecca Blake had already called to tell him that, after consultation with the new sheriff, she supported Aiden's application for the youth diversion program."

"Not a lot of people know about the program," he said, as if that was his only reason for reaching out to Mrs. Blake. "And Aiden's a good candidate, with a father determined to keep him on the straight and narrow."

"How old were you when you lost your parents?" she asked gently.

"I didn't lose them—they lost me," he told her. "My dad was a drunk who took off before I was born. Apparently he came back again, around my first birthday, but didn't hang around for more than a few months. My mom stuck it out for a few more years, hooking up with the occasional boyfriend who made my dad look like a catch. Then when I was about six, she decided that taking care of a kid was too much responsibility and dumped me at her mother's house.

"I don't know what excuse or explanation she offered, but my grandmother took me in and, for the next eight years, she raised me. Then she died, and I had no one.

"I bounced around in foster care for a while, because teen boys don't tend to settle easily into traditional families, and I spent some time in a group home, where I started to run with a bad crowd and made some poor choices."

"Like hot-wiring the sheriff's truck."

He nodded. "I know it sounds melodramatic, but I really believe he saved my life that day."

"Did Hank have any kids of his own?"

"A daughter, Patricia. She was a year ahead of me in school—the cheerleader who dated the quarterback." He lifted a hand to rub the slight bump on the bridge of his nose. "One night when I was leaving school late, I saw them together. They were in the middle of a pretty heavy makeout session and I wanted to look away, but something about the situation set off warning bells in my head.

"Long story short—she was saying no, he wasn't listening, so I intervened. He punched me in the face, broke my nose, Trish helped me mop up the blood and drove me home."

There was something different in his voice when he said her name, an unexpected warmth that made Kate wish she'd never asked.

She definitely shouldn't ask the next question that sprang to mind, but there was a time delay between her brain and her mouth and the words spilled out before she could stop them. "You fell in love with her?"

"No," he denied. "But I married her."

He'd been upfront about his divorce from the beginning, but he hadn't mentioned that his wife was the daughter of a man who'd been his father figure, mentor and best friend.

And again, though she wasn't sure she wanted all the details, she heard herself ask, "How did that come about?"

"Hank got cancer," he said bluntly. "When he realized he was dying, his biggest concern was his daughter. He didn't want to leave her alone, without anyone to look out for her. I told him that I would and put a ring on her finger to prove it.

"I wasn't in love with her," he said again. "But it wasn't just a quick ceremony to appease her dad, either. When I spoke my vows, I intended to honor them forever."

Kate knew that marriage required a leap of faith, regardless of the reasons for it. She also knew there were all kinds of reasons that marriages—even good marriages—fell apart, and she couldn't deny a certain curiosity about his. "What went wrong?"

"We wanted different things," he said.

"That's rather vague," she noted.

"There were issues that drove us apart and no compelling reason to stay together."

His follow-up response didn't do much to expand on the first, but she decided to let it go. No doubt it was, if not painful, at least uncomfortable to talk about a failed marriage. And now that she knew some of Reid's background, she could understand and appreciate why he was so determined to be there for their baby.

Childhood wounds inevitably left a mark, and although she hadn't been so young when she'd lost her mother, the sense of loss and emptiness was still with Kate every single day. She suspected that Reid's experiences had left even deeper scars and that his determination to be there for his child was a way of ensuring his son or daughter had a better start in life than he'd been given.

Katelyn was quiet for a long while after Reid told her about his upbringing, probably questioning his suitability as a parent. He didn't blame her for having doubts—he had more than a few of his own. But a few days earlier, he'd heard her argue a case that made him believe she'd give him a chance.

Her client was a father seeking to alter a custody order. If Reid remembered the details correctly, the dad had worked long hours in the mines and wasn't much of a hands-on parent for the first few years of the children's lives. Now he was a manager, with a more regular schedule and weekends off, and wanted increased access to his children. The mother balked at the request because she was in a new relationship and the children were settled into routines that she didn't want to disrupt.

Listening to the lawyers, Reid couldn't help but wonder if he and Katelyn would someday end up in front of a judge, arguing about who was entitled to what with respect to their child. He didn't want their son or daughter to become a pawn in a game of one-upmanship, but he would fight to be part of the child's life.

For now, though, he continued to hope that wouldn't be necessary. There was still time to convince Katelyn to marry him and give their baby a real family, but he understood her reservations. She was in court almost every day dealing with the aftermath of marriages that didn't work—contentious divorces, property disputes, custody fights. Even if they'd fallen in love after dating a while, she'd undoubtedly have reservations about making any lifelong promises—and he didn't know how to overcome those reservations.

How could he claim to know anything about making a marriage work when he'd already failed to do exactly that? Of course, the circumstances of his first marriage were completely different. Hank had been dying and Reid would have done anything to ease the man's worry in those final days.

He hadn't been in love with Trish and he hadn't pretended that he was. And even though she'd claimed to love him, he suspected the feelings she professed to have were born of a fear of being alone. She wanted to love and be loved, and when Reid couldn't give her what she wanted, she found someone who could.

It was ironic that one of the reasons his marriage had fallen apart was that his wife wanted a baby and he didn't. Now, by accident rather than design, he was going to be a father, anyway. The role he'd been certain he didn't ever want was suddenly his.

More surprising was the realization that he *wanted* to be a father to the baby Katelyn was carrying. In fact, he was starting to accept that he wanted to be a father *and* a husband—he wanted them to be a family. But first, he had to convince Katelyn that it was what she wanted, too.

"Did the judge make a decision in that custody variation hearing you had last week?"

"You were in the courtroom?"

He nodded.

"Since when does local law enforcement take an interest in a standard family law matter?"

"I only popped in to check out the hot young lawyer at first," he admitted. "But your arguments were compelling and, afterward, I found myself wondering if you believed them."

"You're going to have to be a little more specific," she told him.

"You said the variation wasn't about the dad's right to spend more time with his children but about their right to have a meaningful relationship with both parents."

"Wow, you were paying attention, weren't you?"

"The case struck a chord," he admitted.

"Yes, I believe it," she said. "It's important for a child to be given the opportunity to develop a strong and lasting bond with both parents."

"What does that mean for us?"

Her brow furrowed as she turned to stare out the window. "I would accommodate whatever reasonable visitation you wanted."

"I don't want visitation," he told her. "I want to marry you and raise our child together."

"We don't have to be married to co-parent our child," she assured him.

"I don't want our child to be co-parented," he argued. "I want him—or her—to have a real family. And I think you want that, too, you're just afraid to admit it."

"Of course it's what I'd want if our situation was different—if our baby had been conceived in the course of something that actually resembled a relationship rather than as a consequence of a broken condom during a one-night stand."

"Two nights," he reminded her.

"A second night doesn't miraculously turn a casual hookup into a relationship."

"And an unplanned pregnancy shouldn't be used as a roadblock to the development of a relationship," he argued.

"Especially not when there are so many other obvious roadblocks," she agreed.

He turned onto Station Street. "Why'd you go to Echo Ridge looking for me?"

She gave up the pretense that she'd been in Texas for any other purpose. "Because you're the father of my baby."

He nodded. "Now let's consider for a minute what might have happened if I hadn't already agreed to take over Jed Traynor's job here in Haven."

"You would have been in Echo Ridge," she acknowledged, not sure where this new train of thought was leading.

"Most likely," he agreed, making the turn onto Main. "And you would have tracked me down at the Sheriff's Office and told me about our baby, right?"

She hesitated, but she couldn't deny the truth of what he was saying or see how that truth would trip her up. "Right," she confirmed.

"Even though we'd gone our separate ways and you could have kept the news of your pregnancy to yourself."

"You're the father of my baby," she said again. "And fathers have specific legal rights and responsibilities."

He nodded and turned onto Page, then into the parking lot behind her building. "And when you told me about your pregnancy, you gave me the opportunity to exercise those rights and fulfill the responsibilities."

"Because it was the right thing to do."

"And maybe," he suggested, "because there was a part of you that wanted me to step up, not just to be a father but a husband."

Kate thought about his supposition for a long time after Reid had gone. Her initial instinct had been to deny it, of course, but there was some validity to his argument.

She believed that a child had a right to a relationship with both parents; she didn't believe that a child's mother and father had to be married to parent effectively. Maybe marriage would make some things easier, but that was hardly a reason to get trapped into a legally binding arrangement.

Except that the more time she spent with the sheriff, the less the prospect of marriage seemed like a trap. In fact, the idea of marrying Reid was starting to hold some definite appeal.

Chapter Twelve

Two weeks later, Reid had made little progress in his efforts to convince Katelyn to marry him. For every step he took forward, she took two steps back. Sometimes it was a struggle to even get her to spend time with him. She seemed to have a ready excuse whenever he called to make plans, but she was less inclined to turn him down face-to-face. He took that knowledge with him to her door early Friday night.

"If you keep hanging around my apartment, people are going to start to talk," Katelyn warned, but she stepped away from the door so that he could enter.

"I've got nothing to hide." He followed her into the living room, stopping abruptly when he spotted the playpen in the corner, an assortment of colorful blocks scattered across the area rug and a blond-haired, blue-eyed, chubby-cheeked baby wearing an orange T-shirt and brown overalls with a giraffe embroidered on the front.

The baby was sitting upright and gnawing on a purple block, but he glanced up at Reid and grinned, showing off tiny teeth. "Da!"

"Was I in a coma for—" he looked at the baby, estimated his age and added that to the time remaining in Katelyn's pregnancy "—eighteen months?"

"Ha ha." She scooped the baby up from the floor and propped him on her hip. "That's not Daddy, that's Sheriff Davidson."

"Da!" he said again.

"Don't worry," Katelyn said. "He thinks every man is 'Da.'"

"And who is he?" Reid asked.

"This is Keegan," she told him. "My godson. I'm babysitting for a few hours while Emerson—his mom and my best friend—has an appointment at the spa."

"Haven has a spa?"

"Well, right now Andria has a modest setup in her basement, but she's in negotiations with Liam to move her business to the hotel when it opens."

Keegan stuck his thumb in his mouth and dropped his head to Katelyn's shoulder, snuggling in comfortably. Seeing her with the baby in her arms, Reid felt something move inside him—an unexpected warmth that seemed to start in the vicinity of his chest and spread outward.

He'd spent a lot of time reading up on pregnancy and trying to prepare for the baby that would arrive in another six-and-a-half months, but he really didn't know what it took to be a father. Watching Katelyn with Keegan, he was reassured that their child would at least have one competent parent.

"You're a natural," he noted.

"He's an easy baby," she said.

His brows lifted. "Is there such a thing?"

"Well, most of the time he's an easy baby," she amended, as the little guy twisted in her arms to reach toward the blocks on the floor. "He did give me some trouble a few months back when he was teething, but once those pearly whites broke through, he was a smiling—and drooling—baby again."

"How old is he?"

She set Keegan down again, and he immediately grabbed the purple block. "Ten-and-a-half months."

"So we've got a while to wait before our baby will be teething and crawling?"

"And opening cupboards and trying to stick toy keys in electrical outlets."

He noticed that her outlets were protected with plastic inserts. There were also clear rubber bumpers affixed to the sharp edges of the coffee table. "Do you babysit often?"

"I try to take him for a few hours every couple of weeks, sometimes just to give Emerson a break, sometimes so that she and her husband, Mark, can have some time alone together."

"You're a good friend."

"Thank you," she said. "Emerson claims I borrow her baby to pretend I have a life outside of work."

"I guess you don't get out much."

"You've been in Haven long enough now to know there's really nowhere to go."

"Maybe that's why I always end up at your door."

She smiled at that. "Why are you really here?"

"Because I was thinking about you, and while I was thinking about you, I realized I was hungry, so I decided to see if you wanted to grab a bite and catch a movie."

"Dinner and a movie—that sounds a lot like a date, Sheriff."

"Maybe, if you had to put a label on it," he acknowledged. "Or it could just be a couple of friends-slash-colleagues hanging out."

"I appreciate the invitation," she said. "But Emerson is picking up pizza and wings on her way back."

"Maybe just the movie later, then?" he asked hopefully.

"Mark's out of town this weekend so we're having a girls' night—no boys allowed."

"What about him?" Reid asked, jerking his head toward the baby, who'd traded in the purple block for a green one.

"He gets a pass because his boy parts are in a diaper."

He sighed regretfully. "Okay, I guess I'll head over to Jo's and get my own pizza to take home and eat by myself."

She led him back to the foyer, a clear signal that his attempt to elicit sympathy and procure an invitation had failed.

But when she opened the door, he found himself face-to-face with a slender woman with curly reddish hair and a stack of three flat boxes in her hand.

"Well, hello, there," she said, her green eyes sparking with curiosity. "You must be Reid."

"I am," he confirmed, stepping back so that she could enter.

"And Reid was just leaving," Katelyn said.

"Oh," her friend said, sounding disappointed. "Have you had dinner?"

"I'm going to pick up a pizza on my way home," he said.

"Why would you do that when we've got plenty of pizza—and wings—right here?"

Keegan, having recognized his mother's voice, abandoned his blocks and crawled to the foyer, where he was now attempting to pull himself up on her leg.

"There's my little man," she said, smiling down at the baby.

Katelyn took the boxes. "How much food did you get?"

Emerson lifted the baby, rubbing her nose against his and making him giggle, then propping him on her hip. "They had a special on two pizzas and wings."

"We're never going to eat all that," Katelyn said.

"Then I guess it's a good thing we've got the sheriff here to help," she said, winking at Reid.

"I was just on my way out," he reminded her, showing his willingness to accede to Katelyn's wishes.

"Don't go without having something to eat first," Emerson protested.

He looked at Katelyn, silently questioning.

"Fine—you can stay for a slice of pizza," she relented, handing the boxes to him. "I'll get plates and napkins."

"Can you hold Keegan for a sec while I grab drinks?" Emerson asked when he'd set the food on the table.

Before he could respond—which would have been to suggest that he'd get the drinks—she'd shoved the baby at him, leaving him with no choice in the matter.

He looked down at the little guy who was looking up at him, lower lip quivering. "Oh, crap. You're going to cry, aren't you?"

As if on cue, the baby's big blue eyes filled with tears.

"Hey, this wasn't my idea," he said, talking fast in the hope of distracting the kid long enough for his mom to return. "And I don't blame you for being unhappy with the situation, but your mom will be right back, she just went to help—I assume, since she's your godmother, you call her Aunt Katelyn, or maybe Aunt Katie—get drinks so that we can have dinner."

To his surprise and immense relief, the monologue seemed to do the trick. Though the tears didn't dry up, Keegan's lip was no longer quivering and he looked more curious than scared now.

Reid kept talking. "What do you like to drink with your

pizza? Is your beverage of choice milk or juice? And do you drink from a bottle or a sippy cup?"

Of course, Keegan didn't respond to any of the questions, but the little guy at least seemed to be listening.

So was Kate, who had paused in the doorway between the kitchen and the dining room, plates and napkins in hand.

"I'm running out of things to say now," Reid continued in the same easy tone. "But I'm afraid if I stop talking, you'll start crying and your aunt Katelyn will realize I don't have a clue when it comes to babies and then she'll worry I'm going to be a horrible father.

"And while I'll admit that's entirely possible—and probably understandable considering that I have no memories of my own father and didn't have any positive male role models in my life until I met Hank when I was seventeen—I'm going to do my best to be a good dad and hope like hell—

"*Heck!*" he quickly amended. "I mean heck. I'm going to hope like heck that I don't screw up too badly. I suspect swearing in front of a baby would probably count as a screwup, so maybe we can just keep that to ourselves?

"And maybe you could actually smile and pretend I'm incredibly amusing and entertaining, and maybe that'll help convince Katelyn to give me a chance—"

Kate felt an elbow in her ribs and glanced at Emerson, who was also observing the sheriff's interaction with her little boy.

"If you had to get knocked up, at least you picked a stand-up guy," Emerson noted in a whisper.

"You're making this assessment after overhearing two minutes of a one-sided conversation with an infant?"

"A conversation in which he demonstrated honesty, vulnerability, self-awareness and determination," Emerson noted. "All that, and those fabulous shoulders, too."

Of course, her friend was right. And the more time Kate spent with Reid, the more irresistible he seemed, which made her question why she was continuing to resist.

She pushed aside those tempting thoughts.

"Come on. Pizza's getting cold."

Keegan sat in his mother's lap, gnawing contentedly on a piece of crust while the adults chatted and ate. When everyone had their fill and Kate got up to wrap the leftovers, Emerson said, "Oh, my goodness—is it almost eight o'clock already? I need to get this little guy changed into his pj's and home to bed."

Then she hurried into the bedroom, where Kate had laid a protective sheet on top of her comforter as a makeshift change table for the baby. Kate, of course, followed.

"What are you talking about?" she demanded. "I thought we were going to hang out tonight."

"Except that I forgot the seventeen loads of dirty laundry waiting at home," her friend said as she stripped away Keegan's overalls and T-shirt.

Kate's eyes narrowed. "Oh, no, you don't."

"But I do," Emerson insisted, pulling a sleeper out of the diaper bag. "Soon enough you'll understand how many onesies and burp cloths a baby goes through in a week."

"I'm sure you do have laundry to wash," she acknowledged. "That's not what I'm referring to."

"What are you referring to?" Her friend expertly slid a clean diaper under Keegan's bottom before unfastening and whisking away the wet one.

Kate folded her arms over her chest. "You're taking off because you think that will push me and Reid to spend more time together."

"If you need to be pushed, you're not nearly as smart as I always thought you were," Emerson chided.

But apparently it wasn't enough to push Kate, because Emerson returned to the living room and said to Reid, "Have you got a ring yet? Because The Goldmine has a sale on diamond jewelry this weekend."

Kate sighed. "Emerson's been my best friend since kindergarten," she told him. "But she's never been subtle."

"I've never understood why anyone would tiptoe around an issue when the direct approach gets you to the same place so much faster," Emerson said.

He nodded in acknowledgment of the point before responding to her question. "I might be new in town, but I've been here long enough to know that buying a diamond at The Goldmine would be as discreet as putting an engagement announcement in the Haven Record."

"Sexy *and* smart," Emerson noted. "Okay, putting aside the question of a ring for the moment—what are your intentions with respect to my best friend?"

"You should be more concerned about my intentions," Kate interrupted. "Because right now, killing you seems to be the only way to shut you up."

Her friend just grinned, unrepentant. "You shouldn't issue death threats in front of the sheriff."

But Reid didn't seem to have any qualms about answering Emerson's original question, because he said, "My intention is to marry Katelyn so we can raise our child together."

"And I still maintain that we don't need to be married to raise our child together," she chimed in.

"Blah blah blah," Emerson said, clearly having heard it all before and not at all concerned about upsetting her friend.

"It's true," Kate insisted.

Emerson directed her next comment to Reid again. "All the time Katie spends in divorce court has made her wary of putting her heart on the line."

"Reid doesn't want my heart," she interjected. "He just wants his ring on my finger to legitimize his claim to our child."

He was stunned by her matter-of-fact tone as much as the words. "Is that what you really think?"

Katelyn shrugged, as if it didn't matter. "We both know you never would have proposed if I wasn't pregnant."

"I can't deny that's true, but I don't just want our baby to carry my name," he said. "I want him or her to have the love and support of both parents, not one or the other depending on where he or she's sleeping on any particular night."

"That's a pretty compelling argument," Emerson noted, as she buckled the sleepy baby into his car seat.

"I thought you were in a hurry to get home," Katelyn said to her.

Emerson hugged her friend. "I'm going," she promised. Then she hugged Reid, too. "Don't give up on her—she'll come around."

"I'm keeping my fingers crossed."

"You might have more luck if you put a diamond on hers instead."

Kate shook her head as she closed the door behind her friend. "I'm sorry about that."

"I'm not," he said. "I like her straightforwardness."

"That's one word for it," she agreed.

"And I'm hoping the direct approach will work for me, too," he said, reaching a hand into his pocket.

Her heart started to beat faster when she recognized what was clearly a jeweler's box, and she took an instinctive step back. "What are you doing?"

"I'm proposing, Katelyn."

"Why?"

"Because while I've frequently mentioned that I want us to be married, I've never actually asked you to be my wife."

"You really bought a ring?"

He flipped open the lid to reveal a stunning princess-cut diamond.

As she stared at the glittering stone, Kate wondered why the prospect of marrying a man she'd known only a few months was somehow less terrifying than the idea of having a baby on her own. That he wanted to marry her and be a father to their child told her a lot about the type of man he was, but even if he was willing to vow to "love, honor and cherish" her, she knew he didn't love her.

And she didn't love him.

The five words hadn't fully come together to form a sentence when her heart bumped against her ribs, as if to contradict her claim.

No, her head insisted. It wasn't possible that she'd fallen in love with Reid.

Was it?

She took a minute to review the evidence. Every time she was going to see him, she felt flutters of anticipation in her belly that she knew—only ten weeks into her pregnancy—couldn't be explained away as movements of the baby inside her. She enjoyed talking to him and even arguing with him, because he challenged her to consider different ideas and opinions. And there was no doubt she was attracted to him. Those little flutters were nothing compared to the way her pulse jolted whenever he gave her one of those lingering looks that said he was remembering her naked. Or the way her pulse would race when he touched her—even just a casual brush of a finger down her arm. And when he kissed her—

Ohmygod.

She *was* in love with him.

But her feelings were only one side of the equation. If and when she ever walked down the aisle, she wanted it to be with butterflies in her tummy and hope in her heart— and looking toward a groom whose eyes were filled with love as he looked back at her.

Reid was looking at her now, but all she could see in his eyes was a steely determination to do the right thing.

"Katelyn Gilmore, will you—"

"Stop!"

"You didn't let me finish the question," he said mildly.

"Because if you don't actually ask, then I don't have to say no and we can pretend this never happened."

He rose to his feet again but continued to hold the box open, the brilliant diamond flashing light. "There is another option, you know—you could say yes."

She shook her head regretfully, her throat tight. "I can't."

Then, because she didn't trust herself to hold back the tears that filled her eyes or the newly acknowledged feelings overflowing from her heart, she turned and walked briskly to her bedroom, closing the door firmly behind her.

Chapter Thirteen

She hadn't actually said no, but Reid knew that if he'd pressed the issue, she would have. Maybe they weren't head over heels in love, but he sincerely liked and respected Katelyn. And then there was the sizzling sexual chemistry between them…chemistry that she'd been determinedly ignoring, causing him to suffer through a lot of cold showers in recent weeks.

If she'd said yes to his proposal, one of the perks would be warm showers with his bride-to-be, sliding soapy hands over the sexy curves of her body. Unfortunately, his erotic fantasies seemed destined to remain just that.

If she was adamantly opposed to marrying him—and rushing away in tears didn't suggest that she was on the fence—he had to respect her choice. Even if he wasn't happy about it.

He didn't want to share custody of their child, with scheduled weekend trade-offs and formal discussions about homework or afterschool activities, but he was determined to be there for his son or daughter as much as possible. To be the full-time father he'd never had as a kid.

Still, he was frustrated with the whole situation, so when he stepped outside Saturday morning and saw Norm Clayton pressing one hand to his back while the other struggled with the cord of the lawn mower, he offered to take over. The old man protested at first—after all, the sheriff was paying rent, he shouldn't have to do chores—but Reid assured him that he didn't mind. So Norm retreated inside to his heating pad and Reid welcomed the roar of the mower drowning out thoughts of his aborted proposal.

The backyard required some maneuvering around the climbing structure and sandbox that Norm and Bev had installed for their grandchildren to enjoy when they visited, which got Reid thinking he was going to need a backyard for his son or daughter to run around in. Because he didn't plan on living in the Claytons' downstairs apartment forever and a child needed space.

And toys to scatter around the yard.

And maybe a dog.

He'd finished the cutting and was pushing the mower back toward the garage when he saw Katelyn on the sidewalk.

She smiled, a little tentatively, as she moved closer. "Moonlighting in yard work, Sheriff?"

"Norm's back was bothering him this morning, so I offered to help."

"Did you sell tickets?"

"What?"

"You have an audience," Katelyn noted, sliding a glance toward the neighbor's porch where Beverly Clayton and Frieda Zimmerman were sipping glasses of lemonade.

"They're not watching me," he denied.

"You don't think so?" She lifted a hand in greeting and both women immediately waved back.

"It's a real scorcher today, isn't it?" Beverly called out.

"It sure is," Reid agreed, wiping the sweat from his brow with his forearm.

"Eighty-seven degrees already," Frieda said. "And supposed to get hotter."

"There's an extra glass here," Beverly told him. "If you want some lemonade to help you cool off."

"Or you could just take off your shirt," Frieda suggested as an alternative.

"Frieda!" Beverly admonished.

"We're not out here to watch the clouds move across the sky," her friend and neighbor said bluntly. "We want to see the sheriff's muscles."

Katelyn bit down on her lip, obviously trying not to laugh.

"Maybe next time, Mrs. Zimmerman," Reid said with a smile.

She let out an exaggerated sigh. "Promises, promises."

He put the mower in the garage, then returned to Katelyn. "Were you just in the neighborhood?" he wondered.

"In the neighborhood...hoping to see you."

Suddenly his day was looking brighter. "Do you want to go inside where we can talk without an audience?"

She hesitated, and he knew she was thinking about Mrs. Clayton and Mrs. Zimmerman and worried what they might think if she was seen going into Reid's apartment.

"It's not even eleven—too early for them to suspect we're going inside for a nooner."

His teasing remark earned a small smile, though she didn't look entirely convinced. Her decision was made easier when Frieda grumbled about preferring to be inside with the air conditioning if there was nothing to see outside and the two old women abandoned their posts.

As Kate followed Reid into his apartment, she could see the perspiration glistening on his skin. She'd never thought she would find a sweaty man appealing, but she couldn't deny that the sight of Reid, his T-shirt stretched over those broad shoulders, a dark V dampening both the front and the back of the fabric, made everything inside her quiver.

"Why do you wear jeans to cut the grass in this heat?" she wondered.

"Because the mower might kick up stones or other debris."

Which made sense but was still disappointing, because his legs could rival his shoulders for Beverly's and Frieda's attention—and even her own.

And then, as if he could hear her thoughts, he lifted the hem of his T-shirt and pulled it over his head, then rubbed the fabric across his chest. Her gaze followed his movements, admiring those incredible shoulders, the sculpted pecs, the rippling abs.

"What are you doing?" she croaked through dry lips.

"I thought you'd probably appreciate it if I took a shower."

"Well, undress in the bathroom," she suggested.

His brows lifted. "I only took off my shirt. And you have seen me naked before."

Yeah, but she couldn't let herself think about "before"— when she'd been naked with him—because she was now dealing with an overload of pregnancy hormones that made her want to do all kinds of wickedly wonderful things to him. And let him do anything he wanted to her in return.

"Of course, it's been a while, hasn't it, Katelyn?" he prompted.

Twenty-two days.

Not that she was counting—not really.

But she was staring—she couldn't seem to help herself.

And the amusement that danced in the depths of those hazel eyes left absolutely no doubt that he was aware of the effect he had on her.

"Do you want to join me in the shower?" he asked. "You're looking a little...flushed."

She swallowed. "I'm fine."

He shrugged, and the casual rise and fall of those amazing shoulders nearly made her whimper.

"Why don't you go relax in the living room then?" he suggested as an alternative.

"I'm fine," she said again, unwilling to go anywhere near the flowered sofa where she'd been naked with him twenty-two days ago.

His quick grin confirmed that he knew what she was thinking. "There are cold drinks in the fridge and ice-cream bars in the freezer. Help yourself to whatever you want."

What she wanted was standing in front of her, but succumbing to that desire—again—would complicate her life exponentially. Instead, she waited to hear the bathroom door close, then went to the freezer to see what kind of ice cream he had.

A few minutes later, Kate heard the water running—a sound that elicited mental images of Reid's naked body. She could picture droplets of water sliding over those perfectly sculpted muscles, caressing his taut skin.

Only when she felt ice cream dripping onto her hand did she shove the images aside and the ice cream into her mouth.

He came out of the bathroom a short while later, wearing a clean T-shirt and a pair of cargo shorts. His hair was still wet from the shower and his jaw was unshaven, and all her girlie parts sighed anew with a combination of pleasure and longing.

He opened the fridge and pulled out a can of cola. "Do you want anything?" he asked her.

Nothing I can have.

But, of course, she just shook her head. "No, thanks."

He popped the tab on the can and lifted it to his mouth to drink. She turned away, wandering toward the living area.

"I thought you were going to get some new furniture."

He shrugged. "It's not a priority right now."

"The last time I was here, you claimed to be allergic to the flowers painted on everything."

He smiled, apparently thinking about the last time she'd been there. "The last time you were here is the reason I've grown quite fond of that sofa—flowers and all."

She felt her cheeks burn.

"Why are you here, Katelyn? Since it's apparently—unfortunately—not for an encore performance."

"I'm here because...I wanted to apologize...for last night."

"Turning down my proposal?"

"Walking away in the middle of our conversation," she clarified. "Apparently pregnancy hormones can cause a woman to become...emotional...and I didn't want to have a breakdown in front of you."

"I can handle a few tears," he assured her. "And I *want* to be there for you—in any way that I can."

"That's the other reason I'm here. I got a call from my doctor's office this morning. Everything's fine," she hastened to assure him. "They were just calling to schedule my first ultrasound."

"Isn't it too soon for an ultrasound? Don't they usually happen between eighteen and twenty weeks?"

"Somebody's been reading up on pregnancy," she mused. "But this is an early scan, to calculate the baby's due date."

"You can't just count the number of weeks from the day the condom broke?"

She shook her head.

"So when are you having this ultrasound?"

"Two o'clock Tuesday at the Battle Mountain Medical Clinic."

"Can I go with you?"

"You can meet me there," she suggested.

"Are you honestly worried that someone might see us together in Battle Mountain?"

"No," she said. "I was actually more concerned that if there was a law enforcement emergency, you might have to take off and leave me stranded."

"I can make it work," he told her.

"Okay, then," she relented. "You can pick me up at one."

Reid was impressed by the modern facility and efficient staff at the Battle Mountain clinic, where they were taken to an exam room only a few minutes after checking in. Katelyn hopped up on the table as instructed, while he was directed to stand on the other side of the table, out of the way but able to see everything that was happening.

A few minutes later, the technician came in and introduced herself to the expectant parents, then briefly outlined the procedure for a transabdominal ultrasound and explained how the measurements she obtained would help accurately pinpoint the baby's estimated date of delivery.

Following her instructions, Katelyn folded back the hem of her top and pushed her yoga pants down to her hips to expose her abdomen. The technician keyed some information into the computer, then squirted warm gel onto the expectant mother's belly. She used what she'd told them was a transducer—a small plastic device that sent out and received sound waves (and, in Reid's opinion, looked a little bit like the upholstery attachment of his vacuum cleaner)—to spread the gel around.

He reached for Katelyn's hand, a silent gesture of support, and she offered a small smile in return.

Then his attention shifted to the monitor as the tech clicked the mouse and keyed in the data she was gathering. But Reid was focused on the grainy black-and-white image on the screen, searching for something that looked like a baby. And then he saw it—although it looked more like a blob than a tiny person. Though on closer inspection, he could see a head distinct from the body with stubby legs and little T-Rex arms. But what really struck him when the technician enlarged the image was that something in the center of the body blob seemed to be pulsing.

Katelyn was watching, too, her grip on his hand tightening. "What…is that…the baby's heart beating?"

"That's what it is," the technician confirmed.

Then she clicked some more keys, and suddenly the baby's heartbeat was displayed across the bottom of the screen, the *woop-woop-woop* surprisingly fast and loud in the small room.

Reid looked at Katelyn, who was trying to focus on the screen through eyes blurred with tears. He had a pretty good idea how she felt, because in the first moment he'd recognized that big-headed alien-looking blob as their child, he'd been filled with emotion. And watching and listening to that little heart beating, he was overwhelmed by the knowledge that he'd played even a minor part in the creation of this tiny person.

Later, as he walked out of the medical center beside Katelyn, she reached for his hand. "Thank you for being here with me today."

"Thank you for letting me be here," he said, truly and deeply touched by what he'd experienced—and grateful that she'd included him.

She smiled. "It was pretty amazing, wasn't it? Actually seeing our baby."

He nodded. "For the past few weeks, I've hardly been able to think about anything else. But still, the baby was something vague and distant. Until today. Looking at the image on the screen, hearing the beat of the heart, it suddenly all became real."

"Morning sickness made it real for me," she said lightly. "But I know what you mean. Even though I've experienced changes in my body, they were just abstract symptoms of pregnancy."

He fished his key fob out of his pocket and unlocked the doors of his truck, but he paused before walking Katelyn around to the passenger side. "I know you have all kinds of reasons for believing that marriage isn't necessary or even desirable, but I want our baby to have a real family. I don't want to miss out on the first tooth or first steps because it's not my turn or my day or my weekend. I want both of us to be there for all the milestones."

"I don't want to miss out on anything, either," she admitted. "And if the best way to be sure that doesn't happen is to get married, then let's do it."

"Really?" he asked, equal parts stunned and hopeful. "You mean it?"

She nodded. "I really mean it."

He opened the maps app on his phone. "If we leave now, we can be in Las Vegas in six hours and twenty-two minutes."

But Katelyn shook her head. "We're not getting married today and we're definitely not getting married in Vegas."

"I'm afraid that if we don't do it right now, you might change your mind," he admitted.

"I'm not going to change my mind," she promised.

"Let's make it official, anyway," he said, and pulled a familiar square box out of his pocket. At her questioning look, he shrugged. "What can I say? I'm an eternal optimist."

Then he dropped to his knee again, right there in the parking lot, and said, "Katelyn Gilmore, will you marry me?"

This time, she didn't back away or cut him off. Instead, she held out her hand. "Yes, Reid Davidson, I will marry you."

He rose to his feet and slid the ring on her finger. Then he kissed her, and Kate closed her eyes and let herself be swept away by the romance of the moment.

He kept his arm around her, holding her close for another minute. "Thank you for giving us a chance," he said.

"You might not feel so grateful in another six months, when you haven't had more than three consecutive hours of sleep because our baby's colicky and screaming," she warned.

"Whatever challenges we face, I know we'll get through them together," he assured her.

"The first challenge will be telling my dad."

He opened the passenger door and helped her climb in. "Do you want to do that today?"

"The sooner the better, so we can pick a date and start planning the wedding."

"This weekend works for me," he told her.

"While I appreciate your enthusiasm, if we're going

to get married, we're going to do this right, and not even my family could pull everything together in four days."

"Okay, how much time do you need?"

"More like four weeks," she decided, crossing her fingers that she'd be able to find a wedding dress off-the-rack and the minister would be free and Marcella could squeeze in making a wedding cake and Naomi could do her flowers and—

"So what changed your mind?"

His question was a welcome reprieve from the details spinning through her head—until she realized that he expected an answer.

Because she definitely wasn't ready to tell him the truth—that the reason she'd changed her mind was that she'd fallen in love with him. Not only because she knew he didn't feel the same way but because she suspected it was a truth he wasn't ready to hear.

Since she'd told him about her pregnancy, he'd been focused on doing what was best for their baby. He certainly hadn't said or done anything to hint that he wanted any kind of emotional entanglements. In fact, he'd made it clear he wasn't interested in falling in love.

But she'd seen the look on his face when he saw their baby on the ultrasound monitor—and she recognized the surprise and wonder and love, because they were the same emotions that filled her heart. And if he could fall in love with their unborn child, she had to hope and believe that maybe, someday, he might fall in love with her, too.

Chapter Fourteen

Reid and Katelyn drove straight to the Circle G to share their news with her family. David Gilmore understandably had reservations about the quickness of their engagement—especially when he learned of their plan to marry before the end of the summer.

"Is there any particular reason for the rush?" Katelyn's father asked them.

"I thought you'd want to be a father-in-law before a grandfather," she responded to his question.

"Grandfather?" he echoed, clearly stunned. "You're... pregnant?"

She nodded. "The baby's due in February."

Her father's brow furrowed as he did the math. He looked at Reid, his scowl deepening. "You didn't waste any time making your move, did you?"

"I made the move," Katelyn interjected, attempting to take the heat.

Reid appreciated the effort, but he wasn't going to hide behind his fiancée. "I'd say we moved together," he countered.

She smiled at that. "Maybe we did."

"Well, I guess what matters now is that you're doing the right thing," David said. "Getting married and giving your baby a family."

Reid nodded. "Yes, sir. And it would mean a lot to both of us to have your blessing."

"Well, of course, you've got my blessing," his future father-in-law said. "And my checkbook for the wedding."

"That's a generous offer, sir, but—"

"No buts," David interjected. "I want Katelyn to have the wedding of her dreams—or as close as possible within your time constraints."

She hugged her father. "Thank you."

David smiled at his daughter, his eyes shiny. "Now you better give your grandmother a call—she'll want to know what's going on and help you with the planning."

So Katelyn did, and a short while later her grandparents and siblings showed up to join in the celebration.

It didn't take long after that for the news to make its way through town, and everywhere they went, they were offered congratulations and best wishes. If people were surprised by the August 30 date they'd set for the wedding, they didn't show it to the happy couple.

And they *were* happy.

Reid's only cause for complaint was that he barely saw his bride-to-be in the weeks leading up to the big day. He knew she was busy taking care of all the details that went into a wedding: drafting the guest list and sending out evites, finding a dress, then fittings for the dress, meetings with the baker and the florist, then tracking replies to the invitations and working on a seating plan for the reception—which was being held at the Circle G under the cover of huge tents rented for the occasion.

Reid's responsibilities were limited. He gave his notice to Bev and Norm, since he'd be moving in with Katelyn after the wedding, packed up his meager belongings and went into Elko with Caleb and Liam to be fitted for their tuxes.

Which meant he had a lot of time to focus on his job, which he generally enjoyed. His least favorite part of being sheriff was playing politics. But if he wanted to remain in the position, and of course he did, then he'd need to run for reelection when Jed Traynor's current term expired. And that meant gritting his teeth and making nice with the voters, even when those voters drove him crazy with incessant nuisance calls.

Two days before his wedding, the call was from Ruth Fielding.

"I'll send Deputy Neal to talk to Mr. Petrovsky about his cat digging up your flowers," Reid promised.

"Talking isn't going to grow me new flowers," Ruth protested.

He made a note on the pad on his desk. "Perhaps some form of restitution can be arranged."

"We need a leash law for cats," she said. "I have to put my Harvey on a leash when I take him out. It's not fair that obnoxious feline—"

A movement at the door caught his eye and he looked up, a ready smile on his face for his fiancée, who was meeting him for lunch.

The smile froze on his lips when he saw that it wasn't his soon-to-be wife standing in his doorway, but his ex.

"—gets to run free around the neighborhood and create havoc—"

"You're right, Mrs. Fielding," he interrupted. "And I'll send Deputy Neal over right after lunch."

Then he disconnected the call to focus on his unexpected visitor.

"Trish—what are you doing here?"

She shook her head, a gesture of undisguised exasperation. "Reid, you're getting married in two days—where else would I be?"

"Home in Echo Ridge with your husband and child?" he suggested.

"They came with me," she said. "Because Jonah understands why I needed to be here."

"I'm glad someone does," he said, but he pushed away from the desk and embraced her. "You look good."

"It's the boobs." She smiled proudly as she glanced down at her chest. "Breastfeeding has added a full cup size."

He winced. "Please spare me the details."

"This town needs a decent hotel," Trish said. "We're staying in Battle Mountain because Dusty Boots Motel sounds like a place that rents rooms by the hour and I wasn't sure that you'd have space for us to squeeze in at your place."

His head was spinning. He was grateful that she hadn't made any assumptions about staying with him—which would have been more than a squeeze—but he had to ask, "But why are you here?"

"Did you really think you could send me a text message telling me that you were getting married and not expect some follow-up conversation?"

"I thought you might call," he acknowledged.

"I wanted to read the expression on your face when you explained to me how this happened."

"I met a girl, I asked her to marry me, she said yes."

Trish shook her head. "That's a very concise summary—too concise."

And then he heard a familiar voice in the outer office as Katelyn and Judy exchanged pleasantries.

Reid had no idea how the next few minutes would play out, but he didn't have a good feeling.

"I really wish you'd called before you got on a plane," he muttered.

"If I'd called, you would've told me not to come," Trish acknowledged.

"You're right," he confirmed.

"Which is why I didn't call," she said logically.

"Did it ever occur to you that showing up—unannounced and uninvited—might not go over well with your ex-husband's bride-to-be?"

"No," she admitted. "Why would she care? She's the woman you're head over heels for and I'm already married to someone else."

"I don't know that she will care, but—" he gave up trying to explain as his fiancée walked into his office.

"Sorry, I'm late, I got caught—oh," Katelyn's explanation cut off abruptly when she realized Reid wasn't alone. "I'm sorry. I didn't mean to interrupt."

"You're not interrupting," he assured her.

She looked from him to the other woman in his office and back again.

"Katelyn, this is my ex-wife, Trish."

Whatever she was thinking or feeling, Katelyn kept it hidden behind a neutral expression. But she took a step toward Trish and held out a hand. "It's nice to meet you."

"And you," Trish said, shaking the proffered hand. "I'm really looking forward to getting to know you."

"That's going to have to wait." Katelyn offered a polite if cool smile. "I've got to run to a meeting with a client."

"But we're supposed to have lunch," Reid reminded her.

"I got the call just as I was heading over here—that's why I was late," she said.

And though it was a plausible explanation, he didn't believe it was a complete one.

"We can go after your meeting then," he offered.

Katelyn shook her head. "I really don't know how long I'll be. It's probably better if you two go ahead."

"I could go for lunch," Trish said as Katelyn disappeared out the door. "You pick the place, and I'll pick up the tab."

Reid decided to let her, because he instinctively knew that he'd be paying for this later.

When Kate checked her phone, there were half a dozen missed calls and an equal number of text messages from Reid. She replied to the last one, letting him know that her meeting had gone late but confirming that she was home now.

He immediately responded: I'll bring dinner.

Which dashed any hope of putting him off until the next day.

Ten minutes later, he knocked at the door. Though she'd given him a key because he'd be moving in after the wedding, he wasn't yet in the habit of letting himself in.

She put a smile on her face and opened the door.

Reid walked in carrying a large takeout bag from Diggers', and the scent of spicy buffalo sauce and fried grease teased her nostrils and made her stomach growl.

"I'm guessing you never got around to having lunch today," he said, proof that he'd heard the rumble.

"I guess I didn't," she admitted, only realizing it now herself.

He carried the bag of food to the table.

"Why'd you run out of my office today?"

"I didn't run," she denied, opening the cutlery drawer. "I had a meeting."

He reached in the cupboard beside the sink for plates. "Since when is Emerson a client?"

"Since today," she told him.

Because she was a terrible liar, and because she hated the idea of lying to Reid, she'd made her friend give her a dollar as a retainer so she could legitimately claim solicitor-client privilege and not have to admit that seeing her soon-to-be husband cozied up in his office with his ex-wife had sent her to her best friend's house in tears.

"How'd you know I was with Emerson?"

"Because after I had lunch with Trish—and thanks for setting that up, by the way—"

She bristled at the irritation in his voice as she plucked napkins from the holder on the counter. "No need to thank me," she said. "You're the one who invited your ex-wife to our wedding."

"I didn't invite Trish to our wedding," he told her.

"Then why is she here?"

"Because she has no concept of boundaries."

She set the napkins and cutlery on the table, by the plates he'd already put down.

"I don't know what else to say," he admitted. "I know you're not happy that she's here, but I'm not sure why it bothers you so much."

"Because she's beautiful," Katelyn said glumly.

"Really? That's it?"

She glared at him. "No woman ever wants to meet an ex-girlfriend, lover or wife who looks like she walked off the cover of a magazine."

"It's funny that you'd say that."

"I'm glad you find this amusing."

"Because—" he caught her as she tried to move past him and pulled her into his arms "—Trish told me that no woman, even a happily married new mom, ever wants to discover that she was replaced by a younger and prettier model."

"She really said that?"

"You know I don't understand the workings of a woman's mind well enough to make this stuff up."

"Apparently I'm shallow enough to let that make me feel a little better," she acknowledged. "But I'm still not happy she's here."

"Do you want me to tell her not to come to the wedding?"

"If you do, then she'll know I was the one who didn't want her there, and she came all this way to—"

"Katelyn," he interrupted gently. "This is *our* wedding. What anyone else did or wants doesn't matter if it's not what you want."

She sighed, feeling irrational and unreasonable and generally miserable because nothing about the circumstances of their upcoming marriage were what she would have planned. But of course, none of that was Reid's fault. Or at least none of it aside from getting her pregnant. "What do *you* want?"

"I want you to be happy," he said, and sounded as if he meant it. "And if that means banning my ex-wife and her new husband from our wedding, I'll do it."

Of course, she didn't want her soon-to-be-husband's ex-wife there, but how was she supposed to admit that to him?

"Did you go to her second wedding?" she asked instead.

He nodded. "In the interest of full disclosure, I walked Trish down the aisle when she married Jonah."

"Whose idea was that?"

"Not mine," Reid assured her. "I thought the request

was a little odd but, in the absence of her dad, I didn't see how I could say no."

"What did her new husband think about that?"

"He had no objections. It didn't take him long to realize that me and Trish are more like brother and sister than ex-spouses—and of course he knew the truth about why we got married."

"Because her dad wanted you to take care of her."

He nodded.

"And now you're marrying me because I'm pregnant."

He didn't deny it. If the condom hadn't failed, they might have gone out on a few dates, and maybe those dates might have led to a relationship, but there was no way they'd be planning to marry only two months after he'd moved to Haven.

"Is there a point?" he asked.

"Maybe we shouldn't do this."

"Really? Two days before the wedding, you've suddenly got cold feet?"

"It's not sudden," she said. "You know I've had reservations about this from the beginning."

"But we both agreed that getting married is what's best for the baby."

She nodded. "You're right. But this is the second time you're getting married for the wrong reasons."

"Giving our baby a family isn't a wrong reason."

"You probably didn't think you were marrying Trish for the wrong reason, either, but look how that turned out."

"There are zero similarities between my relationship with Trish and my relationship with you," he told her.

"So why won't you tell me why you split up?"

"I really wish you'd let this go, Katelyn."

"I don't think I can."

He scrubbed his hands over his face. "Trish and I split up because she wanted a baby…and I didn't."

"Oh." Kate now wished she hadn't pushed so hard for an answer to her question.

He lifted his gaze to meet hers again. "Obviously, our situation is completely different."

"How can you say that when you just admitted you didn't want to be a father?" she wondered.

"Because it *is* different," he insisted. "Trish and I were talking about the *possibility* of having a child. The baby you're carrying—*our* baby—is *real*."

"Putting aside that nebulous distinction for now, why didn't you want a child?"

"Because I didn't want to screw up my child the way my parents screwed me up," he confided.

"And now those fears have miraculously disappeared?" she asked dubiously.

"Of course not," he said. "I'm still terrified that I'm going to do something—or a thousand things—wrong. But over the past few weeks, I've started to trust that we can figure it out together."

"I don't want to do this without you," she admitted.

"You don't have to," he promised. "I'm not going into this reluctantly or begrudgingly. I *want* to be your husband and our baby's father. I want to go to sleep beside you at night and wake up next to you in the morning. I want to argue with you about whose turn it is to get up with a screaming baby in the middle of the night. I want to share each and every one of our baby's milestones—the good, the bad and the cranky—with you."

"Even if the cranky part is mine?"

He smiled and touched his lips to hers. "Even if the cranky part is yours."

* * *

One of the difficulties of a midweek ceremony, Kate discovered, was trying to juggle her professional obligations with the final wedding preparations as the days and hours counted down. She was scheduled to meet her attendants—Sky and Emerson—at the spa Tuesday afternoon, but she spent the morning in the office, catching up on some paperwork.

Just before eleven o'clock, Beth poked her head into Kate's office. "Do you have time for a walk-in?"

"Who's the client?"

"A Mrs. Stilton. She didn't say what it was regarding, only that it was important she talk to you today."

"Okay," Kate agreed. She clicked the mouse to save the memorandum she'd been working on, then stood up to greet the client Beth escorted to her office.

The ready smile on her face froze when she recognized Mrs. Stilton as her fiancé's ex-wife.

"Reid didn't tell me your last name."

"I was counting on that to get me in the door," Trish admitted.

"Then you're not here for legal advice?" she guessed.

The other woman shook her head. "No, I wanted to talk to you, woman-to-woman, and this was the only way I could think to make it happen without Reid running interference."

"What did you want to talk about?"

"I wanted to know if you're uncomfortable with the idea of me being at your wedding," Trish said.

"I'm not sure how I feel," Kate admitted.

"I get why it might seem strange to you that we came all the way from Texas for the wedding. And, truthfully, my husband warned me that we might not be welcome."

"I was just…surprised…when I saw you in his office,"

Kate said. "And I did wonder why he didn't tell me you were coming."

"He claims he didn't know," Trish said, confirming what Reid had told Kate. "But he should have known that I'd be on a plane as soon as I heard, because I'm the only family he has.

"And yes, I know that we're not technically family anymore," she continued. "But the connection to my dad created a bond between us. When Reid asked me to marry him, I was under no illusions about his feelings for me. My dad was dying and Reid married me so he wouldn't worry about me being alone.

"Not that I'm not capable of taking care of myself," Trish hastened to clarify. "But my dad was overprotective, and the local sheriff, to boot."

"Believe me, I understand about overprotective parents," Kate said, with a slightly exasperated smile.

"Good, because Reid will probably be even worse when he's a father."

"He told you...about the baby?"

"He didn't need to tell me," the other woman said. "I've known him too long to believe that he'd jump into another marriage without good reason, and in his mind, there's no better reason than to give a baby a family."

Kate nodded, acknowledging the fact.

"And since we're sharing secrets, I'll admit that I had mixed feelings about your pregnancy at first," Trish confided.

"Reid told me why you split up," Kate said.

"So you know I wanted to have a baby and he...had some reservations?"

"He said that he didn't ever want to be a father," Kate clarified.

"He's nothing if not honest," Trish mused. "Sometimes painfully so."

"And yet he's the one who pushed for this wedding."

"Because he's also honorable and loyal—and he wouldn't ever want his child to grow up feeling unwanted."

"Like he did," she realized.

Trish nodded. "When Reid confirmed your pregnancy, I had a moment—it was brief, but still a moment," she confessed, "when I wondered why, if he had to get someone pregnant, it couldn't have been me."

Kate decided that was a reasonable reaction for a woman whose husband hadn't wanted to give her a child.

"But after I had some time to think about it more rationally," the other woman continued, "I realized that Reid and I having a baby together would've been a mistake.

"Maybe we would've stayed together and made our marriage work—he's too loyal and stubborn to believe otherwise—but then I would never have met and fallen in love with Jonah, who really is the love of my life. And Reid would never have met you."

Kate appreciated that Trish didn't pretend to believe her ex-husband had deep feelings for his bride-to-be, but the honesty did sting a little.

"I would like to be there when you exchange your vows," the other woman continued. "But Jonah and I won't show up if our presence is going to make you uncomfortable in any way."

"I'd like you both to be there," Kate decided. "And Henry, too. Reid's made a lot of friends in the short time he's been in Haven, but most of those people knew me— or at least my family—first, so it'll be nice for him to have someone there primarily for him."

"Thank you," Trish said.

"And thank you," Kate said. "For coming here to talk to me, but especially for being here for Reid."

Trish smiled. "I'll see you at the church, soon-to-be Mrs. Reid Davidson."

Chapter Fifteen

Kate and Reid had opted for an evening midweek ceremony to coordinate with the schedule of the minister who'd married Kate's parents and baptized Kate and each of her siblings. Unable to choose between her sister and best friend as her maid or matron of honor, she'd decided to have both. Because Reid was new in town and didn't have any close friends to serve as groomsmen, he'd asked Caleb and Liam to stand up for him.

The bride spent the morning of her wedding day in court. After that, she had lunch with Skylar and Emerson before they all headed over to the Circle G together to get ready for the ceremony.

Her grandmother was waiting at the house when they arrived—to ensure everyone stayed on schedule, she claimed.

"You look just like a fairy-tale princess," Emerson said, when she'd finished tying the corset back of the bride's dress.

Kate turned to look at her reflection in the mirror, pleased with the overall effect. Her dress was an A-line strapless gown with chapel-length train. The side-drape helped disguise the subtle swell of her belly and the pearl-and-crystal beading on the bodice did make her feel a little bit like a princess.

But before she got too caught up in the fantasy, she reminded herself that Reid wasn't her prince—he was just a guy who wanted to do the right thing. And she knew he'd do everything in his power to make their marriage work—for the sake of their baby. She also hoped that, over time, he'd start to care for her as she cared for him.

She couldn't pinpoint an exact moment when her feelings for him had started to grow and change. There was no denying that the initial attraction had been purely physical, and that attraction was still there. His smile never failed to make her knees weak, the most casual of his touches made her heart pound, and those shoulders…just thinking about those shoulders made her sigh.

But he was also smart and kind and funny. Sure, he could be a little rigid at times and more than a little stubborn, but the more time she'd spent with him, the more she'd suspected that he was a man she could fall in love with. Until the day she'd cut off his marriage proposal, because she'd realized that she'd already fallen.

And in just a few more hours now, she was going to be his wife.

After Emerson's assessment, Grams looked the bride up and down, then shook her head. "Something's missing."

"Flowers," Sky said. "Dad went into town to pick them up."

Grams shook her head again. "Earrings."

Kate instinctively reached a hand to her ear, where she'd fastened the simple diamond studs that had been a gift from her father for her eighteenth birthday. "I'm wearing earrings."

"With your hair up, you should have something a little... more," Grams said, as she took a small fabric pouch out of her pocket. "I know you're wearing Emerson's veil as your something borrowed, but these could be your something old—if you want them."

"Grams, they're gorgeous," Kate said, admiring the delicate diamond-and-pearl drops in her grandmother's hand.

"They were a gift to me from your grandfather on our wedding day, fifty-eight years ago, so they're definitely old," she said. "But they were also your mom's something borrowed when she married your dad."

"Oh." She swallowed hard and blinked back the tears that threatened as she unfastened her diamond studs.

Kate had been thinking of her mom throughout the day, missing her as she always did when she celebrated a milestone event. But as she fastened the pretty pearl-and-diamond drops to her ears, the knowledge that her mother had worn the very same earrings on her wedding day made her feel a little less lonely for her.

"Now you're perfect," Grams declared.

"You're going to knock his socks off," Emerson said approvingly.

"Hopefully a lot more than his socks."

"Grams!" Skylar protested.

Her grandmother just grinned as a knock sounded on the door.

"Flower delivery," her father announced.

"Just on time." Grams took the box from him and distributed the bouquets of hand-tied calla lilies before ushering Skylar and Emerson out of the room so Kate could have a few minutes alone with her father before they headed to the church.

"Oh, Katie." It was all he said, but there was a wealth of emotion in those two words.

"Don't you dare make me cry," she warned her father.

He smiled, though his own eyes were suspiciously bright. "You're so beautiful." Then he touched a finger to one of the dangling earrings. "Your mother wore those the day we got married."

She nodded. "They were her something borrowed from Grams—and now they're my something old."

"Your mom would be so proud of you today. Always," he amended. "But especially today."

"I miss her," she said softly. "Always, but especially today."

"It took me a long time to accept that she was gone, and though the grief has lessened over the years, I will never stop loving her."

Kate pulled a tissue from the box on the dressing table and dabbed at her eyes.

"My greatest wish for you and Reid is to be as happy as we were together."

She kissed his cheek. "Thank you."

"Now, we better be on our way to the church if you don't want to keep your groom waiting. But if you do..." He let the sentence trail off, an unspoken question.

She shook her head. "I'm ready to start the rest of my life with the man I love."

Her response seemed to satisfy her father, who nodded brusquely. "Well then, let's go."

Half an hour before the ceremony was scheduled to begin, Caleb and Liam left the groom to perform their duties ushering guests to their seats.

A short while later, when Reid heard the knock on the door of the anteroom where he was getting ready, he assumed it was one of Katelyn's brothers. But when he said, "Come in," it was Trish who poked her head around the door.

"Have you worn out the carpet yet?" she teased.

"I'm not pacing—I'm trying to pin this flower thing on my jacket," he told her.

"It's a boutonniere," she said. "And the flower is a calla lily."

"Can you help me?"

"Sure," she said, taking the flower from his hand and sizing him up. "You clean up pretty good, Sheriff."

"I'm more comfortable wearing my badge than a suit," he confided.

"The suit looks good on you. Or maybe it's the impending nuptials that look good on you." She positioned the flower on his lapel, slid the pin into the stem—and swore when she pushed too far and stabbed herself.

"You're nervous," he realized.

"A little," she admitted.

"Why are *you* nervous?"

"Because I really want this to work for you, Reid."

He lifted a brow. "And you think I'm going to screw it up?"

"I think you sometimes hold too much back," she told him.

"I think you sometimes share too much," he countered drily.

"I know I do," she acknowledged. "But we're not talking about me—we're talking about you."

"You're nagging me." He handed a corsage box to her when she finished with his boutonniere. "And on my wedding day, too."

"What's this?"

"Katelyn asked me to give it to you."

She looked at the flower inside the box, then at him. "Why?"

He shrugged. "I don't remember exactly what she said—something about traditions and honoring family members who aren't in the wedding party."

"Oh." Trish's eyes filled with tears. "Damn, I really do like that girl."

"I like her, too," he said.

"She's probably too good for you," his ex-wife warned.

"Probably," he agreed easily.

"And yet, I think she could be exactly what you need—if you let her in."

"I'm marrying her, Trish. I'm not sure how much more 'in' there is."

She sighed. "Well, hopefully you'll figure it out."

And with those last cryptic words, she kissed his cheek and walked out of the anteroom.

A short while later, Caleb and Liam returned, then the minister summoned them all to take their positions at the front of the church. The pews were filled with invited guests and other well-wishers from the community, and the pianist was playing something Reid vaguely recognized but couldn't have named.

Emerson came down the aisle first, wearing a strapless lavender dress and carrying a bouquet of long-stemmed flowers that matched the one he was wearing. She winked at him as she took her place on the opposite side of the aisle. Sky followed a few steps behind Emerson, wearing the same style of dress in a slightly darker shade of purple and carrying a similar bouquet. She gave him a quick thumbs-up as she took her place beside Emerson.

The music changed—and Reid's heart started to pound harder and faster against his ribs. Then, finally, the bride was there, at the back of the church, and Reid felt as if all the air had been sucked out of his lungs.

He vaguely registered the presence of her father beside her, but his focus was on Katelyn—absolutely, undeniably the most beautiful bride he'd ever seen.

He didn't know enough about fashion to know the fabric or style of her dress, he only knew that the sparkly bodice hugged her breasts and the skirt trailed behind her as she made her way down the aisle toward him. Her hair was pinned up in one of those fancy knots that always made him want to unpin it, but today there were loose strands that framed and softened her face. In her left hand, she held a bouquet of lilies. Her right was tucked into the crook of her father's arm.

When they reached the altar, David lifted the delicate veil away from her face and leaned in to kiss her cheek, whispering something in her ear that made her lips curve in a tremulous smile. Then the bride's father offered his hand to the groom before stepping back and taking his seat in the front pew.

"We are gathered together today to celebrate the relationship of Katelyn Theresa Gilmore and Reid Thomas Davidson by joining them in marriage…"

Reid held Katelyn's hand and her gaze throughout the ceremony.

The vows he made to her weren't new, but he wanted her to know that they were true. Maybe he didn't love her, but he would honor and cherish her for the rest of their days together.

When they'd both recited the requisite lines and exchanged rings, the minister said, "I now pronounce you husband and wife." Then he nodded to Reid before addressing his next words to Katelyn. "You may kiss your groom."

Reid lifted his brows in response to the not-quite-traditional instruction; Katelyn only smiled as she pulled his mouth down to hers.

"I can't believe you managed to put together this wedding in four weeks," Reid said to his bride as they finished distributing pieces of wedding cake to their guests.

"There are some benefits to being a Gilmore in Haven."

"Such as rewriting the minister's lines?"

"It was a minor amendment, and Pastor Richards likes to go off script sometimes, just to make sure the congregation is paying attention."

"But kissing the bride is the part a groom looks forward to," he said. "So I kind of feel like I was ripped off."

"Do you really need to be told when you can kiss your bride?"

"No," he said, drawing her closer to him. "One of the benefits of putting a ring on your finger is that I get to kiss you whenever I want."

"You think so, do you?"

"Yes, I do," he confirmed.

And he kissed her then to prove it.

"I think I'm going to like being married to you," Katelyn said when he finally ended the kiss.

"I hope so, because you're going to be stuck with me for a very long time." He gestured to the dance floor where her grandparents were dancing, cheek to cheek. "That's going to be us in fifty years."

"They've been married fifty-eight years," she told him.

"They're an inspiration, that's for sure."

"My parents were the same," Katelyn said. "After my mom died, there were days I wasn't sure my dad would survive the grief of losing her."

"It couldn't have been easy on any of you."

"It wasn't," she confirmed. "But they were so...connected.

Like two halves of a whole, each one incomplete without the other. They met at The Silver State Stampede and immediately fell in love, and there was never any question in either of their minds or hearts that it was forever."

He knew that she'd wanted the same thing—love at first sight and happily-ever-after. And though he was sorry she'd had to compromise her ideals, he intended to do everything in his power to ensure she wouldn't ever regret it.

"Even if it wasn't love at first sight between us, there was definite lust at first sight," he said, attempting to lighten the mood.

She tipped her head back, a smile tugging at the corners of her mouth. "At first sight?"

"Oh, yeah," he confirmed. "The minute you walked into that conference room, a hint of black silk peeking above the button of that blue jacket, the matching skirt displaying mouthwatering long legs that went all the way down to sexy black shoes with heels that put your mouth almost level with mine."

"That's some detailed recollection," she noted.

"You caught my attention," he assured her. "And then you invited me back to your room."

"There were a couple of steps in between," she noted. "But the minute I saw you, I wanted you, too. In fact, the prospect of sharing a bed with you weighed heavily in the yes column when I was considering your proposal."

He smiled. "And you said 'click' wasn't a factor."

"I've reconsidered my position on the matter. In fact, I'm hopeful that later we'll be sharing a naked and horizontal position."

He lifted a brow. "You've got ambitious plans for tonight."

"It *is* our wedding night," she reminded him. "And I

don't think anyone at our respective offices would be surprised if we were a little late for work tomorrow."

"About that," Reid said, withdrawing an envelope from his jacket pocket.

"What's this?"

"Open it and see," he suggested.

She lifted the flap to peek inside. "A travel itinerary?"

"I know we said we shouldn't take any time away right now," her new husband acknowledged, "but Connor promised that he could handle anything that came up in the Sheriff's Office through the weekend and Beth managed to clear your schedule for a few days so that we can have a honeymoon, albeit an abbreviated one."

She pulled the pages out to scan them more closely. "The flight is at 5:50 in the morning?"

"Yeah, so we won't be sleeping in tomorrow. In fact, we're probably going to want to skip out of the party early tonight."

"Or now," she said, sounding excited and just a little bit panicked. "We need to go home and pack."

"I've already packed my bag, your sister packed one for you and our boarding passes are printed."

"You've thought of everything."

"I know this isn't exactly the wedding day of your dreams," he told her. "But I wanted to do it right, as much as possible under the circumstances, and not having a honeymoon just didn't seem right."

"Why San Francisco?"

"It's relatively simple to get there from here, it's close enough that we won't lose a lot of time traveling, and it's one of your favorite cities."

"How did you know that?"

"I asked Emerson for some help with the planning," he admitted. "And bribed her not to breathe a word about it to you—and since your reaction assures me that she didn't, I'm going to be carting a ton of Ghirardelli chocolate back from San Francisco."

"Make that two tons," she said.

"You can cart your own chocolate," he teased.

"It's not for me," she said. "It's for the baby."

"You're going to milk that for the next five-and-a-half months, aren't you?"

"As much as possible," she promised.

He smiled as he dipped his head and touched his lips to hers. "Let's go say goodbye to our guests and get this honeymoon started."

As eager as Kate had been to get back to her apartment—*their* apartment—and get naked with her new husband, now that they were alone together, she suddenly felt shy.

Reid shrugged out of his jacket and tossed it over the reading chair in the corner of her—*their*—bedroom.

"Are you tired?" he asked, somehow sensing her hesitation.

"Tired but not sleepy," she said. It had been a long day, and her limbs were weary but her blood was humming with nerves and anticipation.

"The sugar from that cake should keep you revved for a while—" he grinned as he unfastened his tie "—I hope."

She watched as his nimble fingers made quick work of the buttons that ran down the front of his shirt. Her mouth went dry when the fabric parted, revealing a strip of beautiful, bronzed skin.

"Do you need a hand with your dress?" he asked.

"Probably," she admitted. "Emerson tied up the corset, so I'm not sure how to get out of it."

"I think getting my wife out of her clothes is going to be one of my favorite husbandly duties," he said.

"You might not think so in a few months." She turned her back to him, so he could see how the dress was done up.

"I will always think so," he promised, starting to work on the corset.

When the lace had been loosened and the bodice began to drop, she caught and held it in place.

He didn't say anything about her impeding his efforts but only dropped his head to press a kiss to her bare shoulder. The brush of his lips on her skin raised goosebumps on her flesh.

Then he kissed her again, midway between her shoulder and her neck. And again, at the base of her throat.

She shivered.

"Your skin is so soft...so sweet."

Her eyes closed as his mouth moved up her throat, skimmed over her jaw.

"I want to taste you—" he teased her lips "—all over."

Heat pulsed in her veins, melting her resistance.

She let go of the bodice and wriggled out of the dress.

He stroked his hands down her sides, his thumbs gently caressing the slight swell between her hipbones.

"There's our little bean," he said, his tone soft, almost reverent.

"Actually, our baby is the size of a lemon now."

He shook his head. "Little bean sounds better than little lemon."

"Is our baby still going to be 'little bean' when he or she is the size of a honeydew melon?"

He eased her back onto the bed. "Are you growing a baby in there or making a fruit salad?"

"A baby," she assured him.

"*Our* baby," he clarified, then pressed his lips to the curve of her belly.

"Some men are…turned off by the changes in a woman's body during pregnancy," she said cautiously.

"Some men are idiots."

His blunt response made her smile, but still, she wasn't convinced he knew what he was in for.

"This is still the early stages," she warned. "When our baby is the size—"

He touched his fingers to her lips. "I know your body is going to change as our baby grows inside you, but getting naked with you is always going to be a huge turn-on for me."

"Really?" she said dubiously.

"Really," he confirmed. "You are beautiful and amazing and the sexiest woman I've ever known, and it's going to give me infinite pleasure to prove it to you throughout the next five-and-a-half months and beyond. Starting—" his hands moved to her breasts, already a little fuller and a lot more sensitive, his thumbs tracing around the areola "—now."

That night, all through the night, Kate learned that her husband was a man of his word.

Chapter Sixteen

Kate had always loved California—Sacramento and San Diego and every stop in between—but San Francisco was one of her all-time favorite cities. From the Golden Gate Bridge and the sparkling waters of the Bay to Lombard Street and the cable cars, Chinatown and Fisherman's Wharf, there was so much to see and do that she never got bored. And because Reid had never been to the city, she was able to see it again for the first time through his eyes.

Of course, the sheriff wanted to go to Alcatraz, and his wife did not. She told him, without regret, that there wouldn't be any last-minute tickets available during tourist season, because it was usually true. But the hotel concierge worked some magic and Reid presented her with two tickets for the ferry to the infamous island prison—cleverly hidden in a basket of Ghirardelli chocolate. It was a blatant bribe, but one she couldn't refuse, so they went to the island, toured the prison and the grounds, the former being much creepier and the latter much prettier than she'd anticipated.

Another day, they walked to Pier 39 to see the sea lions sunning on the docks and enjoy the talents of street performers. Later, they browsed the shops at Fisherman's Wharf, ate fresh shrimp out of plastic cups from a local food truck and sourdough rolls from the Boudin Bakery. They rented bicycles and cycled across the bridge, walked hand in hand through Golden Gate Park and took a cable car to Union Square to browse the upscale shops.

And when they finally went back to their hotel room, they made love, every night.

The morning sickness that had plagued her daily for several weeks had passed long ago, though it continued to make an occasional appearance—including their last morning in San Francisco.

Reid set their packed cases beside the door and did a quick check around the room to ensure they hadn't forgotten anything.

"Looks like we're good to go," he said.

Kate nodded hesitantly as her stomach decided it was unhappy with the brioche French toast and fresh fruit cup that had tasted so good only half an hour earlier.

"Katelyn?" he prompted.

"I'm sorry, but—" That was all she managed before she raced to the bathroom and slammed the door.

Reid knew she'd suffered from morning sickness earlier in her pregnancy, but she'd told him—with her fingers crossed—that the nausea had finally subsided. Listening to her retch through the door, he thought that her crossed fingers might have been a little premature.

"Katelyn?" He jiggled the handle of the door, frowning when it refused to turn. She'd been in a hurry to reach the toilet but she'd still managed to lock him out.

"Just give me a minute."

He heard the toilet flush, then the water turn on.

He rummaged through the suitcase for her toiletry bag, pulled out her toothbrush and toothpaste and had them waiting when she unlocked and opened the door again.

"Thanks," she said, not looking at him as she retreated with the items into the bathroom again.

They'd planned to take the BART to the airport, but Reid called the front desk and asked for a cab instead, which bought them a few extra minutes and gave his wife a little more privacy to feel miserable. He also took the plastic liner for the ice bucket and tucked it into his pocket, just in case.

When she came out of the bathroom, she looked tired and pale—not at all like a woman who'd enjoyed her brief holiday. She tucked her toothbrush and paste away again and zipped up the suitcase.

"Sorry for the delay," she said.

"Why are you apologizing?"

"Because I've put us behind schedule and if we miss the train, we'll be late checking in for our flight and—"

"There's a cab waiting for us downstairs," he said.

"To take us to the train station?"

"To take us to the airport."

"That's going to cost a fortune."

"Only a small one," he said. "And worth it, because we won't feel rushed and you'll be able to close your eyes and relax for a little while."

"You're taking care of me, aren't you?"

"I'm trying to," he admitted. "But you don't make it easy."

She didn't respond to that.

"One of the reasons we got married was so that we

could raise our child together. Until the baby's born, we both need to take care of you."

"I'll never object to you taking care of our vomiting child," she promised. "But I don't want anyone watching me throw up. It's humiliating enough to know that you could hear me yakking my breakfast into the toilet."

"In sickness and in health," he reminded her.

"I'm not sick, I'm pregnant, and I really thought the morning sickness had passed. I was throwing up almost every day for a few weeks, then it was just once every two or three days, and for the past couple of weeks, it's only been once a week. The last time was last Sunday, so I probably should have been prepared for this today."

"Then it wasn't because we overdid it these past few days?"

She shook her head. "No. I'm sure the nausea isn't linked to anything we did or ate, and I sincerely hope the last half hour isn't what you remember when you think about our honeymoon in San Francisco."

"It won't be," he promised. "I loved being here with you and seeing the sights, but my favorite memories took place in this room— most of them in that king-size bed."

"Maybe we should get a bigger bed—if you think one would fit in the apartment," she suggested.

"I don't mind a queen," he said. "It makes us snuggle closer."

"You'll be closer than you want when my huge belly's taking up all the space between us. I already feel like this baby's getting bigger and bigger every day."

He laid his hands on the slight curve of her belly. "Coincidentally, you get more and more beautiful every day."

"We'll see if you still think so in five months."

"I'll still think so in five months," he promised. "And in five years and in fifty years."

And although he said the words to reassure her, he realized that he meant them.

Yeah, he'd proposed to Katelyn because she was pregnant, and he'd campaigned for her to say yes because he wanted to be more than a part-time father to their child. But sometime over the past few weeks, his motivation had stopped being all about the baby. Over the past few weeks, he'd realized that his life was fuller, richer and happier with Katelyn—so much so that he didn't want to imagine a future without her in it.

Kate was surprised by how easy it was to settle into the routines of married life once they got back to Haven.

Although the legal union between a criminal defense attorney and the local sheriff meant that there were some inherent conflicts between them, they adopted a strict rule about leaving work at the office to ensure that nothing interfered with either of them doing their respective jobs. She was fired by one long-time client who didn't believe she could continue to represent him fairly, but for the most part, her practice continued to grow—and so did the baby.

Aiden Hampton had finished his community service before returning to school for the fall term of his senior year, but he and his father continued to attend the grief counseling sessions that had been recommended by the Diversion Program coordinator. Near the end of September, the teen appeared in court for the final dismissal of the charges against him, after which he thanked the judge, then his attorney and even the sheriff who had locked him up—if only for a few hours.

"Do you have to rush back to the office?" Reid asked Kate when court had been dismissed.

She shook her head. "There's nothing that can't wait until tomorrow."

"Good, then you can take a ride with me."

She hitched her briefcase on her shoulder and walked beside him out of the courthouse. He guided her to his personal truck rather than the official vehicle of the Sheriff's Office and opened the passenger door for her. "Where are we going?"

"It's a surprise," he told her.

"What's a surprise?" she pressed.

He just shook his head. "No one warned me about your impatience before I married you."

"You think I'm impatient? Just wait until there's a child strapped into a car scat in the back asking, 'Are we there yet?' every two minutes," she said.

"I can wait," he said, flicking on his indicator before turning into a distinctly residential area. "Because I'm not impatient."

"Are we there yet?" she asked.

He turned again, onto a dead-end street, then pulled up alongside the curb in front of a two-story brick house with a For Sale sign in the front yard.

"Yes," he said. "We're there."

Kate felt a flutter of excitement in her belly as she looked at the house. She was familiar with the neighborhood, of course. There were newer and fancier homes being built on the south side of town, but this area was established, with bigger lots, plenty of mature trees and within walking distance of both the elementary and secondary schools.

"I know the apartment is really convenient to your office and the courthouse," he said to her. "But it's kind of small—plus it was yours before it was ours, so I thought maybe we could choose another place together. Somewhere with room to grow."

"Hey, I haven't put on that much weight," she protested.

He chuckled softly. "I meant to grow our family. Don't you think little bean should have a brother or sister someday?"

She felt the telltale sting of tears behind her eyes. "You want to have another baby with me?"

"Yeah," he said. "I didn't have any siblings growing up, but watching you with yours, I've learned to appreciate the bond you share, and I want that for our kids."

"Brothers and sisters are great," she agreed. "When they're not a total pain in the a—"

He touched a finger to her lips. "Didn't we agree not to use bad language around the baby?"

"Do you really think our baby is hearing anything yet?"

"The books say that babies start to hear sound at eighteen weeks."

"Even if he—or she—can hear what I'm saying, I doubt he—or she—is comprehending," she said drily.

"I'd rather not take any chances that his—or her—first word might be an inappropriate one."

She linked her arms behind his head. "You're going to be a great dad."

"I'm going to do my best," he promised.

"So…how many kids were you thinking you'd like to have?"

"At least two," he said.

"You might change your mind after the first one's born," she warned. "When you've gone a month with no more than two consecutive hours of sleep and you've changed so many diapers you've lost count."

"Trish called today, didn't she?"

Kate nodded.

"You really need to start screening your calls," he advised.

"I like talking to her," she said. "Usually."

He turned her back toward the house. "What do you think? Do you want to look inside?"

"Don't we have to wait for the real estate agent?"

He shook his head. "I've got the code for the lockbox."

"I guess, since you're the sheriff, she figured you were trustworthy?"

"Good guess," he said, leading her to the front door.

"It needs some work," he warned as he turned the key in the lock. "But mostly cosmetic—fresh paint, maybe new carpet or hardwood, updated appliances—and we could take care of that before we moved in."

As he showed her around the empty house—the owner having already moved to Arizona for a job promotion—she had to agree with his assessment. The decor was a little outdated, but she liked the layout—and she loved the spaciousness of the kitchen and the fireplace in the living room and the master bedroom suite.

"What do you think?" he asked, ending the tour at the backyard, slightly overgrown with grass and weeds.

"It might need more work than you realize, once you scrape off wallpaper and pull up carpets," she warned. "Are you sure you're ready to tackle all of that?"

"I want to tackle all of that," he told her. "I want our kids to have a house with a backyard, the lawn scattered with toys, maybe a swing set or one of those climbing things.

"And a dog," he added impulsively. "We should definitely get a dog."

"Let's see how we manage with a baby first," she suggested.

"But what about the house?" he prompted.

And his expression was so hopeful and his enthusiasm so infectious, she threw caution to the wind. "Let's do it."

Ten days later, they signed the final papers and got the keys. That night, they picked up pizza from Jo's and took it to 418 Sagebrush Lane, where they sat on the floor of the living room and ate their first meal in their new home. But they agreed it would be easier to do the work they wanted done before they moved in, and they'd set an ambitious target date of the end of October.

"Speaking of dates," Kate said, as she wiped pizza sauce off her fingers with a napkin. "It's our one-month anniversary tomorrow."

"Is that something we're supposed to celebrate?"

"Not formally," she said. "But I thought I might actually cook something for dinner—and you could pick up caramel fudge brownie cheesecake from Sweet Caroline's for dessert—and we could have a private celebration."

"I like the sound of that," he agreed.

So Kate talked to Emerson and got a recipe that her friend promised was relatively foolproof. After work, she stopped by The Trading Post to get everything she needed to prepare the meal and then meticulously followed her friend's step-by-step instructions.

Half an hour later, when everything was finally ready, she got a text message from Reid.

Sorry. Got a call. Won't make dinner.

She immediately replied:

Ok. Be safe.

Because as disappointed as she was that their plans for the evening had been ruined—or at least delayed—she understood that being married to the local sheriff inevitably meant there would be times when he didn't make it home for dinner. It was even possible that, his best intentions notwithstanding, he wouldn't be with her when she gave birth.

As if unsettled by that possibility, their baby kicked an angry protest. Well, Kate guessed it was a kick, but all she really felt was a flutter. She was exactly nineteen weeks into her pregnancy now, and Emerson had assured her that what she'd originally described as a feeling of little air bubbles popping inside her belly were actually her baby's first movements.

She couldn't wait until the baby was bigger and those movements were stronger, so Reid could feel them, too. But for now, she put a hand on the curve of her belly, instinctively soothing. "It's okay, little bean. We'll make sure you don't make your grand entrance into the world until Daddy's with us."

Then she went to the kitchen to turn off the stove. And though she wanted to wait to eat with Reid, however late that might be, she scooped some rice into a bowl and added a spoonful of the chicken cacciatore because the baby was hungry now—and desperately craving the cheesecake Reid was supposed to bring home for dessert.

She was putting her empty bowl and fork into the dishwasher when her phone buzzed again.

Anticipating an update from Reid, she immediately snatched it up, only to be disappointed when she saw the message from her answering service.

*Urgent. Client wants to meet asap. 775-555-6728

And Kate figured if Reid was working, she might as well be, too.

She was asleep on the sofa, the baseball game on the television now into extra innings, when Reid got home.

The rich scents of tomato and basil lingered in the air—the remnants of dinner she'd cooked for their one-month anniversary.

His wife.

His brilliant and beautiful, sweet and sexy, amazing and pregnant wife.

Damn, he'd lucked out when he'd signed up for that conference in Boulder City. At the time, he'd considered himself lucky just to get the invitation back to her room. He certainly hadn't been thinking that there might be a wedding and a baby in his future. Truthfully, he probably would have run far and fast if anyone had told him that's where he'd end up, so he was grateful he hadn't known, because now he had everything he never knew he wanted.

He picked up the remote and turned off the TV. Katelyn didn't stir. He lifted her into his arms; she sighed and turned her face into his shoulder. She was almost halfway through her pregnancy now and grumbling about the eight pounds she'd put on. Not that the slight swell of her belly was obvious, but apparently her wardrobe options were shrinking as her waistline expanded.

She was still the sexiest woman he'd ever known. And the changes her body was going through as a result of her pregnancy only made her more appealing.

He loved making love with her. And afterward, he loved to cuddle with his hand on her belly. He loved taking her first cup of coffee—decaf—to her in the morning and exchanging brief text messages with her through the hours they were apart. And he especially loved going home at the end of the day to find her waiting for him.

But did he love her?

He wasn't one to get hung up on words. In his opinion, there was far too much emphasis placed on that one particular phrase and too many people who threw it around frequently and easily.

Truthfully, he didn't know if he loved her, but he would do everything he could to make her happy—though she would claim that she was responsible for her own happiness; to take care of her—though she would insist she didn't need anyone to take care of her; and to protect her— though she would argue that she could protect herself.

Yeah, she could argue the opposite side of any issue, and that was just one more thing he loved about her.

He pulled back the covers and laid her gently on top of the mattress, then quickly stripped out of his clothes and slid into bed beside her.

And fell asleep with her in his arms.

Chapter Seventeen

Katelyn was still sleeping when Reid reluctantly slid out of bed in the morning.

He would have liked to stay with her, but he'd agreed to meet Connor at the Sheriff's Office at eight so they could head to the hospital in Battle Mountain. The young store clerk shot during the robbery at The Trading Post had been in critical condition when he was rushed into surgery the night before. Reid had been in the OR waiting room with the parents when the doctor informed them that the surgery had gone well. An early morning call to the hospital revealed that the victim's condition had been downgraded to "serious but stable" and the sheriff was eager to get his statement.

But first, he brewed Katelyn's decaf coffee, as he did every morning, and carried the mug to the bedroom along with a plate bearing a thick slice of Sweet Caroline's caramel fudge brownie cheesecake.

"Good morning, sleepyhead."

She blinked against the harsh glare of the light when he hit the switch with his elbow, but she pushed herself up in bed and brushed back the hair that was falling into her face.

Her eyes lit up when they zeroed in on his gifts. "You remembered the cheesecake."

He chuckled as he set the mug on the bedside table and relinquished the plate to her eager hands. "Of course, I remembered the cheesecake." Then he leaned over to brush her lips with his. "Happy belated one-month anniversary."

"I'm sorry I didn't stay awake until you got home last night." She picked up the fork and dug into the dessert.

"It's okay," he said. "I'm sorry I was late."

Of course, it wasn't the first time and they both knew it wouldn't be the last.

"You missed really hot anniversary sex," she said around a mouthful of cake.

"I'm even sorrier about that."

"Well, we could have really hot morning-after-the-one-month-anniversary sex…after I finish my cheesecake," she told him.

"Words cannot express how tempted I am," he assured her. "But I'm heading back out with Deputy Neal this morning to do some follow-up to our investigation." He kissed her again. "Rain check?"

"Absolutely," she promised.

Kate didn't complain about Reid having to work, even on a Sunday, because she had plenty to occupy her own time—not the least of which was putting together a defense for her newest client. And though it was just as easy to work on her laptop in the apartment, she generally preferred to work at work.

So after she'd finished her coffee and her cheesecake—and how great was it to be married to a man who indulged her pregnancy cravings?—she showered and dressed and headed to her office.

She only felt a little guilty about representing a suspect in the armed robbery that Reid was investigating. They'd both known before they got married that their careers would occasionally put them on opposite sides of the courtroom, and this was just another one of those times.

She unlocked the office door, punched in the security code to disarm the alarm system, then locked the door again behind her and headed into her office.

Beth always emptied the wastebaskets and put the garbage out before she left the office on Friday afternoons, so when Kate hit the light switch and realized there was something in the basket beside her desk, she was immediately uneasy. Moving closer, she saw what looked like a brown paper lunch bag—certainly nothing that would explain her growing trepidation. But the weight of the basket warned the bag wasn't empty, and she used the tip of a pen to open it so she could peek inside.

Then she put the wastebasket down again, picked up the phone and dialed the sheriff's number.

Reid and Connor were leaving Battle Mountain when Katelyn called, so they stopped at her office before heading to their own. She'd hinted about something that might be relevant to their investigation, and though Reid couldn't imagine what it might be, he knew she wouldn't have interrupted him if it wasn't important.

"I didn't touch it."

They were the first words she spoke when they walked into her office.

"Didn't touch what?" he asked cautiously.

"The gun."

Even without any context, the words gave his heart an unexpected jolt.

"What gun?"

It was Connor who asked the question, as Reid's heart was somewhere in the vicinity of his throat, rendering speech difficult.

She pointed to the trash receptacle beside her desk.

Reid shoved his heart back into his chest, looked into the basket and swore. "How did this get here?"

"I don't know." But her face was pale and there was a slight tremor in her voice. "Beth always takes out the garbage on Fridays, and I didn't have appointments yesterday, but I did, um, meet with a client here last night."

"Who?" Reid demanded.

"You know I can't—"

"Screw solicitor-client privilege," he practically snarled at her. "I want to know who was in *my wife's* office with a weapon."

If he'd been thinking clearly, he would've realized that was the absolute wrong thing to say to her. But he wasn't thinking clearly—he couldn't think past the fact that whoever had callously pulled the trigger to put a bullet in the twenty-three-year-old clerk at The Trading Post had then carried the weapon into Katelyn's office.

Didn't she know that desperate people did desperate things? That the client she was determined to protect could have used the gun on her? Didn't she realize Reid could have left one crime scene and come home to find his wife, not sleeping on the sofa with a baseball game on TV, but bleeding out on the floor in her office?

Just the thought made his whole body break out into a sweat.

But Katelyn only straightened her spine and narrowed

her gaze—a warrior ready for battle. "You do your job, *Sheriff*, and I'll do mine."

He knew her mention of his position was intended to draw a line between them, but it also served to remind him that he was there in his professional capacity—and with his deputy as a witness to their altercation, too.

He drew in a deep breath, battling against the fear and impotence that held him captive, and managed a brisk nod. "I assume you have no objection to us taking this—" he picked up the wastebasket again "—into evidence?"

"Of course not," she said, her tone cool and stiff.

"Why don't I head over to the office to get it logged in and sent to ballistics?" Connor suggested.

"You can both go," Katelyn said, but her gaze never shifted away from Reid's. "I have nothing else to say right now."

"Well, I do." Reid shoved the basket at his deputy.

Connor took his cue—and the evidence—and hurried out the door with only a sympathetic glance in his boss's direction.

"I'm sorry," Reid said, after he heard the exterior door open and close again.

Katelyn sighed and lowered herself into the chair behind her desk. "I know."

"That's it? You're not going to apologize?"

"What am I supposed to apologize for?"

It was a reasonable question, but he still wasn't close to feeling reasonable. "Maybe representing scumbag clients," he suggested. "And, by the way, you are *never* again to meet with any of them here alone at night."

"That's not your call to make," she said, her tone icy.

"If you won't think about your own safety, you should at least think about the baby you're carrying. *Our* baby."

"I would *never* do anything to put our baby at risk."

"Oh, well then, why would I worry?" he said, his voice dripping with sarcasm.

She folded her hands on top of the desk, focusing all her attention on the task of lacing her fingers together. When she spoke again, her voice was carefully neutral. "I think you should probably head back to the Sheriff's Office now."

He decided she was right. They were just going around in circles, he was frustrated by her refusal to acknowledge the recklessness of her behavior, and if he didn't walk away, one of them would say something they'd regret.

Kate blew out a weary breath when Reid finally walked out of her office. She stayed where she was after he'd gone, still shaking—with both fear and fury—and not certain her watery legs would be able to support her if she tried to move.

Thankfully, she'd managed to pull herself together by the time she heard a familiar voice say, "Knock knock," from the outer office.

"I'm back here," she said, hastily wiping at her tears before Emerson came around the corner.

"Hey." Her friend gave her a quick hug. "I had some errands to run in town and saw Reid leaving, so I thought I'd stop by and see how your dinner turned out last night."

"It was a complete bust," Kate admitted.

"He didn't like the chicken?"

"He didn't make it home for dinner."

Emerson frowned. "Why…" And then she put the pieces together. "The shooting at The Trading Post?"

Kate nodded.

"It must be hard, not just having plans ruined but knowing your husband's life could be in danger just because he's doing his job," Emerson said sympathetically.

"Of course I worry about him," she admitted. "But I trust that he'll take all necessary precautions to stay safe and come home at the end of the night. Unfortunately, he doesn't seem to have the same faith in me."

"What do you mean?"

So Kate summarized for her friend the argument they'd had after Reid learned about her meeting with the new client—without revealing any details, of course.

"I know you think he overreacted," Emerson said. "But even I was freaked out listening to the story, and you're not my wife or the mother of my unborn child."

"I'm not unsympathetic to his concerns—I just want him to trust me to do my job the same way I trust him to do his," she said.

"Every marriage has an adjustment period as two people who are used to living their own lives suddenly have to learn to communicate and compromise."

Kate shook her head. "This isn't an adjustment problem."

"What do you think the problem is?"

"He doesn't trust me."

"In all fairness, he doesn't really know you," Emerson said gently. "You've been married for a month, and you dated for only a short time before the wedding."

All of which was true, of course. She sighed. "Maybe I shouldn't have married him."

"Is that really how you feel?" her friend asked.

She considered the question for a moment. Though she and Reid had only been married a few weeks, she already couldn't imagine her life without him in it—she didn't want to imagine her life without him in it. Because despite an overprotective streak that rivaled her father's and a frustrating insistence on doing things for her that she was perfectly capable of doing herself, Reid was the man she loved.

"No," she finally said. "I don't regret marrying him."

"Then you're going to have to be patient—and give yourselves both some time to figure things out."

But it was hard to communicate with a man who was hardly ever around. And after the argument in her office, Reid kept himself busy.

At first Kate thought it was just the ongoing investigation that was monopolizing his time, but when that was complete, he spent every free minute at the new house: stripping wallpaper, tearing out carpets, painting ceilings and baseboards and, after Kate had picked the colors she wanted, walls.

He worked hard—every day. Sometimes he was at the house so late, he would crash on the sofa in the living room when he finally got back to the apartment so as not to disturb Kate's rest. At least that was the excuse he gave, but with every day that passed, she felt the distance between them growing.

She'd stayed away from the renovations, because he was worried the dust from sanding and the smell of paint wouldn't be good for the baby. She decided the distance between them wasn't good for the baby—or their marriage—either.

Ten days after their big argument, and three days before they were scheduled to fly to Texas for Henry's christening, she picked up takeout from Diggers' and took it to the new house.

He looked so sexy in paint-splattered jeans with an old Echo Ridge Sheriff's Office T-shirt stretched across those broad shoulders and a slight hint of stubble darkening his strong jaw—and she missed him like crazy.

"I thought you might want to take a break and have something to eat."

He set the roller in the pan and covered it with the

corner of a plastic drop sheet. "I am hungry," he said. "Thanks."

"Maybe we could sit outside?" she suggested. There wasn't any furniture in the house, but there was a patio set that the former owners had left.

"Sure," he agreed.

"You've been busy out here, too," she noted, as they stepped through the patio doors onto the back deck.

"Norm let me borrow his mower," he said.

"It looks good."

"Better, anyway," he agreed.

She opened the bag of food, handed him a foil-wrapped bacon cheeseburger, a paper sleeve of french fries and a can of cola.

"You're not eating?"

"I had something earlier," she said. Which was true—she just didn't specify that 'earlier' was actually lunch.

"Little bean still craving cheesecake these days?"

She shook her head. "Pineapple mango smoothies."

"A surprisingly healthy choice," he noted.

"Well, it's only been three days," she admitted.

For the next few minutes, he focused on eating, though he nudged the fries toward Kate, silently offering to share.

She selected one and nibbled on the end.

When he'd finished his burger, she ventured to ask, "Are we still going to Echo Ridge on the weekend?"

He picked up the can of soda, sipped. "If you want to."

"Of course I want to."

"Okay then," he said agreeably.

"Do *you* want to?"

"Sure."

He offered her some more fries; she shook her head.

"Are you going to initiate any kind of conversation or just answer my questions as succinctly as possible?"

He popped a couple of fries into his mouth, chewed.

"I heard you talking to Emerson," he finally said. "The day you found the gun, I came back with an evidence receipt, and the two of you were in your office."

"Okay," she said cautiously, trying to remember any part of the conversation that could've caused his withdrawal.

"You said you wished you hadn't married me."

Kate immediately shook her head. "No, I didn't. I don't remember exactly what I said," she admitted. "But I know I wouldn't have said that because it's not true."

"Well, it was something along those lines," he insisted. "And it got me wondering...if you wanted out."

She swallowed, her throat tight. "I don't want out." She folded a paper napkin in half, then again, her heart heavy as she contemplated asking the question she wasn't sure she wanted him to answer. "Do you?"

"No." He answered without hesitation, which loosened the vise around her chest a little. "But I don't want you to be unhappy."

"I'm not unhappy being married to you," she said. Then, remembering what her friend had said about honest communication, she elaborated on her response. "I'm also not happy that my husband of six weeks has apparently moved out of our bedroom."

"I didn't move out of our bedroom," he denied. "But I thought we could both use some space."

"You mean *you* needed some space."

"Maybe I did," he acknowledged.

"Have you almost had enough space?" she asked hesitantly. "Because I'd kind of like my husband back."

"Yeah—" he reached across the table and covered her hand with his "—I've had more than enough space."

The vise loosened a little more. "Since I'm pouring out my heart here, there's something else you should know."

"What's that?" he asked, a little warily.

"I didn't just agree to marry you so our baby would have two parents, but because I wanted a partner to share my life, for the rest of my life. And…because I fell in love with you."

He opened his mouth, then closed it again without saying a word, crushing any tentative hope that he might express similar feelings. And then he withdrew his hand, ostensibly to pick up his soda, but she knew the drink was just a diversion.

She pushed her chair away from the table. "Anyway," she said, pleased that her level tone gave no indication that her heart was breaking. "I just wanted you to know."

Reid let her go.

He sat at the table, the bag of garbage balled up in his fist, and watched her walk away because he was an idiot and a coward.

He should have said something. When a woman told a man she loved him, she expected some kind of response. But he'd said nothing, because he didn't know what to say or what to feel. And yes, because he was afraid—afraid to believe her feelings were real, even more afraid to acknowledge his own.

All the books and articles on pregnancy talked about an expectant mother's heightened emotions. It was possible that the love she felt for the baby growing inside her was being extended to him because he was the baby's father. And if so, her feelings could change when the baby was born.

And maybe, an annoying voice that sounded remarkably like his ex-wife said inside his head, he should give her some credit for knowing her own mind and heart. Katelyn was hardly the type of woman to impulsively express her emotions. If she said she loved him, she obviously believed it was true.

And he wanted to believe it, too.

But even if those feelings were real, would they last?

Trish had told him that she loved him. She'd said the words over and over again, urging him to trust her feelings. But in the end, she'd walked away from their marriage. He understood her reasons—she'd wanted something he wasn't willing to give her. And he certainly didn't blame her for choosing to build a life with someone else. But that experience made him skeptical about his new wife's professed feelings.

He didn't doubt Katelyn believed what she was saying right now, but they'd only known one another a short while. He was committed to her and the family they were building together, but he wasn't quite ready to drop the shields around his heart—not even for the woman he'd married.

Chapter Eighteen

A few months earlier, Kate might have thought she'd feel uncomfortable traveling with her new husband to attend the baptism of his ex-wife's baby with her current spouse. Now that she'd gotten to know the other woman and spent some time with both Reid and Trish together, she understood their relationship a lot better. They truly did act more like siblings than exes, and despite her initial predisposition toward her husband's first wife, she genuinely liked Trish and was looking forward to spending some time with her and Jonah and, of course, little Henry.

Any reservations she had as Reid drove from the airport to the Stiltons' house weren't about her husband's relationship with his ex-wife but his current one. Though they were both making an effort to communicate more clearly, Kate sensed that Reid was still holding back.

They arrived just before dinner and after they'd exchanged basic pleasantries, Trish shooed the men—

including Henry—outside to start the barbecue while she showed Kate the house and the room where she and Reid would be sleeping.

"Wow," Kate said, after the quick tour was finished and they'd returned to the spacious open-concept living area. "And you told me you married for love the second time around."

Her hostess laughed. "I did. I just lucked out and fell in love with a man who has a very well-paying job at Texas Instruments." She sat on the ivory leather sofa and tugged Kate down beside her. "Speaking of married…how are things with you and Reid?"

There were so many ways Kate could have answered the question—fine, great, wonderful—that would have put an end to the topic. Or even "it's an adjustment" or "we're figuring things out," either of which would have been more honest but still not too revealing. Instead, she burst into tears.

"Oh, Katelyn." Trish's arms came around her, offering both comfort and support—and the box of tissues from the antique accent table.

A long while later, when most of Kate's tears had been spent, Trish rubbed her back and demanded to know, "What did that big stupid man do?"

The question made Kate laugh even through her tears. "Why are you assuming he did anything?"

"Because I love him dearly, but I'm not blind to his faults."

So Kate started with the confrontation that took place in her office and concluded with her declaration of love—and Reid's silence.

"The problem isn't you," Trish said. "The problem is that no one in his life has ever stood by him, not when it really counted. No one has ever put him first."

Kate was quiet, considering the other woman's words.

"His father didn't even stick around to see him born," Trish reminded her. "His mother walked out on him a few years later—which might have been the best thing that could have happened because she left him with his grandmother. But then she died, and he was truly and completely alone."

"Until he met your dad."

"Which only happened after he'd spent a few years in foster care. But even his relationship with my dad took time to develop. And then my dad died, too."

"He's lost a lot of people he's cared about," Kate acknowledged.

"I'm not done yet," Trish said. "Because, if I'm being completely honest, I abandoned him, too. I told him I loved him and wanted to have a family with him and, when he wouldn't give me what I wanted, I ignored the vows we exchanged to be with someone else.

"I did love him," she said softly. "But I didn't love him enough to sacrifice what I wanted to make him happy."

"Are you suggesting that I should give up my job? Because—"

"No," Trish interjected quickly, firmly. "You shouldn't change anything that makes you who you are, but you need to work with Reid to figure out a compromise you can both live with. And working with Reid won't be easy."

"I'm already realizing it's an uphill battle."

"Just don't stop battling," the other woman urged. "Don't give up on him."

Kate managed a small smile. "I'm not a quitter."

"Good." Trish reached for the envelope on the table. "I took about a thousand pictures at your wedding," she confided. "And I had prints of some of my favorites made for you. So if your resolve ever falters—" she pulled out one of the photos and passed it to Kate "—just look at this."

She glanced at the photo in her hand and felt a tug at her heart. It was a picture of Reid standing at the front of the church on their wedding day. Trish had zoomed in on his face, and the smile that curved his lips was reflected in the happy light in his eyes.

"Do you know what that is?" Trish asked.

"A picture of Reid," she said, stating the obvious.

But Trish shook her head. "It's a picture of the groom," she clarified. "Taken at the exact moment that he saw his bride appear at the back of the church."

Kate looked at Trish, silently questioning.

"Most guests automatically turn to catch that first glimpse of the bride," she explained. "I was looking at Reid as he was looking at you. And what I saw, what anyone can see in that photo, is a man looking at the woman he wants to share his life with—the woman he loves."

Kate shook her head as fresh tears filled her eyes. "I appreciate the pep talk, but Reid doesn't love me."

"I'm not surprised he hasn't said the words," Trish said. "He's never been good at expressing his emotions. But that doesn't mean the feelings aren't there."

Kate wanted to believe the other woman could be right, but Reid's response—or rather complete lack of response—when she confessed her feelings warned her not to get her hopes up.

The baptism of Henry Jonah Stilton was a formal ceremony at the church where his parents had married followed by a big party in their backyard.

Kate didn't know if it was the change of scenery or being away from the demands of their respective jobs or if her husband had finally got over being mad, but Reid was incredibly sweet and attentive throughout the weekend. As the guest of honor was passed from one willing set of arms to another and they slipped away from the crowd and into the house to get their bags before heading to the airport, she was almost sorry to be leaving Echo Ridge.

"It's not going to be too much longer before we can hold our own baby," Kate said as Reid zipped up his duffel.

"Not that you can tell," he said, touching a hand to the gentle swell of her tummy.

"Wrap-style dresses and print fabrics are very forgiving," she confided.

"And stunning," he told her. "Sometimes I look at you and I'm awed that you're my wife, and—" His eyes went wide and whatever else he'd intended to say was forgotten. "Was that…our baby?"

She smiled and nodded. For a couple weeks now, she'd been aware of subtle nudges that were gradually growing stronger, but this was the first time Reid had witnessed any movement.

His lips curved as he felt another kick. "That's…wow." Then his smile faltered. "Does it hurt?"

"No, it doesn't hurt. It's a little distracting at times," she confided. "I feel the baby move and I get so excited, I forget what I'm doing."

He kept his hand on her belly for another minute, and when he finally lifted his gaze to hers, his eyes were moist.

"I'm sorry, Katelyn."

She looked wary. "Sorry you got me pregnant?"

He shook his head. "No. I'll never be sorry about that," he assured her. "But I am sorry about that day in your office—about my response to the situation, and afterward."

"I'd never do anything to put our baby in danger," she said softly.

"I know. But I wasn't just thinking about the baby—I

was thinking about you, too. And when I understood that you'd been in your office with a suspect in possession of a loaded gun… I've worn a badge for almost a dozen years now and I've seen my fair share of bad stuff, and my mind immediately imagined all things that could've gone wrong.

"The rational part of my brain recognized that the situation was controlled, but my emotions weren't," he admitted. "And the thought—as fleeting as it was—that I could've lost you…it cut me off at the knees."

She touched a hand to his arm. "I'm sorry, Reid. It never occurred to me that you were worried about me."

"That might've been because I was yelling at you," he acknowledged ruefully. "But only because I was shaking inside at the idea of you sitting across from a guy willing to pull the trigger of a Glock 17 for less than three hundred dollars in a cash register."

"I was shaking, too," she admitted. "And more than anything, I wanted you to hold me. I wanted to feel your arms—strong and reassuring—around me. But Deputy Neal was with you, and I didn't want to cross the line we've been so careful to draw between our respective jobs and our personal life."

"Can I hold you now?" he asked.

She moved willingly into his arms.

He held her tight and whispered close to her ear, "I love you, Katelyn."

She was still for a minute, her heart—filled with joy and hope—pounding against her ribs. Then she slowly eased back to look at him, not entirely certain she'd heard the words correctly.

But he looked straight into her eyes and said it again, "I love you."

"How… When… Are you sure?"

He smiled as her muddled brain struggled to put together a cohesive thought.

"Yes, I'm sure," he told her. "I think I'd mostly figured it out the night of our first-month anniversary, when I came home and found you sleeping on the sofa. That might also be part of the reason I overreacted the next day—the feelings were still new and overwhelming and then, suddenly, I was imagining how unbearably empty my life would be without you in it."

"Wow, that's a much more eloquent expression of love than you got from me," she told him.

"All that matters is that you do. If you still do."

She lifted her hands to frame his face. "I absolutely do," she said. "I love you with my whole heart, Reid Davidson— today, tomorrow and for the rest of our lives." Then she touched her lips to his. "Let's go home."

When they got back to Haven, Reid surprised Kate by driving to the new house instead of their apartment. He'd put in a lot of hours and she was eager to see the results of the work he'd done, but she was shocked to discover that the house wasn't just in move-in condition but that their furniture had actually been moved in.

"I gave your sister the keys before we left," he explained. "She rounded up your brothers and cousins and supervised the packing and moving."

"Everything looks fabulous," Kate said.

They hadn't yet picked out furniture for the baby's room, but the walls and trim were freshly painted. Kate had chosen "iceberg"—a pale blue color with just a hint of purple, because although they didn't yet know the sex of their baby, she refused to succumb to gender stereotypes in choosing the decor for the nursery.

She paused in the doorway of the next room, where her

queen-size bed and dressers had been set up. "I thought the master bedroom was the one overlooking the backyard."

"It is." He took her hand and led her down the hall to the master, opening the door to reveal their new bedroom set—including a king-size bed.

Kate laughed. "You are worried that my big belly will push you out of bed, aren't you?"

"Actually, I was thinking a little further into the future," he confided. "A bigger bed means more room for our kids to snuggle in with us on lazy Saturday mornings."

"You really are going to be a great dad," she told him.

"I hope so. In the meantime, we've got a great big bed and hours and hours until morning."

"Did you have an idea about how we might fill those hours?"

"Yeah," he said. "I want to make love with my beautiful wife—the woman I love more and more each day."

"What a coincidence," she said. "Because I want to make love with my handsome husband—the man I love more and more each day."

So that's what they did.

And this time, Kate had no doubts that they were truly making love. With every touch of his hands and his lips and his body, he showed her the truth and depth of his feelings for her.

And she loved him back the same way.

Afterward, when their bodies were finally sated but still entwined, they both felt their little bean kick, as if expressing approval that Mommy and Daddy had finally figured things out.

Epilogue

February 14

As Kate's due date approached, she was more than ready to be done with being pregnant. By early February, she was tired of waddling around with an extra twenty-five pounds in her belly.

Reid tried to be understanding and supportive, and he willingly enabled her most outrageous cravings. He even went to The Trading Post one night to get her a bag of dill pickle–flavored potato chips and a package of gummy bears—from which she ate only the orange ones.

Since the responsibilities of an expectant father were limited, he tried to pick up the slack in other ways. And while Kate appreciated his willingness to sweep the floor and fold laundry, what really helped ease the physical discomfort in the last few weeks of her pregnancy was that he told her he loved her, every single day. And—twenty-five pounds of baby belly notwithstanding—he was still happy to prove it to her.

She left work a little early Wednesday afternoon, because her aching back didn't want to sit behind her desk any longer and because it was Valentine's Day and she figured she should put a little effort into making dinner for her husband. But when she pulled into the driveway, Reid's truck was already there. Apparently he'd decided to cut his day short, too.

She set her keys on the hook inside the closet and kicked off her shoes, then followed the sound of chopping into the kitchen. "What's going on in here?"

"You're not supposed to be home yet," he said, setting aside the knife and green pepper to dry his hands on a towel.

"Do you want me to leave?"

"Of course not. I was just hoping I'd have all of this done before you got home." He drew her close—or as close as her belly would allow—and kissed her. "Happy Valentine's Day."

"Happy Valentine's Day," she echoed.

Then she looked around, saw the vase of roses on the table, the candles in holders waiting to be lit, the bottle of sparkling grape juice chilling in a crystal wine bucket. "This is...wow." Then she sniffed the air. "What are you cooking?"

"Spaghetti with meatballs in a basic red sauce with a mixed field greens salad and chocolate chip cookie dough ice cream for dessert."

"Wow," she said again.

His gaze narrowed on her. "Why are you rubbing your back?"

"Oh." She hadn't realized she was doing so and forced herself to drop her hand. "I've been having some twinges."

He was immediately concerned. "Since when?"

She shrugged. "A few days."

"Can you describe the pain?"

"It's just a backache, Reid."

"Back pain can be an early sign of labor."

"I know, but it's really not that bad and—"

"And the sheen of perspiration on your forehead suggests you're in more pain than you want me to know," he noted.

"I'd say it's discomfort more than pain."

He splayed his palms on her belly. "Are you having any contractions?"

"Just Braxton Hicks," she said.

"How do you know they're Braxton Hicks?"

"Because I'm—" she sucked in a breath as her belly tightened "—still several days from my due date and first babies are almost never early."

"I think we should call Dr. Amaro."

"But you went to the trouble of making dinner, and it's Valentine's Day."

He bent his knees so he was at her eye level, and he could see that hers were filled with tears. "It's okay to be scared."

"Are *you* scared?"

"Terrified."

"You're just saying that to make me feel better."

"I'm saying it because it's true," he said. "This is new territory for both of us. But as scared as I am, I know that we can get through this—and everything that comes after—as long as we're together."

She winced as her belly tightened with another contraction and then, as her muscles went lax again, she felt something warm and wet trickle down the inside of her leg.

"Reid…"

"What can I do?" he asked.

"You can call Dr. Amaro now—my water just broke."

* * *

After that, everything happened really fast.

Or really slow, depending on who was telling the story.

Reid called Dr. Amaro, grabbed Katelyn's bag, then hustled—as much as it was possible to hustle a laboring woman—out to his truck.

Nine hours later, very early in the morning of February fifteenth, Katelyn gave birth to an eight-pound, four-ounce baby girl. They named her Tessa Lorraine Davidson, in honor of Katelyn's mother and Reid's grandmother.

Through most of the next day, Katelyn's hospital room seemed to have a revolving door as her dad, grandparents, siblings and various other relatives and friends popped in to check on the new mom and baby. Reid was content to hover in the background while his girls shone in the spotlight, because Katelyn deserved all the credit for bringing their beautiful, perfect daughter into the world and because Tessa was that beautiful, perfect daughter.

And Reid was the luckiest man in the world, because Katelyn wasn't just his wife and the mother of his child, she was the woman he loved with his whole heart—and he knew she loved him back the same way.

* * * * *

SURPRISE BABY, SECOND CHANCE

THERESE BEHARRIE

Grant.
Thank you for keeping me
steady through my anxieties.

My ROSA Typewriter Club.
I'm so lucky to have found you both.
Thank you for believing in me. Always
remember how much I believe in you.

And Megan.
Thank you for your patience with me.
You've taught me so much. I can't wait
for the rest of our books together—sorry,
I couldn't resist!

CHAPTER ONE

ROSA SPENCER HAD two options.

One: she could get back into the taxi that had brought her to the house she was currently standing in front of.

Two: she could walk into that house and face the man she'd left four months ago without any explanation.

Her husband.

When the purr of the car grew distant behind her she took a deep breath. Her chance of escape now gone, she straightened her shoulders and walked down the pathway that led to the front door of the Spencers' holiday home.

It could have been worse, she considered. She could have bumped into Aaron somewhere in Cape Town, where she'd been staying since she'd left him. And since they'd lived together over a thousand kilometres away in Johannesburg, Rosa would have been unprepared to see him.

Since she worked from home most days, she would have probably been wearing the not-quite-pyjamas-but-might-as-well-be outfit she usually wore when she ventured out of the house during the week. Her hair would have been a mess, curls spiralling everywhere—or piled on top of her head—and her face would have been clear of make-up.

Exposed, she thought. Vulnerable.

At least now she was prepared to see him.

Her gold dress revealed generous cleavage and cinched at her waist with a thin belt. Its skirt was long, loose, though it had a slit up to mid-thigh—stopping just before her shape-wear began—to reveal a leg that was strong and toned: one of her best assets.

Her dress made her feel confident—after all, what was the point of being a designer if she couldn't make clothes that did?—as did the mass of curls around her face, and the make-up she'd had done before she'd got onto the private plane her mother-in-law had sent for her.

She hadn't seen Liana Spencer in the four months since she'd left Aaron either. And perhaps that was part of the reason Rosa had agreed to attend a birthday party that would put her face to face with the man she'd walked away from.

The other reason was because of her own mother. And the birthday parties Violet Lang would never get to celebrate.

Rosa took another breath, clinging to the confidence she'd fought for with her dress. It was a pivotal part of the armour she'd created when she'd realised she'd be seeing Aaron again.

She needed the armour to cloak the shivering in the base of her stomach. The erratic beating of her heart. The combination of the two was so familiar that she didn't think she'd ever truly lived without it. Though that hadn't stopped her from running from it all her life.

The door of the house was open when she got there and Rosa slipped inside, thinking that it would be easier than to announce her arrival by ringing the bell. There was nothing to indicate a celebration on the first floor—just the usual tasteful but obviously expensive furniture and décor—though that wasn't surprising. Liana usually went for lavish, which meant the top floor. The one where the walls were made entirely of glass.

It offered guests an exceptional view of the sea that surrounded Mariner's Island just off the coast of Cape Town. Of the waves that crashed against the rocks that were scattered at the beach just a few metres from the Spencer house. And of the small town and airport that stood only a short distance away from the house too.

Rosa held her breath as she got to the top of the stairs, and then pushed open the door before she lost her nerve.

And immediately told herself that she should have escaped when she had the chance.

There was no party on this floor. Instead, it looked like it usually did when there were no events planned. There was a living area and a bed on one side of the room—the bathroom being the only section of the floor with privacy—and a dining area and kitchen on the other side.

There was an open space between the two sides as if whoever had designed the room had decided to give the Spencers an area to be free in.

But in that open space stood her husband. *Only* her husband.

And the last thing Rosa thought of was freedom.

His back was to her, and she thought that she still had the chance to escape. He didn't know that she was there. If she left he wouldn't ever have to know. What harm would it do?

Except that when she turned back to the door it was closed. And when she looked over her shoulder to see if he'd noticed her she saw that Aaron was now facing her, an unreadable expression on his face.

'Running?'

'N-no.' *Be confident.*

His mouth lifted into a half-smile. 'No?' he asked in a faintly mocking tone.

Her face went hot. The shivering intensified. Her heart rate rocketed. But, despite that, she was able to offer him a firm, 'No'.

'Okay,' he replied in a voice that told her he didn't believe her. And why would he? Hadn't she run from him before? Without the decency to explain why? Hadn't the anxiety of that decision kept her up night after night?

Guilt shimmered through her.

She ignored it.

But ignoring it meant that her brain had to focus on something else. And—as it usually did—it chose his face.

Her eyes feasted on what her memories hadn't done justice to over the last four months. His dark hair, dark brows, the not-quite-chocolate colour of his skin. The mixture of his Indian and African heritage had created an arresting face, his features not unlike those Rosa had seen on movie stars.

But his face had more than just good looks. It spoke of the cool, calm demeanour that had always exasperated her even as it drew her in. He rarely let his emotions out of wherever he kept them, so they seldom claimed the planes of his face.

Except when he and Rosa were having a conversation about their feelings. Or when they were making love. There'd been nothing *but* emotion on his face then.

'Where is everybody?' she asked in a hoarse voice.

Aaron slid his hands into his pockets, making his biceps bulge slightly under the material of his suit jacket. Her breath taunted her as it slipped out of her lungs. As it reminded her that it wasn't only Aaron's face that she was attracted to.

It was his muscular body. It was how much taller than her he was. It was his broad shoulders, the strength of his legs, of everything in between.

He'd always been thrilled by the curves of her body. But his hands were large enough, strong enough, that she'd always thought he wouldn't have wanted her as much if her curves hadn't been as generous.

Aaron took a step towards her.

Which was no reason for her to move back.

But she did.

'Well, if I'm right—and I probably am—everyone's here who's supposed to be.'

'I don't understand. It's just you and…' She trailed off, her heart thudding. 'Did you—did you do this?'

'Oh, no,' Aaron replied, and took another step towards

her. This time she managed to keep her feet in place. 'Why would I want to see the wife who left me with no explanation?'

'Great. Then I'll go.'

She turned to the door again, ignoring her confusion. She'd figure it out when she was off the island that reminded her so much of her husband.

The island where he'd taken her months after her mother had died. Where he'd got down on one knee. Where he'd told her he couldn't imagine life without her.

Where they'd spent time after their wedding. Lounging in the sun at the beach. Lazily enjoying each other's bodies as only newlyweds could.

Where they'd taken holidays. When life had become too much for her and Aaron had surprised her with a trip away.

The island where he'd held her, comforted her, loved her on the bed that stood in the corner, its memories haunting her. Overwhelming her.

Yes, she'd figure it all out when she was away from the island. And far, *far* away from her husband.

A hand pressed against the door before she could open it. She swallowed and then turned back to face him.

Her heart sprinted now. Her body prickled. The scent of his masculine cologne filled her senses. Memories, sharp and intimate, could no longer be held back.

Again, she tried to ignore them. But it was becoming harder to do.

'Why are you stopping me from leaving?' she managed in a steady voice.

'Did you think you were just going to walk in here, see me, and then...leave?'

'I thought I was attending your mother's sixtieth birthday party.'

'Which I would have been at too.'

'And we would have seen each other there, yes. But you're the only one here. I've seen you. Now I want to leave.'

'Just like that?'

'Just like that.'

He inched closer. 'You're not the slightest bit curious about why you and I are alone here?'

'Sure I am. But I'm also pretty sure I can figure it out on my way to the airport.'

'The airport?' His lips curved into a smile. 'Honey, the airport's closed.'

'No,' she said after a beat. 'No, it can't be. I just got off a plane. Your mother said it would be waiting for me when I was done here.'

His smile faded. 'She lied. Your flight is likely to be the last one until Monday. The airport's closed this weekend.'

Panic thickened in her throat. '*All* weekend?'

'Don't sound so surprised, Rosa,' he said mildly. 'You know Mariner's Island doesn't work the way the rest of the world does.'

'Yes, but...but it was a *private* plane. Yours.'

'It still needs somewhere to take off from. To land at. And since the airport's closed we won't have that until Monday.'

She ducked under his arm, put distance between them. But it didn't make breathing any easier. 'So...what? Your mother just decided to leave her guests stranded here until Monday?'

'Not guests,' he corrected. 'Just you and me.'

'Did you know about this?'

'No.'

'Then how did you not suspect something was off when the main route off the island would only be viable again on *Monday*?'

'She told me that the party would be going on for most of the weekend.'

'And you *believed* her?'

'Yes,' he said coldly. 'It's not unusual for one of my mother's parties to continue for an entire weekend. You know that.'

'Okay,' she said, and lifted the curls off her forehead with a shaky hand. 'Okay, fine.' Her hand dropped. 'Then I'll take a boat home.'

'It's too late to get one tonight.'

'I know,' she said through clenched teeth. 'I'll take one tomorrow morning.'

'There's a storm warning for tomorrow. Starting tonight, actually.'

She looked beyond the glass walls, saw the dark clouds rolling in. Her stomach tumbled. 'That's fine.'

'It'll be a rough storm, Rosa. It's anticipated to last until tomorrow evening at least. Do you still want to take a boat?'

'Yes.'

He laughed softly. 'You're so determined to get away from me you'll take an almost two-hour boat ride in a storm? Even though you get sick when the water is calm?'

She hesitated. 'I'll be fine.'

His half-smile mocked her. 'I'm sure you will be.'

He was right, she thought, and hated herself for admitting it. Hated him for being right.

Except that what she felt in that moment was anything *but* hate.

Confusion, yes. How had this happened? Had Liana really orchestrated this on purpose?

Guilt, of course. She'd walked away from him. From their relationship. She hadn't even said goodbye.

Anger, *absolutely*. She *hated* feeling trapped. It reminded her of her childhood. Of being caught in her mother's world.

But hate? No, she thought, her eyes settling on Aaron again. There was no hate.

'Why are you so calm?'

'I'm not,' he replied in a tone that gave no indication that he wasn't. 'But I know my mother. And I know this scheme is probably well-thought-out. Much like the first time we met. Or don't you remember?' His voice was soft, urgent. 'Have you run away from the memories too, Rosa?'

She didn't reply. There was no reply she could give. She couldn't tell him that she hadn't been running away from him, not really, but *saving* him. From the anxiety, the stress, the worry of being with someone who was terrified of losing the health of their mind, their body.

Rosa had spent her life looking after someone like that. She knew the anxiety, the stress, the worry of it. She knew the guilt when the fear became a reality.

She'd saved him, she thought again. She'd saved him from going through what she'd gone through with her mother's hypochondria. She'd saved him from having to take care of another person. From having it break him.

The moment she'd felt that lump in her breast, she'd known she couldn't put him through all of that. So she'd walked away. Had tried to move on.

But the memories wouldn't let her. No, the memories were always, *always* there.

'Great,' Rosa said loudly. 'No one's here.'

But that didn't make sense. Her mother had told her there was a Christmas ball for cancer patients that night. Had asked Rosa to be her partner at the ball.

Of course, Rosa had agreed. Her father wasn't in Cape Town, though she doubted he would have agreed to accompany her mother even if he had been. Irritation bristled over her, but she forced her attention to the matter at hand. She'd spent enough of her time being annoyed at her father.

The room was decorated as if there was supposed to be a ball. A large crystal chandelier hung in the middle of the ceiling, white draping flowing from it to different spots on the walls. It lit the space with soft light, brightened only by the small Christmas trees in each corner of the room that had been adorned with twinkling lights.

There was only one table at the end of the room, standing next to the largest Christmas tree Rosa had ever seen, with champagne, canapés and desserts spread across it.

'Am I early?' Rosa wondered out loud again.

But, like the first time, she got no response. Throwing her hands up, she turned to try and find someone who could explain what was happening. As she took a step towards the door, it opened and her breathing did something strange when a man joined her in the room.

'Who are you?' she blurted out.

He lifted an eyebrow. 'Aaron Spencer. Who are you?'

'Rosa Lang.' She swallowed. How had the air around her suddenly become so charged? 'I'm, um, here for the Christmas ball...'

'Me too.' His eyes lazily scanned the room. 'Either we're really early or—'

'Or our mothers have decided to play a game on us,' Rosa said, his name suddenly registering with her.

He was Liana Spencer's son. Rosa had only met the woman a few times during her mother's group chemotherapy sessions but she'd been charmed. Not only by the woman's energy—which she envied greatly—but because she'd done an amazing job at keeping Rosa's mother's energy up, despite the fact that she was going through chemo too.

Liana had been vocal about wanting Rosa to meet her son, and Violet had tried to get Rosa to agree to it just as passionately. The dress Liana had sent her—along with the make-up, hair and car she'd arranged—began to make more sense. And seeing Aaron now had Rosa regretting that she'd resisted an introduction for such a long time...

'I wouldn't put it past my mother,' Aaron replied darkly. It sent a shiver down her spine. But she didn't know if that was because of what he'd said or the fact that she felt inexplicably drawn to him. Even though he didn't seem quite as enamoured.

'This does seem like an excessive prank though.'

'My mother's speciality.'

'Really?' She tilted her head and, for once, let herself lean into what she wanted to do, refusing to give the doubt that followed her around constantly any footing. 'How about we have a glass of champagne and you can tell me all about it?'

She wasn't sure how long he studied her. But when his lips curved into a smile—when his expression turned from reserved into one she couldn't describe but *felt*, deep in her stomach—she knew she would have waited an eternity for it. And thought that—just maybe—he was drawn to her too...

'I remember,' Rosa said softly. 'It was a hospital Christmas ball. Or so we thought. Our mothers told us they wanted us to go with them. That they'd meet us there because they wanted to have dinner before. But there was no hospital Christmas ball. Just a party for two that our mothers had arranged so that we could meet.'

There was a tenderness on Rosa's face that didn't fit with the woman who'd left him four months ago. An indulgence too, though he suspected that was for her mother who'd passed away a year after that incident. And for his mother, who Rosa still had a soft spot for, despite what she'd seen Liana put him through over the years.

Aaron clenched his jaw. The emotion might have been misleading but her actions hadn't been. She'd left him without a word. Without a phone call. Without a note. He'd got home from work one day to find her clothes gone. She'd taken nothing else, and he'd had to face living in the house they'd furnished together—the home they'd *built* together—alone.

'I imagine my mother wanted this to be much the same,' Aaron said curtly. 'She forces us to be alone together but, instead of starting to date this time, we work things out.'

'But it's not like before,' she denied. 'There actually was a ball then. Sure, no one else was there, but there was food and drink, and the place had been decorated for a party. This—' she gestured around them '—is so far away from that.'

'But she sent you a dress again?' He tried to keep what seeing her in that dress did to him out of his voice.

'No. I designed this one.'

'You've never made anything like this for yourself before.'

'I know. It was...a special occasion. Your mom's sixtieth birthday,' she added quickly. But it was too late. He'd already figured out that she'd made the dress because of him.

He wasn't sure if he was pleased or annoyed by the fact. He'd been trying to get her to make something for herself for years. Now, when they were...whatever they were, she'd chosen to listen to him.

Perhaps that was why she'd left. Because he'd been holding her back. He'd add it to the list of possibilities. A list that spoke loudly—accusingly—of his faults.

'I'm sure she would have if you hadn't told her you'd sort yourself out,' he said to distract himself. 'And she arranged the plane for you. And the car to get you here. She's a regular old fairy godmother,' he added dryly.

'No. No,' she said again. 'That can't be it. She wouldn't have arranged all of this just to play at being a fairy godmother.'

'She did it before. When we met.'

'That was just as much my mom as it was yours.'

'Somehow, I think my mother had more to do with it.' His shoulders tightened. 'She likes to think she doesn't live in the real world. And now, with this, she gets to play the

perfect role. The good guy. The fairy godmother. To orches-
trate a happy ever after.'

'For you and me?'

'Who else?' he asked sharply, hating the surprise in her
voice. She winced, stepped back, brushed at her hair again.
It spiralled around her face in that free and slightly wild
way her curls dictated.

'You're saying your mother tricked us into being here
together because she wants us to…reconcile?' He nodded.
'Why?'

'I don't know,' he said sarcastically. 'Maybe because we
were happily married until I got home one day to find you'd
disappeared?' She blanched. 'Or maybe I'd fooled myself
into believing we were happy.'

She bit her lip, looked away. 'Did she tell you that she
wanted us to have a happy ever after?'

He gritted his teeth, then forced himself to relax. Control
was key. 'Not directly. But she's been urging me to contact
you for the last four months.' He cocked his head. 'How
did *she* contact you?'

'My…email. I've been checking my emails.'

Tension vibrated between them. As did the unspoken
words.

*I've been checking my emails. I just haven't replied to
yours.*

'I was always going to attend her birthday, Aaron,' Rosa
said softly. 'You know this is about more than your mother.
More than you and me.'

He did. Rosa's mother had made his mother promise to
celebrate each birthday with vigour. A reminder that they'd
lived. That they'd had a *life*.

That had been a deathbed promise.

It angered him even more that his mother would use her
birthday as an opportunity for her scheme. In all the years
she'd manipulated situations—in all the years she'd blamed

her 'zest for life' for interfering in other people's lives—she'd never done anything this…*conniving*.

And in all the years since he'd taken responsibility for Liana since he'd realised she wouldn't take responsibility herself, Aaron had never felt more betrayed.

Or perhaps the betrayal he felt about Rosa leaving was intensifying his reaction.

Whatever it was, he wouldn't allow it to control him any more. He walked to the door…and cursed when he found it locked.

CHAPTER TWO

'WHAT?' ROSA ASKED, anxiety pounding with her heart. 'What is it?'

'It's locked.'

'It's—what?' She strode past him and tried the handle of the door. It turned, but no amount of pressure made it open. 'No,' she said, shaking her head. 'This is not happening. We are *not* locked in here. There must be some mistake.'

Panic spurred her movements and she reached into the clutch she'd forgotten was in her hand. She took her phone out. 'I have signal!' she said triumphantly. 'Only a few bars, but it should work. Who should I call?'

'I suppose we could try the police.' His calm voice was a stark contrast to the atmosphere around them.

'Do you have the number?'

'No.'

She stared at him. 'How do you not have the number of the police?'

'It's on my phone. It's dead,' he said, nodding in the direction of the table where it lay.

'You didn't charge it,' she said with a sigh. It was something he did—or didn't do—regularly. Which had driven her crazy on good days. This day had been anything but good.

But if he was going to pretend to be calm—if he was going to pretend he wasn't freaking out when she knew that he was—she could too.

'Okay, so we don't have the number for the police station. I'm assuming that covers all emergency services?' He nodded. 'I guess we better hope that nothing happens during this storm,' she muttered, and scanned her contacts for the number she was looking for.

As if in response to her words, a streak of lightning whipped across the sky. It was closely followed by booms of thunder. Rosa closed her eyes and brought the phone to her ear.

'Liana, we're locked in,' Rosa said the moment she heard Liana's voice—distant, crackling—on the phone.

'Rosa?'

'Yes, it's Rosa. Aaron and I are trapped on the top floor of the house.'

'What?' Static dulled the sound of Liana's voice even more. 'Did you get to the house safely?'

'I'm fine. But we're locked in, so we can't get off the top floor.'

Liana didn't reply and Rosa looked at the phone to see if they'd been cut off, but the call was still ongoing.

'Here, let me try,' Aaron said and she handed him the phone. And bit back the response that *him* speaking to his mother couldn't magically make the connection better.

'Mom? We're locked on the top floor of the house. Hello? *Hello?*'

Rosa waited as Aaron fell silent, and then he looked at the display on the phone and sighed. 'It cut off. I don't think she got any of that.'

'We could try someone else—'

She broke off when thunder echoed again, this time followed by a vicious flash of lightning. And then everything went dark.

'Aaron?'

'Yeah, I'm here.'

Her panic ebbed somewhat with the steadiness of his voice. 'Does this mean what I think it means?'

'Yeah, the power went out.' She heard movement, and then the light of her phone shone between them. 'The generator should be kicking in soon though.'

Silence spread between them as they waited.

And relief took the place of tension when the lights flickered on again.

'I think we're going to be stuck here for a while,' Aaron said after a moment.

'We could just try calling someone again.'

'Who?'

'Look up the number for the police,' she snapped. Sucked in a breath. Told herself her confident façade was slipping. Ignored the voice in her head telling her it had slipped a long time ago.

Aaron didn't reply and tapped on the screen of the phone. Then he looked up. 'There's no signal. It must have something to do with the electricity being out.'

'That's impossible. We can't *not* have a connection.'

'It's Mariner's Island,' he said simply, as though it explained everything.

And, if she were honest with herself, it did. Mariner's Island was tiny. The locals who lived and worked there did so for the sake of tourism. And it was the perfect tourist destination. In the summer. When the demands on power and the likelihood of storms were low.

There was a reason the airport had closed over the weekend. A reason the lights had gone out. The island thrived during summer, but survived during winter.

A clap of thunder punctuated her thoughts and she turned in time to see another flash of lightning streak across the sky. She badly wanted to try the door again, but when she turned back she saw Aaron watching her. And if she tried the door again she would be proving him right. She would be proving to him that she *was* running. She would look like a fool.

She didn't want to look like a fool. A fool desperate not to be in the same room with the husband she'd left.

With the husband she still loved.

* * *

Again, Aaron found himself enthralled by the emotion on her face. She looked torn, though he didn't know between what.

It wasn't the ideal situation, them being locked in this room together. But it was what it was. And, since the storm was probably going to keep the good folk of Mariner's Island in their homes, no one would be saving them for a while.

They'd have to accept that fact and do the best that they could.

It almost seemed as if he were okay with it. As if being alone with the woman who'd left him wouldn't remind him of all the reasons he'd given himself for why she'd left.

His reluctance to be spontaneous. His caution surrounding their lives. How he always had to clean up the messes his mother created. How he did so without a word.

She hadn't seemed to mind any of it before. But then she'd left, so what did he know?

'You should turn your phone off.'

'What? Why?'

'Preserve the battery.' He took off his jacket, loosened his tie. Threw them both over the couch. 'We're not calling anyone for a while, but we'll have to do so tomorrow.'

'But what if someone tries to contact us?'

'No one is going to contact us.'

He opened the top button of his shirt, and then narrowed his eyes when he saw two suitcases in the corner of the room. He'd known something was up when he'd got to the top floor and saw that it hadn't been set up for a party. Instead, it looked as it usually did when they visited normally.

Perhaps that had dulled his suspicions. He'd thought his mother had wanted them to share a meal, or that they'd meet there before going to the actual party.

He should have known better.

The pieces had only fallen into place when he'd seen

Rosa. And he'd barely managed to see the whole picture those pieces painted when he'd been battling the emotion at seeing her again.

He walked over to the cases and laid them both on the bed. The first held men's clothing. The second, women's.

'Is that *lingerie*?'

His lips twitched. 'Yes.'

She'd come over from where she'd been standing on the opposite side of the bed and now began to throw the offending items out of the case. 'Well, at least there are some other things here too.' She paused. 'Did your mother pack this?'

He shrugged.

'The other things—' she pulled out a casual-looking dress, holding it between her index finger and thumb '—are less... seductive, I suppose. But I don't think any of them would fit me.' She frowned. 'If it was your mother, this makes no sense. She knows what size I am.'

'Maybe the selection was meant to seduce anyway.' He fought to steady his voice. 'You'd be able to wear that, but it would be tighter than what you're used to. Or more uncomfortable. So you'd—'

'Be encouraged to wear the lingerie?'

'I was going to say you'd look different.' He said the words deliberately now, determined not to show her how the conversation was messing with his head.

'There's nothing wrong with how I usually dress.'

'No,' he agreed.

'So...what? Tighter, more uncomfortable—*different*—clothing would seduce you? And then we'd reunite.' She said the last words under her breath, as though saying them to herself. 'There isn't anything I can wear here that's appropriate for this.' She gestured around them.

'I don't think my mother intended this.'

'Us being trapped?'

He nodded. 'She probably wanted us to go out and enjoy

the island like we have in the past.' He let that sit for a moment. 'You're free to use whatever she's packed for me.'

'It'll probably only be jeans and shirts.'

You could wear the lingerie, if you like.

The words seared his brain. Out loud, he said, 'You're welcome to help yourself.'

He walked to the other side of the room, as though somehow the distance would keep him from remembering her in lingerie. And what had happened after he'd seen her in lingerie. It would do nothing for his need for control to remember that.

He eyed the alcohol his mother had left on the counter of the kitchen—at least she'd done *that*—and reached for the rum and soda water, adding ice from the freezer. He was sipping it when he faced her again, but her back was towards him and the memories he'd tried to suppress struggled free, even though he couldn't see her front.

But he didn't need to.

Because, from where he stood, he could see the strong curve of her shoulders, the sweeping slope of her neck. He'd only have to press a kiss there, have his tongue join, and she would moan. She'd grab his hands as his mouth did its work and pull them around her, over her breasts, encouraging him to touch them…

He gritted his teeth. Reminded himself—again—that he needed to be in control. But his reaction wasn't a surprise. His attraction to Rosa had always goaded him in this way. When he'd first seen her—her curves, the curls around her face, the golden-brown of her skin—it had kicked him in the gut.

He'd managed to ignore it for a full year, and only because both their mothers had been going through chemotherapy and acting on his attraction had seemed inappropriate. But their year of friendship hadn't been enough for him.

And their chemistry had constantly reminded him of its presence.

Stalking him. Mocking him.

It was why control was so important now. He couldn't act on his attraction this time. He couldn't show Rosa how much she'd hurt him when she'd left. And how shaken he was to see her again. He'd only just begun to face the fact that the morning she'd left might have been the last time he'd ever see her…

Control meant that he had a plan. And plans were how he lived his life. How he made sure his law firm remained successful. How he tried to make sure his mother hadn't created another problem for him to fix.

He hadn't had a plan in his marriage, and he'd wondered if that had contributed to how—and why—it had ended so abruptly.

Or had his need to plan been the cause of its end?

He took a long drag from his drink and shook the feelings away. He might not know if his plans—his need for control—had contributed to Rosa leaving, but having a plan was the only way he'd survive the night.

Now he just had to come up with one.

CHAPTER THREE

'Do you have any intention of offering me a drink?' Rosa asked when she turned back and saw Aaron sipping from a glass. It was filled with golden liquid, the kind she was pretty sure would help steady the nerves fluttering in her stomach.

'What do you want?' he asked flatly.

She almost winced. 'Whatever you're having is fine.'

He nodded and went about making her drink. She walked towards him cautiously and then busied herself with putting the bottles from the counter into the cabinet beneath. It wasn't necessary, but it was a way to keep her hands busy. Especially since something about his expression made her want to do something remarkably different with her hands.

Or was that because the clothing—the lingerie—had reminded her of all the times she'd *wanted* to seduce him? Of all the times it had worked?

Her hands shook and she waited for them to steady before she packed the last bottle away.

'You don't have to do that.'

'I know.'

But I was thinking about all the times we made love and I needed a distraction.

'Do you think your mother left something for us to eat?'

'Try the fridge.'

She did, though she wasn't hungry. Again, it was just because she wanted something to do. To distract from the ache in her body. From the ache in her heart.

She found the fridge fully stocked.

'How nice of her,' Rosa said wryly. Her patience with Liana had dropped dramatically after the seductive clothing thing. And now, finding the fridge filled with food, she couldn't deny that Liana had planned this any more.

She'd indulged Liana over the years she'd got to know the woman. Understandably, she thought, considering Liana's history with her mother. With *her*, during Violet's declining health. And…after.

But Rosa had let that influence her view of Liana's actions. Actions that Rosa had condoned by not speaking out. She wouldn't let that happen again—once they got out of their current situation.

'It's full?'

'Yeah.' The hairs on her neck stood when Aaron moved in behind her to look for himself. 'There's this dish—' she took it out, handed it to him—anything to get him away from her '—which I assume is something readymade for this evening. And the rest is ingredients to make meals. Eggs, vegetables, that sort of thing.'

'There was some meat in the freezer.'

Rosa closed the fridge. 'She's thought of everything, hasn't she?'

'She generally does,' Aaron said and handed her the drink. She braced herself for the contact, but it didn't help. A spark flared anyway. She'd never really been able to come to terms with the attraction she felt for him. That she'd felt for him since day one.

Or with your love for him, a voice whispered in her head, reminding her of why she'd had to leave—before either of those things had tempted her into staying.

Staying wouldn't have done either of them any good.

'She just doesn't think about consequences.'

'Oh, I think she knows.' She removed the foil that covered the top of the dish and found a rice and chicken meal of some kind. She took out two plates and, without asking him if he wanted any, dished portions for both of them. 'That there are consequences, I mean.'

'But she never stops to consider *what* those consequences might be.' His voice was steady, but there was frustration there. He'd never been able to hide it completely when he was talking about his mother. 'You know how many times I've had to deal with consequences that weren't favourable. Like the time she gave her car to a guy she met at a conference she attended.'

Rosa nodded. 'She thought it would be easier for him to get to his job in the city if he had a car. And that would make sure he didn't lose his job, and that he'd be able to look after his family.'

'Instead, the man *still* lost his job because *he couldn't drive*, and he ended up selling the car, which then got him into trouble with the police because she hadn't transferred the car into his name.'

'And you had to sort it all out,' she said softly. The microwave sounded, and she handed Aaron the heated plate before putting in her own. 'I'm sorry, ba—'

She stopped herself. She'd been about to call him 'baby'. And it wouldn't have been like the 'honey' he'd called her when she'd first tried to leave. No, that had been said sardonically. This? This would have been said lovingly. Endearingly.

It was because of the routine she'd slipped into. Dishing for him, heating his food. Normal parts of what had been their life before. But that life was gone. She'd walked away from it. It didn't matter why or how—she *had*. Which meant accepting that she couldn't just *slip* back into routine.

The microwave finished heating her food and she used it as an excuse to turn her back to him. To ignore the emotion that was swirling inside her.

'You didn't change,' he said into the silence that had settled in the room. She took her plate and drink to the couch and tried to figure out how to sit down without the slit revealing her leg.

'No,' she replied after a moment, and then gave up and lowered to the seat. She set her food on the coffee table in front of them, covered as much leg as she could and then took a long sip of the drink before she answered him. 'As I predicted, there were only a couple of shirts in there and jeans. The jeans wouldn't fit me.'

He settled at the opposite end of the couch. 'You could have worn one of the shirts.'

She lifted a brow. 'And that wouldn't have been...distracting?'

'What you're wearing now isn't?'

His eyes lowered to the leg she'd been trying to cover, and then moved up to her cleavage.

'I'll go change,' she said in a hoarse voice, setting her drink down.

'No, you don't have to.'

His gaze lifted to her face, though his expression didn't do anything to help the flush that was slowly making its way through her body.

'It's probably for the best.'

'Are you afraid I'll do something neither of us wants?'

'No.'

Because both of us would want it.

'I just think it would be better for us not to...cross any boundaries.'

'Are there boundaries?' he asked casually, though she wasn't fooled by it. She could hear the danger beneath the façade. 'I didn't realise a married couple had boundaries.'

'That's not quite what we are now, though.'

'No? Did I miss the divorce papers you sent to me while you were in Cape Town?'

Bile churned in her stomach. 'There are no divorce papers.' She frowned. 'You knew where I was?'

He nodded. 'I needed to make sure you were okay.'

She closed her eyes. 'I'm sorry. I didn't think—'

'That I'd want to know that you were alive?'

'I took my clothes. I thought—' She broke off as shame filled her. 'I should have let you know.'

A chill swept over her as she took in his blank expression. 'You said we aren't *quite* married, but you haven't asked for a divorce.' He stopped, though she clearly heard the *yet* he hadn't said. 'Which is it, Rosa?'

And, though his expression was still clear of emotion, the danger in his voice was coming out in full now. She swallowed and reached for her drink again.

'I don't want to get into this,' she said after she'd taken another healthy sip. She'd need a refill soon if she went on like this.

'You can't get out of it. We're stuck here.'

'I know.' Couldn't forget it if she tried. 'I also know that if we start talking about this stuff, being trapped here is going to be a lot harder than it needs to be.'

'Stuff,' he repeated softly. Her eyes met his and she saw the anger there. 'Is that what you call leaving me after five years of being together? After three years of marriage?'

'I call it life,' she replied sharply. 'Life happened, and I had to go.' She stood. 'There's no point in rehashing it now.'

He stood with her, and the body she'd always loved cast a shadow over her. 'Where are you going to go, Rosa?' he asked. 'There's nowhere to run. This room is open-plan. The only other room is the bathroom, and even then you wouldn't be able to stay there for ever.'

She took a step back. Lowered to the couch slowly. 'You're taking too much joy from this.'

'This isn't joy.' He sat back down, though his body didn't relax. She nearly rolled her eyes. What did he think he was going to have to do? Tackle her if she tried to get past him?

'What would you call it then?'

'Satisfaction. Karma.'

'Karma?' she said with a bark of laughter. 'I didn't re-alise you believed in karma.'

'I didn't. Until today. Now. When it's become clear how much you want to run from this—from me—and can't.'

Now she did roll her eyes. 'And what are *you* paying for? What did *you* do that was so bad that you deserve to be locked in a room with the wife who left you?'

His features tightened. 'Maybe I don't believe in karma then.'

'Sounds like you're taking the easy way out.'

'Or like I'm doing whatever the hell suits me.' His voice was hard, and surprise pressed her to ask what she'd said that had upset him.

But she didn't. She didn't deserve to know.

'Doing whatever the hell suits you *does* sound like you're enjoying this.'

'Maybe I am. Hard to tell since I've forced myself not to feel anything since you left.'

And there it was. The honesty, the vulnerability that had always seeped past the coolness he showed the world. The emotion that showed her how deeply he cared, even when he pretended he didn't.

It had always managed to penetrate whatever wall she'd put up with him. Or whatever wall he'd put up to make her believe he didn't feel. But he did. Which made her actions so much worse.

She'd done many stupid things in her life. Most of them because she'd wanted to find out who she was after giving so much of herself to her mother.

Like dropping out of college because she didn't think they were teaching her what she needed to know about design.

Like moving out when she was tired of being responsible for her mother's mental health.

Like ignoring her mother's phone calls for almost two

months after she moved out, because she thought Violet was trying to manipulate her into coming back home. When really her mother had been calling to tell her about her cancer.

She hadn't thought anything about her relationship with Aaron had been stupid. At least she hadn't until she'd found the lump. Until it had reminded her of how stupid she'd been by choosing not to be tested for breast cancer when her mother's doctors had advised it.

And suddenly all the uncertainty she'd battled with in the past about her decisions had returned. Maybe they'd never really gone away. And the disaster scenario of what that lump could mean had echoed her mother's own anxieties so closely that it had reminded Rosa that she was her mother's child.

It would have been selfish of her to stay. To put Aaron through what she'd gone through with her mother. To put him through anything that would cause him to suffer as he had when his mother had been ill.

'Maybe that's for the best,' she told him, kicking off her shoes. 'If we don't feel anything, we don't get hurt. And since we're already in this situation—' she waved between them '—committing ourselves to not getting hurt doesn't sound so bad, does it?'

He stared at her. 'Are you...are you serious?'

'Yes,' she said, and lifted the plate she'd set on the table, resting it on her lap as she leaned back into the couch. 'Doesn't it sound appealing to you? Us not hurting each other?'

'Is that why you left? Because I hurt you?'

She toyed with the food on her plate. 'No,' she said, lifting her gaze to his. 'You didn't hurt me.'

'Then why did you leave?'

'Because I would be hurting you by staying.'

'Why?' But she shook her head. 'Rosa, you can't just

tell me something like that and not give me *anything* else.'
Still, she didn't answer him. He clenched his jaw. 'You don't
think you're hurting me now? With *this*?'

'I know I am.'

'And that doesn't mean anything to you?'

'It…can't.'

He wanted to shout. To demand answers from her. But
that would only keep her from talking to him.

And he needed her to talk to him. He needed to know
why she was saying things his wife never would have said.
The Rosa he'd married would never have given up on anything. She would never have settled for backing away from
the possibility of pain when there was a possibility for joy.

Or perhaps this was karma, like he'd said. Maybe this
was *his* karma. For not acting with reason when it came to
Rosa. She'd only been twenty-three when they'd married.
He'd been twenty-six. Older. Wiser.

At least old enough to know that she might not have
been ready to marry him. She'd still been grieving for her
mother when he'd proposed. Her decision might not have
been entirely thought through.

But as he thought back to the moment he'd proposed he
couldn't remember any hesitation from Rosa…

He wanted everything to be perfect. Simple but perfect.
That was his plan. And, since only he and Rosa were on the
beach in front of the house on Mariner's Island, there'd be no
one but himself to blame if everything didn't go perfectly.

He took a deep breath and Rosa looked up at him. 'Are
you okay?'

'Yeah.'

'You're sure?' Her brow furrowed. 'Because you've been
quiet since we got here. I mean, quieter than usual.'

She gave him a small smile and his heart tumbled. Even
her smile could make his heart trip over itself. No wonder

he was proposing to her when he'd never thought he'd get married.

'I'm thinking.'

'About?'

'This. Us.'

'Really?' She pressed in closer at his side when the wind nipped at their skin. It was cooler than he would have liked, but he supposed that was what he got by wanting to propose just as the sun was going down on an autumn day. 'And what have you come up with?'

'You're amazing.'

His feet stopped, though they weren't close to the place where he'd planned on proposing. This was good enough. Waves were crashing at their feet. Sand around them. The sun shining over them as though it approved of his actions.

Besides, none of that mattered anyway. Not any more. All that mattered was her. And that he couldn't imagine another moment going by without knowing that she'd one day be his wife.

'Well, yeah,' she said with a smile that faded when she saw his expression. 'What's wrong?'

'I have something for you.'

'Okay.' Confusion lined every feature of her beautiful face, but there was trust in her eyes. He hoped he would never betray that trust. 'Aaron?' she asked quietly after a moment. 'Are you going to tell me what it is?'

Instead of replying, he stepped back from her and removed the rose petals he'd been keeping in his pocket. It had been a silly idea, he thought now as the confusion intensified on her face. But it was too late to stop now.

He cleared his throat. 'I got these from the house.'

'You stole...petals from the garden?' Her lips curved. 'Just petals? Not the actual flowers?'

He smiled. 'I wanted to take a picture of you standing in a shower of petals.'

'Aaron,' she said after a moment. 'You realise you're being weird, right?'

His smile widened. But he only nodded. She let out a frustrated sigh. 'Okay, fine. Should I just—' She cupped her hands and mimicked throwing the petals into the air.

'Yes. But throw them over your shoulder.' He handed her the petals, careful to protect them from the wind. 'So, turn your back to me while I get the camera ready.'

There was impatience in her eyes now, but she didn't say anything. Only turned her back to him. She was indulging him, he thought. Because that was who she was. Always putting him first, even when she didn't understand why.

He took the ring from his pocket and took another deep breath. And then he got down on one knee and said, 'I'm ready.'

She threw the petals into the sky and turned, a smile on her face for the picture she'd thought he was about to take. At first the confusion returned. Her eyes searched for where she'd thought he'd be as the petals swirled around them. Then, as they were carried up and away by the wind, her gaze lowered, settling on him.

She sucked in her breath and then, on an exhale, said his name. The surprise had turned into something deeper, more meaningful, as she did. And suddenly all the fear, all the uncertainty disappeared.

It was going to be perfect.

That was the last thing he thought before telling her why he wanted to spend the rest of his life with her.

No, he thought as he closed his eyes briefly. There had been no hesitation when Rosa had accepted his proposal.

But hadn't his mother shown him that he would need to take responsibility for others at some time in his life? So why hadn't he realised Rosa might have needed that from him too?

But now that he thought about it, he wondered if it was because he *had* been responsible when it came Rosa. He'd promised her mother that he would look after her. And, since he'd loved her so damn much, marriage had seemed like the perfect way to do it.

But maybe *that* had been his mistake.

Or maybe *he* was the mistake…

'Okay,' he said curtly, ripping himself out of the web his memories had caught him in. 'Do you want another drink?'

She blinked at him, and then silently nodded and handed him her glass. He deliberately brushed his fingers against hers as he took it, and saw the slight shake of her hand as she drew it back to her lap.

He turned away from her, satisfaction pouring through him. Whatever it was that she was going through—whatever it was that *they* were going through—he hadn't made up their attraction. And that attraction had come from their feelings for one another.

Perhaps he'd made one too many mistakes with Rosa. Heaven knew he had with his mother, so it might not have been different with his wife. But at least he could make sure Rosa didn't forget that they were drawn to one another. Something neither of them had ever been able to deny.

And then what? an inner voice asked as he poured their drinks. Would they just become hyperaware of their attraction, since their feelings were seemingly out of bounds, and then let it fizzle out between them?

There was no way that was happening. And if they acted on it…what would that mean for him? For them? Would she just walk away from him again? Would he just let her go?

An uncomfortable feeling stirred in his stomach and he walked back to her, setting her glass down on the table to avoid any more touching. He had no idea what he wanted to achieve with her. With his marriage. And he'd never thought he would be in the position to have to worry about it.

He'd thought he'd done everything right in his life. He'd looked after a mother who hadn't cared about looking after herself. About looking after him. He'd got a stable job. Succeeded in it. He'd fallen in love—though it had been unplanned—and he'd married.

And still everything had gone wrong.

Though, if he was being honest with himself, perhaps that had started when his mother had been diagnosed with cancer and he'd realised the extent of his mistakes.

Now, the fear that had grown in the past four months pulsed in his chest. Had him facing the fact that everyone in his life who was supposed to love him had left him. His mother. His father. And now Rosa...

He couldn't deny that he was the problem any more.

CHAPTER FOUR

'So, WHAT HAVE you been doing these last four months?'

Somehow, she managed to keep her tone innocent. As if she wasn't asking because she desperately wanted a glimpse into the life he'd made without her.

It was veering into dangerous territory, that question, and yet it was the safest thing Rosa could think to ask. Something mundane. Something that didn't have anything to do with what they'd been talking about before.

Feelings. Emotions. Their relationship.

But the expression on his face told her that perhaps the question wasn't as safe as she'd thought. Still, he answered her.

'Work.'

'Work?' When he didn't offer more, she pressed. 'What about work? New clients?'

'New clients.'

She bit back a sigh. 'And?'

'We're expanding.'

'Oh.'

Expanding? He'd never spoken about the desire to expand before. His law firm was one of the most prestigious family practices in Gauteng. He had wealthy clientele, made sure his firm helped those in need, and he'd always spoken about how content he'd been. Proud, even. So why was he expanding?

She waited for him to offer an explanation. He didn't. And she didn't have the courage to ask him. Not when she would have known if she'd just *stayed*.

'You?'

Her gaze sprang to his. She hadn't expected him to engage. 'I've been working on a new line. Evening gowns.'

'Like the one you're wearing.'

'Exactly like the one I'm wearing. For women like me.'

His eyes swept over her, heating her body with the faint desire she saw on his face. He was controlling it well, she thought. He never had before. She'd always known when Aaron desired her. It would start with a look in his eyes— much more ardent than what she saw there now—and then he'd say something seductive and follow his words with actions.

She'd loved those times. Loved how unapologetic they had been. How freeing. And since they both had problems with being free—no matter how much she pretended that she didn't—those moments were special.

And now she'd lost them.

'It'll be popular.'

'I hope so.' She paused. 'I did a sample line. I've been promoting it on the website for the past month, and it's got some great feedback. I might even do a showcase.'

'I told you it would be great.'

'You did.'

Neither of them mentioned that for years he'd been telling her that she needed to make clothes for herself. For others like her. But that wasn't why she'd got into fashion. At least, not at first. She loved colours, patterns, prints. She loved how bold they could be, or how understated. She loved the contrast of them—the lines, the shapes.

She hadn't wanted to confine herself when she'd started out. She'd wanted to experiment, to explore, to learn about everything. And, because she had, she now had momentum after being labelled a fresh and exciting young designer. Enough that she could finally design the clothes she wanted to. For women who looked like her. Who were bigger. Who weren't conventionally curvy.

She'd shared all her worries, her fears, her excitement with Aaron. And she wanted nothing more than to tell him about the challenges, the joys she'd had creating this new line now.

But the brokenness between them didn't lend itself to that discussion.

Her heart sank and her eyes slid closed.

How had her *safe* question led to *this*?

Watching her was going to be the only way he'd figure out what was going on in her head. It was clear she wasn't going to tell him. And, since he hadn't exactly been forthcoming himself, he could hardly ask her what was causing the turmoil on her face.

But he couldn't be forthcoming. How was he supposed to tell her that his expansion plans had started the moment his mother had informed him of where Rosa was? He hadn't been interested in finding her...at least, that was what he'd told himself. But then he'd received Liana's email telling him Rosa was in Cape Town.

And suddenly he was planning to expand his firm to Cape Town.

How was he supposed to tell her all that?

'Oh, look,' she said softly, her gaze shifting to behind him. The pain had subsided from her face—had been replaced by wonder—tempting him to keep looking at her.

Dutifully—though reluctantly—he followed her gaze and saw that she was watching the rain. He didn't know what she found so fascinating about it. Sure, it was coming down hard, fast and every now and then a flash of lightning would streak through it. But still, it looked like rain to him. Regular old rain.

And yet when he looked back to Rosa's face he could have sworn she had just seen the first real unicorn.

She got up and walked in her beautiful gown to the glass

doors, laying a hand on them as though somehow that would allow her to touch the rain. It was surprisingly tender, but he refuted that description almost immediately. What he was witnessing wasn't *tender*. How could his wife watching the rain be tender?

But he couldn't get the word out of his mind as she spent a few more minutes there. Then she walked to the light switch in the kitchen and turned it off. The entire room went dark and she murmured, 'Just for a moment,' before returning to her place at the door.

He still wasn't sure what was so special about it. About watching the rain in the dark. But her reaction had cast a spell around him. And now he was walking towards her, stopping next to her and watching the rain pour from the sky in torrents.

'I don't think I've ever seen a storm more beautiful,' she said softly from beside him.

'An exaggeration,' he commented with a half-smile.

She laughed. Looked up at him with twinkling eyes. 'Of course it is. But I like to think that I use my opportunities to exaggerate for effect. Is it working?' she asked with a wink.

His smile widened and, though his heart was still broken from her leaving, and his mind was still lapping up every piece of information she'd given as to why, as they looked at each other, he was caught by her.

He told himself it was the part of him that wanted things to go back to the way they'd been before. The part that mourned because it was no longer an option. Not with how things had shifted between them. Not when that shift had confirmed that they were no longer the same people they'd been before she'd left.

And still he was caught by her.

By her brown eyes, and the twinkle that was slowly turning into something else as the seconds ticked by. By the angles of her face—some soft, some sharp, all beautiful.

He didn't know why he still felt so drawn to the woman beside him when she wasn't the woman he'd fallen in love with any more. Or was it himself he didn't recognise? He'd spent the four months since she'd left racking his brain for answers about what had gone wrong. And what he'd come up with had forced him to see himself in a new light. A dim one that made him prickly because it spoke of things he'd ignored for most of his life.

'Why do you still make me feel like this?'

He hadn't realised he'd spoken until her eyes widened. His gaze dipped to her mouth as she sucked her bottom lip between her teeth. It instantly had his body responding, and he took a step towards her—

And then suddenly there was a blast of cold air on him and Rosa was on the balcony in the rain.

'Rosa! What are you doing?'

But she turned her back to him and was now opening her palms to the rain, spreading her fingers as though she wanted to catch the drops, but at the same time wanted them to fall through her fingers.

'Rosa!' he said again when she didn't answer him. But it was no use. She didn't give any indication that she'd heard him.

He cursed and then took off his shoes and stepped out onto the balcony with her, hissing out his breath when the ice-cold drops immediately drenched his skin.

Her eyes fluttered open when he stopped next to her, and he clearly saw the shock in them. 'What are you *doing*?'

'The same thing as you, apparently,' he said through clenched teeth. 'Care to explain why we're out getting soaked in the rain?'

'I didn't think you'd—' She broke off, the expression on her face frustratingly appealing. Damn it. How was that possible when their lives were such a mess?

'Rosa,' he growled.

'I wanted to get out of that room,' she said. 'I wanted to breathe in proper fresh air and not the stifling air in *that* room.'

'That room is over one hundred and fifty square metres.'

'You know that's not what I meant,' she snapped. 'I just felt…trapped. With you. In there.'

'You felt trapped with me,' he repeated.

'No, not like that,' she said. 'I felt… It's just that room. And the fact that resisting you—resisting us—is so *hard*. Everything between us is suddenly so hard.' She let out a sound that sounded suspiciously like a sob. 'Mostly I feel trapped by what I did to us.' She closed her eyes and when she opened them again he felt the pain there as acutely as if it were in his own body. 'I threw what we had away.'

He took a step forward, the desire to take her into his arms, to comfort her compelling him. But then he stopped and told himself that he couldn't comfort her when he didn't know why. That he couldn't comfort her when, by all rights, she was supposed to be comforting him.

She'd left *him* behind. She'd hurt *him*.

And yet there he was, outside, soaking wet in the rain because of *her*.

He moved back. Ignored the flash of hurt in her eyes.

'We're going to get sick if we stay out here,' he said after a moment.

'So go back inside,' she mumbled miserably.

It was a stark reminder that she hadn't asked him to come outside in the rain with her. And it would be logical to listen to her and go back inside.

Instead, he sighed and held his ground. Tried to commit the experience to memory. He suspected that some day he'd want—no, *need*—to remember this moment, however nonsensical it appeared to be.

To remember how she looked with her curls weighed down by the rainwater, the make-up she wore smudged dramatically on her face. How her one-of-a-kind dress clung to her beautiful body, reminding him of all that he'd had.

To remember how this—standing on a balcony while it poured with rain—spoke of her spirit. The passion, the spontaneity. How he'd never consider doing something like this and yet somehow he found it endearing.

Heaven only knew why he wanted to remember it. Because the feelings that accompanied it *gutted* him. The longing, the regret. The disappointment. Heaven only knew why he was thinking about how incredibly beautiful she was when empirical evidence should have made him think otherwise.

'Why are you looking at me like that?' she demanded.

The misery, the pain in her voice had disappeared. Had been replaced with the passion he was used to.

'Like what?'

'Like *that*,' she told him, without giving any more indication of what she meant. 'You know what you're doing.'

Was he that obvious? 'I'm waiting for you to decide to go inside.'

She stepped closer to him. 'No, you weren't.'

'You'll get sick.'

'And you won't?' He lifted his shoulders in response. She took another step forward. 'You're not helping me feel any less trapped than I already do, Aaron.'

Again, he shrugged. Again, she took a step forward.

'And you're not as unaffected by all this as you're pretending.'

'What are you doing?' he asked, clasping her wrist just before her hand reached his face. Somehow, she'd closed the distance between them as she'd said her last words without him noticing.

'I'm trying to show you that you're not as aloof as you believe,' she said, and dropped her hand with a triumphant smile. 'I told you.'

He didn't reply. He couldn't do so without telling her that she was right—unaffected was the *last* thing he felt. But he showed her. Slid an arm around her waist and hauled her against him.

'Maybe you're right,' he said, his voice slightly breathless, though measured, he thought. But he could be wrong. Hell, he could have been imitating the President of South Africa right then and he wouldn't have known. 'Maybe I was thinking about the first time we kissed.' He dipped his head lower. 'You remember.'

It wasn't a question. And the way her breath quickened— the way her hand shook as she wiped the rain from her brow—confirmed it.

'Aaron, wait!'

He turned back just in time to see Rosa running towards him. His stomach flipped as it always did when he saw her. And he steeled himself against it. He couldn't fall into the attraction. He hadn't for the last year. He could survive whatever she was running to tell him.

'Would you give me a lift home?' she asked breathlessly when she reached him. As she asked—as he nodded—a menacing boom sounded in the sky before rain began pouring down on them.

'Here, get in,' he said, starting towards the passenger's side of the car. But she put a hand on his chest before he could make any progress, and he held his breath.

Control. Steel.

'No,' she replied tiredly. She leaned back against his car, dropping her hand and lifting her head to the sky. 'No, this is exactly what I need.'

'To be drenched in rain?'

She laughed huskily and need pierced him. 'No. Just… a break.'

'Hard day?'

'Isn't every day?'

She glanced back at the hospital where her mother was staying overnight. His mother had a chemo session but she'd left the book she'd wanted to read at home. And since Rosa's mother—Liana's usual companion—had started a new course of treatment, she wasn't in Liana's session to keep her company.

And because Liana knew Aaron would do anything to make what she was going through easier, she'd asked him to fetch her book.

'But today was particularly hard,' Rosa continued with a sigh. 'I had to meet a deadline for a couple of designs. And my creativity hasn't exactly been flowing over the last few months.'

'I'm sorry.'

'It's okay.' She smiled at him, and then something shifted. He didn't know what it was, but he felt it. It had need vibrating through him again.

'We should go,' he said hoarsely, clenching a fist to keep from touching her.

'What if I'm not ready to go?'

'I'll wait until you are.'

Now, he saw the change. Her eyes darkened. Her lips parted. And he realised how his words had sounded.

'Rosa—'

'No, Aaron,' she said softly, taking a step closer. 'I don't want to—' She broke off. Shook her head. And when her gaze rested on him again, he saw heat there. 'I'm too tired to keep myself from wanting this.'

In two quick movements she gripped the front of his shirt and kissed him.

'It was outside the hospital,' he continued, the memory and his words weaving the web tighter around them. 'On a rainy day, just like this. You were exhausted after a deadline, but you still came to visit your mother in hospital.' He brushed a thumb over her lips, feeling the shiver the action caused go through them both.

'You asked me to take you home, and for the first time you let me see that you were attracted to me. And then you closed the space between us and told me you were too tired to run from it.'

She was trembling now, though he couldn't tell if it was because of the rain or the memory. It didn't stop him.

'And then you stood on your toes and pressed your lips—'

He stopped when she took an abrupt step back, breaking the spell.

'You're going from "I don't want anything to do with you" to *this*?'

'I wasn't the one who said they didn't want anything to do with the other,' he replied gruffly, forcing himself to take control again. Now, he took a step back and the railing pressed into his back.

'I know that was me. I wanted space. Why won't you give it to me?'

'I didn't plan for us to be locked in together.'

'But you won't even give me a moment to be alone. Why?'

He didn't answer.

'I'm fine out here. Alone,' she said again with a clenched jaw. 'I just wanted some…space. I wanted to feel the rain. I wanted to stop feeling trapped.' She turned away from him, but not before he saw a flash of vulnerability in her eyes. 'You should go inside before we say something to hurt one another even more. '

'So you *are* hurt?'

She shook her head and took another step away from him. Aaron immediately got a strange feeling in his stomach. A familiar feeling. Hollow, sick. The kind of feeling that usually preceded his mother telling him she'd done something stupid. Or him getting the call that confirmed that she had.

Except now he wasn't sure how to understand it. He didn't think Rosa had done something wrong. And if she had he was sure she'd be able to figure it out herself. Unless...

'Are you in trouble?'

'What?' She turned slightly to him. 'No.'

'You don't have to lie to me.'

'I'm not.' But she shifted in a way that made him think that she was. The feeling in his stomach tightened.

'Rosa—'

'Go back inside, Aaron.'

For a moment he considered it. But then he realised he didn't *want* to go back inside. She'd pushed him away before. Then, he didn't have a say in it. If he let her push him away now, he'd be having a say. And he'd be saying that he didn't care about her.

He might not know where they stood with each other, but he *did* know that not caring wasn't the message he wanted to give.

He took a step forward.

CHAPTER FIVE

'ROSA.'

'Go back inside, Aaron.'

'Not until you tell me what's going on with you.'

How many times would she have to tell him that it was nothing? That nothing was wrong? Would she have to keep convincing him? She wasn't sure she could. And her impulsive decision to come outside in the rain was fast becoming one of her worst ones.

She'd just wanted some space, like she'd told him. And she'd wanted to breathe something other than the tension in the air between them.

Now she was sopping wet, the rain finally penetrating her skin. She was cold. She was miserable. And yes, she was in pain. She didn't want things to be the way they were between them. But what choice did she have?

She was doing this for the good of them. She was doing it for *him*. Why couldn't he just leave her alone to do that in peace?

She turned to him now, took in his appearance. He was as soaked as she was, and yet he gave no indication of it. She'd always admired how at home he seemed to be in his body. How he owned the space around it, even though he was taller, stronger, more intimidating than most. He never seemed out of place. Even here, in the rain, soaked to the core, no doubt, he looked as if he belonged.

With me, she thought, and nearly sobbed.

'Let's go back inside then,' she managed quietly, and walked past him before realising she would soak the entire floor if she went in wearing her dress.

The small carpet at the door would probably soak up

some of it. But the rest of the floor would not escape unscathed. Forcing herself to be practical, she undid the ties of her dress at her waist. And then she dropped it to the floor before stepping out of it.

She refused to look back. Knew what her actions would seem like, and after what had happened outside...

She was just being practical, she thought again as she turned on the lights and went to the bathroom for towels. When she handed one to Aaron his expression was unreadable.

But the silence between them flirted with the tension that was still there. Wooing it. Courting it. Reminding them of what would have happened at any other time had she stood in front of him in shapewear that clung to the curves of her body.

It was the dress kind that plunged at her breasts and stopped mid-thigh, and hastily she patted down the water from her body before picking up her soaking dress and fleeing to the safety of the bathroom.

She released an unsteady breath when she got there and then squeezed the excess water from her dress, wincing at the destruction it didn't deserve. Making the best of the situation, she hung it over the door and then stepped into the shower. She made quick work of it, knowing that the door was open a smidge now because of the dress. She didn't want to take any more chances with Aaron.

Not that he'd cross that boundary. Not when his control was back in place after what had happened on the balcony. It was stupid to feel disappointed, she admonished herself, and reached for another towel—there seemed to be plenty of them, fortunately—and then tied it around herself before opening the door widely.

And walking right into Aaron.

His hands reached out to steady her, though her own hands had immediately lifted to his chest to steady herself.

Only then did she notice that her face was directly in line with his chest. That fact wasn't a surprise. He was significantly taller than her.

No, the surprise was that his chest was bare.

She blinked. Stepped back. And then saw that he wore only the towel she'd given him around his waist.

Her mind went haywire. Memories overwhelmed her. Suddenly she was thinking about all the times she would have jumped into those arms, wrapped her legs around his waist, kissed him. And how those kisses would have turned into something more urgent as soon as she had.

Her breathing went shallow and she told herself to step around him. To ignore how his body hadn't changed. How the contours of his muscles were still as defined, as deep. How his shoulders were still strong, still broad. How his torso was still ripped.

She loved his body. Loved how big and strong he was. How he could pick her up, carry her around and not lose so much as a breath as he did.

Like the time she'd teased him about not wanting to accompany him to some event. He'd threatened to carry her there and, when she'd goaded him, had made good on the threat, though the event hadn't been for hours.

He'd picked her up and tossed her over his shoulder. She'd complained, squirmed, called him a caveman for doing it. But she'd loved it. And when he'd set her down she'd given him a playful punch to the chest before launching herself into his arms and—

'Excuse me.'

His deep voice interrupted the memories and she nodded. Stepped around him. And let out a sigh of relief when some of the tension inside her cooled.

She figured out her clothing options quickly. She'd have to wear the lingerie Liana had packed for her as underwear and, since none of the other clothing would be comfortable, she'd wear one of Aaron's shirts over it.

She was buttoning up the shirt when Aaron emerged from the bathroom, again in nothing but that towel.

Her heart started to thud. She forced herself to focus on something else.

'I'm going to try the kitchen and hope your mother left coffee.' That was something else, she thought gratefully. 'Would you like some?'

He nodded and she walked away as fast as she could. Fortunately, Liana had left coffee and she busied herself with the task. But her mind wandered and, since she didn't want to slip back into memories, she thought about why she'd stepped out into the rain in the first place.

She'd felt claustrophobic. And plagued by the connection she and Aaron had shared. The rain had offered an alternative. An escape. It had seemed like a perfectly logical thing to do at the time. And yet it wasn't.

She'd made too many decisions like that in her life. Because she'd wanted to test herself. To see how those spontaneous decisions made her feel.

It was a form of control, she thought. The only kind she'd had. She'd been lost in the world of her mother's anxiety for the longest time, and those spontaneous decisions had been a reprieve. Even though some of them had been stupid. Even though some of them had got her into trouble. They were *her* decisions. And when she made them, for the briefest of moments she felt free.

But freedom had come at a price. And that price had been—when she'd felt that lump in her breast in the shower— leaving her husband.

Because that lump had made her think she had cancer. And how could she put Aaron through that again when she didn't think he'd fully recovered from his mother's illness?

Especially when hers could have been prevented if she'd just made the right decision when she'd had the chance.

But, like so many other moments in her life, she didn't know what the right decision would be. Uncertainty clouded every one she'd made. Even running away to protect Aaron seemed uncertain. And now, as she thought about it, her stomach turned, her heart thudded at the doubt…

'It always used to drive me crazy, how quiet you were,' she heard herself say suddenly. She closed her eyes, told herself it would be better to speak—even if she was speaking about things she should leave in the past—than to let her mind go down that path again.

'I know.'

She whirled around, then shook her head. 'You always know.'

He was wearing jeans and a shirt, though somehow he looked just as gorgeous as he had in his suit. Perhaps because he hadn't buttoned the shirt up entirely, and she could see his collarbone, the start of his chest…

'Not always,' he responded quietly. 'But this, you told me. Too many times to count.'

He walked to the couch, sank down on it with a fatigue she'd rarely seen him show. Her fault, she thought. And added the guilt to the sky-high pile she already had when it came to him.

She sighed. 'You should have told me to stop harassing you.'

'You weren't harassing me.'

She set his coffee on the table and took a seat on a different couch. 'It didn't bother you?'

'How could it? You said it to me before we got together. I can't fault you for something I knew about when we met.'

It was ridiculous to feel tears prick at her eyes, and she took a gulp from her coffee—burning her tongue in the process—to hide it from him. But she'd been reminded of how unselfishly Aaron had loved her.

He wasn't like her father. He would have accepted her anxiety about her health. He would have supported her decision not to get screened for breast cancer. He wouldn't have given up on their relationship, like her father had on his marriage. But she couldn't be sure.

She'd often asked herself why her mother hadn't left her father because of his lack of support. The only answer she had come up with was that her mother had been scared. And that that fear had been rooted in selfishness. Violet hadn't wanted to go through her illness alone. And her marriage— even the illusion of it—prevented that.

But Aaron didn't deserve that. Again, Rosa thought that it would have been selfish for her to stay. To do what her mother had done. And it would have been worse for Aaron because he wouldn't check out like her father had. Worse still because he'd already been through so much.

The decision seemed clear now, though she knew it wasn't. Not when she looked into his eyes. Not when she saw the pain there.

'I didn't mean to drive you crazy.' Aaron spoke so softly Rosa almost thought she'd imagined it.

'I loved it,' she said immediately. 'Not in that moment, of course, because your quietness would always make me run my mouth off about something.' *Like now.* She stared down into her cup. 'But I loved it.'

'But...it annoyed you.'

'No. Driving me crazy and annoying me are two different things. You being okay with things being quiet between us? That drove me crazy. You taking my car to work without telling me? *That* was annoying.'

His lips curved. 'It was more economical.'

'Sure, Mr Big-Shot Lawyer.' She rolled her eyes. 'You were thinking about being *economical.*'

'I was.'

'No, what you were thinking was that my car would help make some of your clients feel more comfortable. Which, after I got through my annoyance at finding myself with your massive SUV when I had to go into town where the parking spaces are minuscule, I'd forgive you for.'

'You always did forgive quickly.'

'Not always,' she said softly.

'Rosa?' She looked up. 'What did I do? What couldn't you forgive?'

CHAPTER SIX

'IT WASN'T YOU,' she replied after the longest time. Her heart ached at the look on his face.

'You keep saying that, but how can I believe you?'

'Because it's true.' She set her cup on the table and went to sit next to him, drawing his hands into her own. 'It wasn't you. It was—' She broke off, closed her eyes. Could she tell him she couldn't forgive herself? 'It was me. It *is* me.'

'No,' he said. 'No, it's not. It has to be me. It's always me.'

She opened her mouth as he pulled his hands from hers and stood, staring at him. But no words came out.

'Wh…what do you mean?' she said when she managed to get over her surprise.

'Nothing.'

'No,' she said standing. 'That definitely meant something. What are you talking about, Aaron?'

When she joined him in front of the glass door—just as they'd stood earlier, watching the rain—she felt his entire body tense. She lifted a hand to comfort him, then dropped it, hating how uncertain things had become between them.

He didn't answer her question but she had to make him see that it hadn't been him. And the words spilled from her mouth before she could stop them.

'I found a lump in my breast.'

Aaron immediately snapped out of his self-indulgent moodiness. 'What? When? Are you okay?'

'Yes. I'm fine.' But she crossed her arms over her breasts, her hands on her shoulders. Her self-protective stance. 'It was just over four months ago.'

'Before you left?' She nodded. 'Why didn't you tell me?'

Her eyes lifted to his, but he didn't know what he saw there. It killed him. Just as he feared his lack of oxygen would if he didn't catch his breath soon.

'Because it turned out to be nothing.'

That wasn't the reason, but he let it slide. It was more information than he'd thought he'd get. And when finally he'd caught his breath he asked, 'What was it?'

'A milk duct.'

He lifted his eyebrows as the air swept out of his lungs again. 'A milk duct?' he rasped. 'As in—'

'No! No,' she said with a shake of her head. 'Not a baby, no. It was just something that happened. Hormonal.'

He nodded. Tried to figure out why he felt so...disappointed. Was it because she wasn't pregnant? Or because she'd gone through this hellish ordeal and hadn't told him about it?

'You should have said something.' He left his spot at the door and headed for the drink he hadn't finished earlier. He downed it, ignoring his coffee.

'I didn't want to worry you.'

He turned around. 'Were *you* worried?'

Confusion spread across her features. 'Yes.'

'Then you should have told me. When you're worried, I should be worried too. That was the marriage *I* signed up for.'

'Yes, but sharing my concerns about—' she threw her hands up '—my career isn't the same as sharing my concerns about my health.'

'Why not?'

'I don't know. This is more important.'

'And you didn't want to share something important with me?'

'No, Aaron, come on. I didn't mean it like that.'

'How did you mean it?' She didn't answer him and he

nodded. 'Maybe it's better if you and I just don't talk and get some sleep. You can take the bed. I'll take the couch.'

He spread the throw that hung over the couch over it. Not because he wanted to sleep there—he almost laughed aloud at the prospect of sleeping when things were like this between them—but because he wanted her to realise he didn't want to talk any more.

Everything she'd said tore his broken heart into more pieces. He could almost feel the shredded parts floating around in his chest, reminding him that he hadn't done enough in their marriage. That he hadn't managed to get her to trust him. To tell him about the *important* things.

She sighed and then switched off the lights again. Moments later, he heard her settle on the bed and he settled on the couch himself. His body barely fitted, but he wouldn't take the bed if she was there. It gave him some sort of sick satisfaction that she'd be aware of his discomfort.

Or was that sick feeling a result of what she'd just told him?

He'd been there when his mother had found her lump—had stayed with her right until the moment they'd told her she was in remission—and he knew what havoc it wreaked.

Granted, his mother wasn't entirely the best example of responding to anything with grace. He knew Rosa would be. Or perhaps not, since she hadn't told him about it. Since she'd run.

Still, he wished he could have helped her through it. After what her mother had gone through—after it had led to her death—he could only imagine how terrified she'd been.

And yet she hadn't told him.

No matter what Rosa said, he knew that had something to do with him. His mother had blamed him for everything since his birth. The fact that things hadn't worked out with his father. The fact that his father had walked away from them...

Never mind that he'd never even met the man who'd supposedly left his mother because of *him*.

'I can hear you thinking,' Rosa called over to him. It had been something she'd say to him in bed often, right before they went to sleep. Except then, she'd turn over and force him to talk about it. And he would, because he'd wanted to share it with her.

Now, he didn't.

'You're not going to say anything, are you?' she said a bit softer, though he still heard her. 'I'm sorry, Aaron. I didn't mean to hurt your feelings. It's just… You know my parents didn't have the most conventional relationship. They didn't share things with one another.'

'We weren't like that,' he heard himself say.

'I know we weren't. But that's because—' he heard rustling, and assumed that she was now sitting up '—we weren't like them.'

'Now we are?'

'Now…things have changed.'

'Because you found a lump in your breast.'

'Yes.' Silence followed her words, but he waited. 'You already went through all that with your mother. I didn't want you to have to go through that with me too.'

He frowned, and then sat up. His eyes had adjusted to the dark and he could see the silhouette of her on the bed. She was sitting up, like he'd thought, and had drawn her legs to her chest, her arms around them, her head resting on her knees. He'd found her like that before. Once, when her mother had just died. And again on each anniversary of her mother's death.

He still couldn't resist it. Even though, as he walked to her, as he sat down next to her on the bed, he told himself he needed to.

'I can't imagine how scared you must have been,' he said softly. 'I wish you'd told me.'

'But—'

'I know you didn't want me to worry. And now I know that you were also thinking about what happened with my mother. But you shouldn't have. You should have thought of us first. Of yourself too.' He paused, struggling to figure out how to tell her what he'd thought she already knew. 'We're...stronger together. No matter what we face, we're stronger facing it together.'

'You don't mean that.'

'I do. Why is that so hard for you to believe?'

'Because I was you, Aaron. And I didn't feel the way you claim to feel now.'

'What do you mean?' Aaron asked her in that quiet, steady way he had. And since his quiet, steady presence had already calmed her, she answered him.

'I didn't ask to be my mother's emotional support when she got sick.' She stopped and wondered if he'd know what she meant by that. That she was talking about her mother's mental illness *and* her cancer.

But her mother's mental illness wasn't a subject she'd ever wanted to talk about—it had been too difficult—though she had mentioned it to him once. But could she expect him to remember something she'd only mentioned once?

She shook the doubt away. 'But I had no choice. My father...was useless with that kind of thing—' *with everything that she'd gone through* '—and my brothers used excuse after excuse to keep from dealing with my mother's illness. Or emotions. Or anything beyond their own lives.' She rolled her eyes at that, much like she had to their faces. 'I was forced into being her carer, and I didn't want to do that to you.'

'I took my vows seriously.'

'But you don't know how… You don't know until you know.'

His hand engulfed hers. 'I do know,' he told her. 'I made those vows intentionally. I'd be there for you in sickness and in health.'

'My parents made those vows too,' she responded quietly. 'And look where that got them.'

'They weren't us.'

'It's not that simple.'

He didn't reply. Only drew her into his arms and slid down so that they were lying together on the bed.

She didn't want this. She didn't want to be reminded of how good it felt to share her worries with him. How good it felt to lie there in his strong arms and let him take that burden from her.

But she stayed there and, for the first time in months, felt herself relax.

CHAPTER SEVEN

THE RAIN HAD calmed slightly when Aaron opened his eyes. It was barely light, and it took him a moment to figure out that he'd fallen asleep. Rosa stirred against him, reminding him of how *she'd* fallen asleep first the night before.

He hadn't had the heart to move her then, and now, though he knew he should, he didn't move. She was still sleeping, but it wouldn't be long before she woke up. It was her habit to wake as the sun came up. She'd check to see if he was still in bed with her. If he was, she'd snuggle against him and go back to sleep. If he wasn't, she'd go find him. Miserable, sleepy, she'd creep into his lap, complaining that if he hadn't been working she'd have been able to sleep longer.

It had been one of her endearing qualities. Much like the fact that she couldn't deal with quiet—his preferred state—so she'd keep talking until he'd answer her.

Things had been good between them. But he could see the cracks clearly now. Her running instead of turning to him when she'd found that lump had been the first sign of it. The last four months—and the last twelve hours—had highlighted the others.

All of which seemed to lead to the same conclusion: she didn't want *them*. She didn't want *him*.

He got up, the thought making him too anxious to continue lying still beside her. He'd never given much thought to being unwanted, though his mother had reminded him of it often enough that he should have.

There were days when she'd told him he was a surprise. Others when she'd call him an accident. It was only when she was feeling terrible about herself that she'd call him a mistake.

But he'd brushed it off. It had been easy to do when he'd been raised by his nanny—a kind woman who his mother's rich family had been able to afford. So the idiosyncrasies of the woman who'd showed up twice a day to say good morning and goodnight to him hadn't really mattered.

And since he'd never met his father, he hadn't cared about that either. His needs had been taken care of. His nanny had been there when he was younger. His mother had become more of a permanent fixture in his life when he got older. And when she'd got sick it had jolted him into realising she was the only family he had.

He hadn't needed anything else until he'd met Rosa. Until he'd married her. Until she'd left. And he'd realised how, despite believing otherwise, being unwanted had affected him.

He went about his morning routine as usual. His mother had thought of practicalities like toothbrushes and toothpaste, fortunately—hell, he'd take what he could at this point—and when he was done he went to the kitchen to make coffee.

'Coffee?' he asked when he heard a rustling behind him.

He made another cup after her sleepy, 'Yes, please,' and by the time he was done she'd emerged from the bathroom looking adorably mussed from sleep.

The shirt she wore was creased, her hair piled on the top of her head. It took less than a minute for his body to react to how much of her legs the shirt now revealed.

He took a steadying breath as he set her cup on the table and then moved to watch the rain through the glass doors. It was easier to do that than to watch her. Than to want her.

Than to need her.

'It's better today,' she said softly from behind him. He grunted in response. The annoyance of the situation was catching up with him now.

Sure, that's it, a voice in his head mocked him.

'We're back to this now, are we?' she said after another few moments of silence. He took a sip of his coffee in response. Pretended not to hear her frustrated sigh.

'Aaron—'

'I'm sorry that you had to go through what you did,' he said, turning to her. 'I'm sorry that you felt you couldn't share that with me. Whatever your reasons were,' he added. 'But clearly we have different opinions on this relationship. Now mine is finally catching up to yours.'

Being locked in that room was torture.

She'd thought it before, when she hadn't alienated her only company. Well, she considered, at least not to the extent that she'd alienated him now. And she wasn't even sure how she'd done it. They'd been on okay terms when she'd fallen asleep. Then, when she'd woken up, she'd found Aaron as aloof as always.

Except he hadn't really ever been aloof with her. With other people, yes. But her? No. Being the recipient of it made her heart ache.

And now she'd also have to live with the silence she'd complained about earlier. For an indefinite amount of time. Within the first hour she was antsy. And then antsy turned into bored. She was desperate to run out in the rain again. But she didn't. Because she was a mature, responsible adult who wouldn't deal with her feelings by doing something that stupid. Again.

Instead, she went to the bed since Aaron had claimed the couch. The bedding was rumpled, the indentation of their bodies still there...

'We have to leave this room at some point,' Rosa said, snuggling into the warmth of Aaron's body. He made a non-committal noise, tightening his arm around her, his free hand lightly trailing up and down her arm. 'We're on honeymoon. We should be going to the beach. Exploring the town. Showing off our love to the world.' He didn't reply. She sighed. 'Fine. For food then, at the very least.'

'We don't need food.'

'Really?' she replied dryly. 'You don't think we're going to need fuel if we want to stay here?'

The side of his mouth lifted. 'I suppose you have a good point there.'

'I know,' she said with a laugh. 'Honestly, I'm not sure how we've survived so long without it.'

He looked down at her, his eyes alight with desire and amusement. 'Probably like this.'

His lips were on hers before she could stop him. And then so was his body, the weight of it a comforting and intoxicating pressure on her aching skin.

Suddenly, all thought of food fled from her mind. Suddenly, she didn't want to stop...

She sucked in her breath at the memory. Brief as it had been, it had stung. It had reminded her of the good times she and Aaron had shared. Not only in their marriage in general, but there, in the very room they were trapped in. On the very bed she was looking at.

And she'd given up on that. On them. Because she'd made the wrong decision a long time ago. Because, even now, she didn't know how to make the right one.

Desperate to escape from her thoughts, she began searching through the drawers of the bedside tables, hoping to find paper so she could work on a design that would keep her mind busy.

But, almost as quickly as she'd been swept into that memory of her and Aaron, she was drawn into another memory. This time, though, instead of paper she'd found a picture of her mother, holding the flowers they'd both been named after, smiling up at the camera.

The air left her lungs and her legs crumbled. She sagged down onto the bed.

'Rosa?'

His voice was behind her. She hadn't realised he was so close. The bed dipped next to her. His hand covered the one she'd let fall to her lap.

'I didn't realise your mom had this picture,' she said absently. 'It's the one I put next to my mom's hospital bed. A reminder of the flowers we'd been named for. Forces of nature. Symbols of life.'

She smiled. 'I forgot this picture existed.' She traced her mother's smiling face with a finger. 'She looked so happy here. She was pregnant with me, so it was before she got sick.'

'Long before the cancer.'

'No, I meant the hypochondria.' She set the picture on top of the bedside table. Tilted her head as she looked at it. It had been a long time since she'd seen that smile on her mother's face.

'Your mom was a hypochondriac?'

His question lulled her out of the memories, and she quickly realised what she'd told him.

'Yes,' she forced herself to say lightly, and got up. Away from him. 'I told you that.'

'I'm sure I would have remembered if you had.'

'I told you at the funeral.' Her stomach cramped. 'You asked me why people kept telling me how sorry they were that this had actually become something.'

He swore softly. 'I forgot about it.'

'I know.'

'You didn't remind me either. I don't think you've ever spoken about it.'

'No,' she replied with a thin smile. 'I didn't.'

She walked away, towards the door that showed the light shower that was coming down now. She wanted to escape, but it wasn't from the room any more. Or from him. It was from the memories.

From the reminder of how often she'd held her breath, waiting for her mother to tell her how the rash she'd got from being out in the sun was skin cancer. Or how her headaches were a brain tumour.

Rosa's life had revolved around her mother's anxiety. And that anxiety had spilled over into her own life. Rosa had never been free to do what she wanted to, too afraid that her mother would need her.

It had been easier not to make plans. She'd told herself that, and yet she'd still wanted to do things. And the tension between wanting and telling herself that she shouldn't, that she couldn't, had constantly churned in her stomach.

So she'd done spontaneous things. Things she'd wanted to do. She'd chosen to seize the moment because she hadn't known when those moments would be snatched away from her.

And they would inevitably be snatched from her. And she'd mourn the loss of her freedom even as she'd wondered whether she should have done those things in the first place.

'It hurt you.'

The quiet words said from behind her had tears prickling in her eyes. 'It doesn't matter,' she said. Except that it came out in a whisper, which didn't make it sound like it didn't matter. 'It's over now.'

He moved next to her and she thought about how often they'd stood there, like that, since they'd arrived.

'What was it like?'

She shook her head, fully intending not to answer that question. Which was why, when the words came spilling out of her mouth, it was so surprising.

'Difficult. My mother had always been anxious. But it

was okay, for the most part, because she could deal with it.'
She paused. 'I don't know what changed that. I don't know
why she suddenly started obsessing about her health. But
by then I'd had already taken on the role of soother. I don't
have any memory that wasn't somehow affected by it.'

She blew out a breath. 'People use that term so easily.
Hypochondriac. I remember a friend of mine calling a colleague a hypochondriac because she'd take sick leave often.
And I found myself asking her whether she knew what that
really meant.'

She stepped away from the door now, and began pacing.
'It was terrible, and I felt so bad afterwards. Because her
explanation was so pathetic, and didn't come close to what
it's really like. How the person can feel themselves suffering. Or how they can see themselves dying. The panic, the
anxiety. How they can never truly believe that things are
going to be okay. How they can't fully enjoy life because
one day they believe life is going to destroy them.'

She didn't mention what it was like for the people around
the hypochondriac. How they'd constantly be waiting for the
anxiety, for the panic to come. How that would make *them*
anxious and panicked. How they'd doubt themselves. Had
they handled it properly? Had they done the right thing to
help? Had they helped at all?

How, even after the person was gone, they'd still feel
the effects of it.

She stopped when her legs went weak and bent over,
waiting for it to get better. And when it did she stood, and
saw the conflicting emotions on Aaron's face. He wanted
to help her and yet he didn't know if he could.

Her own fault.

'I'm sorry—I didn't mean to go on about it.'

'I asked.'

'I shouldn't have spilled it all out on you like that.'

She walked to the couch, sank down on it.

'You should have,' he said when he took the seat opposite her. 'You should have told me sooner.'

'Apparently there's a lot I should have told you.' She gave him a wry smile. 'And with all my talking too, I hadn't told you any of it.'

'It's part of the reason you left.'

She stiffened, her heart racing. 'What do you mean?'

'There's a reason why, with all your talking, you didn't tell me about your mother. Or open up about it,' he said quietly when she opened her mouth to protest. 'It's probably why you didn't tell me about the lump in your breast either.'

'No,' she denied. But she'd started shaking. He was awfully close to the truth.

'Yes,' he told her. 'You've had to be brave for your mother for so long. You don't know how not to be.'

CHAPTER EIGHT

Rosa released a sharp breath and nodded. 'I suppose you're right.'

And yet, somehow, Aaron felt as if he'd got it wrong. Not entirely, he thought, looking at the pensive expression on her face. But there was relief there too, which made him think that there was something else.

'You should be able to talk with me. Or you should have been able to talk with me,' he corrected himself when that annoying voice in his head reminded him that they were no longer together.

'I've made a lot of mistakes with you,' she admitted softly, and his chest tightened.

'I know. I'm sorry.'

'Why are you apologising?'

'Some of those mistakes were my fault.'

He threaded his fingers together, braced his arms on his thighs, but he refused to drop his head like he wanted to. No, he would face her. He would face the mistakes that he'd made. Especially now, after hearing about her mother's issues.

He hadn't known before. Or, more accurately, he hadn't been paying enough attention. He vaguely remembered her mentioning her mother's hypochondria but, since he'd only ever heard it used in the way she'd described her colleague using it, he hadn't thought much of it until now.

He should have. He should have been more attentive. He should have done his part for her.

'I don't understand how my mistakes could have been your fault.'

'I shouldn't have let you make them.'

Her eyes narrowed. '*Let me?* I don't think that's the correct phrase.'

'I don't mean it that way.'

'Then how *do* you mean it?'

He opened his mouth to explain, and yet every explanation he could think of sounded wrong. And exactly the way she'd thought he'd meant it.

'I was...older than you when we married,' he tried eventually. 'I should have...helped you.'

'Helped me...with what?'

'Helped you see that perhaps marrying me wasn't the best idea.'

Her expression twisted into one that would have been charming had the words he'd just said not turned his heart inside out.

'I...' She blew out a breath. 'No, Aaron. That's not one of the mistakes I was talking about.' She pushed up from her seat now, sat down next to him, curling her legs under her. 'It wasn't a mistake marrying you.' She closed her eyes. 'At least, not for the reasons you mean.'

'But it *was* a mistake.'

She let out a breath again and leaned forward, taking his hand. 'I don't remember ever being happier than that moment you proposed to me. It was like...a light in a terrible darkness that I couldn't get out of. You helped me get out of it.'

'You were grieving for your mother.' He didn't know why he was still speaking. About his fears. About all the things he'd realised since she'd walked into the room. Since she'd left four months ago. 'I should have given you more time.'

'So why didn't you?'

'Because I—'

'What?' she prompted softly when he broke off and didn't continue. 'Because you what?'

'Because I made a promise to your mother to take care of you.' There was a stunned silence, and then her hand left his. He turned to her. 'She didn't ask me to marry you. Just to make sure you'd be okay. It seemed like a natural thing to do because I loved you. And I wanted to live my life in case... Before it was too late.'

She didn't respond. Instead, she shifted back and stared blankly at her hands in her lap.

'Rosa—'

'No—' she cut him off in a hoarse voice '—you just told me one hell of a thing. I need... I need time.'

'Okay.'

He watched helplessly as she stood and began pacing again. He couldn't say more than he had. Nor could he do anything to make her feel better. So he watched. And waited.

'How do I know?' she asked suddenly. 'How do I know that your proposal wasn't just because of my mother?'

'We'd been dating over a year before I proposed.'

'So what?' She stopped in front of him and rested her hands on her hips. 'So what, Aaron? It was a *year*. Sure, we were friends for a year before that. But what does it matter? We spent most of our time together at the hospital. Can we even call that dating?'

'We got to know each other during that time,' he replied measuredly. 'You got a job designing clothes without any qualifications when you were nineteen. Now you're an incredible success.'

'Because of your mother.'

'My mother might have helped spur it along with her connections, but you got your foot in the door by yourself.'

She clenched her jaw. 'Those are facts. I shared facts with you.'

'I learnt that your drive got you to where you were. And that drive came from a passion to create. That creating calms your mind. That it helps you make sense of things.' Her expression turned softer, and feeling hopeful, he continued. 'I know that your family life was hard. That your father and brothers were hopeless with your mother's disease—and now I realise how deep that goes—but that it taught you to be strong. Brave.'

'Too brave,' she offered with a smile.

'Only when it comes to trusting the person you agreed to spend the rest of your life with.' Silence pulsed between them, reminding them that they were no longer in that place. But neither of them addressed it. 'Besides, I bought the ring I gave you long before your mother spoke to me.'

Her hands curled into fists, but not before he saw that she was still wearing her ring. He wasn't sure how he'd missed that, but the fact had hope beating in his heart, healing some of the pain there.

'You're lying.'

'I had the ring made the day after you showed me how to dance.'

She stared at him. Shook her head. 'Now I *know* you're lying.'

He smiled. 'I'm not.'

'But that went *terribly*.'

'Only because your instruction ability left much to be desired.'

'*Excuse me?*' she said. 'I'm a *terrific* teacher. The entire reason we were able to do our wedding dance was because of me.'

'You, and the dance instructor I hired to show me how to do the steps after each of our lessons.'

She gasped. 'You did *not*.'

His smile widened. 'I did.'

She stared at him a while longer and then shook her head. 'This is a betrayal.'

'Apparently,' he replied, amused. 'Because you've forgotten the reason I mentioned the dancing in the first place.'

'Firstly—' she lifted a finger '—I taught you to dance

out of the goodness of my heart. The reason it went so badly was because you have two left feet. Secondly—' a second finger lifted '—I didn't *want* to teach you our wedding dance. I remembered how badly it went the first time. The only reason I did it was because I didn't want you to look silly when we danced in front of all your fancy colleagues. Though now, of course,' she muttered darkly, 'I wish I'd left you to embarrass yourself. And thirdly—' a third finger lifted, and then she threw both hands in the air '—why on earth would that make you want to marry me?'

He stood now, ignoring the way her eyes widened when he took her hand and put it on his shoulder, before resting one hand on her waist and taking her other hand in his.

'Because,' he said as he started swaying, 'I could smell your perfume when we did. It made me realise I'd be okay if that was the only scent I'd smell for the rest of my life. And having you in my arms made me think that I'd be okay if that was the only thing I could feel for the rest of my life.' He pulled her closer until her body was pressed against his. Something akin to belonging washed over him. 'I also loved how hard you tried to make me think you weren't annoyed with me. And that smile you'd give me every time I'd step on your toes.'

'You're doing pretty great now.'

'That's because I always knew how to dance,' he said with a crooked smile. Felt it widen when she frowned at him.

'But the instructor?'

'Didn't exist.'

'I don't understand.'

'It's simple, really,' he said, and stopped moving. 'I'd lie about anything if it gave me an opportunity to do this.'

He lowered his lips onto hers.

She'd seen it coming. In the way his eyes had first softened, then heated. She could have stopped it. Should have.

Instead, she closed her eyes and let herself be swept away by her husband's kiss.

Oh, how she'd missed it. The way his lips knew how to move against hers. The way his tongue knew how to tangle with hers. It sent shivers down her spine just as intensely as it had the first time he'd kissed her. The butterflies were there too, as was a need she hadn't known could exist inside her. As was a want she didn't think would ever go away.

His arms tightened around her. Pulling her in. Keeping her safe. She could feel the strength in them and then in his hands, when they moved from her waist, down over her butt, squeezing gently before coming back up over her hips.

Her body shuddered under his touch. Her breath hitched as he deepened the kiss. As his hands moved up over the sides of her breasts to take her face in his hands. He was being gentle, sweet, and she would have protested against it—against the control she knew it required from him—if she wasn't so desperate for the taste of him.

As it was, her hands couldn't stay still. They slid over the grooves of his muscles. His back, his shoulders, his arms. Down between them, over his chest. His abdomen trembled under her touch when her hands lowered, and she felt the effect she had on him press against her stomach.

'Wait,' he said, gently pulling away from her. Which was strange, she thought, a bit dazed, since the expression on his face was fierce, obviously pained, and far from gentle. 'I can't do this with you.'

'Do what?'

'This.' His hands tightened slightly on her arms and then he took a step back. Controlled, she thought again, and a violent wave of resentment washed over her.

'You were the one who started this, Aaron,' she said in a low voice.

'It was…a mistake.'

He walked away from her and the pain that spasmed in her chest was so intense she thought her heart had broken.

'I'll add it to the list, I suppose.'

'Another thing that's my fault.'

'Oh, stop that,' she snapped. Hurt and anger had done dangerous things to her patience. 'Nothing that happened between us is your fault. I married you because I wanted to. I left you because I had to. That's it. End of story. I'm not your mother, Aaron. You don't have to take responsibility for me. Or for something that you didn't cause.'

CHAPTER NINE

'IT'S NOT THE SAME.'

'Isn't it?' she shot back. 'Because that's what I'm hearing right now.'

Aaron couldn't describe the emotions going through him. It was a mixture of desire and annoyance. Anger and frustration. All because of her. He shook his head.

'I'm not going to have this conversation with you.'

'What else are you going to do?' she exclaimed. 'Walk out through the locked door?'

'It won't be locked for long,' he said, and made the kind of spur-of-the-moment decision he'd warned himself against. He walked to the door and then took a couple of steps back. Enough so he could plough through it.

'Aaron?' There was panic in her voice. 'What are you doing? Aaron,' she said again when he didn't answer. When he began to move forward, she shouted, 'No!'

It wasn't that she'd shouted at him. It was more the complete panic in her tone that stopped him. A few seconds later, she was standing in front of the door, her back against it, arms spread out, shielding the door with her body.

'Are you out of your mind?' she said in a shaky voice. 'You can't break down this door.'

'Why not?'

'What would happen if it didn't work?' she demanded. 'You would no doubt hurt yourself, and there's absolutely nothing in here that would help me look after you.' Her chest was heaving. 'I wouldn't be able to call for an ambulance, and who knows how long it'll be until we get out of here?'

'Careful,' he said quietly. Dangerously. 'You almost sound like you care.'

'I *do* care,' she said through clenched teeth. 'I wish I didn't, but I do.'

'Then what's the real reason you left?'

'Because I found a lump in my breast. Because I immediately thought I had cancer. Because I remembered a doctor had told me that I should get screened for breast cancer. Because, in some stupid, misguided cling to independence, I decided against it.' She sucked in air. Continued. 'Because I thought about how my life would change while I went through chemotherapy. Because I knew I couldn't put you through that again.' Her voice caught at the end and he cursed himself for forcing her to speak.

'Rosa—'

'I told the doctor that my mother had cancer, that I hadn't been screened for it, and they gave me all the tests. I sat through the whole process fearing the worst and in the end there was nothing. *Nothing.*'

She lifted her hand and let it fall on her last word. 'So I'd insisted, and imagined it all, and there was nothing.' Her eyes shone when she lifted them to his. 'Just like my mother.'

And suddenly Aaron understood why it had affected her so badly. And why she really had left because of the lump. With quick steps he pulled her into his arms and held her as her body shook.

He closed his eyes. Told himself he was an absolute jerk for pushing. And when the shaking subsided he pulled back and saw that her eyes were dry. That it hadn't been tears at all, just…shaking.

'You're not like your mother.'

'You don't know that.'

'I know it just as well as I know that you're not like *my* mother either.'

'And where does that get us?' she asked, pulling away from him now. 'We still have a broken relationship.'

'Because you were scared about having cancer.'

She stared at him and then shook her head sadly. 'No. No, that's not it at all.'

'Tell me then,' he said urgently, an unknown fear compelling his words. 'Tell me what I'm not understanding.'

'I don't want to be in a relationship with anyone, Aaron. That's why I shouldn't have married you. That's why I left.'

How could she have hurt him more than she already had?

She hadn't thought it possible, and yet here she was, watching the hope on his face transform into something uglier. And then his expression went blank, his calm façade back in place.

She hated it.

'I'll file the divorce papers as soon as I get home.'

'No, Aaron—'

'No, what?' he said almost conversationally. 'You don't want to be divorced? Because that's the reality of our situation, Rosa. You don't want to be in a relationship with anyone. You made that clear four months ago. You've made it clear now.'

'But… I don't want to be divorced either,' she replied lamely.

'You have to make a decision,' he said coldly now. The tone she'd heard him use with opposing council. 'You can't have it both ways. If you want to fix this, we'll make that decision together and try our best to fix it. If you don't, I file for divorce when I get back and we end this. Either or. Not both.'

She bit her lip when he turned away from her, the tears she'd resisted earlier threatening to spill over now.

But a sound at the door distracted her. She took a step back automatically, felt Aaron approach, placing himself between her and the door. Seconds later, a red-faced man was standing in front of them.

'Aaron and Rosa Spencer?'

'Yes,' Aaron answered.

'Sergeant Downing.' He showed them his badge. 'Liana Spencer—your mother?—called to say that there might be some trouble here. Was she right?'

Rosa heard the hesitation in the man's voice and for the first time realised how it must look to him. Aaron was wearing a wrinkled shirt and jeans, barefoot, and she wore only his shirt. It looked less like the captive situation he'd thought he'd be stepping into and more like an invasion of privacy.

'She was right,' Aaron replied. Cool. Collected. Always. Though he'd stepped in front of her, blocking her from the sergeant's view. 'The door was locked. We couldn't get out.'

'Not locked.' Rosa peered from behind Aaron to see the sergeant lift his hand to his chin. 'It was jammed and I had to use some force, but it opened.'

'So...no one locked us in?' Rosa asked softly. Aaron stiffened in front of her.

'No, ma'am.'

'And the electricity?' Aaron asked.

'We're working on it.' Sergeant Downing frowned. 'Your mother told us she was worried about you and to check. She told me about the spare key she left with the security company down the street.' He paused. 'The only reason I knew to check up here—' his face went red '—was because I... er...heard voices.'

Rosa could only imagine what those voices must have sounded like to an outsider.

'Thank you, Sergeant.'

Aaron didn't move from where he stood, didn't offer the hand she knew he would have if he wasn't still protecting her. Her heart swelled, though she wasn't sure how. She was certain it had broken.

'We couldn't contact you, and with the storm... We thought we'd be stuck here all weekend.'

'You're welcome,' Sergeant Downing replied. 'Well,

then, the rain's calmed somewhat, but it's still pretty bad out there so I should be off. There's bound to be another emergency somewhere. A missing dog or something.' He winked at them and only then did Rosa notice the shimmer of raindrops on his coat. 'You two try to stay out of trouble for the next twenty-four hours.'

'Twenty-four?' Rosa spoke again, almost without noticing that she had. 'Will the storm be continuing until tomorrow?'

'That's the expectation, though you know what the weather's like on this side of the world.' He paused. 'I know this is probably a much better place to ride out this weather—and since I'm a police officer I'm supposed to tell you that you should stay inside until it gets better outside—but this weekend is our annual heritage celebration.'

'In winter?'

'Yeah,' Sergeant Downing said with an indulgent smile. 'We don't get many visitors this time of year, and our founders rocked up here on the fifteenth of this month, so we celebrate. It's nothing major—just some food, some wine, some music inside city hall—but we'd love to have you.'

'We won't—'

'Thank you so much, Sergeant Downing,' Rosa spoke over Aaron. Again, she felt him stiffen. 'We appreciate the invitation. And your assistance.'

'It's fine. And, while I'm here, I'll write down my number in case things get rough again.' He took out a notepad and pen and wrote quickly before handing Aaron the paper. 'Things should be up and running again in a few hours at best—by the end of the day at worst—so you should be able to call. Otherwise, I'll see you in the city.'

He nodded at them and a few moments later they were alone.

'I'd better go down and make sure he locks up,' Aaron said.

'Do you want to go?' she asked instead of replying.

'Do I want to go to the heritage celebration?' he asked, and then shook his head. 'I can think of better things to do.'

'Like spend your time here, alone with me?'

His expression grew stony. 'You're more than welcome to go.'

'How?'

'Take my car.'

She lifted her brows. 'So you really won't go with me?'

'Rosa, I've told you where I stand. You're on the side that doesn't allow me to go with you.'

He left the room before she could reply.

She wasn't on the top floor when Aaron returned. Which was fine, he told himself, because he was tired of whatever was happening between them.

He wondered if his mother had given any thought to the havoc her plan would wreak. Liana hadn't known why Rosa had left him—*he* certainly hadn't, so she didn't find out from him, at least. Though now that he knew she'd been in contact with Rosa, perhaps his wife *had* told Liana why she'd left...

He dismissed it almost instantly. His mother would have told him if she'd known what had happened. It would have been an opportunity to tell him where he'd gone wrong, and she'd never be able to resist that.

He couldn't describe his relationship with his mother. Liana had kept him at a distance for most of his life. And then she'd got sick and things had changed between them. Probably because *he'd* been determined to change things between them, and he acknowledged that he'd bridged the gap more than she ever had.

But watching her suffer the way she had... His stomach turned just thinking of it. It had been enough to ignore the fact that she hadn't wanted the reconciliation as much as he had. It had been enough to move his life to Cape Town until she got better.

Maybe it was time to face the truth—that his mother still

didn't want the relationship he'd tried to forge with her. Perhaps, this weekend, she'd wanted him to face the fact that the end of his marriage had been his fault. Or perhaps she'd been trying to fix it. Which, if that was true, would have been ironic since he'd been cleaning up *her* mistakes his entire life.

I'm not your mother, Aaron. You don't have to take responsibility for me. Or for something that you didn't cause.

He sat down heavily on the couch, clutching the glass of rum he'd poured for himself, Rosa's words echoing in his head. Maybe he *was* conflating the two issues. Rosa and his mother were nothing alike. And Rosa was right. She had a mind of her own. And she'd never expected him to clean up after her. She'd always taken responsibility for what she'd done, even if what she'd done had been spur-of-the-moment.

'Aaron?'

When he looked up Rosa was hovering in the doorway, wearing fitted jeans and his shirt, which she'd paired with ankle boots. 'Where'd you get the clothes?'

'I found some things I left behind the last time we were here.' She shifted her weight from one foot to the other. Was she remembering how different things had been the last time they were there? 'The shoes are your mother's.'

'No top?'

Her cheeks turned pink. 'No.'

He frowned at her reaction, but didn't ask her about it.

'I'm going to go into town. Are you—' She broke off, cleared her throat. 'You're sure you don't want to come along?' He shook his head. 'Okay. Right. Fine.' She paused. 'Well, I'll try to find somewhere else to stay then.' Her gaze met his. 'Since there's a line in the sand now.' She stepped back and then nodded. 'Take care of yourself, Aaron. I'll make sure your car gets back to you in one piece.'

And then she was gone. Seconds later he heard the garage door opening and then closing again. He didn't move.

Just kept wondering if this really would be the last time he'd see his wife.

If it was, it would be his fault. He'd been the one who'd drawn a line in the sand. Who'd given them sides to stand on. He was the one who'd told her that she needed to decide between saving or ending their marriage.

Really, it had been selfish. Because he'd hoped that his ultimatum would force her into letting him in. She had—a little. She'd told him about her mother's illness, how she'd thought she was becoming like her mother when she'd found that lump.

But it was so obvious that she *wasn't* like her mother.

Why hadn't she believed him?

And what had she meant when she'd said she shouldn't be in a relationship with anyone?

Clearly, she'd been right when she'd told him he didn't get it. He didn't. He didn't understand how she could claim that marrying him had *and* hadn't been a mistake. He didn't know how she could say she didn't blame him and yet not want to be with him.

It was hopelessly messy. He hated it. Hated how much it reflected the messiness of his mother's life.

With a sigh, he went downstairs to try to find the suitcase he'd brought with him when he'd thought he'd be staying at the house for the weekend. He found it in the room he and Rosa had shared when they'd been there last. He ignored the memories that threatened and was on his way to the shower so he could change when he glanced into the closet Rosa had used the last time they'd been there.

She was right. There were extra clothes of hers there. Including three or four long-sleeved tops, any of which she could have worn out that night.

So why had she worn his shirt?

CHAPTER TEN

Rosa pulled in to the city hall's car park with a sigh of relief. Sergeant Downing hadn't been joking when he'd said it was still pretty bad outside. She'd driven forty the entire way, praying that she wouldn't bump into anything since the visibility was so bad.

Which was probably for the best. She didn't want to be reminded of all the things she and Aaron had done together on the island in happier times.

Things hadn't ended particularly well between them now, but she hoped that he'd realise her leaving hadn't been his fault. Though she didn't think that was the case. She'd botched the explanation. Partly because she couldn't say that she was a *hypochondriac*. Not out loud. She could barely think it. The other part was because she didn't think he'd respond well to her saying she'd done it for his own good.

So, really, she'd given him all that she could.

Her fingers shook as she unbuttoned Aaron's shirt. It was pathetic, lying to him about why she was wearing it. Especially since he could so easily figure out that it *was* a lie. But she didn't care.

The shirt would remind her of the last day they'd spent together. Even if it wasn't exactly his, she could still smell him on it. Remnants of sleeping together the previous night, which proved that he'd held her while they'd slept.

She pulled it off, held it to her chest for a moment, and then folded it neatly and set it on the passenger seat. Then she pulled at the long-sleeved top she'd put on under Aaron's shirt and hurried into the hall, her handbag the only protection she had against the rain.

She worried she'd made a mistake when she walked in

and saw only unfamiliar faces, though that feeling in itself was familiar. It had accompanied all of her spur-of-the-moment decisions. And when Sergeant Downing had told her about this event, right after she and Aaron had had such an immense argument, it had seemed like the perfect escape.

And since that was what she did—ran, escaped—she'd come.

She shook the water off her clutch and then walked further into the room as though she belonged.

'Ms Spencer?'

She whirled around, felt a genuine smile on her lips when she saw Sergeant Downing. 'I hope you meant it when you invited me.'

'Of course,' he replied with a smile. He was handsome, she noticed for the first time. He had short curls on his head, dimples on either side of his mouth that became more pronounced when he smiled. If she hadn't been so entirely enthralled by her husband, she might have been interested.

'This place is pretty big for such a small town.'

'Yeah.' He stuffed his hands into his pockets, looked around, 'It's meant to hold the entire town. We're about six thousand, so it has to be pretty big.'

'It's lovely,' she said, taking in the hall.

It was decorated informally, with stands throughout the room that held food and other goodies. A makeshift bar stood against the wall on one side. There was an elevated platform on the other side, where children chased each other and screamed, and parents soothed and chatted in groups.

The windows were high—almost at the roof—and were spattered with rain, though they provided enough light for the room that the fairy lights that had been haphazardly draped throughout weren't entirely necessary.

'You have generators here?'

'Yep.' He lifted his shoulders. 'City hall is also the designated safe venue for disasters.' He gave her a chagrined smile. 'Small town.'

'Oh, no, I love it. Apart, you know, from the fact that I was locked in a room with my husband for a day because we couldn't make any calls.'

He laughed. 'Speaking of your husband...'

'He's not coming,' she said, her body stiffening. 'He's tired, and me being out the house is giving him the chance to...rest.'

He studied her but only nodded. 'Shall we get something to drink?'

Relieved, she said, 'Sure.'

She followed him to the bar but, when she saw that there was a hot drinks stand right next to it, pivoted and ordered a hot chocolate instead of the alcohol she'd first wanted. Sergeant Downing seemed well-liked by the town—certainly well known, though in a town of six thousand that was expected—and when he began to introduce her as 'Ms Spencer' she automatically corrected him.

'It's Rosa,' she said while she took the hand of the elderly woman who'd handed her the drink.

'That's a lovely name,' the elderly woman—Doreen—said.

'Thank you. I was actually named after my mom's favourite flower. It's a tradition in our family. For the daughters, at least.'

'How lovely.' Doreen beamed. 'It's almost like our Charles over here.'

Rosa glanced over just in time to see Sergeant Downing wince. She cocked an eyebrow. '*Charles?*'

'He was named after his mother's favourite royal,' Doreen offered enthusiastically.

Both her eyebrows rose.

'My mother's always been unique,' Sergeant Downing told her grimly. 'Thanks for that, Doreen.'

'It's a pleasure.'

Rosa laughed. 'Thanks for the hot chocolate, Charles.'

'Charlie,' he replied with a smile. 'You're welcome.'

The whole encounter made some of the sadness that inevitably came when she spoke about her mother ease. Which was strange, considering that she barely spoke about her mother outside of her family. Hell, she barely spoke about her mother *in* her family.

Her father and brothers' lives had pretty much gone on as usual after her mother had died. They lived in Mossel Bay, a small town on the Garden Route in the Western Cape. She'd grown up there, and had then gone to Cape Town when she'd started college. And then, when she'd dropped out, she'd started working for a commercial chain as an intern, before working up to a junior and then senior designer, with help from Liana's connections.

She'd only gone home a couple of times since she'd left for college. The first to pick her mother up and take her to Cape Town so that she could help take care of her as she went through her treatment. Her father and brothers would visit once a month, sometimes twice, which was hopelessly too few times, and yet every time she'd told them that they'd told her they had their own lives to live.

And so that had been that. Even after her mother had died, and Rosa had gone home to pack up her mother's things, it had been Aaron who had been by her side, helping her through it all.

Her brothers hadn't been interested. Her older brother had just started his own business and was more interested in Aaron's legal advice than their mother's belongings. And her younger brother had just got married to someone Rosa had only met once, and he'd been no help whatsoever.

And as for her father... Well, he'd been living a life separate from his wife for a long time by then. Now, of course, he was living with the title of 'widower' and enjoying the attention.

No, Rosa thought again. She hadn't been able to talk about her mother in the longest time. She hadn't wanted to bring it up with Aaron because… Well, because she hadn't wanted to remind him of how terrible their experience with cancer had been.

It had been long after his mother had gone into remission and her mother had passed away that Aaron had relaxed. She'd only then realised how negatively he'd been affected by it all. He'd finally started eating properly. He'd smiled more. He wouldn't toss and turn as much at night.

She hadn't wanted him to slip back into the person he'd been before. Hadn't wanted that for herself either. So she'd left. Protected him from going back. And felt *herself* revert as she did. She'd been foolish to believe it was possible for her to do otherwise when her life was still shadowed by what she'd gone through with her mother.

'Rosa?'

She blinked and then offered a smile to Charlie when she saw his questioning look. 'Sorry. It's been a rough morning. What did I miss?'

He gave her a sympathetic look. 'I don't think I'm going to be making your day any easier, I'm afraid.' He hesitated. 'Your husband managed to get hold of me just now. He says he has your phone, and asked whether I could pick it up for you.'

Aaron was waiting at the front door when Sergeant Downing rang the doorbell. There was surprise on the man's face when Aaron opened the door almost immediately after the bell sounded.

'Hi,' the sergeant said cautiously. 'You called.'

'Yes. Thank you for coming.'

'Rosa insisted.'

Aaron paused as he reached for Rosa's phone on the table next to the door. 'You spoke with her?'

The man's face turned a light shade of red. 'Yeah. I was with her when I got the call.'

Now Aaron turned to face the man fully. 'You were with my wife when you got my call,' he repeated.

'Not like that,' Sergeant Downing said quickly. And then he straightened his shoulders. 'I was the one who invited her. Both of you,' he added. 'And when I saw you weren't with her...' He trailed off. 'Well, I didn't want her to feel alone. Like she was amongst strangers.'

'She was. Is.'

'Yes, but she didn't have to be.'

Aaron considered it for all of a minute. 'You're right I should probably come back with you. I'll give Rosa the phone myself, and make sure that she isn't amongst strangers any more.'

CHAPTER ELEVEN

ROSA SMILED WHEN she saw Charlie walk through the door of the hall, but the smile froze in place when she saw Aaron following closely behind him.

'What is it, dear?' Doreen asked worriedly when she turned back to Rosa with an outstretched hand that Rosa was meant to supply with a cup of hot water.

'Nothing,' she said, and quickly turned to pour the hot water from the dispenser. She cursed quietly when she saw her hand shaking and told herself to stay steady when she turned back to Doreen. 'Sorry about that,' she murmured, and kept her eyes on the woman who was now making tea for a customer.

After Charlie had left, Rosa had wondered around aimlessly until deciding that her mind would be put to better use if she was working. So she'd asked Doreen if she could help, and had been doing so for the last twenty minutes.

But suddenly working with hot liquids didn't seem like such a great idea.

'Charles, you're back,' Doreen exclaimed, and Rosa was forced to look up and into her husband's eyes.

They were steady as they met hers, as if he hadn't an hour ago told her he'd be filing their divorce papers when he got home.

'I didn't realise you were picking up my phone *and* my husband, Charlie,' Rosa said, pleased with how calm she sounded.

'Your husband?' Doreen exclaimed—the woman really only seemed to have one way of speaking. 'I thought you were here with our Charles.'

'No, Doreen,' Charlie interrupted quickly. 'We're not

here together. I actually invited Rosa and her husband, Aaron, to come here this evening when I was on a call to their house.'

'Which house is that?'

'The Spencer property off Main.'

'You're Liana Spencer's son?' Doreen asked, her voice raised even higher.

'Yes, ma'am,' Aaron replied with a nod.

'Why, son, let me give you a hug.' Doreen walked around the table and made good on her word. Rosa's lips twitched. Her husband didn't feel comfortable with public displays of affection, let alone displays with *strangers*. It was kind of adorable to watch.

The older woman's head barely reached Aaron's chest and she gave him an unexpectedly tight squeeze. Rosa hadn't imagined the woman's body had had the strength to give it.

'Thank you,' Aaron said when Doreen pulled back, and Rosa didn't bother trying to hide her smile.

'No, dear, that was me saying thank you to you.' Doreen dug into the front of her apron and pulled out a crumpled tissue which she pressed to her face. 'Your mother let me and my boys—all three of them, and their wives and my seven grandkids—stay in that house for a month after the place we'd all been staying in burnt down.'

'That was the Spencer place?' Charlie asked now, interest alight on his face. 'Yeah, I remember. I'd forgotten about it.'

'We didn't have any money to spend on staying somewhere else, and we lost everything in that fire. The insurance was giving us a hard time—' Doreen cut off, sniffled. 'And then one day, out of the blue while I was talking to someone in the grocery store, your mom came by and told me she'd heard what had happened and that we could stay in her house until we found something else.'

'Where did she go?' Aaron asked after a moment.

'Not sure. She was gone by the time we got there, and she didn't once check in with us.' Doreen pressed the tissue under both eyes before stuffing it back into her apron. 'Of course, that didn't mean we took advantage. I made sure that house stayed spick and span. And that nothing broke, even though all the grandkids are under ten.'

Aaron's eye twitched. 'I appreciate that, ma'am.'

'Your mother is a good woman, boy.' Doreen reached up and patted Aaron's cheek. 'Now, if you want anything from me or my boys, you can have it for free. Make sure they know it's you and that I told you that, and they won't give you any trouble.' She cocked her head. 'They're good boys too.'

The only thing Aaron had wanted to hear less than an old woman telling him she'd thought Sergeant Downing and Rosa were on a date was that his mother was a good person.

'Bet you didn't expect that,' Rosa said when they finally managed to escape the woman. The sergeant had wisely found someone else to engage with.

'No.' He led them to a less populated area in the corner of the hall. 'You seem to be having a good time here.'

'It's been okay.' They took two empty seats and, for the first time, Aaron noticed she wasn't wearing his shirt.

'You've changed your clothes.'

She looked down. Immediately colour spread over her cheeks. 'I...yes.'

'The shirt?'

'Is in the car.'

'I thought you didn't have anything else to wear?'

She shrugged, which would have annoyed him if he hadn't already known that she'd had something else to wear. And maybe that was part of the reason he'd decided to accompany Sergeant Downing. Because she'd seemed to... want something of him.

Though the tinge of jealousy at Sergeant Downing's words and the panic that had risen with the D-word had contributed to his decision too.

'You know that's technically not my shirt.' She made a non-committal noise. He almost smiled. 'So you stole it for nothing.'

'I didn't steal it.' She looked over at him and something on his face made her roll her eyes. 'You're teasing me.'

'I'm asking.'

'I didn't steal it,' she said again. 'I…kept it. As a memento.'

'Of what?'

'This weekend.'

'It's been terrible.'

She laughed. That sound had always weakened something inside him. And he realised that she hadn't laughed nearly as much as he'd have liked since they'd been on the island.

'You're right,' she answered. 'But… If this was going to be the last time you and I spend any time together, I wanted to remember it.'

'Even if it was terrible?'

'Even if it was terrible.'

'Why?' he asked after a moment.

'Because it hasn't always been terrible,' she replied, surprising him with her answer. 'We were happy.'

'Yeah, we were.'

'The way things ended,' she said suddenly, her eyes meeting his. The emotion there stole his breath. 'It had nothing to do with the way things were, okay?'

'I'm not sure I can believe that.'

'You have to.' She reached out, took his hand. 'I told you. All of it… It's my fault. I'm the reason things ended badly. Me. It has nothing to do with you.'

'You felt like you had to leave.'

'It's not that simple.'

'It is to me.'

He turned his hand over so that their fingers intertwined.

'I know you see things in black and white.' Her gaze was on their hands. 'If something went wrong between us, it's because someone did something wrong. But…that isn't what happened here.'

'Maybe,' he said. 'But you said it was a mistake marrying me.'

'Only because I shouldn't have put you in this position in the first place.'

'This is—was—a marriage, Rosa. You didn't put me in any position. I chose to be here. We both did.'

'But I shouldn't have.' Her words were soft. Insistent. 'You deserve more than this. You deserve more than *me*.'

His grip tightened on hers as surprise fluttered through him. 'That's not true.'

'It is.'

She blinked and stared ahead at the crowds of people, though he didn't think she saw any of them. And suddenly he thought how strange it was that they were sitting here, in the corner of a hall in a small town, surrounded by strangers, having the kind of conciliatory discussion they hadn't been able to have when they'd been alone.

'I might turn out just like her, Aaron.' She said it so softly he thought he'd imagined the words. 'I might turn out to be exactly like my mother.'

'You won't.'

She turned to him, the smile on her lips unbearably sad. 'You don't know that. The cancer scare…it could be the first of many. Or it could lead to actual cancer.'

'Because she had it?'

'Yes.' She paused. 'And because I refused to take the test to screen for it after she died.'

Silence slithered between them. He wanted to break it.

To keep the momentum of their conversation—her honesty—going. But his mind was still processing what she'd said. He couldn't think what to say to keep the silence from choking them.

He saw her more clearly now. Understood the extent of the terror she must have gone through. The blame she'd taken on herself. Her cancer scare took on a deeper meaning. Again, he wished he could have been there. Didn't understand why she hadn't turned to him.

'Why did you refuse?'

She lifted her shoulders. 'I'm not sure.'

But he could see that that was a lie. She knew why she hadn't taken that test. She just wasn't ready to talk about it. Pain drenched his heart.

'Did your mother ever see someone about…' He trailed off, unsure of whether she'd answer. But she didn't seem to mind.

'Sometimes. When it got really bad I'd be able to talk her into seeing a psychologist.'

'Did it help?'

'For as long as she went.' She paused. 'But when she got to that point—when she actually decided to go—it had already got so bad that she had no choice but to acknowledge something was wrong.' She wrapped one arm around herself, held her chin up with the other. 'The therapy would help, then she wouldn't experience such intense symptoms for long enough that she could convince herself that she was fine.' Her eyes met his. 'It was a vicious cycle.'

He nodded. 'And you…?'

'Have I seen someone?' She laughed dryly and dropped the hand at her chin. 'No. That would entail admitting something was wrong.' The laughter sobered. 'No, I'm too much like my mother to let that happen.'

'You've already told me,' he reminded her softly.

'Only because I wanted you to know that none of this—'

she waved a hand between them '—is because of you. And, trust me, it was hard enough telling you.'

He knew it had been. Which was why it meant so much to him. Even if there were some things she was still keeping from him.

Hope began to bandage some of the pieces of his heart together again. Perhaps foolishly. But his black and white view of things told him that they'd identified the problem. And, since they had, maybe they could find the solution...

'We should probably stop being so antisocial,' he said suddenly.

She blinked. 'What?'

'Let's go talk to your friend.' He stood, held out a hand to help her up.

'My friend—Charlie?' He nodded, and was proud that he managed to keep himself from rolling his eyes. 'Why?'

'Because when I walked in here you looked happy to see him.'

She gave him a strange look, but took his hand and stood. 'You're not going to try and get on his good side and then beat him up, are you?'

He smiled. 'No.' Though that wasn't a bad idea.

'I'm not sure I trust this change in attitude.'

'You should,' he said, serious now. 'You need happy. If happy means you talk to a man and the old woman who believes that the two of you should be together, then that's what we'll do.'

She stared at him and then a smile crinkled her eyes. It hit him as hard as her laugh had. More, when she reached a hand up to his cheek and stood on her toes to press a kiss to his lips.

'I knew I didn't deserve you,' she said softly, the smile fading. And then she took his hand. 'Come on. Let me introduce you to some new friends.'

CHAPTER TWELVE

ROSA HAD THOUGHT that the term 'new friends' would cause Aaron to give up his appeasing mood and run far, far away.

Except it hadn't. In fact, right at that moment, she was watching him engage in a conversation with Charlie about some legal show they both happened to enjoy.

Of course, for Aaron that meant that he said one sentence—sometimes that sentence would take the form of a single word—and letting Charlie speak several others before he spoke again.

It was charming—though it drove her crazy when it was directed at her. But since it wasn't now—and since he was engaging for her sake—she found it extra charming. Found *him* extra charming.

She'd been talking to another friend of Charlie's while said engaging was happening, but the woman had excused herself minutes ago, leaving Rosa to witness Charlie and Aaron's conversation. But it also gave her time to think. To consider what it meant that she'd told him the truth of why she'd left and he hadn't reacted the way she'd expected.

Except now that she'd told him, and had seen his reaction, she wasn't sure what her expectation had been. Had she thought he would agree to end things between them because she might be ill like her mother? Or had she expected him to stay, to support her, and *that* had been what she'd feared?

She didn't know. Both seemed equally fearsome to her now. Both seemed like valid arguments.

Because of what she'd been through with her mother, she still couldn't make a decision to save her life. Literally. She didn't want that for Aaron. Nor did she want him to go back to being afraid of life, of love because his life had taught him to be. Because the people in his life—because almost losing his mother—had forced him to protect himself.

Aaron's eyes met hers and he gave her a small, indulgent smile. Something swelled inside her. Guilt, she thought. Because, by leaving, she hadn't proven to Aaron that living and loving were worth it. Danger, too. Because something swelling inside her meant that she wanted to.

'Rosa, you've never watched *City Blue*?'

Her eyes flickered up to Charlie's, her mind taking a moment to play catch-up before she shook her head. 'No. Legal dramas are more Aaron's thing.'

'And what's your thing? *South Africa's Next Top Model*?' Charlie asked with a wry grin, but her gaze had already met Aaron's and they were both smiling when she answered.

'Yes, actually.'

Charlie looked between them. 'You're serious?'

'Rosa's a designer,' Aaron said. 'Shows like *South Africa's Next Top Model* are like drugs to her. Either she gets ideas for her new designs or she gets to picture herself designing the clothes the models wear.'

Charlie blinked, though Rosa couldn't tell whether it was because that was the most that Aaron had said during their conversation, or because he was surprised by the information her husband had supplied.

'I immediately regret my dismissive comment now,' Charlie said, rubbing a hand over the back of his neck.

'Don't worry,' Rosa said with a chuckle. 'It takes more than that to offend me.'

As she said it, the lights in the room flickered. Moments later, a woman walked into the hall and announced that the electrical grid was up and running one hundred per cent again.

'Storm's calming too,' Charlie said, looking up at the windows. There was barely a beat between his words and his radio crackling. He spoke in quick, short sentences and, by the time he was done, he offered them an apologetic smile.

'Duty calls. It was lovely meeting you both.' He shook their hands. 'When are you guys leaving?'

'Monday,' Aaron answered.

Charlie nodded. 'Well, shout if you need any more help. Though I wouldn't recommend shutting yourselves in rooms any more, okay?'

He gave them a quick smile before walking off, leaving a strange, not quite awkward but not easy silence behind him.

'We should probably get back too,' Aaron said finally.

'And I should find somewhere else to stay.' But she didn't move.

'You know you don't have to.'

Her gaze met his. 'You're…okay with having me there?'

He nodded. She bit her lip and wondered what she would be getting herself into if she agreed to go back to the house with him.

Danger.

Except not going back with him would be throwing away the progress they'd made that evening. She wasn't sure why that progress was suddenly so important—what did it matter, if she still intended to leave him when this was all over?—but it had her nodding and handing him the keys to the car.

They made the trip back to the house silently and when they pulled into the garage Rosa held her breath. She didn't know what to expect from him. Didn't know what *he* expected. And holding her breath seemed to help still the sudden drastic beating of her heart. And the sudden trembling anxiety in her stomach.

'We should go in.'

She forced herself to breathe. 'Yes.'

Silence pulsed between them for another few moments, and then he turned to her. 'How does a movie night sound?'

* * *

It was like old times. Which was probably a thought he should steer away from, especially since old times hadn't involved Rosa pressed against one side of the couch with him at the other.

Old times would have her curled up against him. Old times would have meant they wouldn't be resisting the electricity sparking between them. If it *had* been old times, Aaron would have pulled Rosa into his lap ages ago and done something constructive—something enjoyable—with the restless energy flowing through his veins.

But it *wasn't* old times. Though there *was* something between them now that hadn't been there before. He couldn't put his finger on what. Couldn't place how he felt about it. Or how the divorce discussion they'd had earlier had contributed to it.

How it had shifted something inside him. As though that something was desperately shunning even the *thought* of ending their marriage.

So he sat there, ignoring it all, pretending to watch the movie.

An explosion went off onscreen—the final one, thankfully—and the movie ended with a close-up of the hero and heroine kissing.

He rolled his eyes.

'You didn't like it?' Rosa asked with a slanted smile.

'I've seen better.'

'Yeah?' That smile was still in place. 'Like... *City Blue*?'

'Movies,' he clarified. '*City Blue* is a series.'

'And it doesn't compare?'

'It's much better than this.'

'Oh.' Her smile widened now, and his heart rate slowly increased.

'You're teasing me.'

'How can you tell?'

His lips curved. 'I've missed this.'

He cursed mentally when the easiness of their banter dissipated and her smile faded.

'Me too,' she replied softly after a few moments, and when their eyes met he swore he felt fire ignite between them.

Suddenly, he was reminded of that kiss they'd shared earlier. How it had been comfortable but had displaced something inside him. How it had soothed him just as it had spurred him on.

His fingers curled into his palms as he remembered how soft her skin had felt under them. As he remembered the way her curves felt. Slopes and indents and bumps unique to her that made his body ache and his heart race.

'Maybe...' she said hoarsely, before standing up slowly. She cleared her throat. 'Maybe I should make some tea.'

'The only kitchen that's stocked is the one on the top floor.' His voice was surprisingly steady.

'Okay. Just don't let the door shut behind us.'

She left him without checking that he was following and, a little helplessly, he did. He worried when a voice in his head questioned whether he'd follow her anywhere. Felt alarm when his heart told him he would.

Run, he told himself. It would be best to run, to get away from the temptation of her. But his feet kept following. And his eyes ran over the curves his hands had only just remembered touching.

She had swapped her jeans for pyjama pants he'd found in his cupboard, though she'd kept the top she'd worn earlier. The pants were baggy, ill-fitting, and yet he could picture the lower half of her body so clearly she might as well have been naked.

He shook his head and stayed at the door when they reached the top floor. He leaned against the wall. Watched her go through the motions of making tea.

'I didn't mean you have to stand there like a stalker,' she told him after putting on the kettle.

'I'm keeping the door from shutting.'

'Which I'd appreciate more if you didn't look like a creep doing it.'

He shifted his body. 'Better?'

Her lips curved. 'Was that your attempt at making yourself less creep-like?'

He smiled. 'It didn't work?'

She laughed. 'Not as well as I think you think it did.'

They smiled at each other, and then she drew her bottom lip between her teeth and turned away.

'Rosa?' he asked softly.

'It's nothing,' she replied. And then the click of the kettle went off and she sighed. 'I just... I keep thinking about what Doreen said about your mother. About how she did good things sometimes.'

He stiffened. 'What about it?'

'Well, don't you think that maybe this is one of those things?' She poured the water into two mugs, avoiding his eyes.

'I don't know what you mean.'

'You do.' Now she did meet his eyes, but she looked away just as quickly and replaced the kettle on its stand. 'But, since you're probably going to keep pretending you don't, I'll tell you.' She stirred the contents of the mugs before removing the teabags and adding milk. 'Bringing us together this weekend. Forcing us to talk.'

'She might have brought us here together, but she didn't force us to talk.'

'We both know it would have happened.'

'Not in the way it has.'

She walked to him with the two mugs, handed him his before switching off the lights. Everything went dark except for the stars in the sky, clear now that the rain had stopped.

'It really is beautiful up here,' she said after a moment. He looked around the room his mother had designed with an architect and grudgingly agreed.

'Better now that we're not trapped.'

'Yes,' she said, turning back to him. His eyes had adjusted to the darkness, allowing him to see her half-smile. His heart shuddered as their eyes held, and then she looked away. 'We should get back down before our tea gets cold.'

'You don't want to have it up here?'

'And have you stalk me while I drink it?' She smiled. 'No, thank you.'

His lips curved as he followed her down the stairs, careful not to spill the tea. She led them to the living area on the first floor. It was pretty here too, he thought, taking in the tasteful décor, the view of the beach through the windows.

His family had owned this house for decades, though his mother had made a lot of changes over the years. Some—like the top floor and the décor on the current floor—he'd agreed with. Others—like the incredibly excessive water feature she'd installed in the garden—she should have let go.

'I get that the talking is us,' she told him. Her expression was careful, and he wondered what she saw in his face when he hadn't realised she'd been watching him. 'But would we have talked if your mother hadn't tricked us into being here?'

He didn't reply immediately. 'I know that sometimes she means well.' It was almost painful to admit. 'But this—you and I—and Doreen... Those cases are few out of many.'

'Don't they count?'

He gripped the mug between his hands. 'My mother hopes for the best when she does things. She doesn't think them through.' He stilled. 'Those people she invited to live here could have been criminals. They could have taken everything in here. Or worse.'

He tried to relax his jaw, and then continued carefully.

'You have to think about the consequences of your actions. That's how life works.'

'Speaking as someone who can act without thinking about consequences,' she said slowly, 'I think you need to give her a break.'

'You might act impulsively sometimes, Rosa, but you don't expect other people to bear the brunt of those decisions.'

'Sometimes I do,' she said quietly. 'I have. With you.'

CHAPTER THIRTEEN

'WHAT DO YOU MEAN?' There was an urgency in the question that had the answer spilling from her lips.

'Things would have been different for us if I'd had that test done.'

'How?'

'I wouldn't have worried as much about the lump. I wouldn't have felt as though I had to leave to protect you from it. From me.' She rubbed her arms. 'I wouldn't have doubted my decisions. Every one of them, since my mother died.' She laughed breathlessly. 'Since long before it, actually. But then it was for different reasons.' She shook her head, hoping her words made sense to him. She took a breath. 'We wouldn't be here if I'd had that test done.'

'Wouldn't we?'

It was the only comment he made. She'd ripped her heart out to tell him that—and that was all he said.

Not that she could blame him. He was right. Their relationship would have taken this turn eventually. There'd been too many things left unsaid between them. Too many cracks in their foundation. Neither of them had noticed it before. But it would have come out eventually. And their relationship would have crumbled down around them, just as it had now.

'I'm tired of hoping with my mother.'

'What?'

'It started when I was so young I can't remember anything other than the hope.' Something unreadable crossed his face. 'But, as I got older, I realised that I'd keep hoping, even when she'd prove to me that it wasn't worth the pain. Like when she got sick. I hoped she'd change.'

Understanding he was offering her something with this, she nodded. 'But she didn't.'

He shook his head. 'It wasn't that I was hoping for too much. I just wanted her to change her behaviour so I wouldn't have to keep fixing things for her. And—' he hesitated '—I wanted her to be there for me like I'd been there for her.' He paused. 'I put my life on hold when she found out she had cancer. It made me realise how much the fact that she was my mother meant to me, however complicated our relationship was. But even a life-changing event like cancer couldn't make *her* change.' Another pause. 'She used her *birthday* to manipulate us, knowing how important it would be to you.' He shook his head again. 'It's not as easy to forgive her as you've made it seem.'

She wondered what he would say if she told him that this was part of why she'd left. He'd never told her this before, but it had clarified things for her. Because she'd sensed some of how he felt. Enough to understand that Aaron would have put his life on hold for her too, if she'd had cancer.

And if she'd had cancer she would have become the person she'd been running from her entire life. Anxious, bitter. Terrified of death. She would have become her mother.

The lump had catapulted her in that direction anyway. Had awoken the seed of fear she hadn't known had been buried inside her. But it had grown so quickly Rosa had known she couldn't stay. She couldn't let him see her become her mother. She couldn't let him go through that pain. Because now, hearing him say this… It made her fully appreciate how painful it would have been for him to be at her side.

'Aaron—'

'We should get to bed,' he said, not meeting her eyes. He set his mug down, his tea untouched.

'You don't want to—' She broke off when he sent her a beseeching look, and she nodded. He'd given her enough.

He didn't want to talk about it any more. And, if she were honest with herself, neither did she.

'It's probably for the best to get to bed. To finally get a decent night's sleep.'

'You didn't sleep well last night?' he asked in a wry tone that sounded forced.

'It'll go better tonight, I'm sure.' After the briefest hesitation, she leaned over and brushed a kiss on his forehead. 'I'm sorry. For all of it.' She left before he could reply.

As she climbed into bed she heard Aaron's footsteps pass her door. When the sound stopped, she held her breath, anticipation fluttering through her. But then the footsteps continued, and she blew out the air she'd been holding in her lungs.

She wasn't sure why she'd reacted that way. Or what she would have done if Aaron had entered her room.

No, she thought, shutting her eyes. She knew *exactly* what she would have done.

And that was part of the problem.

When the sun woke Rosa the next morning, she wasn't surprised. Cape Town was famous for its unpredictable weather. And, since Mariner's Island was only thirty kilometres from Cape Town, the weather was pretty much the same there too.

Which was great, she mused, since the restlessness she'd felt the night before—when she'd thought Aaron might be coming into her room to seduce her—was still with her. But sunshine meant escape. And, right now, escape meant going for a run on the beach.

It wasn't ideal running gear, she mused as she looked at herself in the mirror. Most of what she was wearing had come from Liana's closet and, since her mother-in-law was smaller than her, the outfit wasn't quite appropriate for a run.

But the tank top would keep her boobs in place, and she'd

replaced her ridiculous lace underwear with Liana's yoga tights. Again, not ideal, but it would have to do. Though she breathed a sigh of relief when she found a long, loose T-shirt of her own that would cover most of it.

When she'd tied her running shoes—Liana's—she stepped out of the room and made her way to the front door.

'Rosa?'

She spun around, her heart racing when she saw Aaron on the couch in the front room. His shirt was only half buttoned, revealing smooth muscular skin. It stopped just below his crotch, which she hadn't noticed before. Perhaps because, before, he'd been wearing *pants*.

She cleared her throat. 'You slept here last night?'

He lifted a hand to his hair and she fought to keep her eyes on his face. 'Yeah. None of the bedrooms were…comfortable.'

She nodded. 'I'm…er…going for a run.'

'A run?' He arched a brow. 'That bad, huh?'

She managed a smile. 'Just some restless energy.'

'Up for some company?'

She shook her head. 'It won't be for long.'

'Okay.'

Though his expression was unreadable, something in his tone gave her pause. And then it hit her. He hadn't been *uncomfortable*. He'd been watching out for her. He'd slept in the front room because he'd thought *that she might leave*.

Guilt knocked the breath from her and she forced herself out of the door before she did something about it.

He kept himself busy. Which was exactly what he'd done when she'd left the last time—so he wouldn't go crazy.

Now, though, it seemed ridiculous. He'd seen what she was wearing. And she'd left without any of her things. She wasn't *leaving*, leaving. Besides, where would she go? It was Sunday; the airport was still closed. She couldn't escape Mariner's Island even if she wanted to.

He clenched his jaw and continued preparing their breakfast. Ignored the voice that mocked him for being so desperate about not letting his wife leave him that he'd slept on the couch.

When he heard the front door open, the air began to move more easily in and out of his lungs. He made coffee and, by the time she came upstairs after a shower, had a cup ready for her.

'Did it work?' he asked as he handed her the cup. Her mouth curved. So, she wasn't going to pretend she didn't know what he was talking about.

'A little.'

'You were gone a while.'

'I was coming back.'

'I know.'

But something pulsed between them that confirmed she knew he hadn't been sure of it.

'How is it outside?'

She quirked a brow. 'Are we talking about the weather now?'

A faint smile claimed his lips as he nodded. 'Unless you have something else you want to talk about?'

'Oh, no,' she said dryly. 'The weather's fine. It's cool, with a south-easterly wind. Not quite swimming weather, folks.'

His smile widened. 'You sound exactly like her.'

'Cherry du Pont,' she said with a smile. 'The weather woman we listened to every morning for years.' She lifted a shoulder. 'I should hope I know what she sounds like.'

'Have you been listening to her by yourself?'

He wasn't sure what had made him ask it. And when she tilted her head, studied him, he was sure she didn't want to answer it. Surprise fluttered through him when she did.

'Some days. When I felt—' her eyes swept away from him '—when I felt lonely, or missed you.' She shifted away from the table, went to the glass door overlooking the beach. 'Most days, actually,' she continued. 'But then I'd force myself out of it, and start working. I managed to do an entire line that way.'

She gave him a cheeky smile over her shoulder and looked back at the beach before he could smile back. Good thing, as he wasn't going to smile back. No, he felt as if he could barely move, could barely *think* over her words echoing in his head.

When I...missed you... Most days...

He wanted to ask her why she hadn't come back then. Didn't she think they could be saved? Didn't she think that whatever she was going through they could go through *together*?

'It was because of you that I did it,' she said, breaking through his thoughts.

He cleared his throat. 'What was because of me?'

'The line.' She turned back now and walked to the stack of French toast he'd made earlier. She put two slices on a plate and squeezed honey over it.

'What does the line have to do with me?'

She looked at him and he saw understanding flood her eyes. She knew what her words had done to him. Perhaps that was why she kept talking.

'The line. For bigger women.' She went to the couch with her coffee and her toast.

He stacked his own plate with toast and bacon, and then went to sit opposite her. 'Why now?'

'I don't know.'

'Rosa.'

She looked at him. 'It's not an easy reason.'

His stomach clenched. 'Tell me.'

'I don't think—'

'Rosa,' he said again. He injected as much patience as he could into his tone, and unspoken words passed between them.

Tell me.

You won't like it.

Tell me anyway.

'I guess… Well, at first it was practical. And the reasons that had kept me from doing it were no longer much of an issue. Being a prominent lawyer's wife had done wonders for my own designs. And the people who wore them because of your mother.' She gave him a smile that was marked by sadness. 'Anyway, it seemed like the right time to do it.'

'At first,' he said quietly. 'You said at first.'

'And you would pick up on that, wouldn't you?' she asked in the same tone. But she nodded. 'It also…made me feel close to you.'

Surprise and emotion punched his heart. He nodded. 'Okay.'

'Okay,' she repeated, though it wasn't a question. And that was the last thing either of them said for a while.

They started eating in silence and by the time they'd finished their meal he realised it was his turn. He debated what would be the best way to tell her. Began speaking before he'd fully decided.

'The expansion,' he said, setting down his plate. 'It's a firm in Cape Town.'

'Cape Town?'

He nodded. 'Frank's been nagging me for a while. It seemed like the right time.'

They'd both used that phrase to explain what they'd been doing while they'd been away from one another. And now that Aaron had said it he realised that the 'right time' merely meant that they'd needed to occupy their time. With things that felt like work but reminded them of each other.

'In hindsight, maybe going for a run wasn't such a good

idea,' Rosa said suddenly. He turned in time to see her set down her empty cup and plate and push back her hair. Her face was a bit pale and when she looked at him her eyes were dim.

'You're not feeling well?'

'I feel…off.' She shifted to the front of her seat. 'Though that could be because I went for a jog. It's…been a while.' She gave him a weak smile.

'You should rest.'

'Maybe,' she replied with a frown. And then she stood and when he saw that she wasn't entirely steady he moved beside her and told her to lean on him.

'This is probably an overreaction.' He grunted in response. 'I'm fine, really.'

He looked over at her as he led her to the bed. 'You're tired.'

'So are you.'

He grunted again.

'We're not letting each other sleep very well, are we?'

'You're going to sleep now.'

'That sounds like a threat.'

'It is.' But he smiled at her and said softly, 'Get some sleep.'

'Okay.'

He watched as she settled down. Felt an ache in his heart that he'd ignored for months but couldn't any more. He didn't know how long he sat at the edge of the bed, making sure she was okay. But when he shifted to leave he felt a hand on his forearm.

Her eyes were still closed when he looked back, but her grip on his arm was firm. And after a short moment of deliberation he let himself relax beside her.

A mistake, he knew instantly. There were boundaries, as she'd said, and he wanted now, more than ever, to keep those boundaries. He understood them. Because they didn't know where they stood with one another. *He* didn't know.

And, he considered as he held his breath as Rosa snuggled back against him, he didn't think she did either.

What he needed to do was get up and go downstairs. He needed to put distance between them. So that when, the next day, they left and went back to the separate lives they'd forged for themselves it wouldn't hurt as much.

And he thought it might not. Now that he knew the circumstances of why she'd left, he realised that it had less to do with him and more to do with her. Logically. Except it still *felt* as if it was to do with him. Just like he'd thought it was for every moment of those last four months.

Since he couldn't stop himself from feeling it, he figured there must be some truth in it, regardless of what she said. And, honestly, he couldn't blame her.

CHAPTER FOURTEEN

WHEN ROSA WOKE it wasn't entirely dark, but it wasn't light either. She took some time to realise that she'd slept most of the day away, and it was now dusk.

But it seemed the sleep had done its work. The fatigue she'd felt earlier had lifted somewhat and she didn't feel as listless. It wasn't a surprise that she'd felt that way. She had stepped into the rain like a fool—and she swore she'd feel the effects of that soon—and she hadn't slept well over the last two nights.

She should thank Aaron for forcing her to sleep, she thought, and then started when there was a movement next to her.

Her breath whooshed from her lungs. It was *Aaron*. Aaron was *sleeping beside her*. She searched her mind for any memory of how that had come to be, and nearly groaned when she remembered grabbing his arm as she'd fallen asleep.

It had been a reflex, and she hadn't meant much by it. No, she thought with a silent groan. That was a lie. Her sleepy self had just had the courage to do what she couldn't when she was awake.

Cling to him. Ask him not to leave her.

It was ridiculous, she told herself as she shifted so that she could see him better. She'd left him. And for good reasons too. Though, for the life of her, at that moment Rosa couldn't remember one of those reasons.

Her hand had lifted without her noticing it and now her fingers were tracing his forehead, down the side of his cheek. Her thumb brushed over his lips and her heart thudded at the memories of what those lips had done to her.

Moreover, it craved the healing those lips had done. How they'd kissed away her tears when her mother had died. How they'd comforted her as he'd kissed her temple at her mother's funeral.

She'd got through so much because he'd been there for her. Those lips, kissing, comforting, yes, but because of *him*. Because of his presence. Because of his steadfastness.

She blinked at the tears that burned in her eyes and her hand lowered. Over the curve of his Adam's apple, into the cleft at the base of his neck. Her fingers fluttered over the collarbone on each side, before resting between them. He wore another shirt, though this one was flannel, the kind she knew he wore on casual occasions.

The top buttons were open and she saw her fingers shake more as they scooped down to the edge of the skin that those buttons revealed. It was just enough for her to see the slope between his pecs, and she remembered all the times she'd rested her head there, listening to his heart, being calmed by it.

Without thinking about it, she undid another button and was about to slide her hand in, so that she could feel his heart again—so that she could have that calmness again— when his fingers closed over hers.

She sucked in her breath, felt her skin flush with the embarrassment of being caught caressing the man she'd left while he was sleeping.

'What are you doing?' His voice was husky, sexy, sending a shiver down her spine.

'Nothing,' she replied, breathier than she wanted.

'It didn't feel like nothing.' His eyes opened and she nearly gasped at the need she saw there. At that intense look in his eyes that had always meant one thing.

Resist.

But she could feel herself falling.

'It…wasn't nothing,' she said helplessly. She tugged at the hand he held in his grip, but he wouldn't let go.

'What was it?'

'Memories,' she whispered, giving up now. She flattened her hand under his, let her fingers spread across his chest.

'Of…us?'

'Of you. And how often you've made me feel…better than I should.'

'When?'

'Always.'

'That can't be true.'

'It is.' She took a breath and shifted up so that their eyes were in line with one another's. 'You know now that I didn't leave because of you.'

His eyes darkened and his other arm went around her waist, pressing her closer to him. It was seduction, though she didn't understand how it could be.

'No.'

'Aaron—'

'Rosa.' His expression was serious and she stopped herself from interrupting him, knowing that he needed to speak. 'You left because there was something about me that you didn't want.'

'I left because I didn't want you to see how broken I was,' she corrected him softly, and used her free hand to press against his cheek. 'I didn't want you to be me and I didn't want me to be—'

'Your mother.'

'Yes.'

'You didn't have to leave,' he said after a moment.

'I know. And if I'd told you whatever I was feeling you would have told me that too. But I know you. And I know that you're…committed to making things better for other people.'

'I'm committed to you,' he replied simply. 'You're my wife.'

'And that's why I had to leave. I didn't want you to have to…to have to be responsible for me too. To take care of me when you shouldn't have to.'

'That's what you thought?' He pushed himself up against the pillows. 'You thought that this—us—would somehow end up being like the relationship between me and my mother?'

'I didn't at the time,' she admitted softly. 'Up until last night, I don't think I did. I thought I was doing it because I was saving you from something. Protecting you from being me in the relationship I had with my mother. But I see now that part of it was just trying to keep you from… from being *you*.'

His face tightened and a pain she didn't understand shone in his eyes. 'I'm sorry.'

'Why are you apologising?' she demanded, unsteady from the emotion.

'I've made you cry.' His hand lifted to brush the tears from her cheeks.

She blew out a breath. 'That wasn't you.'

'Hard to convince me of that when you're crying in my arms while talking to me.' He smiled, but it wasn't the easy smile he usually gave her. And it…bothered her.

'Aaron, it's never you.' She moved again, and this time she propped her head on his chest, on her hands, and looked him in the eye. 'You're the best thing that's ever happened to me.'

He nodded, though she didn't think he believed her. She was about to open her mouth to try and make him understand again when he looked beyond her and a more genuine smile claimed his lips.

'We might just have weathered a bad storm on Mariner's Island, but that won't keep the locals from celebrating.'

She followed his gaze and sat up with a gasp when she saw the fireworks go off on the beach. Though it was some distance away, they could see it clearly and the silence as they watched made the tension following their conversation settle.

She leaned back against him and sighed with pleasure at the simplicity of the moment. Somewhere in her mind she thought that perhaps she hadn't only been tracing the shape of his face, letting the memories wash over her when he'd been sleeping. No, now she thought that she'd been memorising it. Just like she was memorising that very moment so she could go back to it some day.

And with that thought something loosened inside her and, though her mind told her it was a terrible decision, she ignored it. Much like she ignored every warning it would give her when she was about to do something rash. When she was about to do something possibly stupid.

'You never needed an excuse, you know,' she said, turning to him and moving until she was sitting on her knees facing him.

'For what?' he asked carefully.

'To kiss me.'

His eyes went hot. Seduction, she thought again. 'You mean I don't have to dance with you to kiss you?'

'Yes.'

'Okay.' But he didn't move.

She cleared her throat. 'That was an invitation.'

'I know.'

'So…?'

He shook his head. 'You don't need an excuse either. If you want me to kiss you, you're going to have to do it yourself.'

She understood why he wanted that from her. He wanted her to make the decision. He wanted her to cross the line. Which was fair, she considered. He'd kissed her the first time, when they'd been dancing. And she'd been the one who had put the line there in the first place.

With an exaggerated sigh, she leaned forward and slid a hand behind his head. 'Just like our first kiss,' she whispered as she brought her lips closer to his. 'Seems like I have to do everything myself.'

And then they were kissing—falling—and it didn't matter who'd started it, only that they had.

He hated himself for what he was about to do. Hated it because he'd slept on a couch the night before to prevent *her* from doing it. But he didn't have a choice. And though the voice in his head told him that that was a lie—that it was an excuse and he *did* have a choice—he was going to do it anyway.

With one last look at Rosa sleeping naked beside him— accepting the longing, the guilt—Aaron got up and made a few calls. Then he packed everything he'd brought with him and forced himself to leave the house without saying goodbye to her.

She'd understand, he told himself as he got into his car and drove away from the house—from his wife. She'd understand that he couldn't deal with what had just happened between them. What he saw now had been inevitable from the moment he'd seen her—in that gold dress, in her sexy shapewear, in his shirt, her jeans, that running gear.

From their *kiss*.

But she'd understand that he couldn't deal with the intimacy, the passion, the *love* that had been clear in what they'd just done. That he didn't want any of it to be spoilt by a discussion of what would happen next.

So he'd left.

It was Monday morning—early, yes, but the airport would be open—so he *could* leave. He'd called his plane and, though it would take some time for it to get there, he'd rather wait at the airport than at the house. With the prospect of Rosa waking up. Realising what was happening. The inevitable confrontation. The inevitable conversation…

He was trying to avoid all that. For both of them. He would be saving them both from the pain, the heartache.

So why did he still hate himself for doing it?

CHAPTER FIFTEEN

IT HAD BEEN a month since Aaron had left her alone in that bed. A month since they'd made love. A month since she'd woken up to find herself naked and alone.

The last thing Rosa wanted was to be in Aaron's office now, *especially* thinking of that weekend. It made the fact that *he'd* left *her* this time worse than when she'd left him.

At least that was what she told herself.

But she *had* to think of it in that way. In *any* way that would make her feel better about the turn her life had taken in the last month. If she'd had a choice, she'd still be in Cape Town. Safe, away from Aaron. She'd still be working on her line. On her life.

Instead, she was in Johannesburg, in her husband's office—*the husband who'd left her alone and naked after they'd made love*—waiting for him so that she could tell him her news and return to that life she'd created for herself in Cape Town.

Her stomach tumbled when she thought that that might not happen after she told Aaron her news.

The door opened, distracting her as Aaron entered the room. Just as handsome as ever, she thought. More so when he was surprised. She almost smiled at his widened eyes. At the way he tensed.

Good.

And then her stomach heaved in a way that had nothing to do with nerves, and she gritted her teeth. She would do this without throwing up. She couldn't give him that power too.

'Rosa,' he said in a calm tone, but she heard the subtle quaking. 'What are you doing here?'

Fairly certain the contents of her stomach were back where they belonged, she replied, 'I've come to see you, darling husband.' She stood up—dramatic flair had always made her feel more confident. 'At least that was what I told your secretary. Turns out he still believes we're a married couple.'

'Of course he still believes it,' he said in a low voice, closing the door behind him. He set his briefcase on the chair next to the door and walked directly to his bar. 'That's what we are.'

'Could have fooled me,' she said through her teeth. 'I didn't realise married couples left each other naked after a passionate night of reconciliation without so much as a word.'

His skin darkened slightly. 'Don't.'

'Why not?'

'You're not as innocent as you're making it seem.'

He took a healthy sip of the alcohol. Jealousy stirred inside her. She would have liked to have something to dull her nerves before she told him. Hell, she would have liked to dull everything inside her. Except, in her current state, she couldn't.

Which brought her back to the real reason she was there.

'Fortunately, I'm not here to discuss the tit-for-tat turn our marriage has taken,' she said swiftly. She walked around the desk, stood closer to the door. Closer to escape when she needed it.

'Then why are you here?'

'Because it seems our—' she swallowed and told herself it would be best just to get it out '—because our night together has led to a…consequence.'

'What con—?' He cut himself off, his eyes lowering to her stomach, and she resisted an urge to put her hand on her abdomen. She wasn't sure where that urge had come from. She'd been strangely detached from the news that there was a life growing inside her since she'd found out. Detached. Alone. The way that life had come to be—how *that* had ended—was the only explanation she could think of for why she felt that way. Or the only explanation she *allowed* herself to think of.

'Are you...' he started, and then his voice faded before he cleared his throat. 'Are you telling me you're pregnant, Rosa?'

'Yes.'

She straightened her shoulders. Drew up her spine. This was the reason she'd worn another one of her designs. Confidence. Courage. This time it came in the form of high-waisted pants and a blue shirt.

'How...how... Are you sure?'

She'd rarely seen her husband so frazzled. 'I've taken multiple pregnancy tests.' And had hated herself for it. It seemed like something her mother would have done. 'And had it confirmed by my GP. It's still early, as you can imagine. But it's there.'

'But...how did this happen?'

'I wasn't taking the Pill any more. It didn't seem necessary.'

He made a disbelieving noise. It felt as if he'd slapped her. '*What?*'

'I didn't say anything,' he snapped, and began to pace the length of the room.

'No, you didn't,' she said. 'But that sound you made implied something. Almost as if getting pregnant was some kind of plan. As if the unwilling and unknowing part I played in your mother's misguided fairy tale plan was meant to end up like *this*.'

Her stomach turned again and she held up a finger when he opened his mouth, pressing her other hand to her own mouth. The wave of nausea had barely passed before another took its place and she strode to the door of his bathroom—

thank heaven it was adjoined to Aaron's office—barely making it to the toilet in time to empty her stomach.

Which was strange, she thought as she heaved, since the only thing she'd managed to choke down that morning was a dry piece of toast and black rooibos tea. But there it went, followed by a few extra lurches of her stomach.

She flushed the toilet and sank down to the floor. It was refreshingly cool, though a moment later she felt an even colder cloth pressed to her forehead. She knew it was him before she opened her eyes. Saw the concern—and something else she couldn't place—on his face.

'I'm fine,' she said and tried to stand, incredibly aware of the fact that she hadn't rinsed her mouth. Steady hands helped her up and, exhausted, she couldn't summon the energy to be annoyed at his assistance.

She'd expected it, hadn't she? It was part of why she'd left him in the first place. Because she hadn't wanted this to be her life—to be his—if she were sick like her mother.

Ignoring the irony that had brought them to this point anyway, she asked him to get her handbag. And when he left gave herself a moment to take a quick breath before she washed her face and patted it down with the dry end of the towel he'd given her.

She was pale, she thought as she looked at herself in the mirror. The skin under her eyes looked bruised, and the light brown of her hair somehow looked darker because of it.

But she told herself not to be too concerned about it. She'd already been there, worrying about all the possibilities that had made her look and feel that way. It had pushed her into making an appointment with a psychologist, but then she'd missed her period and postponed *that* appointment in lieu for one with her GP.

Aaron returned with her handbag, and thankfully gave her space when she rummaged around in it to find the travel toothbrush and toothpaste she'd started carrying when throwing up had become the norm.

She made quick work of it, and then took another breath before walking out to face Aaron again.

'Better?' he asked in a clipped tone. She frowned. How had she possibly annoyed him by throwing up?

'For now,' she answered mildly. 'You?'

His expression darkened, and there was a long pause before he said, 'I'm sorry. I shouldn't have reacted that way.'

'You didn't really react. Besides when you implied that I somehow tricked you into making me pregnant.' At his look, she shrugged. 'You know that's how you made it seem. And, if I recall, you were as much into the activity that got us here as I was.'

Though she hadn't thought it possible, he looked even more peeved than he'd been before. Not that it surprised her. She was purposely being contrary, but it was the only way she could cope with what was happening. And again, she'd give herself permission to do just about anything if it helped her cope.

'Does this mean you're not accepting my apology?' he asked quietly, and she lifted her shoulders. 'Rosa,' he said more insistently now, and she blew out a breath.

'Yes. Fine. I accept your apology.'

He folded his arms and leaned against his desk, looking at her evenly. Back to being in control, she thought, resenting it.

'What did you hope to achieve by coming here today?' he asked.

She frowned. 'I didn't hope to achieve anything. I just came to let you know.'

'You came all the way to Johannesburg to let me know that you're pregnant?'

'Yes. Or would you have liked that information over the phone?'

He didn't react to her sarcasm. 'Thank you for coming to tell me in person.' He paused. 'But I suppose what I'm actually asking is whether this was a planned trip, or whether it was spur-of-the-moment?'

It *had* been spur-of-the-moment, something she'd convinced herself to do before she lost the nerve. So she'd booked the ticket, put on the sample suit she'd made for her line, and now she was here.

But she wouldn't tell him that.

'I came here to tell you that you're going to be a father,' she said, and saw that he wasn't as unaffected as he was pretending to be. 'Other than that... Well, no, I suppose I didn't know what else *to* achieve.'

'But you didn't think you were going to tell me and then just leave?'

Her heart started thudding, reminding her of when he'd said something similar when she'd first arrived at the house on Mariner's Island. 'I know we have to talk about things.'

'Yes,' he agreed. 'But more than that, Rosa. We're going to have to fix this marriage.'

She inhaled sharply, and then let the air out between her teeth before she replied.

'That's a high expectation from someone who didn't have any intention of doing that a month ago.'

'Did you?' he asked softly, the haughtiness of her statement not putting him off. In fact, it did the exact opposite. It told him that she was scared. And he'd contributed to that fear by leaving.

'Did I what?'

'Did you have any intention of fixing things between us after we slept together?'

She opened her mouth and then cleared her throat. It was enough of an answer. Enough that he didn't need her to say anything else.

'So I was right to make it easier on the both of us by leaving.'

'Oh, is that why you did it?' Her eyebrows rose. 'I thought you left because you wanted to make me know how it felt to be the one left behind.'

'I'm not that vindictive.'

'I didn't think so either. But I had to wonder. Karma, and all that.' She was throwing his words from the first night on the island back at him. Then she abruptly changed the topic. 'Your mother called me.'

'You…you didn't tell her?'

'No. I didn't answer, actually. And then she sent an email saying she hadn't heard from you since you got back. Asked me whether that was some form of payback. Karma?' she asked lightly.

Annoyance bristled through him. 'You know better than to listen to my mother.'

'She's right about some things, Aaron,' she said. 'She was right to bring us to that island.'

'Look where that got us.'

Her hand shifted, moving towards her stomach before she jerked it back. Something about the movement irked him. 'Yes, we're in a…situation now, but this situation is proof that we couldn't just walk away from things and hope to never face them again.'

'I didn't walk away f—'

'First?' she interrupted him. 'Yes, I know I did that. And I know that I was wrong to do that, especially without any explanation.' She bit her lip, and then blew out another breath. 'I saw that on Mariner's Island when we were talking. And I realised that I should have told you about what I was going through so that, at the very least, we were on the same page.'

Why was she being so calm now? He almost preferred the haughtiness.

'So you would have tried to fix things between us?'

'No,' she said after a moment. 'But I would have tried to make you understand why I couldn't. So that when we walked away from one another I'd be able to move forward with a clear conscience. We both would.'

'Is that what you want to do now?' he forced himself to ask. Was proud of how he'd managed to ask it without revealing the emotion that was choking him.

'Partly, yes. We have even more reason to be on the same page now. Without the past clouding things.'

'What does that mean, Rosa?' He pushed off from the table. Took a step closer to her. 'What do *you* really mean?'

'We can't fix this,' she said stiffly. 'So maybe your idea of ending things—of filing for divorce—was for the best.'

CHAPTER SIXTEEN

HE WASN'T EMOTIONALLY prepared to hear that Rosa wanted a divorce. Hell, he wasn't emotionally prepared for *anything* that had happened in his office since he'd walked in and found her there.

He'd been on somewhat of a high when he'd got there too. The case he was working on was a particularly dirty one. The husband had more than enough money and power to force his wife into divorcing him quietly. And he would have succeeded too, if Aaron had agreed to be *his* lawyer.

But the moment Aaron had met the man he'd known no measure of money or power could make Aaron represent him. Instead, he'd reached out to the man's wife and had offered to take on her case pro bono.

It had been a rocky ride—would be for some time—but that day the judge had ruled on custody. And since the husband was the ass Aaron thought he was, he'd gone for full custody based solely on the fact that his wife wanted the kids. But that day the wife had won. *They'd* won. And it had felt *damn* good.

Until he'd seen the wife he'd walked out on a month ago, found out she was pregnant and that now she wanted a divorce.

It was his own fault. He'd mentioned it before. And that had set the events in motion that had culminated in their night of passion.

But she *was* right. Things were hanging mid-air between them, and they couldn't live like that for ever. Particularly not if they were going to raise a child together.

A child.

He pushed the thought aside and told himself it wasn't

the time to think about that. Or to remember how disappointed he'd been when she'd told him about the milk duct in her breast—the lump—and that that hadn't meant she was pregnant.

One problem at a time.

Since he'd had an appointment shortly after Rosa had dropped her bombshell, he'd had to deal with work first. But they'd arranged to have dinner together that night. So they could talk about *getting on the same page.*

She was already there when he arrived, and he fought the feeling of nostalgia at seeing her there. The restaurant had been his suggestion—it was the first one that had come to mind. Unfortunately, it was also one they'd been to often when they were together. And often she'd be waiting for him to get there.

Except then she'd had a smile on her face. Her expression would be open, warm, as soon as she saw him. That was not the case now. His heart took a tumble when he saw her wary expression. The tightness, the nerves. He'd done that, he thought again, and then forced it aside and took his seat.

'You came,' she said after a moment.

'You thought I wouldn't?'

'I...wasn't sure. After what happened today.'

'We don't have many choices any more, Rosa. You and I are in this together, whether you like it or not.'

She winced, but nodded. She was still pale, and when the waiter took their drinks order she asked for black tea and water. Not her usual.

'How are you feeling?'

Her eyes lifted. 'Fine.' They were tired. And he knew that she was lying.

'Rosa.'

'What?'

'If we're going to have this conversation, then we should be honest.'

Colour flooded her cheeks but she nodded. 'It hasn't been the best experience.'

'Obviously you're suffering from morning sickness.'

'Obviously,' she repeated dryly. 'And I'm tired. Even when I wake up. Par for the course.' She lifted her shoulders, but the gesture looked heavy and a sympathy he didn't understand pooled in his belly. A fear too.

He frowned. 'I'm sorry.'

She opened her mouth and then caught him off-guard with the smile that formed there. 'I was going to say it's not your fault, but then I realised it's at least fifty per cent your fault.'

His lips curved. 'I suppose.'

Her gaze suddenly sharpened, and then she released a breath. 'It is yours.'

It took him a moment to figure out how to reply. 'I didn't think it wasn't.'

She nodded. 'I know some... Well, thank you for not doubting that.'

'Things might not be in the best state between us,' he said stiffly, 'but I don't suddenly think that you've changed.'

'And changing would be sleeping with someone else?'

The air was charged, but he couldn't tell if it was because of her words or because of the way things were between them.

'Changing would be lying to me.'

And she'd never done that, he thought, seeing the confirmation of it on her face. At least there was that. They'd had honesty between them for the longest time. And if somehow that had changed it was just as much his fault as it was hers.

It might very well have been his fault alone.

'I'm sorry,' he said after the waiter brought their drinks. He waved the man away when he mentioned food, seeing Rosa recoil at the suggestion. 'I shouldn't have left you the way that I did.'

'Why did you?'

'I already told you.'

'You told me that you left because I was going to leave.' She was watching him closely. He shifted. 'I don't believe that, Aaron.'

'You should. It's the truth.'

'Not the whole truth.' She paused. 'If you've changed your mind about being honest…'

He clenched his teeth and then reached for his drink, which thankfully had alcohol in it. He nearly hissed as the liquid burnt down his throat and then he pushed it aside, no longer interested in the courage it offered.

Fake courage, he thought, since he still had to steel himself to answer her question.

'It seemed easier.' He didn't look at her. 'And what we shared…was special. To me, at least.' He paused. 'I knew that whatever we'd say to each other about it would spoil that, and I didn't want that memory to be destroyed. So I left.'

She took a long time to answer him. Because of that, he forced himself to look at her face. Her expression was unreadable, though her hands trembled slightly as she put some sugar into the tea in front of her, stirring the liquid much longer than it required.

'You're right,' she said eventually. 'It would have.' The stirring stopped. 'But then, I don't think you leaving the next day did much different.'

She lifted her eyes and their gazes met. Clashed. But in them Aaron saw the acknowledgement that what they'd shared *had* been special. He didn't know if the effect that had on his heart was good or bad, all things considered.

'I'm sorry.'

She lifted her hand, as if to brush his apology away, and then dropped it again with a nod. 'Okay. It's in the past. Let's move on.'

There was an expectant pause after those words, as if she were waiting for him to say something that would do just that. Except he couldn't. Not immediately. His thoughts were too closely linked to the past. His feelings too.

He fought through.

The child.

'What are we going to do about the baby?'

She'd lifted her cup to her lips, but lowered it slowly after his question. Still, her hand shook. He resisted the urge to lean over and grip it.

'We're going to have it.' He nodded. He hadn't been concerned about that. He knew where they both stood on that issue. 'But, other than that, I... I don't know.'

Her grip tightened on the cup and he watched as she forcibly relaxed it.

'So let's take it one step at a time,' he said slowly. The temptation to make the decisions for her—to take the pain of it away from her—was strong. 'Your pregnancy.'

'Yes.' She blew out a breath.

'Where do you want to live during that time?'

'I...haven't thought about it. I have a flat in Cape Town. I suppose I'll live there.'

Panic reared its head, but he reined it in. 'Okay. Do you have friends out there?'

She gave him a strange look. 'Yeah, a few.'

'So they'd be able to help you through...this.'

'I suppose. I mean—' She broke off. 'It's not their responsibility.' He waited as she processed it, and then she sighed. 'Not this again.'

'What?'

'You know what, Aaron.' She pushed away her cup. 'You're trying to make me think that this—that I am your responsibility. I thought we were over that. I'm not your responsibility. I make my own choices.'

'I didn't say that you don't,' he replied with a calmness

he didn't feel. Her words spoke to that inexplicable fear he'd had since seeing her on the ground after she'd thrown up at his office. After she'd told him how poorly she was feeling now. 'But didn't you tell me that I'm at least fifty per cent responsible for this?'

She narrowed her eyes. 'I hate that you're a lawyer.'

He smiled thinly.

'So, what?' she asked, wishing with all her might that she could wipe that smile off his face. 'You're saying that you want me to move back here? To go through my pregnancy here?'

'It's an option.'

'No. No, it's not.' She shook her head, and then rested it in her hands when the movement caused her head to spin. She shut her eyes, and then opened them again in time to see a drop of water fall onto the tablecloth.

She lifted one hand to her face and realised that the water was coming from her eyes. Was she crying? Damn it, she thought, and pushed her chair back, determined to make it to the bathroom before it became obvious.

But her head spun again when she stood, and pure panic went through her when she thought she'd fall down in the middle of the restaurant. But steady hands caught her and soon she was leaning against a rock-solid body.

'I'm fine,' she said but it sounded faint, even to her.

He didn't say anything, only lowered her back into her chair. Then he gestured for the waiter.

'What are you doing?' she asked through the spinning. 'We're not done yet.'

'No,' he agreed, his face etched with concern. 'But we'll continue some other time. You need rest.'

'There is no other time,' she said and closed her eyes. When he didn't reply, she opened them again. He was watching her with an expression that told her he wouldn't indulge her, and then he was speaking to the waiter and settling the bill.

Soon he was helping her up and out of the restaurant.

She wanted to pull away and tell him that she could walk by herself. But she wasn't sure that was the truth. The last thing she wanted was to fall down and make herself look even more of the fool. It was bad enough that she was basically being carried out of the restaurant.

'You can call me a taxi,' she said when they got outside. The air was crisp, and it helped to clear her head.

'You can ride with me.'

She debated wasting her energy on arguing with him, and then nodded. 'Fine. I'm at the Elegance Hotel.'

'You'll stay with me.'

'Aaron—'

'It's just one night,' he said, cutting off her protest. 'For one night you can stop fighting and just come home.'

Home. It sounded amazing, even though she wasn't entirely sure where home was any more. And perhaps it was because that made her think of her mother and sadness rolled over her in waves. Or perhaps it was because he'd been referring to *their* home and longing and nostalgia went through her.

Or perhaps it was just because his face was twisted in an expression she'd never seen on him before. And the concern—the only emotion she could identify in that expression—was as strong as on the day he'd been beside her when she'd buried her mother.

Whatever it was—all of it, most likely—it had her agreeing.

'My flight leaves tomorrow evening.'

His expression tightened, but he nodded. 'Fine.'

'Fine,' she repeated as she got into his car. And then she closed her eyes and wished she were anywhere in the world but there.

CHAPTER SEVENTEEN

AARON COULDN'T HELP the ripple of anger that went through him as he remembered how helpless Rosa had looked at that restaurant. It took him some time to realise the cause, and even then he could only put his finger on one small thing: the fact that he'd let things go too far.

He shouldn't have slept with her. He knew that and yet, every time he thought back to the day it had happened, he didn't see how he could have avoided it.

They'd somehow woven a spell around themselves that weekend. Though he didn't know how that spell had gone from hurt and accusation to a deeper understanding of their issues. Their fears.

What had been missing in their marriage to make them end up like that? It had gone so wrong, and he'd thought things had been *good* between them. But clearly there'd been layers they'd barely explored.

Those questions had kept him up at night, and each time the buck had stopped with him. And he'd been forced to realise that he'd been doing something wrong. That maybe his approach of keeping his thoughts, his feelings to himself until Rosa extracted them from him had been wrong.

He'd got it wrong. Again.

He still felt the stirring of anger when he pulled into his driveway, though now it was tainted with guilt that tightened in his stomach. He took a breath and then got out of the car, moving to the other side so that he could carry Rosa into the house.

But she was already opening her door when he got there. The look in her eyes had anger and guilt spinning in his body again, making tracks he didn't think would ever go away.

Her gaze met his, and there was a recognition there that was replaced so quickly with caution that it did nothing for the way the emotions churned inside him.

'I can walk.'

He didn't reply. Instead, he stepped aside and waited for her to get out, standing close enough that if she needed him he'd be there. It sounded like a metaphor of some kind, but he couldn't find the energy to figure it out.

She staggered slightly when she stood, and she braced herself with a hand against his chest. And then she looked at her hand, removed it and straightened.

'Thank you,' she mumbled. He made a non-committal noise in response. He waited for her to walk in front of him, and then followed. He didn't bother guiding her. He'd driven to their house; she knew her way around.

He watched as she left her handbag on the kitchen counter, kicked off her shoes and took off her jacket, hanging it on the coat rack. It was so familiar his heart stuttered, nearly stopped. He needed to get a grip.

But then, it *was* his fault. He'd been the one to bring her here. And then she went straight to the couch, sat there gingerly, and he knew he'd made the right decision.

'What can I get you?'

'Nothing.' Then she shook her head. 'Actually, I didn't get to finish my tea, and that's about all I can keep down these days.'

He nodded and went to the kitchen to make her tea. He made himself a cup of coffee, thinking that he'd had enough to drink, though a part of him disagreed.

He handed her the tea and then sat down on the adjacent couch. There was a moment of silence, when he thought they were both thinking about how weird it was. The last time they'd been there together, they'd been happy. Or not, he thought, reminding himself that the last time they'd been there together, she'd left.

His hands tightened on the coffee mug.

'I really would have been okay,' she said into the silence.

He acknowledged her words with a nod. She bit the side of her lip, held the mug between her hands.

'Thank you.'

'You're welcome.'

More silence. They should go to bed, he thought. But now, with her there, going to bed didn't feel right. Not to the bed they'd shared, and not to any of the other rooms in the house. Because she was there. She should be with him. In his bed. In *their* bed.

He hadn't spent much time there in the four months she'd been gone. He'd worked late, stayed at the office as long as he could stay awake. And when he did come home he'd sleep on the couch she was now sitting on, unable to go to their bedroom alone.

When he'd returned from Mariner's Island, he'd tried. Told himself that he had to, since *he* was the one who'd made the decision to leave now. But when he hadn't been able to sleep for the fifth night in a row, he'd realised that he hadn't made that decision at all. That it hadn't been a decision. More, it had been a defensive move. He'd leave before she left him. Again.

The thought made him nauseous.

'I'll think about staying here.' She broke the silence again. 'Which was probably your plan all along.'

'My plan would have involved more than you just staying here,' he told her. 'But I appreciate it.'

'You knew I'd agree. You've been much too quiet...'

The corner of his mouth lifted. 'It's not that easy.'

'No.' She sighed. 'But you're right. I don't have people there. Not like I do here.'

'Then why did you go there?'

If she was surprised by the question, she didn't show it. 'I didn't really have much of a plan when I left here.'

'Spur of the moment.'

Now her lips her curved. 'Partly. But mostly it was me

trying to run from what scared me most. Then,' she added almost as an afterthought, and he watched again as her hand lifted, almost moving to her stomach, and then dropping back to the mug again.

'And now?' he asked softly, compelled by her gesture.

'Now I have much more to fear.' The vulnerability in her eyes when she met his gaze knocked the breath from his lungs.

'You don't have to be scared of it. Of this.'

'Of course I do. There's so much we don't know. And this wasn't planned—'

'Isn't that when you work best?'

'Not with this. Not ever, really.' She frowned. 'I don't do the unplanned because I don't want a plan. I like plans. But for most of my life, plans haven't worked out. Or they involved things I wanted to do but that my mother's illness...' She trailed off. 'I had to be flexible. Or rebellious.'

'And...marrying me?' He forced himself to say it. 'Were you being rebellious?'

She didn't say anything for long enough that he thought their conversation was over. He was about to stand up, excuse himself when she started speaking.

'I've done a lot that I've called spontaneous. I probably would have continued calling it that if it hadn't been for our conversations. On the island. Now.' She ran a finger over the rim of her cup. 'The right word would probably be rebellious. Because that's what I was.' She lifted her eyes to his. 'Small moments of rebellion against the fact that I couldn't control so much of what was happening in my life.'

He breathed in slowly, deliberately letting the air in and out of his lungs. If he didn't, he'd probably pass out waiting for her to speak.

'Because of it, whatever I chose to do felt wrong. Whether I did it for myself or for my mother.' Her gaze fell again. 'If I did it for myself, guilt and uncertainty followed me. If I did it for my mother, it...wouldn't change anything. She'd still be sick.' She paused. 'Even after she died, I was rebelling. I didn't get the test because of it. And now I have to live with the guilt and uncertainty of that decision.'

She took a breath. 'I did things that weren't planned. Rebelled. But marrying you—loving you—was never part of that.'

The air he inhaled grew thicker, though by all rights it should have been easier to breathe. She'd told him their relationship hadn't been a mistake. Yes, things had fallen apart towards the end, but at the beginning things had been good. So why didn't that make him feel any better?

Maybe it was because all he could think about was how she'd told him she'd left because of *him*. Because of who he was.

He'd thought about that often over the past five months. Had figured it was the reason his mother hadn't responded to his efforts to make a better relationship with her too. It was probably why his father—

No. That made no sense. He didn't know his father. His father didn't know him.

His father not being around had nothing to do with him.

Except maybe it did.

'Aaron?'

It was messing with him. This whole thing was messing with him.

'It's been a rough day,' he said gruffly. 'We should get some rest.'

She opened her mouth, but then nodded. 'I'll take one of the spare bedrooms.'

'No. Take the main bedroom.'

'That's not—'

'Rosa,' he said firmly. 'Take the main bedroom.'

She let out a breath. 'Okay. I'll see you in the morning.'

She disappeared around the corner to the passage that led to the bedroom, and Aaron waited until he heard the click of the door before moving. But, instead of walking to the room he'd planned on spending the night in, he went to the sliding door, opening it to let the fresh winter air in.

He stepped outside onto the deck that gave him a perfect view of the dam the houses in their security estate had been built around. He'd known he wanted to live there the moment he'd seen it. And when one of his clients who knew the owner of the security estate had given him the details, Aaron had jumped at the opportunity to buy a property.

Months later, it had been his and Rosa's.

His and Rosa's. He'd taken that fact for granted. He'd believed that they were going to be a unit, a him-and-her-forever. But he'd been sorely mistaken. He realised now how often that happened. How he'd ignored it to protect himself.

He'd been mistaken when he'd thought his mother would change after recovering from cancer. That she'd be more responsible. That she'd begin to value her only son.

He'd been mistaken when he'd thought his wife would be with him for ever. When he'd believed that she hadn't left because of him—as she'd led him to believe in the early part of their visit on the island.

He'd been mistaken when he'd slept with her. When he'd been so overcome by the love he still had for her that he'd let his feelings cloud his judgement.

And now he was here—so raw that he felt as if he were made entirely of abused nerve-endings. What was wrong with him that the people in his life didn't want him? What more could he do to make them love him as much as he loved them?

He hung his head as the pain crawled through him. As it ripped its nails down him as on a chalkboard.

Because the answer was simple. He *couldn't* do anything more. Because nothing he did would change who he was. And who he was wasn't enough.

CHAPTER EIGHTEEN

IT FELT GOOD. That was the first thing Rosa thought when she woke up. Being home, waking up in her own bed… It felt good. The only thing that was missing was Aaron.

Her second thought was she was going to throw up, followed closely by the fact that she needed to get to the bathroom. She scrambled to it and made it just in time. After a solid fifteen-minute heaving session—her record so far—she brushed her teeth and stumbled into the shower.

The motions of it were so familiar that she had to close her eyes against the tears that burned. Hormones, she told herself. The intense nostalgia—the even more intense regret—were hormones.

It was the only way she could comfort herself. The only way she could lean away from the doubt. She had to believe she'd done the right thing. She *had* to.

She went back to bed after her shower, collapsing there in only her towel. The sun was shining through the glass wall opposite the bed when she clicked to clear the glass, and she almost groaned aloud when its rays hit her body, warming her skin.

She loved the light, the sun in the mornings. Loved the view of the water rippling out on the dam. She'd missed it. Hadn't realised how much until right that very moment.

Almost as much as you missed the man you shared it with.

A knock on the door interrupted her thoughts.

'Come in,' she called as she sat up. She had no energy for modesty, and was glad when Aaron's face didn't change from its usual unreadable expression when he saw her.

But her heart did soften when she saw that he had a tray with him, and that it held the usual delights for a pregnant woman. Dry toast—butter on the side as an option—and black tea.

'I wasn't sure if you were awake.'

'You didn't hear the retching noises?' she asked wryly, accepting the tray from him.

'No.' He paused. 'Were they bad?'

'No worse, no better.' She took a tentative bite of the toast and, when her stomach didn't recoil after swallowing, took another. 'Though I am beginning to feel like I'm on some cruel reality TV show where this is a delicacy.' She lifted the toast.

'*Torture*—the new show where people who love food are forced to eat only dry toast.'

She smirked, though his words had been said with a straight face. 'Sounds like a winner to me.'

Silence followed her words, and Aaron walked to the window, staring out with his hands in his pockets. He was wearing jeans and a flannel shirt again, and she studied him as she chewed the toast mechanically.

Something about his movements—his posture—worried her. Maybe she shouldn't have mentioned her morning sickness. She knew things like that bothered him.

'I'm sorry. I didn't mean to upset you.'

'You haven't.'

'No?'

He turned. 'Why do you think that you have?'

'Because...' It sounded silly now that she had to say it aloud. She took a breath. 'I know this is difficult for you.'

'What?'

'Seeing me like this.'

'Why?'

'You know why.'

'No, Rosa. I don't think I do.' He walked back to the bed and sat at its edge. 'Tell me.'

She set her unfinished toast aside and took another breath. 'Seeing me sick. It must bother you.'

'It does. But that's because I…care for you,' he finished slowly.

'And because it reminds you of your mother.'

He frowned. 'What?'

'You can't tell me watching me throw up, feeding me this—' she gestured to the toast '—doesn't remind you of how things were when your mother was ill. My mother suffered like that too,' she reminded him softly after a moment. 'I know this is…similar to the reaction to chemo. And that it must be difficult for you.'

Emotion kidnapped his once unreadable expression. It felt like an apt description when Rosa knew he wouldn't have willingly allowed his emotions to show. Nor would he have wanted her to witness it. When he met her gaze, there was a realisation there that stole her breath.

'When you found that lump—when you left—you were thinking about this?'

'I told you that.'

'No, you didn't. Not like this.' He stood. Ran his hand over his head. 'You were worried that if you'd had cancer it would remind me too much of my mother.'

She had to tell him the truth. They were long past the point where she could deny it. She nodded. 'I was protecting you.'

'From myself?'

'From…hurting like you did.' She blinked, surprised at the tears prickling her eyes. 'I saw what your mother's illness did to you. Only realised how bad it was when you started coming out of it. I couldn't do that to you, Aaron. It would have been my fault if I had too, because I chose not to get that test and—'

'And what?' he interrupted. 'If you'd got that test, the result would have changed things?'

'Yes.'

'If it had been negative, maybe. What if it had been positive?'

She had an answer for him. Of course she did. She'd thought all this through. She'd known that not taking that test had been a mistake. Had known it as soon as she'd found that lump.

But when she didn't have the words to offer him, she realised that she'd been fooling herself. That taking that test would have only changed things if, like Aaron had said, the result had been negative. There was no way she'd have been able to stay if it had been positive.

He was right. It wouldn't have changed things.

'I… I need to take a walk,' she said suddenly. 'I need some fresh air.'

He didn't answer immediately, and then he gave her a curt nod. 'I'll come with you.'

'No.'

'Last night you almost fell over in a restaurant. I'm coming with you. Thirty minutes.'

He left before she could respond, and she sucked in air as the door closed behind him. Hoped that somehow the oxygen would make her feel better about what she'd just discovered.

There was no more running from it. She had to face things now. Not only for her own sake, but for the sake of her child. Because she was having a *baby*. And that baby was dependent on *her*.

Her heart stumbled at that, and fear joined tenderness as she finally let herself acknowledge she was going to be a *mother*. She forced herself to breathe, to let air into her body again. And then, when she'd managed that, forced herself to think about her reaction.

This had all started with her own mother. All the things in her life could somehow be traced back to Violet. Rosa's decisions had been dictated by her mother's anxiety, by her illness, and then by her death. She feared making decisions because she could never figure out whether they were right. Because she'd always been torn between what she wanted to do and what she thought she should do. And that was so closely tied to her mother too.

Was it any wonder thinking about becoming a mother herself had caused her to react so strongly?

But when would she stop using that as an excuse? When would she face that *she* made her own decisions now? That *she* lived with the consequences of them?

It didn't matter what her decisions were, she always had to live with the consequences. Good, bad, she had to face them. She was facing them now. The aftermath of leaving her husband. Of conceiving a child with him.

And that last part she couldn't blame on her mother. No, *that* had all been her.

The realisation jolted her. Made her realise the extent of the excuses she'd been making for herself. Her indecisiveness had come from fear—had led to her anxieties—because she hadn't known how to live her life outside of her mother's world.

But, without her realising it, she *had* been living outside of her mother's world. She'd made a life with Aaron outside of it. But she'd left him because she'd blurred the lines between her mother's world and the one she'd created for herself. And it was time that she stopped doing that.

She could no longer use her mother's disease as an excuse not to live her life. She could no longer let it weigh down—or dictate—her decisions. She couldn't let the fear of what had happened to her mother—what might happen to her—turn her into the parent her mother had been.

She took a deep breath as tension tightened in her body. She might know these things now, but living them... That was an entirely different thing.

* * *

They were walking in silence.

He wanted to say something to break it, but nothing he thought up seemed good enough. So he waited for her to say something. Waited for her to save him from his thoughts.

They were taunting him. Chiding him. Had kept him awake all night. And now he had the added complication of knowing what she'd meant when she'd said she'd left because of who he was.

It stripped him of every illusion he'd had about himself. And he didn't know how to face it.

'I've missed this,' she said softly, closing her eyes and opening her arms to the sun.

It was so typically Rosa that his heart ached in his chest. Her eyes met his and something jumped in the air between them. And then he looked away, kept his gaze ahead of him, and heard her sigh next to him.

'Don't you get tired of it?'

'What?'

'Thinking so much.'

He almost smiled. 'Always.'

'Then why do you do it?'

'You're saying there's a way *not* to think?'

'Yep.'

'I don't think that's true.'

'Really?' The challenge in her voice made him look over. 'Because I've been known not to think, Aaron. And I have to say I'm pretty good at it.'

Now, he did smile. 'Sure.'

'Remember when I called out that guy who was acting like a complete ass at your end-of-year function?'

'My top paying client,' he offered dryly.

She grimaced. 'Sorry about that. But at least I wasn't thinking.'

'Oh, you were thinking. You just weren't thinking about the consequences.'

There was a beat between them, and he realised that that was exactly what he'd said about his mother. He opened his mouth to take it back, but she was speaking before he could.

'I was thinking that no amount of money should entitle you to treat other people like they're less than you.'

'I think my employees would disagree with you.'

'But *you* didn't,' she challenged. 'You were annoyed at losing him. And yes, I'll give you that. You had the right to be. But you didn't disagree with me. And, if I recall,' she added, 'you replaced him pretty quickly with the guy who helped us get this amazing place.'

She did a twirl with her hands out at her sides. He looked around lazily, enjoying her energy, since it seemed she'd lost some of the fatigue that she'd greeted him with that morning. In fact, he hadn't seen her like this since…since before she'd left.

Neighbours greeted them as they walked, and he nodded while Rosa waved. It was the kind of neighbourhood where people worked from home. Or ran their companies from home, he corrected himself as he took in the borderline mansion properties.

'Hey,' she said suddenly. 'Aren't you supposed to be at work?'

'I pushed my meetings for today.'

'No court?'

'Not today.' He paused. 'The mid-year function is tonight.'

She stilled beside him. 'Are you going?'

'What time is your flight?'

'Seven.'

'It begins at six-thirty.' He considered. 'I probably won't attend then.'

'You're their boss, Aaron. You can't not go.'

'I have more important things to deal with.'

'Like dropping me at the airport?' He nodded. 'No, that isn't as important as this. This...this sets the tone for the rest of the year. And it's been a rough one.' As if he needed a reminder. 'Some might even say it sets *the bar* for your company.' She nudged her shoulder against his.

He chuckled, surprising himself. Though a voice told him he shouldn't be surprised. This was exactly why he'd fallen for Rosa. Because during the worst of times—the most hectic of times—she could make him laugh.

'You have to go,' she insisted softly.

'And who's going to take care of you, Rosa?' he replied.

He'd meant who was going to take her to the airport, but instead the question came out more sombrely than he'd intended. But he realised then that he'd meant the question. And he wanted to know the answer.

Because, since the night before, he'd realised one thing: he was no longer the right person for the job.

CHAPTER NINETEEN

ROSA DIDN'T KNOW how to answer him. Her instinctive response had been that she could take care of herself. But that didn't seem like the best option any more. Not when she wasn't the only one she needed to think about.

Her hand immediately went to her stomach, and she gripped her shirt there. She felt his gaze on her before her eyes caught his, and again something shifted between them. She opened her mouth, but thunder boomed above them and they both looked up.

The sun of that morning was gone and the clouds were now an ominous grey.

'Why does it feel like everywhere we go there's a storm brewing?'

'A metaphor for the way things are between us?'

'Aaron...' She stopped when she saw the smile on his face. Felt her own follow. 'Was that a *joke*?'

'I've been known to make them,' he replied seriously, and her smile grew.

'Really? By who?'

'Everyone.' He looked up when the thunder boomed again, and held out his hand as they turned back. She took it without saying a word. She *deserved* this, she thought. She deserved this short period that had somehow turned light-hearted. That had somehow turned into a normal day for them.

'Everyone?'

'Everyone. I'll probably get the mid-year award for office jokester tonight.'

She snorted. 'Maybe...*if* everyone who used to work there has been fired and replaced by a bunch of morticians.'

'Are you saying I'm not funny?'

'No. I'm just saying that there are funnier people in the world.' She paused. 'In the country. The city. This conversation.'

She laughed when he sent her a look, and the rest of the walk was in companionable silence. She hadn't expected it, but she was enjoying it.

Though she shouldn't be, she thought. She *had* to speak with him. She had to share what she'd realised earlier that morning. It would entail putting her cards on the table. All of them. Except now, there seemed to be more cards than what she'd started with. Cards she hadn't expected.

Ones that held his laughing face, or the serious expression he'd had when he'd been trying to convince her he was funny. Ones that held that quiet, caring look he'd had when he'd asked her about who would look after her, or the annoyed expression he'd had when she'd said she'd been fine and obviously hadn't been.

Cards that reminded her how in love she still was with her husband.

They arrived at the house just as the sky opened and rain poured down. She settled into the couch as Aaron put on a fire, and felt the tension build as she prepared to be honest with him.

'How are you feeling?' he asked when he sat beside her.

'Okay.'

'Are you sure?'

Something in his voice had her frowning. 'Yeah, why?'

'Because I've been thinking,' he said softly, and her breath caught when she met his gaze. 'And I don't want to think any more.'

In a few quick movements she was on his lap, his mouth on hers.

He shouldn't have done it. And if he had been thinking properly he wouldn't have. But, as he'd told Rosa, he was tired of thinking.

He didn't want to think about how her leaving that evening sat heavily on his chest. Or how he couldn't stop thinking that he needed to convince her to stay. How he couldn't stop wanting to help take care of her, even when he might not be the best person to do so.

He didn't want to think about how close taking care of her and taking responsibility for her were. Or how much that reminded him of his mother.

He didn't want to think about the baby.

He didn't want to think about being a father.

He didn't want to think about *his* father.

He only wanted to kiss her.

And so he had.

She made a soft sound in her throat when their lips met, and it vibrated through him as his mouth moved against hers. As he savoured the taste of her—a fire, a sweetness, a combination of the two that made no sense unless he was kissing her and tasting it for himself.

She shifted so that her legs were on either side of his and tilted her head, both movements allowing their tongues to sweep deeper, allowing their connection to become more passionate.

She kissed without reservation. Without the heaviness that had always weighed each of his actions. The only time he did anything without reservation was when he was with her. When he was kissing her. Because then the only thing that mattered was that he was kissing her.

And that was the only thing he thought about.

About their lips moving in sync, and their tongues taking and giving. About the stirrings in his body, of his heart. Even in this physical act—in the touches, caresses—there was emotion. Memories. Reminders of why he'd fallen for her, and how hard. Reminders of what they'd shared and, now, of what they'd created. Together. Always together.

They were better together.

He fell into the kiss when that made him want to think again, and let his hands roam over the curves of her. He couldn't get enough. Of kneading the fullness beneath her skin. Of the bumps there, the faint feel of her stretch marks beneath his fingers. It had never been enough. It never would be. And so he took, letting his hands speak for him. Letting his touch, his kiss, say what he couldn't.

And when she pulled back, her chest rising and falling quickly, he let his hands linger on her hips, ready to take, to give when she gave the word.

But when her eyes met his he knew that that wouldn't happen. No, the anguish there, the agitation told him so.

'I made a mistake,' she whispered as tears filled her eyes. 'I made a mistake and I don't know how to fix it.'

Let me fix it for you, he thought, but didn't say. Instead, he lifted a hand to her face and let his heart take the lead. For once. 'What mistake?' She shook her head and he took a breath. 'The baby?'

'No.' A tear fell down her cheek and he brushed it away. 'No, not the baby. You.' His throat closed. His breathing stopped. And then she said, 'I shouldn't have left you, Aaron.'

A long time passed as his lungs figured out how to work again.

'How... Why...?'

It was all he could manage.

'I was scared. And I realise that now because I'm just as terrified. More.' She squeezed her eyes shut and more tears spilled onto her cheeks. 'I left because I thought I was protecting you. But I was just deciding for you.' She wiped her tears away, and his hand fell back down to his lap.

'I have an anxiety problem. Struggling to make decisions—being unable to trust them—is only a part of that. Another is being afraid I'm going to get sick like my mother did. That I'll suffer with being unable to trust my body. That

some day it'll betray me anyway.' Her voice had lowered
to a whisper again. 'I'm scared, Aaron. I'm scared that this
baby will be born into the same kind of world I was born
into. That he or she might go through what I went through.
That because of me—like me—they'll worry excessively
about things they don't have control over too.'

Her eyes lifted to his, the lashes stuck together because
of her tears. 'I'm scared that you'll become indifferent to me
like my father was to my mother. That this—' she gestured
between them '—will never happen again once you realise
that the uncertainty, the anxiety—the *sickness*—might not
go away. That you'll stop caring.'

She'd barely finished before he pulled her closer, tightening his hold on her. He understood now that leaving him,
protecting him, had been her way of trying to prevent that
he'd stop caring for her.

He hoped that his embrace told her she didn't have to
worry. That he would always care for her. That he'd be
there for her whether she was sick or not. And that their
kid would be too.

But he knew that this time actions weren't enough. So
he loosened his hold and, when she pulled back, took her
hands in his.

'You're right. You did make this decision for me and it
wasn't the right one.' He paused. 'I know that part of the
reason you left was because you thought you were protecting me. But I don't need protection. Not from this.'

'But—'

'Rosa,' he interrupted. 'My mother's sickness hit me so
hard because...our relationship was difficult. Finding out
she had cancer made me realise she was my only family. So
I fought for that.' He took a breath. 'I lost some of myself
because of it. I can see that now. But you helped me find
that part of myself again. Because of that, I *can* be there for
you. Through whatever happens.'

He struggled for his next words, unsure of how to make her see what he saw. 'Everything that happened with your mother was…terrible. But you chose to stay. Even though it was difficult, and you sacrificed a lot because of it,' he said when she opened her mouth to protest. 'Even though now you're still living with the effects of it. You stayed because your mother meant something to you. There's nothing wrong with that.'

She blinked, and another tear made its way down her cheek. It fell, dropping to his lap before either of them could brush it away.

He wanted to say more. He wanted to tell her that she meant the world to him. That he'd asked her to marry him because she did, and that he'd stand by her side for ever—that he was strong enough to—because that was what he'd vowed to do on their wedding day.

But he couldn't make that promise to her. How could he stand by her side for ever when he knew he wasn't enough for her? When his genes carried things like his mother's flightiness? With his father's disregard for family?

And how the *hell* was he supposed to be a father when the only thing he knew about fathers was that they *weren't* there?

'Aaron?' she asked with a frown. 'What is it?'

The doorbell rang before he could answer.

CHAPTER TWENTY

'You HAVEN'T BEEN answering my calls,' Liana said as she brushed past Aaron. She stopped when she saw Rosa on the couch, and then her face split into a smile. 'And if this is the reason, I suppose I'll forgive you.' In three steps she was in front of Rosa, pulling her into a hug. 'It's lovely to see you, darling.'

'Liana,' Rosa said with a smile. Forced, since she was suddenly feeling queasy again, and it was only partly because of her pregnancy. At least she didn't have one of those faces that stayed blotchy for long after crying. 'It's lovely seeing you too. Though I was hoping to see you a month ago. At your birthday party, which turned out to be a ruse.'

Rosa caught Aaron's look of surprise before focusing her attention back on Liana. She had the decency to look guilty.

'It's in the past now, isn't it?'

'Not quite,' she muttered, and then shook her head at Liana's questioning look. 'I wasn't able to give you your gift.'

'Oh, you know that gifts aren't necessary,' Liana said, and then waved a hand. 'Do you have it here?'

'No. I sent it by courier though. It should have been delivered by now.'

'Oh, I haven't been to the house in a while,' Liana replied vaguely, and Rosa wondered whether she should ask. But then, since Liana was there, she figured they'd find out about it soon enough. The expression on Aaron's face told her he figured the same thing.

'How long have you been here, darling?' Liana settled on the couch.

'Just since yesterday.'

Liana frowned. 'But I thought you two...' She trailed off,

likely realising that she was opening herself up to another attack by mentioning the island reunion she'd tricked them into. 'Well, then,' she said instead. 'Why haven't you been answering my calls since you got back, Aaron?'

'I was afraid you wanted something,' he replied. 'Since you're here, I suppose I'm right.'

Liana's brows lifted and Rosa felt the surprise echo in her chest. This wasn't the Aaron who dealt with his mother with resignation. Which confirmed her suspicions that something was wrong.

'I didn't realise I was such a burden,' Liana said with a huff. She didn't mean the words, Rosa knew. Liana was more self-aware than she gave herself credit for. She knew her actions burdened Aaron. Though Rosa didn't think she knew how much they hurt him.

'I'm sorry,' Aaron replied curtly. 'You're here for a visit. Do you want me to make some tea? Coffee?'

Liana's expression turned pensive, and Rosa almost smiled at how smoothly Aaron was handling his mother. They all knew now that if Liana said she wasn't there for a visit, she'd expose her lie. So Liana wouldn't come clean, though at some point she'd find a way for Aaron to fix whatever she'd done.

Again, Rosa thought about how blind she'd been to Liana's manipulations. And how much it must have bothered Aaron. How much it must have *hurt* him. But he hadn't shared any of that hurt with her because he'd known how much Liana had meant to her. That was just the kind of man he was.

Rosa would always thank the heavens that Liana had decided Cape Town held the best chances for her recovery. She would always be grateful because it had meant that Liana had been able to make the end of her mother's life better. Liana had done so much for her, for Violet, and Rosa would always love her for it.

But perhaps it was time for her to take her husband's side.

'No, thank you, darling,' Liana said. 'I was just making sure that you were still alive, really. I didn't know what to think after you stopped replying to my messages.'

'I've been busy.'

'Yes. Well.' Liana paused. 'Since you're alive and well, I suppose I can leave. Rosa, it was really lovely to see you. And—' Liana hesitated slightly '—does this mean that I'll be seeing you again in the future?'

'Always,' Rosa answered honestly, and then made a split-second decision. 'Though I was wondering… What are your plans for the rest of the day?' She saw Aaron step forward—to protest, she thought—but ignored him. 'Aaron has a function this evening and I don't have anything to wear. Would you mind taking me to find something appropriate?'

Liana clasped her hands together. '*Of course* I will. I can have Alonso drive us to the boutique immediately. I'll call Kitty. She'll have a couple of dresses waiting when we get there.'

Almost vibrating with glee, Liana took out her phone and went to make her phone calls in the kitchen. When Rosa moved to follow, Aaron caught her arm.

'What are you doing?'

'Being your wife,' she replied simply. 'And doing it the way I should have a long time ago.'

His grip tightened slightly. 'What does that mean?'

'I'm going to accompany you to your function tonight.' It was the easiest explanation.

'What about your flight?'

'I'll change it.'

Or cancel it.

'Rosa,' he breathed, and her name was a warning now.

'Don't worry,' she said, and stood on her toes to give him a kiss. When she pulled back, she saw Liana watching them with a smug smile. 'Ready?' Rosa asked her mother-in-law, and she nodded. 'See you later,' she told Aaron, and ignored his confusion as she picked up her handbag and followed Liana out of the door.

Rosa had never been a schemer, but when she'd left with his mother that afternoon she'd *definitely* been scheming.

If her answer about why she was doing it was anything to go by, she was scheming for him. And he couldn't figure out what that meant. Or how it made him feel.

All he knew was that her scheming wasn't like his mother's scheming. He trusted that, even if the very fact that she *was* scheming worried him. But Rosa was nothing like his mother. Especially since his mother had never, *ever* done any of her scheming for him.

No, he corrected himself immediately. She had. She was the reason he and Rosa were in this situation in the first place. How had he forgotten that? But then, that made it one scheme for him out of *hundreds* of schemes for other people. So perhaps this one had really only been for Rosa's sake.

He paced the floor, waiting for Rosa to return, and realised why the fact that his mother didn't scheme for him bothered him so much. Because if his mother was going to scheme for him, he wished she'd done so a long time ago.

Like when he'd been younger, and had still cared about growing up in a happy family. When he'd wanted a father, and needed a mother. But none of her schemes had done that. Which told him that she wasn't interested in scheming for him.

Because she'd never wanted him.

Just like his father had never wanted him. And just like he'd thought Rosa had felt when she'd left him.

Now that she was back—now that she'd told him why she'd left—he had to figure out how to get over all the flaws he'd discovered in himself when he'd been trying to figure out why she'd gone.

It left him feeling hopeless. As if he couldn't be a good son, a good husband, a good *father*, no matter how hard he tried.

He choked back the emotion when the door rattled and Rosa walked in. And then a different kind of emotion settled inside him, soothing what had been there before, though he knew it shouldn't.

She wore a royal-blue gown. It had a high neckline adorned with an amazing piece of jewellery, and then creased at one side of her waist before flowing down regally to the floor. The bold necklace was accompanied by matching earrings that he spotted through the spiral of curls around her face.

The colour contrast—the blue of her dress, the bronze of her skin—was striking, and his breath went heavy in his lungs, as if weighed down by her beauty. He'd always been struck by that beauty. It had knocked him down, and then out, and he'd never fully been able to get up again.

It was no different now.

'Are you going to say anything?' she said softly after a moment. Only then did he realise he was gawking at her.

'I…yes. Sorry.' He shook his head. 'You look amazing.'

A small smile played on her lips. 'Thank you.'

'You meant for me to react this way.'

The smile widened. 'Well, I was hoping.' And then faded. 'Just like now I'm hoping that I don't end up being sick in this dress.'

He took a step forward. 'Is there anything I can do?'

'To keep me from throwing up?' She smiled kindly. 'No. But I appreciate the attempt. I'm just going to have to…well, hope.' She paused. 'How are you doing?'

'Fine. Good.' He frowned. 'Why?'

'I haven't seen you all afternoon. Is it a crime to check in?'

'No. But you're checking in for a reason.'

She gave him a look that told him she had no intention

of sharing that reason. He bit back a sigh. 'How were things with my mother?'

'Fine. I gave her the opportunity to play fairy godmother with me. Willingly, this time.' She tilted her head. 'Honestly, she loved it. The dress, and then the shoes.' She swept the dress from her leg—nearly stopping his heart as he realised the dress had a slit and he could ogle her leg freely—revealing a shoe that sparkled up at him. She let the dress go. 'Plus, she was thrilled that her plan to get us back together had worked.'

'And you let her believe that.' The dry comment wasn't meant as a question.

'No, actually, I didn't. I told her that she needed to think about her actions. That she wasn't a real fairy, which meant those actions had consequences. And that those consequences affected you.'

He couldn't formulate a reply.

'You're welcome,' she said with a smirk.

'I... I don't know what to say.'

'I just told you you're welcome. You don't have to say anything.'

'Why?' he asked, when his mind still couldn't grasp what was happening.

'Because someone needed to tell her.' She paused. 'I didn't tell my mother that her actions were affecting me. I expected her to know somehow, or I wished... I wished my father would say something. But he didn't, and she didn't, and now—' She broke off on a slow exhale of air. 'I wish I'd said something to her. Maybe our relationship would have changed. Maybe I wouldn't have felt the way that I do now.'

Her eyes had gone distant with the memories, but when she looked at him they cleared. 'So I thought that if I said something to your mother it might make a difference.'

'Did it?'

'She was surprised to hear it.' She bit her lip. The first

show of uncertainty. 'She didn't expect anyone to call her out on it.'

'I never did.'

'I know.' She gave him a small sad smile. 'You just did what it took to make it go away. And while I get that—I did it too—it's not going to be as easy to do when the baby gets here. And your mother needs to know that.'

'You told her about the baby?'

'No. I just said that we're working things out, and that that means we have to have boundaries.'

'And she agreed?'

'We'll have to see.' The uncertainty was back. 'Did I... did I overstep?'

'No.' He moved forward and kissed her forehead. 'No, you didn't.' He paused. 'Thank you.'

'You're welcome,' she said again, and rested her head on his chest.

The movement should have comforted him, but instead it sent a ripple through his already unsettled feelings. He wasn't upset by what she'd done, but he also didn't know why she'd done it. Or why it felt as if another weight had been added to what he was already carrying on his shoulders.

CHAPTER TWENTY-ONE

HE WASN'T UPSET with her.

He'd told her he wasn't, and the way he engaged with her seemed to suggest the same. But he'd been distracted on the way to the hotel that was hosting his function. And his usual collected demeanour seemed frazzled.

His colleagues had noticed too. At one point, his partner Frank had spoken about the expansion and Aaron had just looked at him. Had just *stared*. And then he'd asked Frank to repeat the question, and Frank had shot her a look of concern before replying.

Rosa was worried. She was also beginning to think Aaron's strange mood had something to do with her. He'd been that way since they'd kissed that afternoon, and she'd broken down in his lap and spilled her deepest, darkest fears to him. Maybe he regretted what he'd said now.

If he did, would it affect how comforted she'd felt because of what he'd said?

She smiled at one of Aaron's colleagues, accepting their curiosity as a part of the event. She didn't imagine her absence over the past five months had gone unnoticed. And then the previous day she'd shown up at his office and now she was attending the company function.

It was too good to pass up, and so she forgave the people who looked at her as if somehow that would give them the answers they were hoping for.

She focused her attention back on Aaron, but now he was preparing to give his speech for the evening, and he'd gone even quieter. Her chest ached and her stomach rolled, and she pleaded with the new life growing inside her to give her an evening without throwing up. If she did throw up it would no doubt give the people who were looking at her the answers they wanted.

So perhaps they were right to stare at her.

Thankfully, she made it through Aaron's speech. Smart, concise, motivating. He was an excellent boss, she thought, and would make an excellent father.

But was he still interested in being an excellent husband?

The evening moved into a more casual phase after Aaron's speech. The band began to play, the alcohol began to kick in and people were moving to the dance floor. Aaron had been intercepted by one of his employees on his way back to the table, which made it easier for Rosa to excuse herself.

She made her way to the bathroom and then, when she saw the queue to the ladies' room of the venue, pivoted and went to the elevator. She almost pressed for the first floor, but then someone might have the same idea as her, so she pressed for the third floor instead.

It was the top floor of the hotel, and she thanked the heavens when she was able to make it there and locate a bathroom before anyone else saw her. She was also grateful that her baby had allowed her to close the door of the stall before she or he demanded that Rosa be sick.

There was more in her stomach than usual, since she'd felt obliged to eat some of the meal they'd served to avoid suspicion, which made the experience longer and more unpleasant. When she straightened her head started to spin, and she had to spend even more time in the stall to make sure she wouldn't fall over when she exited.

It was all of thirty minutes later by the time she left the bathroom—breath fresh and make-up fixed, thanks to the contents of her bag—and she knew that Aaron would be worried about her. But she still felt a little clammy, and she eyed the door to the balcony before deciding that fresh air might help steady her.

She didn't know what the sound was at first when she

got there. Thought it was in her head, the harsh, unsteady breaths. But when her eyes adjusted she saw a shadow in the corner.

She blinked, realised it was a person sitting hunched on the floor, and was about to leave when she realised that that person was her husband.

He couldn't breathe.

It was the damn tie, and the shirt, and the suit jacket. And though his brain was fuzzy and there were a million thoughts going through his mind—or none—some part of it knew he couldn't throw off all his clothes. So he threw off his jacket, loosened his tie, opened his top button and tried to breathe.

The attempt sounded ragged to his own ears. He was dimly aware of someone else on the balcony and, though he wanted to, he couldn't bring himself to care. If his employees saw him like this it would break something he didn't think could be fixed.

He didn't care.

If Frank saw him it would put their partnership at risk.

He didn't care.

And yet, when he felt the person crouch down in front of him and he lifted his head and looked directly into Rosa's eyes, he found himself caring.

'Rosa,' he rasped. Why did his voice sound so strange?

'It's okay, baby,' she said, settling some of the spinning happening inside him. 'It's okay. You're okay.'

As she wrapped her arms around him he wanted to tell her that it didn't feel as if he was okay. That his head hurt with all the thoughts, and his lungs felt as if they couldn't hold the air he was breathing.

But the thoughts he'd believed so coherent in his mind came out as a garbled mess of air and words. Her hold tightened on him but her voice stayed calm and after some time had passed—he didn't know how long—he looked up at her, and followed her instructions to breathe.

'In,' she told him, 'and out.' She smiled. 'See, you're doing it. Just keep breathing. Inhale on a count to five, exhale on a count to five. You've got this, baby. You can do this. I know you can do this.'

He didn't know how long it took before he believed her. Or how long after he believed her that his breathing actually reflected it. And when he was still—when he felt his mind and body still—she was on her knees and somehow he was cradled in her arms.

'I'm sorry,' he said quietly. She pulled back, her eyes sweeping across his face, and then she shook her head.

'What are you apologising for?'

'That…that you had to see this.' The words were more helpless than he'd intended, and only succeeded in making him feel even more of a fool.

'If by "this" you mean whatever happened out here, don't apologise.' She shifted, and it tugged him out of whatever was going on in his head. The position she was in must have been uncomfortable, and he wasn't sure how long she'd been sitting there like that.

He helped ease her off her knees and then pulled her forward so that she sat on his lap. She didn't protest, just lifted a hand and swept hair from his forehead.

'You don't have to apologise, Aaron,' she said again, her hand now playing with his hair.

'You shouldn't have—'

'Do you think I wanted you to see me after I threw up yesterday?' She clenched her jaw, and then relaxed it again. After taking a breath, she continued. 'Or have you witness what my anxiety is doing to me? What it *could* do to me?' She lifted her shoulders. 'I've run away—hid—from you before because I didn't want you to see that. But you showed me that was wrong.' She paused, as if she were letting her words sink in. 'Talk to me. Let me in.'

Her words shook him. And again he realised how complicated her decision to leave had been.

But he'd just had a panic attack. The first he'd ever had, and he didn't know where it had come from. He needed time to process that. And what she'd told him. He couldn't find the right words to explain that to her.

'Okay,' she said when the silence stretched. 'Tell me what happened before you came up here.'

'I… I was just talking with Lee about—' He broke off when he realised Rosa would learn nothing about what had caused him to react like that from a discussion he'd had with one of his associates.

Because his panic attack had had nothing to do with what he'd been talking about with Lee. At some point during the conversation his head had started spinning and it had felt as if he couldn't get enough air into his lungs. And his mind…

He'd been thinking about all the promises he'd wanted to make to Rosa, but that he'd never be able to keep.

And about how he couldn't keep lying to her. About how she had the right to know that he wasn't worthy to be her husband. He was barely worthy of being a father to their child.

'Aaron—' her soft voice interrupted his thoughts '—talk to me.'

He looked into her eyes and could only see the things he couldn't give her. 'I can't be there for you, Rosa. Not in the way you need.'

Her heart dipped almost as violently as it had when she'd seen him in that corner. It was still bruised from holding her stoic, strong husband in her arms as he shook, as he struggled for air. It could barely bear the weight of him telling her now he couldn't be there for her.

'I'll get it under control,' she said, her voice just above a whisper. 'No,' she said almost immediately. 'I don't know if I have what my mother had. I don't know if I'm a hypochondriac. Or about the cancer. So I'll get it diagnosed. I'll see a psychologist, and get screened for the breast cancer gene. I'll keep my anxieties in check. I'm already trying,' she added, desperation fuelling her words. 'I go to the doctor if I feel off, and it almost always *is* something. It isn't in my head.'

The last words were said in a whisper, and her hands reached for his, gripping them tightly. 'I'll fix it, Aaron. Just don't…don't leave me.'

'Rosa,' he said, his voice shaking. But it wasn't from whatever had happened to him. No, it was because of what she'd just told him and she immediately felt guilt crush her.

'I'm sorry. I'm being selfish. I'm being…' The words drifted and she felt tears follow them down her cheeks. 'I'm sorry.'

'I wasn't talking about that,' he replied, and he let go of one of her hands and slid an arm around her waist. 'I should have thought you might think that.' His expression softened. 'That's another part of why you left, isn't it? You thought I'd leave you too. Like your dad did with your mom.'

Not trusting herself to speak, she pursed her lips. Nodded.

'I won't,' he said softly. Firmly. 'Not because of that. Not because of you.' He pressed a kiss to her lips that calmed some of the frantic beating of her heart. 'It's because of me, Rosa. It's always because of me.'

'That's what happened earlier.' Somehow her reaction had made him see the reasons for his own more clearly. 'I was thinking about how I wanted to promise you I'd always be there for you.' He took a breath. Wondered how, over the last month, he'd shared more with her—had delved more into his emotions—than he ever had before.

'Lee's been working on a case where a mother who desperately wants custody of her kids won't get it.' And now that he thought about it—now that his brain was steadier—he realised his discussion with Lee had contributed to his reaction after all. 'She promised them they'd be able to live with her, but her two jobs won't make that possible. She broke down in Lee's office because she'd have to break that promise to them.'

The more he spoke, the clearer it became. 'It's not fair. She works two jobs to make sure that they have everything they want. Except her.' He paused. 'And because of that broken promise they're going to spend their lives not trusting her.'

'Aaron, it's not the same thing—'

'No,' he interrupted. 'That's not what...' He blew out a breath. 'What happened here was partly because of the promise I couldn't make to you, and partly because those kids... They're going to wonder if *they* were the reason that promise was broken. If they did something wrong, or if she really wanted them in the first place.' Emotion, strong and heavy, sat in his chest. 'They're going to be angry with her at first, and then they're going to feel responsible for making sure she believes their existence was worth it.' He looked at her. 'It'll make them take responsibility for things they shouldn't have to. It'll affect their entire lives. And everything that goes wrong from this point in their lives will make them wonder if it was their fault.'

'Like if their wives leave.'

'Yes.'

'Even when it's clear their wives have problems, fears of their own, that contributed to why they left?'

How did she always see what he couldn't say? 'Yes.'

'And at what point do they start believing that there's

nothing wrong with them? That their wives love them more than anyone else in the world, and that they would do anything to make them believe that?'

'I'm broken,' Aaron said, and the pain in his chest agreed with him. 'You saw that. You left because of it.'

'But you've shown me that I was wrong, Aaron. The way you've dealt with all this.' She made a vague gesture towards her stomach. 'And with your mom today.' She paused. 'What you said to me this afternoon. You've grown. I just didn't see it.'

'Or you did, and—'

'No, Aaron. I was wrong. Scared.'

'But my mom took so little interest in me, and my dad… He wasn't even there.'

'That's more about them than it is about you,' she said gently. 'You've learnt that with me this past month.' She squeezed his hand. 'It doesn't mean you're the one who's broken. And if you are… Well, then, all of us are.'

'But your mother and father didn't leave—' He broke off with a shake of his head. 'I'm sorry. I wasn't thinking.'

'No, it's okay.' She leaned back against the railing, making him think about how ridiculous they must look. Her in her beautiful gown, and him in his tux. Broken, shaken, on the floor of a balcony.

'I don't think I ever thought that there might have been something wrong with *me* because my parents…were who they were. Are, I guess, in the case of my dad. Not until I found that lump and freaked out.' She lifted a hand to his face now. 'I understand why you feel this way. And now, with the baby on the way, why it's an issue.'

'Because I'm going to be a terrible father?'

'What? No!' She straightened. 'I meant it made you think of your parents. Of your father. No,' she said again. 'You're going to be a terrific father.'

'I don't know if I can believe that.' He was so tired of

saying it, and yet it haunted him so that he couldn't do anything *but* say it.

'Well, I'm telling you.' She paused. 'I know your relationship with your mother is…difficult. And unfair. But she's done a pretty decent job of teaching you how to be responsible.' She wrinkled her nose. 'Silver linings.'

'Yes, I know how to be responsible. I've been responsible my whole life. But look where that got me.' He felt helpless saying it. And, despite what she'd told him, he couldn't believe her. He couldn't believe that he'd be good for them. For her and the baby.

'I'm having a panic attack during a work function, Rosa. I can't face that I'm going to be a father. The responsibility is…easy. I'll look after the child. I'll be there, which is more than what my mom and dad did.' He paused. 'But what is responsibility going to teach this child? That I *have* to love them?'

'Is that how you feel?'

He shrugged. 'I don't know.'

Silence followed his words and, though he knew she would never say it, he sensed that he'd hurt her with his answer. Felt it confirmed when she drew herself up and tried to stand. He helped as much as he could, and was already standing when she turned back to him.

'You have to figure this out, Aaron,' she told him softly, kindly, though he'd hurt her. 'We—me and your baby—don't want to feel like you're just there for us out of some warped sense of responsibility.'

'I wouldn't be.'

'No? There isn't a part of you that feels like the only reason you're open to getting back together again is because I'm pregnant?'

'I… I didn't realise that was on the table.'

She laughed lightly. Mockingly now. 'You didn't realise that getting back together was an option? Not when I sat on your lap and kissed you back? When I fell apart and told you enough to help you put me back together again?' Any pretence of humour left her face. 'You didn't think me speaking with your mother, me staying here to accompany you tonight, that *any* of that meant I wanted to get back together again?'

'I... I didn't want to hope. After what happened,' he finished lamely.

'After I left.' He nodded, and she sighed. 'Maybe I was stupid for thinking that we'd be able to move past this.' She lifted a hand to her forehead. 'Or maybe we just need to clear it up.' She straightened her shoulders. 'You know why I left. And I know where I went wrong in making that decision.' She paused. 'I'm going to manage my anxiety. Or do my best to try. You said you'd be there for me.' He nodded. 'Did you mean that as the mother of your child, or as your wife?'

He hesitated only briefly. 'Both.'

She gave him a sad smile. 'If this is going to work we have to be honest,' she said, reminding him of his words at the restaurant the night before. But he didn't respond. Couldn't, since he was still trying to figure out what had happened that had got them to this point.

Hope and guilt made a potent shot, he thought, and wondered why he'd downed it.

'Aaron... I want to stay married to you. I love you—' her eyes went glossy as she said the words '—and I'll always regret how stupid I was to leave you instead of opening up to you. But this whole experience has taught me that there were things that we were going through by ourselves that we shouldn't have gone through alone. That we should have shared.'

She blew out a breath. 'So maybe, in some weird way, this was a good thing.' She went silent, her face pensive, and then she shook her head. 'But we know what we know

now. And the actions of the past have brought us here, to make this decision. So, if you want me—' her voice broke and she cleared her throat '—you're going to have to move past what happened and—' she threw up her hands '—and hope again. Because, right now, I'm choosing you again. Not because of the baby. Because of *me*. Because I love you, and I was foolish to believe that I could go through life without you.'

She stepped forward, laid a hand on his cheek. 'But I will, if you can't choose me too. If you don't *want* to be responsible for me and our child. Because that's what it is, isn't it?' She didn't wait for an answer. 'Wanting to be responsible for someone instead of feeling like you *have* to be. Can you say that about us?'

He opened his mouth to agree, to tell her how much he wanted their lives to go back to being how they'd been before. But he knew that he couldn't. Because, as she'd said, they knew what they knew now. And the things he knew about himself worried him more than anything he'd found out about her.

He couldn't be sure that he *wanted* to be responsible for them. Couldn't be sure because he didn't know what *wanting* to be responsible looked like. His entire life had been spent doing things he *had* to do. Except for Rosa. He'd wanted her, but now even that had felt like a compulsion of sorts.

Had he felt obliged to be with her because that had been what their sick mothers had wanted? What her mother had asked of him? Or had it been the attraction, the heat, that had dictated their relationship? Their love?

Her eyes filled again as the silence grew. Her hand dropped and she hung her head. He wanted to comfort her, to draw her in and promise that he'd made a mistake.

He couldn't.

When she looked up at him again her eyes were clear,

though there was still that unbearable sadness in them. She lifted up onto her toes, put both hands on his cheeks and kissed him.

It tasted like goodbye, and somehow that taste felt familiar to him. He found himself swept away by it. Felt the emptiness fill him when she pulled away. Felt his hands go to her hips as she lowered to her feet again. As he kissed her forehead.

He didn't know how long they stood like that, but he knew he'd remember for ever what happened next.

'Be happy,' she said hoarsely. 'Find out what that means to you and go for it. I'll be in touch about the baby. We can figure things out once you've had time to…' Her voice faded and it was a few seconds later when she said, 'When you've had time.'

And then she was gone.

CHAPTER TWENTY-TWO

'AND YOU DON'T think it's normal?' The delicate older woman waited patiently for Rosa's reply, and Rosa took a deep breath, preparing herself to answer the question honestly.

She had been the one who'd decided to make good on her promise to get her anxieties under control. She might not have a husband to do it for—she swallowed at the pain that quaked through her body—but she had a child. Or she would have a child. And since her anxiety had spiked since she'd returned to Cape Town the week before, she'd finally decided to go to the psychologist.

'Normal?' Rosa asked. 'The fact that I worry incessantly about what's happening in my body? That I can't trust it?'

'Yes,' Dr Spar replied. 'You don't think, after what your mother went through, it's normal to have your concerns?'

'Well, I suppose that's why I'm here. Because it's normal coming from where I come from.' She bit her lip. 'But the worrying extends to my decisions. And I can't trust them either.'

'Which bothers you?'

'It's affected my life.'

Dr Spar nodded. 'Have you thought about how not trusting yourself might have come from your mother being unable to trust herself?'

'Not quite so specifically. But I know my indecisiveness, or struggling to trust my decisions... I know that's because of my mother.'

'You told me that you didn't want to use your mother as an excuse for your actions any more.'

'That doesn't mean I magically know how to stop doing that.'

'Except being here of your own accord—for your child—means that you have, in some way. Can you see that?'

She lifted a shoulder. 'Maybe.'

'You struggle with it.'

'With seeing that I'm not my mother?' Rosa asked.

'Yes,' Dr Spar replied. 'But also with seeing yourself for who you are.' She paused. 'You're not your mother, Rosa. You can see where your fears and anxieties come from. And you're facing them. Do you think your mother could do that?'

Rosa shook her head silently as she thought it through. The rest of the appointment passed in a blur after that. It had been her second appointment—the first had been spent sharing what Rosa thought she needed help with—but already she knew that it was helping.

She wasn't foolish enough to think she was cured. She was still anxious. Still doubted herself. And she still couldn't bring herself to be screened for the breast cancer gene, though she was using her pregnancy as an excuse for that. So she made her subsequent appointments and patted her stomach as she walked out of the building.

We're going to get through this, pumpkin, she told her baby silently.

She bit her lip and tried to push past the tears that always seemed to be close by recently. Partly because she'd been worrying about what kind of mother she would be. Worrying that she'd be similar to *her* mother. But having Dr Spar point out how differently she'd reacted to her anxieties compared to her mother had made her feel better.

As she headed home she told herself that it was okay that she didn't want to be like her mother. That she wasn't betraying her mother by wanting that. She'd loved her mother. She wouldn't have put herself through what she had for Violet if she hadn't.

But that didn't negate the difficult experience Rosa had

had with Violet. No, that experience and that love could co-exist. And there was nothing wrong with Rosa not wanting her child to live in a world where it did.

It was harder to convince herself that the other part of what had brought her to tears recently was okay. The fact that her child would grow up without his or her parents being together. Especially because Rosa knew how much she'd contributed to that fact.

Her decisions had brought her to this point. Long before she'd found that lump too. And now she knew she'd always fear inheriting her mother's hypochondria. The anxiety, the mistrust of her body, of her decisions, would stay with her.

But she could deal with that. She'd fight for her mental health just as hard as she'd fight for her physical health. Even though that battle would probably extend throughout her life.

She wouldn't let it control her life, her actions. Not any more. She would continue her therapy and learn how to manage it. Learn how to look after herself properly. And see who she really was.

But before she'd got to that point she *had* let it control her life, her actions, her decisions, and she couldn't ignore that she had a part in breaking up her marriage.

She hadn't spoken with Aaron since that night at his work function. She didn't think she was strong enough yet. Not for that. She'd left immediately after that conversation with him. She'd gone back to the house, not particularly caring about what people would say about her departure; she'd packed and had been at the airport an hour later.

The whole thing had cost her a fortune, and there had been no fairy godmother to pick up her tab. But then, her life with Aaron felt like a made-up tale to her now anyway. The clock had struck twelve on her—her carriage had turned back into a pumpkin and she'd turned back into a normal woman with no prince at her side.

'But we don't need a prince, do we, pumpkin?' she murmured softly, laying her hand on her stomach. Ignoring the voice that said, *Liar*.

She *did* need a prince. *Her* prince. But the clock had struck twelve.

She choked back the grief.

It had been two weeks since he'd last seen her. Two weeks without a phone call or message. Of course, he'd gone without either for much longer. But things were different now. Because of the child, he told himself. Because she was pregnant.

Was she okay? Was the baby okay? How was she feeling?

Those questions—and variations of them—had plagued him since she'd left. And he could have got the answers to them with one simple phone call.

That was how he knew he was lying to himself. Things weren't different between them because she was pregnant. At least, not *only* because she was pregnant. They were also different because things had changed between them. Things had become more intense.

He missed her. He missed sharing with her. Regretted how rarely that had happened when they'd been happily married.

Happily.

He didn't think he could use that word any more. Not knowing what he knew now. Not considering the depths their relationship had sunk to before he'd been stupid enough to let her go.

He took leave from work when he realised his usual strategy of throwing himself into his cases was no longer effective. And if he'd managed to pass off his colleagues' concerns when he'd returned to their function that night two weeks before without Rosa, he wouldn't be able to now.

He *never* took leave. And he'd had to convince Frank that he was fine.

But he wasn't.

He spent his days on menial manual tasks. He went to the gym, ran. Fixed things in the house that needed fixing. At some point he found himself at the hardware store purchasing wood, and when he'd got home he'd started building a treehouse. He hadn't given it much thought, had just done it, and he'd been halfway through when he'd realised he was building a treehouse.

Anything to avoid your problems, a voice in his head told him mockingly. But he didn't think he was avoiding his problems. No, he was avoiding his *mistakes*. Because if how miserable he was without Rosa was any indication, he *had* made a mistake. And he didn't know how to fix it.

Which was why he was now at his mother's house.

He had a key, but he didn't want to use it. He'd dodged whatever his mother had wanted because of Rosa the last time, and he hadn't heard from her since. But that didn't mean that he wouldn't. For all he knew, he could be walking into another family staying at his mom's house.

His mind had created such a convincing picture of it that he was mildly surprised when he found his mother alone.

'So, this is the reason for the weather today,' his mother said when she saw him. She stared pointedly out at the rain through the windows before meeting his eyes again. 'You're visiting me.'

'Yes.' He wasn't in the mood for dramatics, though he understood the sentiment. 'I wanted to talk to you.'

'I assumed so, yes. Something to drink?'

When he shook his head she asked for tea from the housekeeper, who'd been hovering in the room since she'd opened the door for Aaron.

When they were alone, Aaron continued, 'What's wrong with me?'

'What?'

'Why didn't my father want me?'

To his mother's credit, she didn't look nearly as surprised as he'd thought she would. Though she did get up and start pacing. When she finally answered him, she had taken her seat again.

'It wasn't you. It was me.' There was pain in her eyes that he had never seen before. 'Your father didn't want *me*.'

'He walked away from his son.'

'Because he didn't want to have a child with me.' She cleared her throat. 'Because he was married.'

'He was…' Aaron couldn't quite process the words, though he'd half repeated them. It took time, during which his mother's tea had been brought and now sat untouched on the table in front of her. 'You slept with a married man?'

'I didn't know he was married when we met.' Liana looked out of the window as she spoke. 'It was a one-time thing too. And when I found out I was pregnant it was hard to find him. The only reason I could was because I had money. Which, thankfully, he didn't know about.'

'He was a one-night stand?' he asked slowly. 'You didn't know him?'

'I was young, Aaron,' she said coolly. 'It was a mistake.'

'You mean *I* was mistake.'

'I've said that in the past, yes.' She looked at him now and her expression softened. 'Though I doubt I meant it. I was just…angry. At myself for making such poor decisions. At you for—' she took a breath '—for reminding me that I should have been responsible.'

'Because I was responsible.'

'Yes.' She brushed a non-existent hair from her face. 'Even though I knew responsibility was your coping mechanism. Responsibility and control.' She smiled sadly. 'Because your mother was irresponsible and out of control.'

'Is that…' He closed his eyes. Opened them. 'Is that why you didn't want to spend time with me when I was younger?'

Her lips pursed. 'I wouldn't have made a good mother. You didn't need me around.'

'I did,' he disagreed softly.

'No, you didn't. Look what's happened to your life since I've been around.'

'It didn't have to be like that. After you got sick—'

'You tried to salvage our relationship,' she interrupted. 'But I saw what that cost you, Aaron.' Her breath shuddered through her lips. 'I said that your father was a one-time mistake, but I've made so many more. I forced you to become someone you shouldn't have had to be. I hurt you beyond measure. I've made you doubt your worth. I'm… I'm sorry.'

He didn't know where her candour was coming from. Didn't know what to do with the emotions it caused inside him. What he *did* know was that his mother's apology meant something to him. That it shifted something inside him.

'You didn't deserve us as parents,' she interrupted his thoughts softly. 'You're a good child. And you have been better to me than I deserved. And your father…' She sighed. 'He's missed out on getting to know you. But that wasn't because of you. That was only because of the circumstances you were born into.'

'Thank you.'

'You don't have to thank me. I should have done this for you a long time ago.'

'Be honest?'

'Yes. And not punished you for my actions. My mistakes.' She leaned forward. '*I* should have been responsible for *you*. Because you were my child, yes, but also because I love you.' She cleared her throat. 'I shouldn't have hurt you the way I have. I should have put you first. I'm sorry.'

'Mom—'

'I knew she'd be good for you,' she interrupted. 'I didn't realise she'd be good for *us*.'

His heart began to sprint. 'Rosa?'

'Of course. She told me all this, you know.' He nodded. 'And she said you'd come here soon. To prepare myself.'

Though his mother's honesty began to make sense now, the reason why surprised him. Again, something shifted inside him. Again, he thought about the mistakes he'd made.

'I see a bit of myself in her.' His eyes lifted and she met his gaze. 'Is that why you're here, and not with her?'

'How—'

'I keep track of my family,' Liana said.

'You knew she was here when you visited me a few weeks ago.'

She nodded. 'I promised Violet that I would look out for Rosa too.'

And yet he was beginning to think that Rosa looked out for them more than they ever had for her.

'She's not like you.'

'No,' Liana agreed. 'She's better. And she's shown you that being spontaneous doesn't have to be a bad thing.' She paused. 'Perhaps she'll help you to let go a little.'

He didn't reply immediately, his mind racing. And finally, when he looked at his mother again, there was a knowing glint in her eyes.

CHAPTER TWENTY-THREE

'WHY DID I decide to live on the top floor of this stupid building?' Rosa wondered out loud, speaking to no one in particular. The elevator of her building had broken. She was almost seven weeks pregnant, and so tired she was barely able to lift a hand to her face, let alone her feet up three floors.

And so she sank down next to the broken elevator, ignoring the looks of the other residents as they easily made the journey up the stairs. She sighed, leaned her head against the wall and closed her eyes.

She was probably going to get mugged. Her handbag was on her lap. The bags from her grocery haul sprawled around her. Toast and tea, ginger biscuits and prenatal vitamins—the extent of what her stomach would hold. And then there were the sample dresses that she'd had to get for her show in two weeks' time.

Why she'd decided to showcase her new line during her first trimester she'd question for ever.

Because you're desperate to prove that you can move forward with your life without your husband by your side?

She groaned, and pleaded with her thoughts to stop bringing Aaron up. It happened too often for her liking, at the most inopportune times—

'Rosa?'

And now she was hearing his voice. She opened her eyes with a soft curse, and then felt them widen when she saw Aaron right in front of her, crouching down with a concerned look on his face.

'Are you okay?'

She frowned and then reached out, touched his face, to make sure he was really there.

'*Aaron?*'

'Rosa,' he said again, his voice firm. 'Are you okay?'

'If you're really here…' She paused, gave him a moment to confirm it.

There was slight amusement on his face when he nodded.

'Yes, I'm fine.' She straightened now. 'What are you doing here?'

'What are you doing on the floor?' he countered. There was a beat of silence while they both waited for the other to answer, and then she sighed.

'The elevator's broken, and I'm too tired to climb the stairs.'

'That's it?'

'Nauseous, dizzy too. But yes, that's it.'

'So you sat on the floor of an apartment complex?'

She pulled a face. 'I would have moved eventually.' She blew out a breath. 'And yes, I know it's disgusting and I was putting myself in danger, but—'

She broke off when he placed the grocery bags in her one hand, slid her handbag over her shoulder and put the garment bags in her other hand.

'What are you—?'

Again, she broke off. This time, though, it was because he'd scooped her into his arms, holding her as she held the bags easily.

'You're not going to carry me up three floors.' He answered her by turning to the stairwell and doing just that. 'Aaron, you don't have to do this. I'm fine. Just let me down—'

'Are you going to complain the whole way?' he asked, pausing to look down at her. He didn't even sound out of breath, she thought, and cursed him silently for always doing the kind of thing that made her swoon.

'No,' she answered sullenly, and his lips curved. 'It's not funny.'

'No,' he agreed, and kept walking.

Rosa told herself not to get too excited by the fact that he was there. It was probably for the sake of the baby, and she pushed back against the guilt that swelled up inside her. She should have called him, as she'd said she would, and given him an update. But there was no update. She still felt crappy. She still wished that things were different between them.

She couldn't bring herself to call since she didn't trust what she would say. She'd told him she could live without him that night, but her courage had faltered terribly since she'd left Johannesburg.

Besides, what was wrong with his phone? He could have called her too.

Happy with that, and ready to defend herself if she had to, she barely noticed that they'd reached her floor until he stopped in front of her door and set her down gently.

She stared at him. 'How did you know this was my apartment?'

'My mom.'

Rosa's forehead creased. 'Your mother? How did she... Is that how you knew I was in Cape Town the first time?'

He nodded. 'She always knows where her family is. Her words, not mine,' he said with a shrug when her face twisted into a questioning look.

The day was becoming stranger and, since she didn't want to waste her already limited energy on arguing about something that wasn't worth it, she merely nodded. She handed him the garment bags and reached for the key in her handbag to open the door.

He was still holding the garment bags as he walked in and looked around. She closed the door and tried not to fidget. She lived there, but nothing about the flat was hers.

She'd rented it furnished. The quirky colours, odd furniture and weird paintings weren't her choices.

In fact, they'd almost deterred her before she'd remembered the flat had a view of Table Mountain and was located close to the factory that made her designs. She'd realised then that those were her only two priorities.

'Are these for your show?' he asked when she took the bags from him. She didn't bother asking him how he knew.

'Yep.'

'Can I see them?'

'Why would you want to?' she asked tiredly. 'You didn't come all the way here to look at the clothes I designed.'

'No,' he agreed again, and she nearly sighed. Why did he have to be so damn amicable?

'So why did you? Come, I mean.'

'To fight,' he answered slowly.

'What are you fighting for?' she asked after a stunned silence. He'd expected some version of that question, though it was still a punch to the gut.

'You.'

She stared at him. 'There's nothing beyond "you"?'

'I…' He took a deep breath, and then plunged. 'No, there is. I'm sorry, Rosa. For…everything. You shouldn't be here. You should be home. You should be with me.' He gave her a moment to process. 'It's my fault that you're not.'

Her expression remained unreadable. 'How does this change things?'

'I'm here, aren't I?' It came out in a surlier tone than he'd intended. And of course she picked up on it.

'Really? You're annoyed because you're here? Aaron, you've barely said anything beyond *I'm sorry*. And I appreciate your apology, I do, but what am I supposed to do with it? Things haven't changed, which means you're probably here because you think it's what you should do.'

'No,' he said after a moment. 'I'm here because I'm… choosing to be. And because I didn't think about it. I just booked a flight and came here right after I spoke with my mother.'

'You…spoke with your mother?' she asked slowly, before shaking her head. 'No, wait, you *just* booked a flight?'

He clenched his teeth, and then forced himself to relax. 'I was being spontaneous.' He hissed out a breath. 'So yes, I suppose I am annoyed to be here. I'm annoyed that I don't have anything better for you than *I'm sorry*. Because that's what happens when I don't have a plan.'

'But you're here,' she said softly. 'And that means something.'

The emotion in her eyes told him that it did. And suddenly all the uncertainty didn't feel so overwhelming.

'Tell me about the visit to your mother,' she urged softly, when silence took over the room.

'I asked her about… Well, I asked her about my father. And about her.' He cleared his throat. 'About why they didn't want me.'

'And she told you it wasn't you.'

'Yes.' She always knew. 'He was married.'

'Oh, Aaron.' She took a step forward, and then stopped. 'I'm sorry.'

'Don't be,' he said, his heart aching at her hesitation. 'It made me realise that the things I've believed about myself, about my life, weren't entirely correct.'

'And you're okay with that?'

He thought about it. 'No. I don't think I will be for a long time. But I have answers now, and they'll help me figure it out. That's enough for now.' He paused. 'I think that's why you leaving—why all of this—hit me so hard. Because I thought all of it was me. Because I didn't have answers.'

'But you know better now,' she said. 'You have answers.'

'Yes.' He cleared his throat. 'She told me you told her I'd come.'

'A guess,' she said, but angled her face as if she didn't want him to see her expression.

'No, it wasn't a guess.' He walked towards her, stopping only a few metres away. 'You know me. How?'

She laughed hoarsely. 'You're my husband.'

'And you're my wife.' He stepped closer. 'Yet somehow I didn't realise how important that was until you walked away from me. When I saw you again, and I couldn't keep my heart or body from you. And when you told me you were pregnant—'

He sucked in air. Let it out slowly.

'My mother told me she should have been responsible for me because I was her child. But also…because she loved me.' He closed the distance between them now. 'And I love you, Rosa. Being responsible for you and our child… It's because I *want* to be. I'm choosing you.' He lifted his hand, brushed a finger across her lips. 'No matter what happens in my life, Rosa, I always end up choosing you.'

She sucked her lip between her teeth and then blew out a breath. 'You really know how to sweep a woman off her feet, don't you?'

His lips curved. 'I'm only interested in sweeping one woman off her feet.' His hand dropped to her waist. 'You have questions.'

'So many,' she said on a little outburst of air. 'But I also have to tell you… I've been seeing someone about my anxiety.'

'Has it been helping?' he asked carefully.

'Yes. But it's not just going to go away.'

'I know.' He took her hand. Squeezed. And let go.

'And I haven't done the test yet.'

'The screening?' She nodded. 'Can you do it while you're pregnant?'

'I… I haven't seen a doctor about it, so I don't know for sure. But I wanted you to know, so that—'

'I can be there for you if and when you choose to go?'

Her mouth opened, and then she swallowed. 'I'm going to do it.'

'Okay.'

'So there's no *if*.'

'Okay.'

Her brow furrowed. 'You're really okay with all this?'

'They're your decisions, Rosa. I'll support you, no matter what you decide. And we'll deal with the consequences of whichever decision you make.'

Her eyes filled. 'Thank you.' Seconds later, she said, 'You mean it, don't you?'

'Yes.'

'You're choosing it. You're choosing me.'

'Rosa, I had a heart-to-heart with my mother about my father, and her actions in the past.' He stroked her hair. 'And then I flew here on the spur of the moment with only my mother's word that you'd be here. I have no clothes, no toiletries, no place to stay. I only have you.'

'But—'

'I don't want to waste my life like my parents did,' he interrupted. 'Their choices—the fact that I'm here—were a series of mistakes. And yes, we've made mistakes too. But *we* were never a mistake.'

His hands moved to her waist again, and tightened there. 'And, if you'll have me, I'll believe that nothing that's brought us here has been a mistake either.'

Now he placed a hand on her abdomen and felt his entire body warm when she covered his hand with both of hers.

'I still love you, Rosa,' he said again, quietly. 'I've never stopped—'

He was silenced by her lips on his. It was a long, sweet kiss, free from the anguish that had plagued them for longer than either of them knew. Only when the doorbell rang did they come up for air.

'I'm not expecting anyone,' Rosa said breathlessly as she moved to open the door. He caught her waist.

'I am.'

'What? Who?'

'I…ordered some camellias.' He swallowed. 'I remember you said you liked them. I know they're not your favourite, but they're sometimes called the rose of winter.' He waited nervously but she didn't say anything. 'If we have a daughter,' he added quickly, 'the name would be perfect to fit into your family's tradition. Because yours is Rosa, and she was conceived in—'

Again, she silenced him with a kiss. Tears glistened on her face when she drew back. 'I… I can't tell you how much that…' She stopped, offering him a watery smile. 'Thank you.' She laid her head on his chest. 'I love you, Aaron.' She paused. 'We're going to figure it all out, aren't we?'

He kissed the top of her head. 'Together.'

She looked up at him and smiled. 'Together.'

* * * * *

LET'S TALK
Romance

For exclusive extracts, competitions
and special offers, find us online:

- facebook.com/millsandboon
- @MillsandBoon
- @MillsandBoonUK

Get in touch on 01413 063232

For all the latest titles coming soon, visit
millsandboon.co.uk/nextmonth

MILLS & BOON
A ROMANCE FOR EVERY READER

- **FREE** delivery direct to your door

- **EXCLUSIVE** offers every month

- **SAVE** up to 25% on pre-paid subscriptions

SUBSCRIBE AND SAVE

millsandboon.co.uk/Subscribe